# CASSIE EDWARDS
# THE SAVAGE SERIES

**Winner of the *Romantic Times*
Lifetime Achievement Award
for Best Indian Series**
"Cassie Edwards is a shining star!"
—*Romantic Times*

# SAVAGE LONGING

"I will go with you," Ashley said, anxiously searching Yellow Thunder's eyes for answers. "I owe you so much for having rescued me. Let me go with you and help you find your sister."

She lowered her eyes. "I am alone in the world now," she murmured. "No one will miss me if I travel with you."

Touched by her words and her feelings of abandonment, Yellow Thunder lifted her chin with a finger and lowered his mouth to her lips.

Ashley was at first surprised by this action, yet soon became lost in helpless surrender when his mouth covered hers in an all-consuming kiss.

She had never experienced such bliss before.

A half moon was shining overhead, encircled by a great hazy ring. Ashley drifted into Yellow Thunder's arms, oblivious of time and place and of her reasons for being there.

Other *Leisure* and *Love Spell* Books by Cassie Edwards:

**TOUCH THE WILD WIND**
**ROSES AFTER RAIN**
**WHEN PASSION CALLS**
**EDEN'S PROMISE**
**ISLAND RAPTURE**
**SECRETS OF MY HEART**

The *Savage* Series:

**SAVAGE SECRETS**
**SAVAGE PRIDE**
**SAVAGE SPIRIT**
**SAVAGE EMBERS**
**SAVAGE ILLUSION**
**SAVAGE MISTS**
**SAVAGE PROMISE**
**SAVAGE PERSUASION**

# SAVAGE Sunrise

# CASSIE EDWARDS

LEISURE BOOKS   NEW YORK CITY

# A LEISURE BOOK®

Published by
Dorchester Publishing Co., Inc.
276 Fifth Avenue
New York, NY 10001

*Affectionately, I dedicate SAVAGE SUNRISE to my friends in Harrisburg, Illinois, especially—*

*Nadine and Jim Wintizer*
*June Partain Hill*
*Billy Paul and Grady Ewell*
*Betty and Ed Towle*
       *and*
*Mary and Bill Kent*

                         *—CASSIE*

# SOFTLY, A STORY

When your eyes first looked into mine
The world stood still, lost in time,
Neither of us knowing why,
Just knowing love was ours to try.
We held each other into the night,
Our hearts were soaring, as if in flight,
Whispered words upon the air
We told each other we would always care.
Even though we were worlds apart,
One cannot deny feelings of the heart,
We have loved in rain and snow
We have made a place for our love to grow.
As time goes by the world will understand
Why I put my heart into your hands.
Some day, with spoken glory,
We, together, will tell the world softly, a story.

—HARRI GARNETT, Maine
A friend, poet, and reader
of romance.

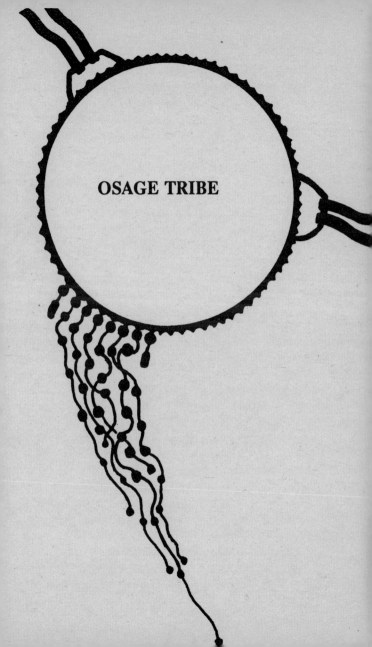

OSAGE TRIBE

# *Chapter One*

*1779—The lower Mississippi Valley*

The room was filled with smoky shadows. A lantern hanging from the low ceiling cast a faint, golden light on Star Woman as she sat huddled in a corner with many other Osage women. A baby wrapped in soft buckskin lay in Star Woman's arms, his tiny lips suckling at her exposed copper breast.

Star Woman lifted her proud, desperate eyes and tried to ignore the droning voice of the auctioneer as he stood before a crowd of men, extolling the better qualities of each of the Osage women as they were forced up onto the bidding platform, to be sold into slavery.

Although she was trying to keep her dignity, Star Woman's heart was aching. She bit her lower lip to keep herself from screaming at the white men taking liberties with the Osage women, touching and fondling them familiarly as their lust-filled eyes roved over the women's bodies sheathed in clinging buckskin dresses.

When a man suddenly tore the dress from one of the Osage captives and began stroking her copper flesh with groping fingers, Star Woman looked quickly away, disgusted. Her turn was soon to come.

How could she bear the humiliation? She was the wife of a proud chief—Chief Eagle Who Flies.

The tattoo of a spider on the back of her hand was a mark of distinction—proof of her marriage to the great chief. It had taken many horses, robes, and blankets to pay an Osage artist for the task.

Tears that she did not want to shed streamed from Star Woman's eyes as she gazed down at her infant son. Yellow Thunder had been but a few months old and she was still carrying him in his cradleboard on her back when they were abducted from the garden patch near her Osage village.

Thinking that a child would only cause complications to the slavers who had stolen Star Woman and several other of her friends away that day, she had feared for Yellow Thunder's life. But she had been allowed to keep her son. Until today.

Would she and her son be separated? Would he be slain?

She cuddled Yellow Thunder closer to her bosom as his tiny fingers rested trustingly on her breast and his lips continued to suckle. She gazed down at his perfect features and at the beautiful copper coloring of his skin. He was a handsome son, the replica of his chieftain father in all respects. And had her son been given the chance, he would have been a great leader of his people!

But now that would never be. He had been robbed of his heritage the moment the white men had set foot on Osage soil. . . .

Star Woman heard movement close by, and her insides froze to think that the auctioneer had come so soon for her. She closed her eyes and clutched tightly to Yellow Thunder.

But she could not hold him tightly enough, it seemed. Her eyes flew open wildly when Yellow Thunder was suddenly wrenched from her arms, and the child's sudden, frightened wails tore at her heart.

When Star Woman looked up and saw a white woman, instead of a man, standing there holding Yellow Thunder, her heart skipped a beat and she felt faint, for the woman was holding Yellow Thunder as though he were her own flesh and blood— her very own son!

"He's so beautiful," Corinne Wyatt murmured as she stared down at the tiny child that was going to take the place of the babe she could never bear herself. "Jacob. We will name our son Jacob." She looked at her husband, who looked back at her with adoration in his blue eyes. "Peter, do you approve of the name I have chosen for our son?"

"Jacob will do just fine," Peter said. A diamond ring flashed as he drew the buckskin blanket back to take a closer look at the child. The child no longer cried; instead he gazed up at the stranger quizzically. "He's pure Osage, but we can raise him to accept our culture as his."

"Thank you, Peter, for buying the child for me," Corinne said, ignoring the woman who looked so pityingly up at her, thus far speechless over the transaction. "I could hardly stand being childless any longer."

Corinne gazed down at the infant again. She shrugged. "What does it matter that he is an Indian?" she said. "At least he is a child—my Jacob!"

Then she gazed about her with a haughty air. "Let's get out of this wretched place," she said. "Let's get our son home, out of this insufferable atmosphere."

"Yes, let's take Jacob home," Peter said, turning to walk away.

Until now, Star Woman had been unable to move or to speak, so stunned was she by what was happening.

She knew so little English—but she did know the word "son" and understood how it was being used.

She also understood that Yellow Thunder was no longer her son and that his heritage and his name had been taken from him!

She scrambled to her feet and reached out for Yellow Thunder. "*A-i-i-i!* No!" she cried in her Osage tongue. "Do not take him from me. He is mine! He is *Wa-saw-see*—Osage!"

The white woman turned and gave Star Woman an annoyed glance, then walked away with her husband.

Two men came and yanked Star Woman toward the bidding platform. She knew that it was useless to struggle. She had seen those who had tried receive severe beatings.

"His name is Yellow Thunder!" she screamed in English as the couple continued walking away with her child. "Do not call him by a white man's name! His name is Yellow Thunder, the son of the great chief, Eagle Who Flies!"

The white woman gave Star Woman another lingering glance, as if the name Eagle Who Flies seemed to her a strange name to be called. She turned and went outside, wrinkling her fastidious nose at the murky swamp air, as if that stench was as ugly to her as the Indian names she had heard.

Star Woman's pleadings were ignored. Now hands fell on her heavy, milk-filled breasts, and Star Woman straightened her back and stared blankly ahead, over the heads of those men who were familiarizing themselves with her body. She forced her thoughts elsewhere, to a better time, to a better place.

She was a young girl, laughing and running through the forest—free, so wonderfully, beautifully free and innocent. . . .

As she was yanked from the platform and rough hands moved her along until she was outside and she caught her last glimpse of Yellow Thunder as he was being carried into a fancy carriage, Star Woman reached out to him and tears filled her eyes again.

"*Kipanna, kipanna,*" she whispered mournfully. "My child, I love you. I shall always love you. . . ."

# *Chapter Two*

In the dim, cool interior of the St. John Chapel, several yellow candles were burning before the altar. The walls were hung with small tablets bearing the word *merci*, for the church was a wishing shrine where people came to pray for whatever they happened to desire—and for those whom they had lost.

Yellow Thunder stood in the deep shadows inside the church, watching Calvin Wyatt as he ushered a lovely young lady to the altar of candles. For days now, since Yellow Thunder's arrival in New Orleans, he had stalked Calvin, watching his every movement.

This beautiful lady with Calvin had seemed to occupy the center of the slaver's attention even more than his business dealings, and this confused Yellow Thunder. His trusted contact in New

Orleans had brought him the news about Calvin's association with Indian slavery, and indicated that perhaps Calvin could lead Yellow Thunder to his sister, Bright Eyes.

Many sunrises ago, the warriors of Chief Eagle Who Flies, along with Yellow Thunder, the son of this great Osage chief, had gone away on a hunt, leaving only a few warriors behind to keep watch on the women and children of their village. The warrior assigned to watch Bright Eyes had been slain, and Yellow Thunder's sixteen-year-old sister had been abducted from her tepee.

If Calvin Wyatt was responsible for his sister's abduction, Yellow Thunder hoped that his actions would soon prove his guilt and that he would lead Yellow Thunder to his sister!

But Yellow Thunder had not expected a woman's interference in his plans. He watched even now as Calvin and the entrancing lady took turns at lighting candles, thinking that perhaps this was their way of joining hands in marriage.

A bitterness claimed Yellow Thunder's heart toward this man Calvin, and not altogether because he might be guilty of abducting Yellow Thunder's beloved half-sister.

Yellow Thunder's resentment toward Calvin had begun many moons ago, when Yellow Thunder had been called by the white man's name—Jacob! That was when Yellow Thunder, the very young Jacob, had learned about prejudices against people whose skin was red instead of white. That particular day, when he was four, a boy child had been born to his white adoptive

17

parents—a baby with skin as white as alabaster and eyes the color of the sky . . . a son they had named Calvin.

Yellow Thunder could hear now, as it had happened then, how his adoptive mother had called their new boy a *miracle* child. They had only taken the Indian baby to raise as their own because they had thought that Corinne's womb was meant to always be barren of children! Then suddenly she had discovered that she was with child, after having already raised the Indian child as their own for four winters.

Yellow Thunder had overheard them later, talking about him, calling him by the name Yellow Thunder. Corinne did not see how she could raise their "normal" son with an Osage brother. Yellow Thunder had immediately realized that the difference in his skin coloring was to make all the difference in the world to him for the rest of his life, for it was this skin coloring that set him apart from those who had professed to love him for the first four winters of his life.

It had been his adoptive parents' final decision to return Yellow Thunder to his true people, so that they could raise their white child without always having to explain why he had an Indian brother, possibly to be laughed at and scorned for it.

As Yellow Thunder saw it, his adoptive parents' hearts had not been big enough to allow their white son to be raised with an Indian brother, but they had been thoughtful enough to at least return him to his true people instead of sell him into slavery.

For that, Yellow Thunder was grateful.

For that reason alone he had not totally hated and resented them. When he had joined his people, he had become whole again, a true person.

Yes, for that he was most grateful.

But somehow he could never forget his resentment toward Calvin for having taken his place in their hearts; and now he was to soon come face to face with him again.

He was not sure if that was at all wise.

If he were not so determined to find his sister, he knew that he would never subject himself to the scorn of this white man, who was known to hate all Indians.

Yellow Thunder feared that he might kill Calvin for all of the wrong reasons!

As for his white adoptive parents, they were both dead now, a loss that truly meant nothing to Yellow Thunder. When they had turned their backs on him, he had closed his heart to them forever.

Until his sister's abduction and the news brought to him that Calvin and Peter Wyatt were deeply involved in the slave trade.

This had forced Yellow Thunder to return to the city in which he had spent the first four years of his life. It had also forced him to accept the fact that his adoptive father, along with his son, Calvin, had surely been involved in the slave trade for many years.

Peter and Corinne Wyatt had procured *him* in such a way, had they not?

Yellow Thunder shook off these thoughts. They were a waste of his precious time. He turned his attention again to the white woman with hair the color of a copper sunrise and watched her with even more interest. Her red hair was parted demurely in the middle and caught at the nape of her neck by a ribbon bow, then fell from the tied ribbon to her waist in a cascade of curls.

His gaze raked slowly over her, admiring the delicate texture of her skin and her slender figure that was displayed beautifully in her blue silk organdy dress.

His gaze went admiringly to her high, well-rounded breasts, and then her slim waist.

Then he found himself gazing intently into her lustrous green eyes as she turned to look slowly around the room, feeling as though he were being pulled into them, as a moth is drawn into the flames of a fire.

He shifted his gaze quickly, but not before he saw much about her expression of angelic innocence that reminded him of his sister—except for differences in the color of their skin and eyes.

Even if this young woman was not Osage, he could not look away from her loveliness—yet he pitied her for not having the insight to realize what kind of man she was marrying.

Perhaps she was even in on his schemes herself, he thought bitterly to himself. Perhaps she even approved of stealing innocent Osage maidens away in the night!

A sudden thought struck him. Yellow Thunder could steal *her* away from Calvin. He could take her back to his Osage village and force her to live with the Osage and obey his every whim and desire!

painstaking craft of making lace, of the romance of "bobbins."

She glanced at Calvin again, frustrated over having to wait until Calvin's return from his upcoming business excursion on the Mississippi River before setting up shop in New Orleans or finding her own little cottage in which to make her residence. Upon the death of his father, Calvin had immediately sold the Wyatt mansion and pocketed the money, choosing to make his residence in a suite in one of the plushest hotels in New Orleans.

Since the death of both of their parents, so much had taken precedence over finding housing for Ashley, or a decent shop for her business. And having to wait even longer unnerved her.

But while she waited for Calvin's return in a hotel suite of her own, she would spend the time organizing in her mind what she would need to set up shop, and how many people she would employ.

Her very own precious laces were packed away until she found a small cottage she could call her own—until she found the proper gentleman with whom she would share her life.

Ashley's attention was drawn to a movement in the shadows to her right. Her lips parted in surprise when she found a stranger lurking there, watching her and Calvin with what seemed an unusually keen interest. The cause of her dismay was not so much in finding someone else in the chapel at this time of day. It was a sanctuary for everyone to come and give thanks, or to pray, at any hour of the day or night.

It was because of what the soft candlelight revealed to her. The man was an Indian. And this was not the first time she'd seen him. In the last few days she had noticed him several times.

And although the mere presence of an Indian lurking about frightened her, she could not deny that he was the most handsome man that she had ever seen. Sheathed in fringed buckskin, he was tall and vigorously muscled, with a smooth copper face displaying hard cheekbones, a bold nose, and sculpted lips.

He wore a beaded headband, his long, dark hair flowing over and framing his noble shoulders.

Mesmerized, Ashley could not help but stare at the Indian's eyes. They were as intense and dark as midnight and seemed to brand her as he gazed back at her. She was not sure why, but her knees had weakened and her heart was racing out of control.

Was it fear that had caused these strange sensations within her? she wondered.

Or was it the stories she had heard about an Indian who had once been a part of Calvin's family's lives?

She recalled how Calvin had spoken about Jacob, whose real name had been Yellow Thunder, and how Calvin had laughed about the Indian being returned to his people because he was not good enough to share the same roof with a white-skinned brother.

A coldness seized Ashley, wondering if this Indian lurking in the shadows could be Yellow

Thunder. Had he returned to seek vengeance against the Wyatt family for abandoning him as a child after having allowed him to live with them for four years?

But she cast such foolish notions from her mind and turned her eyes away from the Indian. If Yellow Thunder had wanted revenge, surely he would not have waited so long.

She glanced back at the Indian again, another thought seizing her. If Yellow Thunder had heard of Peter Wyatt's death, would he have come to New Orleans thinking that he deserved some of the inheritance because he had been raised as Peter's son for four years?

The thought teased her brain. If this were so, Calvin would be furious at the possibility of having to deal with an Indian in this capacity. It was well known that Calvin hated Indians—*all* Indians, but especially Yellow Thunder, who had still been spoken of at the dinner table, a subject that had never seemed to fade from the guilty memory of Peter Wyatt.

Ashley's gaze slowly lowered, stopping at the rifle clutched within one of the Indian's powerful-appearing hands, and then at the huge knife sheathed at his waist.

Then she looked away from him, torn with what to do. A part of her wanted to warn Calvin, yet a part of her felt that wasn't wise. When Calvin hated, he hated with a vengeance! And if this Indian was just an innocent bystander, she did not want his death on her conscience. She feared that Calvin would kill the Indian for the merest excuse, for it did seem that Calvin would as soon kill as look at an Indian.

She bowed her head to say a soft prayer before leaving the chapel, but the presence of the Indian was causing her thoughts to become scrambled. She willed herself not to look and see if he was still there. She didn't have to. She could still feel his eyes on her, dark and imploring.

Oh, but what did he want? she fretted. Why was he there? If he was there to pray, why were she and Calvin the object of his attention?

She smiled up at Calvin, who was asking her if she was ready to leave. He wanted to take her shopping before escorting her back to her hotel.

"Yes, I'm ready to leave," Ashley murmured. "I've made my peace."

"I apologize again for having to leave you at the hotel alone while I'm away," Calvin said, taking Ashley by the elbow and gently ushering her up the aisle toward the door. "But I have immediate business to attend to. My riverboat awaits even now, for my business lies up the Mississippi."

Ashley glanced up at him, wondering how he could attend to business so quickly after the burial of his father? Yet, it had been two weeks now since the funeral, and Calvin had not shown the same remorse that she had felt. Anyone as driven as he could not be expected to sit idly by for long.

Not even to mourn.

"Calvin, have you made your peace?" she asked, not able to stop herself. "Are you bearing up to your loss? Your father was a great man—a wonderful father."

A coldness seemed to enter Calvin's eyes, as it always did at the mention of his father. What alarmed her was that the coldness did not seem to originate from a sad memory of someone he loved. It seemed to be more from the annoyance of hearing about his father at all.

It made her want to question Calvin further about his feelings, for she had only known him for four years.

"Enough talk of parents and death," Calvin said icily. He ushered her from the chapel. "We have some shopping to do, Ashley. We shall buy out the stores today."

"Calvin, I have enough clothes to last a lifetime," Ashley said, stepping outside where the air was clear, the sunshine burning. "I did not befriend you these two past weeks with the selfish intent of bettering my wardrobe."

She could not help casting a quick glance over her shoulder, her heart reacting capriciously when the handsome, mysterious Indian stealthily left the chapel behind her and Calvin, staying in the shaded part of the building, where the sunlight slanted beneath the roof.

When their gazes met and momentarily held, Ashley's blood quickened and something told her that this was not the last time she would be held spellbound by this man's night-black eyes. The thought intrigued her. . . .

Again feeling foolish, wondering what was compelling her mind to conjure up such wild thoughts, she wrenched her eyes away, but not so quickly that she did not see the whole of him. His buckskins were fringed on the sleeves and across the shoulders of his shirt and down his trouser legs. His trousers were so close-fitting, they showed the play of his muscles and lean thighs as he stepped deeper into the shadows.

Again, Ashley was torn with what she should do, and whether or not she should tell Calvin about this Indian, who seemed to have become their shadow.

Again, she chose to say nothing, fearing more for the Indian than herself, should Calvin be alerted to his presence.

"No matter what you say, I will purchase you a wardrobe that will be the envy of all the women in New Orleans," Calvin said, helping Ashley into the carriage waiting at the curb. "And, my dear stepsister, if one wants fine, imported goods, one goes to the shops along Canal Street in New Orleans. You shall have your choice of shops in which to choose your wardrobe."

Later, walking among the fascinating shops, Ashley was able to forget the Indian, for she was now absorbed in her surroundings. She had driven past these four-story buildings many times before in her buggy after her stepfather had lavished her and her mother with new purchases. They were lovely buildings with their intricate facades and wrought-iron galleries over the sidewalks.

And the women!

On any fine day the streets were thronged with pretty, well-dressed women going in and out of the shops. Surely nowhere in all of America could one behold such brightly colored muslins, such smooth silks and roseate ribbons.

Stopping to stare through a window, Ashley let her eyes feast on the display. There were such nosegays of hats, such cobwebs of laces, such fans, shawls, and brocades!

Then she turned to Calvin. "Although everything I see is lovely, I truly don't need any more clothes or hats," she said wearily.

"Hogwash," Calvin said, taking her by an elbow and guiding her inside the shop. The merchandise was expensive, but the shop was old and shabby, an odor of mildew hanging heavily in the air.

Calvin took her to a fine display of hats of all designs and colors, most liberally garnished with poufs of lace, yards of ribbons, and bouquets of flowers.

"Let us first choose you a hat," he encouraged. "The sun should never be allowed to touch your silken tresses."

She looked up at him. "I truly don't want to do this, Calvin," she whispered, annoyed, as he smoothed her hair beneath a lovely straw hat with flounces of lace across the brim.

Calvin took Ashley to a mirror, and she finally resigned herself to the task at hand and placed hat after hat on her head. She cocked her head one way, and then another, admiring them all. There was a morning hat, a toque with a satin bow; a tailored toque with a velvet brim, silk crown and bow; and an evening hat in flowered silk and plaited chiffon.

Ashley sighed when she tried on an afternoon hat with an egret plume and satin-faced brim. She had never before seen anything as exquisite, or as tempting.

Then her hands trembled as she lifted the beautiful hat from her head. In the mirror, she had gotten a quick glimpse of the Indian as he had moved into view, then quickly away again. Her lips parted in a slight gasp and she paled.

Turning quickly, she looked into the dim shadows of the shop, finding the Indian gone, yet realizing now that his being there was no coincidence. He was there for a purpose, and she still could not find it in her heart to tell Calvin.

"What is it?" Calvin asked, turning to follow the path of her troubled gaze. "Did you see someone?"

Ashley gazed innocently up at Calvin. "No," she murmured, forcing a smile. "It was nothing."

But she knew that it was more than nothing, for the thumping of her heart revealed to her exactly how seeing the Indian again had affected her.

Suddenly she was afraid more than intrigued.

# *Chapter Three*

Still shaken from having seen the handsome Indian again, and now almost certain that he was following them, Ashley walked stiffly beside Calvin into the St. Charles Hotel, looking warily around her for any signs of the Indian again, even there. Under any other circumstances than having to be there because of her mother's death, added to her wariness about the Indian, she would have been thrilled over staying at such a grand hotel. It was surely the largest and handsomest in the world. Taller than any other building in New Orleans, it boasted six stories and a raised main floor, the raised and recessed portico giving guests a place to stroll without having to go into the dirty street.

Acutely aware of her misgivings today about so many things, Ashley could not enjoy the hotel, even though she was dressed as expensively and handsomely as any other guest.

Her eyes became fixed on the spiral staircase that led up to the hotel suites, now troubled by something besides the Indian. As before, since the first day she had made residence in this hotel, each time she entered it something told her that it was wrong to be here with Calvin, even if she did have a legitimate reason and a separate suite—*and* that Calvin would soon be gone on his riverboat excursion.

She could not help being suspicious that Calvin's recent kindnesses to her had all been pretense. She had seen the way he had looked at her since the death of her mother and his father. It was a look of possession, of ownership that until the recent accident had been beyond his grasp.

But now all that had changed.

Still, he had never approached her sexually before. Why would he now?

Except that now, she thought to herself, for the moment at least, she was certainly at his mercy. . . .

Never had she felt so suddenly trapped—so threatened. . . .

Ashley stood aside, her hands clasped tightly before her, when Calvin handed over his bundles of purchases to a bellhop. She did not want to watch Calvin go and ask the clerk if there were any messages for him. She would rather be anywhere but this hotel at this moment.

To avert her attention from Calvin's activities, she looked slowly around her. The main floor on which she now awaited her stepbrother was divided into a central salon, dominated by Ionic columns and a marble statue of George Washington. She could see a gentleman's *ordinary*, or dining room, and also a smaller *ordinary* for ladies, a gentlemen's sitting room, a ladies' parlor, and a ballroom which was said to be one of the handsomest in the country.

"My dear sister, shall we?" Calvin said, taking Ashley by the elbow. "Your new purchases have already been taken to your room. Now let me escort you there. I have paid for the plushest suite in the hotel for you. We must see to it that we get our money's worth."

As he ushered her toward the spiral staircase, Ashley stiffened, yet she began to feel more hopeful that she had been wrong to suspect him of being guilty of anything but being kind to her. His voice was smooth and filled with caring. His hold on her arm was gentle, not the sort that one would expect from a man who was the devil in disguise.

Still, she could not shake the feeling of foreboding that had claimed her.

Now on the stairs and moving toward the third-floor landing, Calvin looked somberly down at Ashley. "You are so quiet," he said, pausing on the stairs a moment to let their eyes meet and hold. "Don't you trust me? Have I given you cause not to?"

Ashley swallowed hard and forced a smile. "It has nothing to do with you," she said meekly. "I seem to get these moments when I am so saddened over my recent loss."

"That will pass in time," Calvin said softly. "You'll see."

Goosebumps rose on Ashley's flesh as he peered down at her intensely for another moment.

Then she went on up the stairs with him and walked down a narrow corridor until Calvin stopped at a room at the far end.

"Your key?" he said, offering his hand on which to place her key.

"Calvin, it isn't necessary for you to go into my suite with me," Ashley said, her spine stiffening as suspicions arose within her again. "Just be on your way. I shall be anxiously awaiting your return from your riverboat excursion. I would like to get on with my life. As it is, I feel as though I am in limbo."

Calvin's jaw tightened and his eyes narrowed. "The key, damn it," he said, glowering down at Ashley. "I am not going to be forced to say my goodbyes to you out here in this damnable corridor."

Ashley paled. "But, Calvin, why does it matter where we say our goodbyes?" she said guardedly.

"Goodbyes should be private between a brother and sister," Calvin said, glancing nervously from side to side, then again glaring down at Ashley. "You trust me, don't you? After all I've done for you since your mother's passing, you don't trust me? I'm hurt deeply over this, Ashley. Deeply."

Stunned by his attitude, wanting to get rid of him as quickly as possible, and seeing that giving him his way was the quickest method, Ashley sighed and reached inside her dress pocket for her key.

Her fingers trembled as she gave him the key, yet she felt foolish. He had been in her suite before. He had been nothing less than a gentleman then.

But now seemed different.

He was behaving peculiarly. He seemed *too* eager, and she didn't like to be made to feel as though she owed him anything.

Fumbling with the key, unable to get the door unlocked, Calvin uttered some profanities beneath his breath, then shoved the door open with his booted foot when the lock finally gave way.

Ashley hesitated for a moment, then stepped into the room, again finding it breathtaking. It was well-carpeted, with luxurious carved and highly polished black walnut furniture and drapes of rich blue damask. There were snow-white mosquito curtains draped above the bed, endless rocking chairs and *Psyches*, Grecian-style settees.

"Do you still find it grand enough?" Calvin asked, looking around the room approvingly.

"Yes. It's beautiful," Ashley murmured, walking stiffly into the room.

Calvin followed her, then reached a hand out to her wrist and turned her to face him. "We must do something about your tenseness," he said. He walked away from her and looked at her over his shoulder as he opened the door. "I shall return shortly with a bottle of wine. That should relax you somewhat. We shall also use it to toast my newest excursion on the Mississippi."

"I don't want—" Ashley began, but he was gone before she could finish telling him that she wanted no wine, that what she truly preferred was her privacy. She had to wonder if, when he did return, he would find more excuses to delay his departure?

Clasping and unclasping her hands, Ashley went to a window and looked out over the teeming city, at the great brown river with its heavy traffic of steamboats and sailing ships, and the swampy horizons in every direction.

Farther up the river, some cabins stood among weeds and willow and rank swamp growths, hamlets surely infested with mosquitoes, snakes, frogs, and an occasional snooping alligator.

The giant, murky stream seemed to reflect her mood—sullen. The waters of the Mississippi were a dull yellow, like liquid mud.

Below Ashley, on the wharves where there was always something new and interesting going on, a banana vessel had just discharged its cargo. Stevedores stood in half a dozen lines, each man with a bunch of fruit on his shoulder, carrying them from the vessel. Some waste fruit was being thrown into the water. Close under the steamer hull was a rowboat with a couple of boys in it, one at the oars, his companion capturing the floating plunder with a scoop-net.

Ashley's eyes scanned the wharves again, and then looked past it at the busy streets of the city. Her thoughts drifted to the handsome Indian again and where he might be at this moment. Just the thought of him made her fear of him wane, replaced by a strange sort of melting sensation.

How foolish she was to allow herself to put any value on this fantasy that she was creating within her mind—a fantasy built around a stranger whom she would surely never meet again.

But she could not help closing her eyes and envisioning the handsome Indian there with her, whispering sweet nothings in her ear instead of threats.

Her thoughts were drawing her more and more into the spell of the man, as though he were there, his hands warm, his breath hot on her flesh. . . .

Hands suddenly moving around her and curving over her breasts took Ashley by surprise. She opened her eyes wildly and parted her lips in a gasp, for a moment thinking that her fantasy had come true and that the hands on her breasts and the hot breath on her neck were the stranger's.

But the voice breaking through the silence told her who it truly was.

Calvin!

He had returned.

And with him a daring that he had never revealed while their parents were alive.

Trembling, Ashley shoved Calvin's hands away from her breasts, turned with a start, and faced him. Fire leapt into her eyes; anger seethed in their depths. "How dare you!" she said in a low hiss. She began inching away from him. "Don't you touch me again!"

Ashley felt faint when Calvin laughed hoarsely and reached for her, jerking her roughly against him. "Surely you knew what I had in mind when I bought you those clothes and housed you in this hotel," he said. He took one of her hands and forced her to touch the bulge in his breeches.

"See what you do to me?" he said huskily, his breath coming in short, raspy intervals. "I've wanted you for a long time, Ashley, and now, by God, the waiting is over. I'm going to *have* you."

Repelled at being forced to touch his hardness through his breeches, her fear of him growing, Ashley managed to jerk her hand away. "All along you were planning this? You were planning—to seduce me?"

"If you want to call it that," Calvin said, grabbing her wrists and forcing her to walk backwards toward the bed. "And, my dear *sister*, say no more. I've wasted enough time. My boat and crew await me."

When they reached the bed, Ashley was surprised that he released her wrists and took a step away from her. Her heart pounding, her eyes wild, she stared at the door, then up at him, knowing that she had no chance of escaping unless . . . unless she found a way to trick him.

She began searching through her scrambled brain for a way.

"Undress me," Calvin suddenly said, holding his arms out and spreading his legs. His eyes were dark and lust-filled as he glared down at her. "Did you hear what I said? Undress me, damn it."

Ashley placed a hand at her throat, feeling trapped. Then an idea sprang to her mind.

"Calvin," she managed to say, forcing her voice not to give away how she truly felt. "Please undress yourself for *me*. Do you not know that seeing a man disrobing himself excites a woman into wanting him even more hungrily?"

Calvin's lips parted in a surprised gasp, then he smiled smugly down at her. "And how would you know that?" he said, chuckling low. "Am I not the first man with you? When have you sneaked from the house for a rendezvous? With whom did you meet?"

Ashley stiffened, seeing how the thought of her being with another man excited Calvin even more. "And would you prefer that I am not what you thought I was?" she forced herself to say, to further her scheme of trapping *him*. She smiled to herself as he slipped off one of his boots, knowing that he was being drawn into her scheme, yet unsure what she would do when she was given the opportunity.

"I have seduced many virgins in my time," Calvin said, now barefoot, his fingers eagerly unbuttoning his shirt. "It's exciting, yet it's much simpler to have an experienced woman share my bed. There isn't all that sobbing and squirming to deal with."

Ashley stared blankly at Calvin, wondering how she could have ever seen any good in this man. All along he had been an evil man who sought pleasure in forcing innocent women into his bed.

It would not happen to her.

She would not become another of his conquests!

Now bare-chested, with dark and kinky hairs swirling around his nipples, Calvin eyed Ashley greedily as he began lowering his breeches. "It's time for you to see the gift I give you today besides an expensive wardrobe," he said, his thick manhood springing forth as he dropped his breeches to the floor to rest around his ankles.

Oblivious of anything but escape and seeing that her chance had finally come, Ashley paid no heed to that part of Calvin's anatomy that he was so proudly flaunting in front of her. While his breeches were still draped clumsily around his ankles, she broke into a mad run toward the door.

Her heart skipped a beat when he yelled at her.

"Where the hell are you going?" Calvin shouted, surprise in his voice.

Ashley fumbled with the doorknob, then sighed with relief when the door finally opened. "Away from you, you monster—you *cad*!" she screamed as she turned and momentarily faced him. "How could you have thought I'd ever want you. You—you make me ill just to look at you."

With that, she turned and fled into the corridor, fear her companion as she worried about how long it would take him to dress again and come after her. She had to find a place to hide, at least until after she knew that he would have given up the search. He didn't have that much time. He would have to get to his paddlewheeler and oversee it being loaded for its journey down the Mississippi.

After she was certain that he was gone, she would return to the hotel suite, get her belongings, and totally escape his wrath.

She would go to another city and make her hopes and dreams a reality there!

Her eyes lit up with an idea. "The haunted house!" she whispered to herself. "No one ever goes there. I can hide there."

As she fled down the stairs, she went over again in her mind the tales that she had heard about the haunted house.

Long, long ago, the house had been owned by a cruel French madame. She had had much money and had bought slaves just to torture them. It was said that she would hang them up in the garret by their thumbs and whip them. She had thrown the slave babies into the cistern. After she was gone, they had found the cistern full of babies she had drowned.

Now, it was said that if anyone listened at the doors of the haunted house at night, they swore that they heard the cries of the dead slaves.

A shudder soared through Ashley; then her chin firmed. She knew that most tales told about haunted houses were not true. Normally they were stories exaggeratedly blown out of proportion to tell around a midnight fire.

"I'm not afraid," she whispered to herself, rushing outside, where the sun was too low in the sky for her liking. She swallowed hard, looking at the darkening heavens. "Truly, I'm not afraid."

Not taking the time to look over her shoulder for Calvin, Ashley quickly mingled with the other people on the planked sidewalk, hiding among them, then ran away from them and escaped behind the towering houses until she finally saw the haunted house a short distance away.

The sky was aflame with a brilliant sunset. The air was drawing the cool dampness from the river, chilling Ashley through and through as she entered a wide gate and crept across a tangle of vines that had grown over the front walk that led to the house.

The vacated mansion loomed above her, like some dark monster ready to swallow her whole.

She shivered as the whine of the wind swept through the gnarled and twisted limbs of the gigantic live oaks that circled the house, moss like fine lace swaying eerily from them.

At the steps that led up to a leaning porch, Ashley looked upward and felt engulfed by the overwhelming size of the house. The wind sounded lonely as it whistled around its corners, making her realize her aloneness. But then she remembered her stepbrother and knew she must hide herself.

He was probably even now searching for her.

Hurrying up the steps and across the porch, Ashley went to the massive wooden door with its ornate brass ornamentation. Before she had a chance to touch the doorknob, the door creaked open a fraction, causing her heart to jump with alarm.

But when another gust of wind lifted Ashley's hair from her shoulders and the door creaked open another inch or so, she sighed with relief, realizing that the wind was opening the door for her—not ghosts.

Swallowing back her mounting fear, Ashley shoved the door open more widely. Squeaking, rusty hinges greeted her as she entered the house, stepping lightly into the gloomy, damp rotunda.

Shadows and silence seemed to close in on Ashley. She stopped and inhaled a nervous breath as she gazed around her at the dark interior of the house. Peeling wallpaper hung loosely from the walls; the floors were bare, silky with age; and there were no traces of furniture anywhere.

Again recalling the morbid tales about this house, Ashley could not help but listen for the cries of the dead slaves. The stone walls of the house were surely so thick that they must have imprisoned the crying and pleading of the slaves all those years ago.

Even now, should anyone appear with plans to accost her, no one would hear her cries for help.

She paled when she heard a noise from somewhere close by. Her pulse racing, she edged herself against the wall of the corridor. Hugging the wall with her back, she peered into the gloom, seeing movement, then stifled a shocked gasp behind her hand when she discovered exactly what was wandering aimlessly toward her. It surely had to be the strangest thing that had ever strayed through this deserted house—a brown, broken horse, lean, with sore-looking, sunken flanks, and a head of tremendous size. It stopped and gazed at Ashley, as though expecting her to give it something to eat, and when she offered nothing, it passed on by her, stumbling into a room off the corridor.

Bewildered, Ashley crept behind the horse to see where it was going and what it might do next. When it left the house through opened French doors at the far end of the room and wandered on outside, Ashley rushed to the doors and closed them.

Leaning against the wall, Ashley closed her eyes to catch her breath, then walked slowly toward the door that would lead her once again to the corridor.

But before she got to the door, someone grabbed her from behind and soon had her hands tied behind her. Before she could look to see who her assailant was, her eyes were blindfolded and she was gagged.

Numb from fear and unable to fight back because her wrists were tied tightly together, Ashley felt herself being dragged across the floor.

Someone had followed her to the haunted house!

At first she thought the assailant was Calvin, then discarded that thought, for she did not see why he would need to blindfold and gag her. He would more than likely boast of having found her and finish with her what he had started in the hotel room.

No, she did not think this man who was treating her so roughly was Calvin.

The only other person who might have cause to abduct her was—was the Indian who had been following her and Calvin!

Oh, how could she have forgotten to be wary of him? she despaired to herself. Surely it was he who was treating her as less than a human being.

Her thoughts returned to earlier in the day when she had taken leave of her senses and had fantasized about the Indian in shameful and reckless ways. She had been wrong ever to let her guard down.

Yet why would the Indian want to abduct her? she wondered as she felt the cool night air splash against her face as she was taken roughly out of the house.

She went limp with fright as she was slung over the back of a horse, as though she were no more than a sack of potatoes. She kicked and swung her legs, then lay still as her assailant swung himself in the saddle and soon rode away with her.

She scarcely breathed, trying to guess where the horse was traveling. They were not on the streets of the city, for she could hear no sound of hooves against cobblestone.

It was apparent to her that she was being taken through the forest, her beautiful dreams of all her tomorrows gone forever.

# *Chapter Four*

Soon after the horse was drawn to a halt, Ashley cringed as rough hands took her from the animal and began carrying her away from it. She squirmed in an effort to get free, but the assailant's hands just dug more deeply into her and his arms held her tightly against him.

Finally giving in to her fate once again, knowing that it was useless to struggle any longer, Ashley lay limp in her assailant's arms, yet quite aware of something different in the surroundings. She could tell that she was no longer in the forest. She could hear the slapping of the waves against the pilings of the wharves close by. The scent of the water that was so heavily perfumed with fish teased her nostrils. And she could feel the dampness blowing in from the river as it settled on her face.

She scarcely breathed when she realized that her assailant made a sharp turn, and her ears picked up the sound of his footsteps as she was being carried across something wooden. Her assailant's gait was now less steady.

Her nerves tightened when she recognized another sound—the creaking of a ship. She had heard it often enough in the ships that lay moored at the quay. As she recognized this sound, she also knew what her assailant was carrying her across—a gangplank that led to a ship!

Again she squirmed and fought to get free, aware now of men laughing and mocking her as her assailant reached more solid footing and began walking more determinedly across what she now knew had to be the deck of a ship.

And then she felt the strain of her assailant's muscles as he seemed to be descending a staircase. Her heart pounded, her pulse raced, and she felt him make contact again on solid flooring.

Soft sobs soon reached her ears, making her eyebrows arch. Ashley's mind swirled with questions.

Who was crying? Where were they? Had they also been abducted?

When Ashley was finally placed on her feet, she teetered for a moment, then reached out and grabbed hold of something with which to steady herself. Her heart seemed to turn to ice when she realized that she had just circled her fingers around the cold steel bars of . . . a cell.

She jumped with alarm when she heard a loud clanking sound close by. Pain shot through her hand when her fingers were jerked away from the bars, and she found herself being shoved, falling to her knees onto a wood floor.

She flinched when a knife cut the ropes at her wrist, freeing them. She began rubbing the rawness of her flesh, glad when the gag was removed from her mouth and she was able to breathe normally again.

Her blindfold was the only thing that was left in place and by the time she had reached up and jerked it away from her eyes, her assailant was gone, the door to her cell locked.

A faint glow from a lantern hanging outside the cell gave off enough light for Ashley to look slowly around her. She found herself being eyed by several other women, who were standing behind bars on both sides of her, just as frightened as she.

She pushed herself up from the floor and moved to the bars of her cell, clutching them tightly. "Why have we been brought here?" she asked, keeping her voice low, looking from woman to woman. Most appeared to be her own age, and some were even more frightened than she as they huddled on the floor against the far wall of their assigned cell, sobbing.

One of the girls in the cell next to Ashley came to stand close beside her and said through the bars, "My name is Juliana." She extended a lean, long-fingered hand through the bars. "And you are—"

Ashley reached her hand to the woman's and shook it gently. "I'm Ashley," she murmured. "Ashley Bradley."

"Ashley, I was abducted from the streets only moments ago," Juliana said, her dark eyes locked with Ashley's. "Suddenly, out of nowhere, two men grabbed me and brought me to this boat.

But . . . I don't know why."

"Two men abducted you?" Ashley said, nervously running her hand up and down the side of her dress. "I was abducted by only one man. I think I know who . . ."

"You do?" Juliana asked anxiously. "Who?"

"I don't know his name," Ashley said, in her mind's eye seeing the Indian as he had watched her with more than half interest. She had not known then that she was the center of his focus. She had thought that it was Calvin he was interested in.

She looked guardedly ahead, into the dim, far reaches of what she gathered to have once been the hold of a ship, now turned into a prison, yet still seeing no one. Surely the Indian had been paid to abduct her and bring her here, and after being paid he had already left the ship to find another unsuspecting lady.

But for what purpose, she could not fathom! She should have known the Indian was stalking her, not Calvin. How foolish of her not to have told her stepbrother.

Yet hadn't Calvin proved to be just as evil?

Calvin had obviously planned this day well, except that he had not realized that she would not cooperate.

Even now he was probably moving down the muddy waters of the Mississippi in his lovely riverboat, trying to figure out what had gone wrong with his scheme. He was probably even now scheming how he would right this wrong once he returned to New Orleans after his business excursion was completed.

When he realized that she had disappeared from the face of the earth, what might he do then? Accept his loss, or search for her until he might just accidentally find her and set her free from this misery, just to offer her another misery—to be forced to live with this man she despised with every fiber of her being?

Actually, she just might welcome anything over having to share a lifetime with her wicked stepbrother.

Another incarcerated woman, at Ashley's right side, came and locked her hands around the cell bars that separated them. "I think I know why we were abducted," she said, her eyes wild as she glanced from side to side, watching for those who had brought her there.

Ashley noticed that she was as lovely as Juliana, yet more frail. Her lovely velveteen dress did not cling to her, but hung away from her shapelessly. Her face was pale, her shoulder-length hair a sort of washed-out blond.

"You know why we were brought here?" Juliana said, her voice anxious. "Why? Tell us why."

"Have you heard of the chopper settlements down the river?" Lisa said shallowly, still looking anxiously around her.

"Yes," Juliana said, nodding.

"No, I don't believe I have," Ashley said, leaning eagerly closer to the bars. "What is a chopper settlement?"

"It's a place where lumberjacks settle," Lisa said, raking her fingers nervously through her drab hair. "I—I heard the men who abducted me talking and laughing about it. They said that the lumberjacks would welcome this boatload of women. That means they must be going to place us on the auction block, to be sold to the highest bidder. We are surely going to be the lumberjacks' slaves."

Ashley gasped and felt faint at the thought. Then her attention was drawn elsewhere when she was startled by a noise behind the crates at the far side of the room. Her heart skipped a beat when she heard the noise again. She began backing away from the door that led into the cell, not sure what to expect next. She, along with the other women, *had* been brought there for a purpose, and perhaps they were about to find out who was responsible.

Ashley wasn't sure she wanted to know, fearing the knowing.

When someone stepped into the light from the lantern, Ashley paled and took another step backwards. "You!" she gasped, her eyes wide as she watched the handsome Indian moving stealthily toward her, guarded in his movements, as though he were sneaking about, not wanting to be seen or heard.

Yellow Thunder's eyes widened, yet he seemed not at all surprised to find Ashley and the other women incarcerated in the hold of the ship, prisoners of the evil slaver, Calvin Wyatt.

It was now apparent to Yellow Thunder that Calvin not only dealt with Indian slaves, but also white ones.

These innocent women had been abducted, to be auctioned off!

But where? Yellow Thunder puzzled to himself. He had to find out! That was most surely the exact place that his sister had been taken. Perhaps even his mother, so many years ago.

But he had involved himself in things other than family when he had taken it upon himself to see why this lovely white woman had been taken blindfolded and gagged onto Calvin Wyatt's riverboat. It puzzled Yellow Thunder how she might marry the man, and then that same night manage to be abducted and placed in the hold of his boat. It did not make any sense.

But all he knew was that while he had been hiding, watching the activity around Calvin's riverboat, he had seen Calvin board, and then sometime later, his wife had been taken aboard in a most unwilling fashion!

All that Yellow Thunder could surmise from this was that this lovely lady had innocently trusted Calvin Wyatt, and was now paying the price for her innocence. And although rescuing her might jeopardize his own plans, he had to take that chance. He could not allow anything to happen to her. There was something about her that made his heart beat more soundly than ever before in his life.

He did not know if it was her genuine innocence—or her genuine loveliness!

No matter which, he had taken it upon himself to see that no harm came to her—even if it *was* fear he saw in her eyes as she stared at his stealthy approach. He would soon dispel her fears of him when she realized that he was working for her good.

Grabbing a ring of keys from a peg on the wall close to the cells, Yellow Thunder rushed to Ashley's cell. As he turned the key in the lock, he glanced at all of the other incarcerated women, seeing them also as victims who needed to be set free—and he would, if time allowed it.

For the moment, all that mattered to him was to set this lovely lady free, whose face and innocent eyes warmed him in parts long left cold by women who had not stirred anything within him that was remotely near to how it should feel to love a woman—to feel passion.

As she gazed at him now with eyes filled with questions, his gaze trailed slowly over her, seeing the soft contours of her breasts pressed against the inside of her dress, struck anew by the richness of her hair that was the color of flames and the brightness of her lips.

No. He would not allow her to become Calvin Wyatt's victim.

Her heart racing, the blood drained from her face, Ashley cowered against the back wall of the cell as she watched the Indian throw the door open and step inside the cell. Although his handsomeness and majestic presence stole her breath away, it was the danger that his being there caused her that made her press her back hard against the wall, scarcely breathing as he came toward her.

"*Hiyu-wo*, come forward," Yellow Thunder said, reaching a hand out for Ashley. "*Iho*. Come to me.

Now. There is not much time. The escape must be done quickly!"

Ashley's eyes widened. "Escape?" she murmured. "What do you mean? You—you brought me here, and now you speak of escaping? I don't understand. Why are you *truly* here?"

Yellow Thunder stopped to stand only inches away from her, towering over her. "You say I brought you here?" he said, forking an eyebrow. "That is not true, and why would you think that it was? You see me now. Do I not differ in skin coloring and dress from other men on this boat? Would you not tell me apart from them and know that it was not Yellow Thunder who stole you away in the night to the fate that lies in store for any woman robbed of her freedom tonight?"

Ashley's mind was scrambled, unsure what to believe, yet how could she believe *him*? He knew that she had been blindfolded—he had placed the blindfold himself. Why he wanted to take her away now was what puzzled her, unless he had decided that he wanted her all to himself!

"You are a clever one, aren't you?" she said, placing her hands on her hips. "You know that I cannot describe my assailant because I was blindfolded."

Yellow Thunder nodded. "That is so," he said. "I now recall having seen the neckerchief around your eyes. You could not see who brought you here. Your heart is what will guide you now in what or whom to believe. Let it speak to you now. Let it tell you that you should not delay longer in agreeing to leave this boat of hate. To wait much longer could be—"

His words were stolen from him when he felt the motion of the boat and could hear the sudden splash of the great paddlewheel, knowing that the riverboat was moving away from the wharf. He felt suddenly trapped himself.

He gazed at Ashley, then at the other women.

He knew, and regretted, that he had time to save only himself and the one lady.

He grabbed Ashley by the wrist and yanked her to him. "There is no more time for talk," he said grimly. "Follow me if you seek freedom. Even now you may have waited too long. Your arguments and doubts have placed not only my plans in jeopardy, but also your life."

Ashley tried to wrench herself free, but his grip was too firm. She looked up at him, torn with what to do. She couldn't understand why he was releasing her, but felt that she had no choice but to chance anything to get free from this dreaded boat.

As Yellow Thunder ushered her away from the cells, Ashley glanced over her shoulder at Juliana and the others. "Can't we release them, also?" she cried, now looking up at Yellow Thunder with pleading eyes. "Can't we?"

"There is no time," Yellow Thunder said, half dragging her now as they began going up the narrow staircase that led to the top deck. "Now say no more. Follow my lead. Do as I show you. We must escape over the rail into the water." He gave her a quick, questioning glance as he stopped on the top step. "You do know how to swim, do you not?"

Ashley nodded her head eagerly. "Yes," she whispered, her heart thumping, fearing capture at any moment. "I can swim."

"*Wasteste*—good," Yellow Thunder said, sighing with relief. "Very good."

He grabbed her hand and in a mad dash urged her to the top deck and across it, taking advantage of all of the dark corners and the shadows of boxes stacked here and there. When they heard a footstep drawing close, they would stop and hide in these shadows, both scarcely breathing until they were once more in the clear.

While stopping for one of their needed pauses, Yellow Thunder leaned down into Ashley's face. "Why were you on the streets of this city?" he asked in a low grumble, his dark eyes flashing into hers. "What made you run from your husband? When I saw that you had been abducted, I was forced to follow you onto this boat and leave my valued horse behind. The boat is now too far from the wharf for me to be able to go back for my horse."

"You speak of your horse as though you value it over the life of a human being," Ashley accused him hotly. "Why did you take the time to release me, if not for your own selfish gain?"

"Nothing about what I do is selfish," Yellow Thunder said, then thought better of what he had just said, because in a sense he was being selfish. He wanted to make sure that no harm came to her, for if ever he could put his life back in order, he wanted to make room in his life for *her*.

"And I will have you know that Calvin Wyatt is not my husband," Ashley said before Yellow Thunder had the chance to say anything else. "I even hate to admit that he is my stepbrother, the cad that he is."

Yellow Thunder's eyebrows forked, finding this information much to his liking, for now he had the right—and *she* had the freedom—for them to one day mean something special to one another.

But there was no time now to say anything else. Yellow Thunder saw the path clear for their final attempt to escape, and he yanked on Ashley's hand and took her to the boat's rail.

"It is now time to jump—or else never," he said, giving Ashley a grim stare.

Ashley stared down at the sullen murkiness of the water. It was a dull yellow color that looked like liquid mud. She shuddered, held her breath, then climbed over the rail and jumped alongside Yellow Thunder into it.

# *Chapter Five*

The night world was brimming with moonlight, and every tree was splashed with silver. The river was a path of white, deceptively calm, as Ashley plunged downward toward the murky water. Fear grabbing her at the pit of her stomach as she plunged into it. She fought against the current that pulled at her like clawing fingers—and then she realized something else.

The paddlewheels of the boat were splashing dangerously close beside her as she began pushing herself back to the surface!

Then, as she breathed the night air again, she silently thanked God as the paddlewheeler moved on past her, realizing how close she had come to being chewed up by the large, spinning wheel of the boat.

Treading water, chilled to the bone from the icy temperature of the river, Ashley looked desperately around her for any sign of Yellow Thunder, then sighed with relief when he came swimming toward her out of the dark shadows.

Although she still could not shake off her suspicion that he had taken her aboard the dreaded ship in the first place, she was glad that he had not been harmed during their escape.

At this moment, she more feared being alone than being with the Indian. And he *had* saved her from a fate she did not want to dwell on. For now, she would not think any more about the reasons, and gladly accepted Yellow Thunder at her side as they began swimming together toward shore.

When they had reached land and scrambled onto the rocky beach, it was then that Ashley realized exactly whose boat she had been on. As she stood there hugging herself, trembling, her teeth chattering, and watched the riverboat smooth its way on down the river, it was the name painted in bold black letters on the side of the boat that alerted her to the fact that her stepbrother was even more evil than she had suspected.

The name *Rose* painted on the side of the boat— the name chosen by her stepfather after her mother's middle name—stood out in the moonlight like a sword reaching inside her heart, tearing it to shreds. Calvin was now the sole owner of the paddlewheeler, and whatever business was transacted on the boat was that which he chose to conduct.

And tonight she had discovered exactly what he was involved in.

Slavery!

Calvin dealt in the flesh of innocent women, abducted from the streets for his own personal monetary gain!

She turned her back to the riverboat and hung her head in her hands, nauseated at the thought. She now realized too who was *not* responsible for her abduction.

The Indian!

He was innocent of that which she had accused him—and at least for that, she was glad.

It seemed at this moment in time that there was not much else to be happy about or to look forward to. She had lost her beloved mother and the stepfather she had grown to adore. And her stepbrother had proven to be diabolical in his schemings against her!

"You are all right?"

Yellow Thunder's voice broke through her sad thoughts like a lifeline, drawing her back to the present—and what almost was. She should be feeling blessed that someone had cared enough to risk his own life for her.

Even though he was a total stranger, she turned to him and flung herself into his arms.

"Thank you for taking me away from that dreaded place," she murmured, then stepped back away from him, embarrassed by her show of affection.

As she looked up into his dark eyes, at the kindness in their depths, she felt foolish ever to have thought that he meant her harm. All those times he had watched her from afar, she had seen the same softness in his eyes—the same tenderness.

Yet she had found it hard to trust him. She was guilty of the prejudices of all white people who felt that Indians were *savages*.

She felt ashamed now for such thoughts, for she was finding out who was the true savage among those whom she knew, and his skin was not of a copper color!

"You *are* all right," Yellow Thunder said, placing a gentle hand to her shoulder. He smiled warmly down at her. "Cold and wet, yet all right."

Ashley trembled violently from the chill that was grabbing her insides. "Yes," she said, her teeth chattering. She managed a smile. "I'm very cold and *very* wet."

"I am sorry for that," Yellow Thunder said, reaching his hand now to her hair, running his fingers through the wet tresses. "But we must travel onward, away from this place. Once you are missed, others will follow, searching for you."

"I don't understand what is happening, but I agree that we'd best move onward," Ashley said, then turned with a start when she heard a stirring in the brush nearby. She peered into the forest that stretched out before her, where the shadows made a blue and purple jungle, the leaves overhead giving off a queer whispering noise as a slight breeze rustled through them.

Yellow Thunder grabbed Ashley by a wrist and moved her quickly and protectively behind him as his eyes raked over the shadows, waiting for another sound. There were many unfamiliar night sounds, but the one she recognized were the loudest of all as the frogs offered up their throaty evening serenade.

And then everything grew strangely, awkwardly quiet.

Ashley stood absolutely still behind Yellow Thunder. Her heart pounding, she tried to quiet her breathing.

Then she looked quizzically around Yellow Thunder and into the purple shadows of the trees again when she heard a horse snort and toss its head.

Yellow Thunder gathered her up into his arms and ran with her behind a large live oak, where moss hung from limb to limb, as if the tree's limbs were draped with a beautiful lace shawl.

Ashley was quickly placed back on her feet and she cowered close to the trunk of the tree as Yellow Thunder began moving stealthily away from her and into the cover of thick clusters of bushes.

For a moment she felt totally alone, and then she heard his voice, as though he were in conversation with someone.

Stunned, wondering who might be out there so close to the dangerous swampy areas of the river, she stepped out from her hiding place.

Her mouth dropped open when she saw Yellow Thunder walking a gentle blond mare toward her.

"Lightning has found us," Yellow Thunder said, beaming from his discovery. "When I did not return to land after boarding the ship to find you, Lightning followed the riverboat. *Ah-hah*. My training has proved good. No other horse could be as loyal as this."

In awe of the horse—and the man who owned it—Ashley went to the animal and reached a hand cautiously out toward it. She watched its big and trusting brown eyes as she moved her hand closer, then melted inside when she was given the opportunity to touch the lovely mane of the blond mare.

"I wouldn't have believed that any horse could be that smart, that devoted," she murmured, now placing the palm of her hand at the horse's mouth, letting it nuzzle her flesh.

Ashley eyed the saddlebags, and then Yellow Thunder. "Perhaps you might have some clothes for us to change into?" she murmured.

Yellow Thunder went to one of the saddlebags and pulled a blanket from it. "There is no time to change into dry clothes," he said. He turned to Ashley and gently placed the blanket around her shoulders. "This will have to do until we are farther from the river. Once we have placed enough distance between us and the man who ordered your capture, we will stop and change our clothes. I have enough to share with you."

Clutching the blanket around her shoulders, welcoming its comforting warmth, Ashley nodded as she gazed up at Yellow Thunder, trust for this man building within her.

But still she was plagued by the memory of the many days he had followed her and Calvin, wondering why, yet knowing now was not the time to question him about anything. They were in mortal danger as long as they stayed close to the river. Talk would come later, and she would most certainly get some answers out of him!

• • •

As he helped Ashley onto the horse, then swung himself into the saddle behind her, Yellow Thunder kept glancing toward the river, knowing now that his many days of surveillance had been wasted.

He then looked at Ashley as she so innocently sat in the saddle in front of him, accepting his one arm around her waist to keep her steady as he began riding through the forest. There was no denying that he was angry at her because of her interferences in his plans, yet his anger was kept hidden, for there was too much about her that made him feel many emotions besides anger and frustration. She was drawing him into feelings for her that he had never experienced before with women. He wanted more than just to have protected her. He wanted to know every essence of her moods, of her hopes and desires, of her *dreams*. He had watched her long enough to know that she was special in many ways, and each day of watching her caused his desire of her to grow into something almost painful.

And now that he knew she was not married, anything with her was possible. Their futures could become entwined.

Yet he could not let feelings for her crowd out concerns for his sister. Somehow he would still find Bright Eyes. Until she was safe again among her people, his sister must remain first in his heart.

Somehow he would find out more about Calvin's plans, especially where he was taking the riverboat. He peered over his shoulder at the river as they left it behind them, thinking that perhaps he was wrong to leave it. If he could follow its course, he would then perhaps find his sister!

Yet it would be impossible to keep up with the speed of the riverboat in the water. There were too many bluffs and swamps that would keep him away from the riverbank.

He looked determinedly forward, knowing that somehow he would find another way to discover the landing site of the riverboat.

But first he must make sure he placed the white woman out of danger.

His eyes widened as a thought struck him.

Hah!

He had not yet asked the woman's name! Too much had stood in the way of simple things like that.

He reached a hand around and placed a finger beneath Ashley's chin, turning her face around so that their eyes could meet and hold. "I am called Yellow Thunder," he said, smiling into her eyes. "What name do I call you?"

The name sprang out at Ashley as though someone had splashed cold water onto her face. Could this be *the* Yellow Thunder of Calvin's past? It did seem likely.

Yet she would not pry just yet. Later, when they had more time and he trusted her more, she would ask why he was in New Orleans now? Was he there because of Calvin? And if so, why?

"Ashley," she murmured, not offering him her last name, for that never seemed important to Indians, who were called by only one name. "My name is Ashley."

"Ash-ley?" Yellow Thunder said, forking an eyebrow. "The name ash refers to something gray—something ugly. You are neither."

Ashley giggled, glad to find a moment of lightheartedness in this time of fear and dread. "My name does not have any connection with ashes," she said. The magic of his eyes almost caused her to forget how cold and miserable she was. His touch seemed to warm her insides as he continued to gaze at her.

"I was named after my great aunt," she continued, her words clumsily tumbling across her lips. "My mother once explained to me that it is a name most often used by men, yet she found it beautiful, so used it anyhow. She went further to explain to me that the name Ashley is an old English name, meaning 'dweller in the ash tree meadow.'"

"One day, when there is more time, I will explain my Osage name to you, and why it was given to me," Yellow Thunder said, moving his finger from her chin. "But now we must concentrate on getting farther away from the river. We must find a safe haven for you before I return to my reason for having left my village."

"What *is* that reason?" Ashley asked softly, then felt she might just as well be speaking to the wind, for Yellow Thunder ignored the question as if it had never been asked. He was looking past her, his eyes squinting as he kept a watch on all sides of them as they rode through this land of virgin timber and occasional canebrakes growing along the small streams.

Ashley was satisfied for now, for she was filled with many more questions that would require much time to answer, for her curiosity about him was building, and for more than one reason. Though mysterious he was, she was finding herself more attracted to the man each moment. The fantasy that she had thought up about him in the fancy hotel room did not seem all that impossible now. The way he looked at her made her realize that he was as attracted to her as she was to him.

Yes, she wanted to know so much about him, particularly how he had learned the English language so well. He only occasionally used his own language while speaking to her.

If this was the Yellow Thunder of Calvin's past, that would be the answer to his knowledge of the language—and so many other things.

Yellow Thunder urged his horse onward beneath the wide umbrella of trees, the stench of the swamp which lay beyond them strong and unpleasant. The wind was growing colder now, and the air was heavy with a fast-falling dew. Fog was creeping along the land like a white blanket stretched out before them.

Having never been so cold before in her life, Ashley trembled almost uncontrollably. She peered over her shoulder at Yellow Thunder. "I'm . . . I'm frightfully cold," she said, pleading up at him with her eyes. "I don't think I can go much farther without being warmed somehow. Can we . . . stop and build a fire? Surely we have traveled far enough from the river now. If Calvin and his men come looking for us, surely it will be on foot and we have traveled by horse. Yellow Thunder, surely we *have* traveled far enough. Don't . . . you think?"

Yellow Thunder frowned down at her, something deep within himself telling him to follow his own instincts that were telling him to keep traveling onward, yet he could see how sufferingly cold she was, and he cast all caution to the wind, for it was she whom he thought about— only she.

Without further thought, he wheeled his horse to a stop. He dismounted, helped her down, then walked his horse on a bit farther until he found a suitable place for a fire.

He led his mare up beside a large oak tree and threw the reins over a branch. "This should do," he said, casting Ashley a look over his shoulder. "Start searching for small twigs that can be used to start a fire. It must be kept small. It must not serve as a beacon in the night to those who would cause you harm."

Ashley anxiously nodded. She clutched the blanket around her with one hand, and with the other began picking up and stacking wood, making sure that she kept Yellow Thunder within eye range at all times.

And after enough wood was gathered and the fire was lit, Ashley stood close beside it, staring down into the velvety flames, the faint crackling of the burning branches a comforting sound to her.

As Yellow Thunder knelt beside the campfire, adding more twigs, he kept glancing at Ashley, finding her hard to resist, her loveliness and innocence causing him to waver in the stiff resolve he had learned early in life as a defense against his feelings in a world he had found to be unjust to the man with the red skin.

It had started early, when he was a young boy being raised by white people, and his playmates had all had lily-white skins. The badgering had started even then as his playmates had mocked him, calling him a savage. . . .

There was no mockery in this woman's eyes when she looked at him. There were no insulting words to send an ache through his heart. She treated him as an equal, as though the color of his skin did not matter.

Ashley was casting Yellow Thunder occasional glances, finding herself relaxing more and more with him. Although he appeared to be a restless man, he had proved that he was someone that she could trust. He was also handsome and seemed quite intelligent.

And he had saved her, risking his own life doing it.

Her thoughts shifted to Calvin, still finding it hard to believe that he could be so vile. He had not only tried to seduce her, but he had been responsible for her abduction! Had he ordered it after she had left him?

Or had it been done by accident, his men having been ordered to bring in a certain quota of women each night?

It sickened her to think that all of those innocent women were still in the hold of the ship, at the mercy of her stepbrother and those who would pay money for them. . . .

She hung her head, feeling guilty for having left them, while she had been fortunate to escape.

When Ashley felt a gentle hand on her shoulder, she looked up quickly and found Yellow Thunder standing there, fringed clothing slung across his other arm.

"We can now change into dry clothes," he said, nodding toward the clothes he held out for her. "There are no women's clothes among my belongings. You will have to make mine do."

Ashley pushed herself up from the ground and took the clothes he graciously offered her. "Thank you," she murmured. She glanced down at the pair of fringed buckskin breeches with bright beaded vine-work running along the outer seams, a fringed and beaded buckskin shirt, and a pair of moccasins. To her they were perhaps the most beautiful clothes that she had ever seen, and only because she knew that they were *his*.

"These will do just fine," she quickly added, again peering into his mesmerizing, midnight-dark eyes. "I so appreciate your kindness."

She walked away from him and crept behind some thick bushes, quickly changing, and when she returned to the fire, she noticed that he had also changed into a fringed outfit, almost identical

70

to the one that she wore. Her heart raced, seeing that his hair had dried sleekly black and was now lying in ripples over his powerful shoulders.

She saw a quick amusement light his eyes as he gazed at her and how she was holding the waist of her breeches that were too big for her folded within her fingers. He found a buckskin thong for her, which she tied around her waist to hold the baggy breeches in place.

After a blanket was spread for her and Yellow Thunder to sit upon close to the fire, Ashley sat down beside him, accepting a piece of jerked meat.

Ravenous, Ashley sank her teeth into the meat and jerked off a bite, feeling awkward chewing it, for she had never eaten anything as tough!

But after her hunger had been fed enough, she lay the uneaten meat aside and felt Yellow Thunder's eyes on her again, making her feel self-conscious beneath the heat of his gaze.

"Tell me why you were with Calvin Wyatt, if not to marry him," Yellow Thunder suddenly blurted out. "I thought I was observing a marriage between you when you lit the candles in the white man's place of religion. I was wrong. So tell me what did it mean?"

Ashley drew her legs up before her and circled her arms around her knees, tears burning at the corner of her eyes at the thought of having to relive her mother's death by speaking about it.

But she knew that if she were ever to expect to get the full truth from Yellow Thunder, so must she tell him everything about her.

She lifted her eyes to him and began telling about her mother's marriage to Peter Wyatt, and how happy they had seemed to be until that fateful day when her parents were run down by a horse and carriage.

Yellow Thunder listened closely, stunned to know that Ashley's mother had married the man who had at one time professed to be Yellow Thunder's father! He had heard of the death of Peter Wyatt and his wife, had been saddened somewhat over it, yet had put any sort of grief that he might have had for the man from his mind because of his, and his son's, involvement in the slave trade.

And now, Calvin, the spoiled white boy of Yellow Thunder's youth, had not only inherited his father's riches, but also his slave trade!

If not for his need to find his sister, Yellow Thunder had to wonder if he would have singled Calvin out anyhow to make him pay for everything in his life that had been evil.

Yellow Thunder explained to Ashley his role in Peter and Calvin Wyatt's life, and how he had been sent back to his true people at the age of four winters. He explained that after he was reunited with his true people, he had become aware of the ever-increasing number of white settlers entering his land of the Ozarks—the adventurers, fur traders, and slavers dirtying the soil of the *Wa-saw-see*. He considered the white men to be poachers on Indian land!

Yellow Thunder went into great detail about the illegal Indian slave trade, in which Calvin and Peter Wyatt were also surely involved. He explained about his sister having been abducted, and everything pointing to Calvin as being the one guilty of the crime.

He explained that he had been watching Calvin, waiting for him to lead Yellow Thunder to where his sister had been taken.

As she listened, Ashley was stunned to realize that this *was* the Yellow Thunder that had been acquainted with Calvin in the past. She was in awe of how their lives had come so close to being aligned with one another. Should Yellow Thunder have stayed with Peter Wyatt, she and Yellow Thunder would now, in a sense, have been brother and sister!

The longer she listened, the more Ashley's heart went out to Yellow Thunder, for the treatment he had received as a child and now for having to suffer the continued injustices of the white man.

But she was glad to know that his reasons for coming to New Orleans were not to demand part of a white man's inheritance, and that his reasons were more noble.

But what stunned her the most was the role that her stepfather had played in slave trading! It did not seem to match the heart of the man that Ashley had grown to love and admire.

"*Ah-hah*, I should be saddened over the death of Peter Wyatt," he continued, his eyes taking on a faraway look. "For four winters I was his son. He taught me many things. At age three, he taught me the skill of reading the white man's books. Yet all the while he was dealing in slaves."

"Not only he, but also his son," Ashley said, an involuntary shudder coursing through her. "And I am not all that surprised to discover this about Calvin. I learned long ago that Calvin was a most unpleasant, deceitful person, yet . . . yet I did not think that his mischievous ways would turn into something . . . something vile and ugly."

Ashley shuddered again. "I hope to never see Calvin again," she said, her voice drawn.

"Yellow Thunder *must* face Calvin once again," Yellow Thunder growled. "He must answer to many things. And I shall show him the Indian's way of vengeance." He picked up a twig and tossed it into the flames of the fire. "You see, although I lived with white people, now that I am Indian again, I feel all things Indian, and among those feelings are those ways of making a man pay for his wrongful deeds."

His words sent fear into Ashley's heart, yet regret was a stronger force within her at this moment—regret that she had interfered in Yellow Thunder's plans.

A thought suddenly came to her. She moved to her knees before him, framing his handsome face between her hands. "I know where Calvin is taking his riverboat!" she said in a rush of words. "I don't know why I didn't think of it before, Yellow Thunder—but one of those women in the hold of the ship was talking about it. She said that she had overheard one of the men on board the riverboat saying something about the boat going to the chopper's settlement. The women on the boat are going to be sold into slavery there. Do you know where the chopper's settlement is?"

Yellow Thunder's eyes narrowed. He took her hands slowly away from his face, yet continued to hold them against his chest. "*Nah*, I know not of such a place," he said. "But I will search until I find it. This might give me a lead to my sister's whereabouts."

Yellow Thunder gazed into Ashley's eyes, her nearness causing his heart to soar. "*Pilamaya*, thank you for sharing this information with me," he said softly.

A troubled look moved into his eyes. "And I must not delay using the information," he said hoarsely. "To delay long might be to lose my sister forever. If I take the time to get you to a safe haven, it might make my delay too long to search for Bright Eyes."

"I will go with you," Ashley said, anxiously searching his eyes for answers. "Please allow it. I owe you so much for having rescued me. Let me go with you and help you find your sister."

She lowered her eyes. "I . . . I am alone in the world now, Yellow Thunder," she murmured. "No one will miss me if I travel with you to find your sister."

Touched by her words and her feelings of abandonment, Yellow Thunder lifted her chin with a finger and lowered his mouth to her lips.

Ashley was at first surprised by this action, yet soon became lost in helpless surrender when his mouth covered hers in an all-consuming kiss.

She had never experienced such bliss before.

## Cassie Edwards

A half moon was shining overhead, encircled by a great hazy ring. Ashley drifted into Yellow Thunder's arms, oblivious of time and place and of her reasons for being there.

# *Chapter Six*

Their kiss was long and sweet, then Yellow Thunder wrenched himself away from Ashley. In his mind's eye he was seeing Bright Eyes, his sister, and remembering how important *she* was to him. It was wrong of him to allow any other woman to blind him of what he had to do.

Not even this vision that he had just freed from his arms, her face flushed with passion, her eyes filled with wonder as he moved away from her, must make him forget Bright Eyes. He must come to his senses and remember painfully what had brought him to this land far from his village in the Ozarks.

Ashley was unnerved by Yellow Thunder's sudden decision to move away from her, yet relieved, for their kiss had been filled with fire, stirring her insides to needs that she had never experienced before. These feelings were deliciously sweet, yet frightened her. She was afraid that she was too vulnerable at this moment, her aloneness perhaps causing her to do that which under normal circumstances she would never allow.

Yet she could not deny to herself that she had enjoyed that brief moment with Yellow Thunder—even ached to still be in his arms. They were powerful, yet soothing.

She knew that, in time, she would be held by them again, and her pulse raced at the thought.

"As soon as you are warmed through and rested enough, we must resume our journey," Yellow Thunder said, placing some more twigs on the fire. "From the moment I left my village, I knew that I did not have all that long to succeed at finding my sister. Soon I must return to my village and join my people. I must ride side by side with my chieftain father on the autumn buffalo hunt. In less than thirty sunrises I must return to hunt for many buffalo to ensure that there will be meat enough for each man, woman, and child of my village for the long winter that lies ahead of us."

Her heart having ceased to pound so erratically, her pulse having slowed to normal again, Ashley scooted closer to the fire and drew the blanket more snugly around her shoulders. "I have heard that if the white men settle in many numbers on your land, the buffalo will quickly dwindle in number," she murmured, her insides sweetly stirring when Yellow Thunder turned his eyes her way again. "Is that true? Could this happen?"

"It is true that the hunt could one day no longer be as easy as it is now," Yellow Thunder said, his voice drawn. "The hunt takes many sunrises now.

One day in the future it could take many, many more days to find the buffalo standing on the horizon, so thick they are a solid black blur against the turquoise sky."

"I'm sorry for all the trouble that the white people have already caused your people," Ashley said solemnly. "From childhood on, you personally have suffered from their greedy ways. When you were wrenched from your mother's arms and taken away by a white family to raise, you were too small to understand the meaning. But when you were returned to your people four years later, how horrible it must have been for you. Surely it was something that even now you cannot totally understand, or accept."

Yellow Thunder gazed at her a moment longer, not offering any comment about this that she had spoken of. In a sense, she was grasping for some way to apologize for that for which she was not responsible. Then he gazed into the flames of the fire.

Ashley's eyebrows rose when he started talking about something else besides his past sorrows, realizing that perhaps she had interfered again in his life where she shouldn't have. When he began talking, it was still of the buffalo, but he was not aggressively angry about their possible slow disappearance from his land. Instead, he spoke dreamily, as though he were somewhere else, perhaps experiencing the hunt even now as he talked.

"I have searched many years for the white buffalo," he said. "An albino buffalo is considered a sacred thing, the special property of the Sun. When one is killed, the hide is always beautifully tanned, and at the next medicine lodge, the great annual religious ceremony, it is given to the Sun with great ceremony, hung above all the other offerings in the center post of the structure. The man who kills such an animal is thought to have received the special favor of the Sun—not only for him, but for his whole tribe."

He turned to Ashley. "And so you see why it is so important for me to find not only buffalo for food, but also the white buffalo?" he asked solemnly. "I wish to bring favor upon my Osage people. And one day I *will* find the white buffalo, as well as my sister."

He paused, then added, "My mother is lost to me forever. No matter if I spent every day of my life searching for her, I would never find her. She was sold into slavery twenty-six long winters ago."

He looked away from Ashley again and stared into the flames of the fire. "Even the mother that I came to love once I returned to my people is lost to me," he said glumly. "After the abduction of her daughter, who is also my half-sister, this mother died from a strange sort of heart seizure."

As he continued to talk, Ashley listened intensely, hoping that perhaps she was giving something back to him for his having saved her, in that she was giving of herself as someone to listen, instead of interfering again by talking of her own woes and heartaches.

As she listened, she admired the strong angle of his jaw; his voice was sad, yet warm and sure.

"It is sad that both of my mothers are lost to me," Yellow Thunder said, his voice low and drawn. "But I will carry within my heart remembrances of both of them. I proudly carry within my heart the teachings of my second mother. I proudly bear the name that my true mother gave me at birth."

He turned and smiled at Ashley. "*Ah-hah*, Yellow Thunder was the name chosen for me," he said with a soft melancholy. "Thunder. You have heard him, he is everywhere. He roars in the mountains, he shouts far out on the prairie. He strikes the high rocks, and they fall to pieces. He hits a tree and it is broken in slivers. He does not like the towering cliff, the standing tree, or living man. He likes to strike and crush them to the ground. *Ah-hah*, yes, of all he is most powerful—he is the one most strong! It is a name I carry proudly."

The wind had become stronger, whipping Ashley's hair about her face. She reached up and smoothed the locks back in place, shivering as once again the wind swept the hair from her fingers and caused it to whip around her shoulders.

Yellow Thunder noticed that the fire did not seem enough to keep Ashley warm. Rising quickly to his feet, he went to his horse and took another blanket from one of his saddlebags.

He went back to Ashley and gently placed it around her legs, snuggling it around her, up to her waist.

"Thank you," Ashley said, smiling up at him. "That feels much better. It seems as though I just can't get warm enough. The river was so cold."

"Sit closer to the fire," Yellow Thunder encouraged.

"No, I'll be fine now," Ashley said, sighing heavily, realizing that not only was she cold, she was sorely tired. Her eyes burned with the need for sleep. Her eyelashes were heavy.

But she was drawn to feelings for someone other than herself as she watched Yellow Thunder sit down on the ground beside the fire again, and she saw a shiver course through him, realizing that he was as cold as she.

Without further thought, she moved to her knees, grabbed both blankets up in her arms, and crawled to Yellow Thunder and sat down beside him. Smiling up at him, she placed one end of one of the blankets around his shoulders, the other around her own, then laid the other blanket across both their laps, sharing them equally with him.

A thrill ran through her as their shoulders touched beneath the blanket, and then their hands as Yellow Thunder reached for hers and circled his fingers around hers. Their eyes locked, and Ashley's heart thundered wildly within her chest as Yellow Thunder's lips moved toward hers.

Yellow Thunder was a man who was constantly at war with his feelings and yearnings, but while so close to Ashley, fighting feelings for her was as hopeless as trying to breathe beneath water for long periods of time! Her large, vivacious green eyes, her inviting lips drew him into wanting to kiss her again. Into wanting even more from her that his body was crying out for.

Melting inside, Ashley crept into Yellow Thunder's arms and clung to him as his mouth covered hers with a kiss that was at first gentle, then fevered and savage.

But the sound of crushing leaves not far from where they sat drew them quickly apart. And before Yellow Thunder could make a lunge for his rifle, he found himself staring down the barrel of a shotgun as several men rushed toward him and Ashley from the deep shadows of the forest.

Everything then happened so quickly that Ashley did not even have the time to scream, or to reach out for Yellow Thunder. A man grabbed Ashley and tied her hands behind her at almost the same moment that Yellow Thunder was also rendered helpless by the same means.

And then Ashley paled and felt nausea overcoming her when Calvin stepped into view, away from the many men standing now in a circle around the campfire, their guns aimed at her and Yellow Thunder.

Calvin came and stood before them, his fists on his hips, his eyes glittering as he looked from Ashley to Yellow Thunder, and then back at Ashley as she was yanked to her feet to stand before her stepbrother.

"Tsk, tsk, Ashley, now don't you think you'd have been better off cooperating with me at the hotel, instead of becoming one of those women stolen from the streets for my own gain anyhow?" Calvin said in a feral snarl. "When it was discovered that one of the women had escaped, I had no idea it was you."

Calvin frowned as his eyes raked over Ashley's Indian attire, then he laughed mockingly. "You stupid bitch," he grumbled. "He not only stole you away from me, but he has tried to make you into a savage too."

Calvin gazed with loathing at Yellow Thunder. "And who might *this* be?" he snarled. "Why'd this heathen savage help you escape? He does have a name, doesn't he?"

Yellow Thunder stood stiffly, trying to will himself not to react in any way as he listened to Calvin's insulting remarks. He was finding it strange to be face to face with him now for the first time since Yellow Thunder was four winters of age and Calvin an infant.

It was expected of Calvin not to know Yellow Thunder, yet he surely knew *of* him, and that he had taken Yellow Thunder's place inside his white parents' hearts.

"I thought heathen savages knew better than to leave a trail for anyone to follow," Calvin further said, laughing boisterously. "Did you actually think you got far? You ignorant Injun, don't you know that you did not leave the river that far behind you? Didn't you know the river winds through the forest, and that while you were thinking you were leaving it behind, you were staying close to it? You made it easy to find you. I sniffed you out myself."

Ashley lifted her chin haughtily. "You have no right to hold me *or* Yellow Thunder hostage," she said, trying to sound brave while her knees were so weak they threatened to buckle beneath her. "Once the authorities discover what you do for a living, you will be hanged."

"The authorities?" Calvin said, leaning his face into Ashley's. "Don't you know that I pay them well enough to make them live like kings? No. Your threats are empty, Ashley, and your struggles to get away from me again are useless. It's pure fate that brought you to my riverboat after you ran away from me, making me look foolish. I won't allow you to slip through my fingers again."

Then something came to him like a bolt of lightning. He glanced quickly over at Yellow Thunder. "She called you Yellow Thunder," he gasped. "Are you . . . ?"

Yellow Thunder glared at Calvin, his jaw tight. "*Ah-hah*, I am the Yellow Thunder of your past," he said darkly. "Do you recall also the name Jacob? Jacob no longer exists, but Yellow Thunder does. I have discovered many truths about you—about your dealings in slavery. I demand that you take me to my sister, Bright Eyes. She does not deserve to be a slave to anyone!"

Calvin took a step away from Yellow Thunder. He kneaded his chin for a moment, then laughed. "I have no idea where your sister is, nor do I ever wish to have my name associated with the likes of you. It was not by choice that you and I shared the same parents, even for only a short time. I had hoped that you would stay away forever!"

Turning on a booted heel, Calvin nodded toward his men. "Take Yellow Thunder away!" he shouted.

"Take him to the ship. Shackle him in the hold!" He turned to face Ashley. "As for this one, I'll take care of her myself."

Ashley swallowed hard and looked pleadingly over at Yellow Thunder as their eyes met and momentarily held.

And then, as Yellow Thunder was forced ahead of her, a man on each side of him, half dragging him through the forest, tears rushed from Ashley's eyes.

"Quit wasting your tears on the likes of him," Calvin said, grabbing Ashley by the elbow and forcing her to walk alongside him through the tangled briars and vines. "I don't know the connection between the two of you, or how he happened to be there to help you escape, and I don't care. It's over and done with. He will be sold into slavery, and you will become my wife."

"You'll never get away with any of this," Ashley said, swallowing back any further urge to cry as she looked over at him. "You dreadful man, your father is surely turning over in his grave because of what you are doing to me. Although I now know he was not the sort of person I had always thought him to be, he was always kind and generous to me."

"My father was no saint," Calvin said, glaring down at her. "So don't preach to me about his kindnesses. I know the true man—neither you nor your mother ever did."

He yanked on her, causing pain to surge up her arm. "And don't give me any nonsense about anything else," he threatened. "If you do, I just might offer you to an alligator for supper."

An involuntary shudder soared through Ashley at the thought of what he threatened. She focused her attention ahead, even away from Yellow Thunder, trying to numb herself to what was happening. It was hard to believe that this was real—that her life had suddenly been turned into something ugly and degrading. If she had only followed her earlier instincts about Calvin, none of this would have happened. She would have refused his offers of help and would have lived with a friend until she had gotten herself established in her small lace business.

But Calvin had been so convincing in his kindnesses to her that she had felt that it was better to accept help from a relative instead of friends.

And now she would never even touch fine lace again, much less manufacture and sell it!

Oh, how wrong she had been about so many things!

Her stupidity, her trusting ways, now had even placed Yellow Thunder's life in jeopardy, and she did not see any way of correcting the wrong she had done him. She knew that he would never allow himself to be sold into slavery. He would accept death before being enslaved.

After they arrived at the ship, Ashley and Yellow Thunder were taken in separate directions. When she was forced into Calvin's master cabin, she tried to run away, but he was too strong and soon had her tied to the bedpost.

"Do not fret, my pet," Calvin said, slipping his belt from his breeches. "You are in my bed, but I don't plan to take advantage of that fact just yet. I want to teach you a lesson or two about how to behave when I do decide to share my skills at loving with you. Tonight you will watch me perform with another lovely lady. I believe you made her acquaintance while you were in a cell next to hers. Do you remember sweet, pretty Juliana?"

Ashley's eyes widened and before she could beg him not to force himself on Juliana, the girl was dragged into the room by two men and thrown onto the bed beside Ashley.

Ashley felt herself scarcely breathing as her eyes and Juliana's met, tears surging down both their cheeks.

They did not have a chance to speak, or beg for mercy. Calvin already had his breeches removed and had tossed Juliana's skirt up and had entered her in one wild thrust.

Disgusted by Calvin, and feeling sorry for Juliana, Ashley turned her eyes away, but that did not stop her from hearing Calvin's grunts of pleasure or Juliana's soft sobs and cries of pain.

"Turn your head back around and keep watching," Calvin grunted as he gave Ashley a twisted, angry stare. "I want you to watch. I want you to want me. Beg, Ashley. Beg to be set free. Beg to take Juliana's place. Do you hear, Ashley? Beg me."

Ashley turned angry eyes back to him. "You absolutely disgust me," she hissed. "Never shall I beg you for anything. Do you hear? Never!"

Again she turned her eyes away, pitying Juliana and herself, dying a slow death inside when she also thought of what Yellow Thunder's fate might be.

He might even be dead by now.

Finally, the ordeal was over, and Juliana was taken away from Calvin's cabin, pale and drawn, her sobs fading away into nothingness.

Scarcely breathing, Ashley hugged the bed with her back as Calvin turned and stood over her. She was glad when he pulled his breeches back on, yet became wary of how much whiskey he was drinking as he sat on a chair beside the bed, leering at her.

After Calvin had consumed a half bottle of whiskey, his head began bobbing, and soon he was slumped over in the chair, asleep.

When the whiskey bottle slipped from his hand and crashed to the floor, the glass splintering into a thousand pieces, Ashley gasped and watched guardedly for Calvin to be awakened by the noise, then breathed easier when he remained asleep.

Ashley lay there for what seemed hours, watching Calvin, and then her eyes drifted slowly closed. She welcomed the dark void of sleep, her only escape from her ordeal, at least for the moment.

# *Chapter Seven*

Shivering from the ordeal forced upon her, Juliana sat on the floor of her cell, cowering against the wall. Wide-eyed, afraid to allow herself to fall asleep, she looked guardedly around her, her gaze stopping on Yellow Thunder where he was shackled to the wall in the cell opposite hers, the soft glow from the lantern hanging just outside his cell revealing trickles of blood from the gashes on his bare chest from the whipping he had received after Yellow Thunder had unsuccessfully tried to wrench himself free from the shackles that held him in bondage.

Tears filled Juliana's eyes anew when Yellow Thunder caught her staring at him. In his eyes there was a quiet, seething anger, but also the look of pain caused by one who had been humiliated, who had been scorned.

Juliana offered Yellow Thunder a weak smile, then shifted her gaze to the guard who sat slouched in a chair just outside the door of her cell. His head hung, his arms crossed, his snores broke through the strained silence in the room.

As though in slow motion, Juliana's gaze moved downward and stopped at the chain of keys that hung from a loop at the waist of the man's breeches. Her heart began to pound, knowing that among those keys were those that could set her free—and also everyone else who had been wrongly incarcerated in this hellhole.

As she stared at the keys, the grinding of the paddlewheel and the splash of the water that was being churned by it seemed to become deafening to her, yet her mind was conjuring up a plan that might get her those keys. If she offered herself to the guard, she could somehow render him helpless and then she could take the keys.

The thought disgusted her, knowing that she would never forget being raped tonight, or the viciousness with which it had been done. She ached even now at the juncture of her thighs and wondered if she would ever again be the same person she had been before being abducted from the streets. Alone in the world, she had just arrived at New Orleans to seek a new life for herself. She had not counted on it being one of degradation.

Her father had been a missionary to foreign countries, his wife always dutifully following him. They had left Juliana in the care of a distant cousin, and when word had been received of the murder of her parents in the jungles of Brazil, Juliana had been catapulted into hurtful decisions.

Having always felt that she was an intrusion on her cousin's life, she had left to seek her own life's journey alone. But because of what fate had handed her, she felt she would never trust men again.

Yet there was Yellow Thunder. He was a man, but he had risked his life to save Ashley. And now he was paying for his chivalrous nature.

It made Juliana feel good to think that perhaps she could right this wrong done to so many tonight. Although disgusted by the thought, and fearing that her plan might not work, and that she might be raped again tonight, she knew that she had no choice but to try.

Pushing herself up from the damp, cold floor, each movement causing pains to shoot through her, as though that vile man had ripped her open in his viciousness, Juliana finally managed to get to her feet.

Her heart racing, her knees weak, she went to the bars and circled her fingers around them. She became breathless as she peered down at the sleeping man, her gaze stopping at the golden hair that hung to his shoulders. Although hidden to her now, she could vividly remember his face and how youthful it was; she had thought earlier that he could surely be no more than sixteen years of age, and wondered how he could have gotten mixed up with such a vile man as Calvin Wyatt.

Perhaps he was homeless, as she now was.

Perhaps he had felt desperate enough to do anything to survive.

Just as she was about to do.

Yet she could not truly find it in her heart to think anything but disgust toward this young man. He was the one who had lifted the whip that had scarred Yellow Thunder's chest. He had laughed mockingly each time the whip had made contact with bare flesh.

"Timothy?" Juliana whispered, reaching a trembling hand to his shoulder and giving him a soft shake. "Timothy, wake up. I . . . I have something to tell you."

Timothy's head moved up with a jerk and he bolted to his feet, his hand quickly yanking a pistol from its holster. He turned and faced Juliana, a warning in his dark eyes. "Get back down on the floor," he said, motioning with his gun toward the floor. "Damn it, can't a person get any sleep around here?"

Knowing that much depended on her keeping her courage up, Juliana moved her face close to the bars and poutingly began speaking to Timothy again. "I don't like sleeping alone," she whispered, licking her lips seductively. "If you come in here and lie down with me and keep me company, we'll both sleep better."

Juliana could feel eyes on her besides Timothy's and glanced Yellow Thunder's way. Although he could not hear what she was saying, he could surely tell by her actions what she was trying to do. She locked her eyes with his for a moment, then gazed back into Timothy's eyes. Hope rose within her when she recognized eagerness in his eyes, and she tried not to move away, repelled by his mere touch when he reached his free hand toward her and ran his forefinger along the curve of her chin.

"Instead of wantin' someone just to keep you company for the night, aren't you truly askin' to be seduced?" Timothy said, chuckling low. "Did the old man show you a good time? Are you wantin' to see if someone young like me can do it better?"

"Yes, something like that," Juliana said in a forced purring voice. "Are you willing to give it a try? Or are you a coward, afraid the old man might have proved to be more of a man than you?"

Timothy quickly placed his hand at Juliana's throat and softly squeezed it, causing her to cough and gasp, her eyes suddenly wild. "You wouldn't be tryin' to trick me, now would you?" he said in a growl.

"No," Juliana wheezed out. "I . . . I wouldn't do anything like that. Honest."

She was beginning to feel trapped, thinking that she had been foolish to ever think she could pull anything like this off. She was not a streetwalker who lifted her skirt to every willing man. Tonight had been her first time with a man, and also her first try at flirting with anyone.

She now feared that it would take someone more skilled at flirting and seduction than herself to carry out this plan and that she had just opened herself up to another rape.

"Just don't you try it," Timothy said, dropping his hand from her throat.

Keeping his pistol leveled at Juliana, he reached for his keys with his free hand and soon had the door open to Juliana's cell. He moved stealthily into the cell, then reached his free hand out to rove over her body, stopping at the gentle swell of her breasts. He smiled smugly, then placed a hand on her shoulder and forced her to her knees before him.

"Undo my breeches," he said thickly.

Juliana gazed up at him for a moment, the fearful pounding of her heart almost swallowing her whole.

"Do it," Timothy growled, aiming the pistol at her head.

Juliana's fingers trembled as she fumbled with his breeches, then tears splashed from her eyes as she slowly drew his pants down his hairy legs. She hated every minute with him, and dreaded what he was going to ask of her.

But she knew that sacrifices must be made to get the keys and escape.

His pants off and kicked away from him, his manhood long and hard and close to her face, Timothy leered at Juliana, who peered up at him, awaiting his next command.

"Well?" Timothy said. "You're the whore. You're supposed to know what to do next. Do it!"

Remembering what Calvin had done to her, and how, she reached for Timothy's free hand and led him down on the floor, where she then lay down beside him. She cringed when he moved over her and lifted the skirt of her dress with his free hand, his hardness soon pressing in on her where she was still inflamed from the earlier assault.

She waited breathlessly for him to enter her, and when he began to and closed his eyes in ecstasy, she knew that the moment had arrived for her to truly test her abilities at tricking a man.

In a flash, she grabbed his pistol from his limp hand and thrust its barrel into his chest. "Get off me this instant," she hissed. "And don't try to get the pistol. My mother taught me to use firearms many years ago just for men like you. She showed me which part of a man should be shot first. Believe me, I wouldn't hesitate to follow my mother's teachings."

Timothy scarcely breathed as he rose away from her, his eyes not leaving the pistol. Shuddering with disgust, Juliana used her free hand to brush the skirt of her dress down to hide her nudity, then rose slowly to her feet.

"The keys," she said, her voice devoid of emotion. "Get the keys and go and release Yellow Thunder."

"You're going to be sorry you ever saw the light of day," Timothy snarled. But he kept his eyes on the pistol, too afraid not to do as she said, for she did seem to have a steady aim on him and a solid grip on the handle; her forefinger rested too snugly against the trigger.

"If you don't hurry up and do what I told you, you won't even recall having a mother," Juliana said, narrowing her eyes angrily. "I can shoot you as easily as stand here, *then* help Yellow Thunder escape all by myself."

"All right, all right," Timothy mumbled. "I'll do what you say. Just watch yourself. You could pull the trigger without even trying."

"And so I might," Juliana said, shrugging.

"Can I put my breeches on first?" Timothy asked, glancing down at them.

"No," Juliana said nonchalantly. "It'll serve you right to be caught with your pants down after we make our escape."

Grumbling beneath his breath, Timothy got the keys and went and unlocked Yellow Thunder's cell, and then the shackles which held him in place against the wall.

"Yellow Thunder, hurry and go and get Ashley. She's in the master cabin to the right, at the top of the steps," Juliana said, not taking her eyes off Timothy. "I'll keep this bastard at bay while you are gone." She swallowed hard. "Then perhaps we can find enough time to release the rest of the women."

Yellow Thunder gave Juliana a grateful smile, then rushed up the stairs that led to top deck. He moved with footsteps as soft as a panther's across the deck to the door that led to Calvin's cabin. When he saw that no one was in sight, he sprang forth and was soon inside the cabin, the door closed behind him. There was just enough moonlight spilling through the small porthole above the bed for him to be able to see Ashley tied to the bed, her eyes open, watching him. Then his gaze fell upon Calvin, who was sleeping in a stupor in a chair beside the bed.

Without saying anything to Ashley, in order to not awaken Calvin, Yellow Thunder went to the bed and untied the knots that held Ashley in bondage, then helped her from the bed.

Taking her by the hand, he led her to the door, then stopped as the moonlight revealed a sheathed knife on a table beside the door. Hurriedly, he grabbed it and secured it at his waist.

He then ushered Ashley through the door and soon they were heading toward the steps that led down to the hold. Then they stopped, startled, when they heard voices approaching.

Half dragging Ashley, Yellow Thunder led her behind a tall crate and hid in the shadows as the men walked on, then he leaned down into her face. "We can't risk going below deck again," he said. "We must leave the ship now or take a chance at getting caught."

"How did you get free?" Ashley whispered back, then gasped when he stepped around to where the moonlight revealed his bloody chest to her. "Oh, Lord, Yellow Thunder. How could they have done this to you?"

"The wounds are small," Yellow Thunder said, glancing at the ship's rail. "We must leave now, Ashley. Juliana will have to find a way herself to leave the ship. Even the other women."

"Juliana?" Ashley said, her eyes widening.

"Yes," he said. "She is the one who set me free. We must hope that she will have time to see that others will follow us."

"Oh, Lord, I hope so," Ashley said, grateful that Juliana had had the courage to help them, especially after having been put through such hell with Calvin.

She glanced over her shoulder at the steps that led to the hold, as Yellow Thunder urged her to the rail. She couldn't get Juliana off her mind. If Juliana didn't get a chance to flee also, there was no telling what Calvin might do to her. He would be so enraged, he might even be capable of murdering her!

When Ashley found herself standing at the rail, gazing once again down at the swirling, muddy water of the Mississippi, all thoughts of Juliana and the others were cast from her mind. She dreaded having to jump into the icy water again. Even now she could feel the chill from her last dip in the river.

The sound of someone talking close by made Ashley and Yellow Thunder exchange quick glances; then, together, they climbed over the rail and jumped feet first into the water.

Afraid that the noise from their splash might alert those on the top deck of the riverboat, Ashley followed Yellow Thunder underwater as they swam side by side toward the riverbank.

When they reached shore, they moved exhaustedly from the water, stopping only long enough to get their breaths, and then they began running toward the shadows of the trees, too soon discovering that they had emerged in swampy terrain.

The mosquitoes buzzed noisily around Ashley's head as she moved clumsily through the ankle-deep murky water, her gaze constantly moving around her, remembering that alligators were known to be prevalent in the Louisiana swamps. Her heart beat erratically as she reached for Yellow Thunder's hand and clasped it as they continued moving steadily onward.

"My horse is now lost to me forever," Yellow Thunder grumbled as he cast Ashley a sour glance. "We must find another horse. We must get to the chopper's settlement before your uncle. I must be given a chance to search for my sister before more women are placed on the auction block. My sister might be among those sold again, for she is a rebellious sort and surely did not cooperate with the first man who paid a price for her. She would only obey a white man's command if . . . forced to."

"Like Calvin forced Juliana," Ashley said, lowering her eyes with the shameful memory of her stepbrother raping Juliana. "He will rot in hell for what he did to her."

Then what Yellow Thunder had said about having to find a horse came to her in a flash. "A horse?" she said, gazing disbelievingly up at him. "How on earth can we expect to find a horse in this swampy mess?"

"We will travel until we come to dry land, then follow the land until we find a white man's house," Yellow Thunder said matter-of-factly. "Where there is a white man, there is usually a horse."

"Oh, I see," Ashley said, sighing heavily. "We will then not only be hunted, but also thieves."

"We will do whatever we must to survive," Yellow Thunder growled out.

Ashley cast him a worried glance, and then focused her attention on her surroundings, always watching for a snake or an alligator, knowing that perhaps they were even more dangerous than her stepbrother and his men. One lethal bite, and she would not see another tomorrow.

They ran onward, occasionally stumbling over roots that arched upward from the ground beneath the water and stepping high over fallen, rotting logs. Ashley was terribly chilled again, her whole body atremble from coldness. When the moon spilled through a leafless tree overhead, Ashley held a hand out before her and saw how purple it was, yet she moved relentlessly onward with Yellow Thunder. She knew that he was her only hope for survival now that she realized that her stepbrother was some sort of crazed madman!

When Yellow Thunder did not return with Ashley, Juliana became frightened. She looked nervously up at Timothy, who was watching her every move, then glanced around her again at the other women, whose eyes were pleading with her.

Then a noise overhead drew her attention, and she knew that time did not allow her to think of anyone but herself. And she did not want to spend another moment on that riverboat! She had to leave now, no matter that she did not know Yellow Thunder's and Ashley's fates.

"Go with me to the deck," Juliana whispered harshly to Timothy. "Now. Get going. And if you make a sound, or even act as though you are going to try anything funny, I will shoot you faster than you can blink your eyes."

"What are you going to do?" Timothy said, refusing to budge.

"Escape from this place," Juliana whispered. She motioned with the pistol toward the opened door. "Go on. I'll be right behind you."

"I ain't goin' anywhere without my breeches," Timothy argued. "I don't want to be a laughing stock."

"You already are," Juliana said, laughing softly. "Now go on. I'm afraid my time and luck might be running out. Perhaps it already has for Yellow Thunder and Ashley, but I can't wait to find out."

Timothy gave Juliana a harried look, then left the cell and moved toward the companionway steps. He stopped for a moment before going up to give Juliana another pleading look, but when she motioned with the pistol again and gave him a cold, determined look, he gulped hard and began slowly climbing the stairs.

When they reached the deck and no one was there to stop them, Juliana forced Timothy toward the rail.

"Now what?" Timothy said, glancing down at the pistol still pointed at him. "You have to know that once you jump overboard I'll yell my lungs out to alert the crew that you've escaped. You ain't got a chance in hell."

"Maybe not, but I'm going to at least try," Juliana said, her voice drained of emotion. She motioned with her pistol toward the rail. "Climb over the rail. Jump in the river and swim to shore. And remember, all the while you are swimming, the pistol will be on you. If you turn and shout at the crew, I will blast you right out of the water."

Timothy paled and cowered against the rail. "No, don't make me jump overboard," he whined. "I—I can't swim."

A slow smile crept onto Juliana's face. "That's even better yet," she said, laughing softly. "That is the best way to guarantee that you won't follow me. If you can't swim, you'll drown even before you can draw the attention of the crew. The paddlewheel will drown out your screams, at least until you go under for the last time."

"You don't mean that you actually want me to die in that—in that godawful water," Timothy said, staring down at the river.

"You have one chance of living through the ordeal," Juliana said, her eyes dancing into his.

He stared down at her. "What?" he said, swallowing hard. "What do you plan to do?"

"I'm an excellent swimmer," she said, shrugging. "If I promise to take you to shore, will you promise not to yell at the crew—at least give me a chance to get a headstart on the men?"

She was confident that after they reached the shore, the riverboat would have gone on far enough down the river so that Timothy's shouts would not be heard anyway, especially above the noise of the paddlewheel.

"If that's the only alternative I have, then I have no choice but to accept," Timothy said hoarsely.

"Then jump overboard and I'll come right after you," Juliana said, goading him along with the barrel of the pistol.

Timothy gave her a sour stare, then climbed over the rail and jumped in the water. She soon followed, dropping the pistol in the process of falling. Once she bobbed back to the surface, she found Timothy floundering, his eyes wild as she swam toward him.

Fitting her arm around him, Juliana swam Timothy to shore, then squeezed the water from her hair as she watched him lie on the ground panting.

"Remember our bargain," she said, her gaze turning to the riverboat.

She smiled as it floated on past.

Timothy leaned up on an elbow and also saw where the riverboat was. He groaned and pounded a fist onto the muddy ground.

"I'll now take my leave," Juliana said, giggling.

She turned and began running, sighing exasperatedly when she soon found herself in ankle-deep swamp water, but she was not dissuaded from wanting to get far, far away from the river. She trudged onward. She was not sure if Ashley and Yellow Thunder had made it safely from the boat, but began saying a soft prayer to herself that they would be safe, and that somehow they would all meet again in this lifetime.

# *Chapter Eight*

Daylight was shimmering along the horizon in great splashes of orange, yet it scarcely penetrated the swampy forest depths of cane, briars, and palmetto scrub. So tired and sleepy that she felt she could not go another step, Ashley reached for Yellow Thunder's arm and clung to it as she trudged relentlessly onward, wading through the murky, dark, silent bayou, crossing now and then on some half-sunken logs embedded in the mud.

"No, not again," Ashley cried as hordes of ravenous mosquitoes once again attacked her. As the creatures lit and clung, they prodded her flesh with their poisoned lances in savage eagerness.

She swatted at them, causing them to take flight again, yet she could not relax, knowing that this was only a moment of reprieve. Already her arms and legs stung and itched with the bites, and she reached a hand up and began scratching at several lumps on her right cheek.

But mosquitoes were the least of her worries now that she and Yellow Thunder were traveling through marshes where alligators more than likely lurked.

Thus far, they had been lucky.

When Ashley gazed at Yellow Thunder and again saw the raw whip marks, she realized that he had not been so lucky back at the riverboat. She ached for him, knowing the pain that he was forcing himself to endure.

She prayed that the herbal medication that he had made from wild herbs would be healing enough to ward off infection.

When Yellow Thunder stopped suddenly, Ashley's heart seemed to leap into her throat, thinking that perhaps he had spied an alligator.

"What is it?" she murmured, paling. She looked guardedly around her, seeing nothing. "Why did you stop, Yellow Thunder?"

"To cut a cane to use as a prod, to test for alligators as we move on through the marshes," Yellow Thunder said, taking his knife and cutting a pole that appeared to be at least fifteen feet long. "It is my hope to find the beasts before they find us."

Ashley hugged herself, still looking cautiously around her. "And if we do?" she asked, gazing up at Yellow Thunder. "What would you do if we are threatened by an alligator?"

"Kill it," Yellow Thunder said flatly.

Ashley said nothing in response, not wanting to let him know that she doubted that he could win any battle with an alligator. She just walked on beside him once his pole was cut to his desired length, grimacing when another swarm of mosquitoes began persecuting her.

She eyed Yellow Thunder, whose chest and back were plagued with bites, and then again her gaze settled on the puffy scars on his chest, cringing when allowing herself to again remember how they had been inflicted.

How could her stepbrother actually order anyone to use a whip on Yellow Thunder, or anyone, for that matter! How humiliating it must have been for Yellow Thunder, to have been treated as no less than a slave.

"We should find dry land and white man's village soon," Yellow Thunder said, trying to ease Ashley's mind, while in truth he was beginning to wonder if this no-man's land would ever end. It was nothing like the land of his people, where the dirt could be used for cultivating gardens, and the grasses could feed not only the buffalo, but also his people's animals.

This stagnant waterway, with its many giant, half-dead trees reaching aloft their gaunt, moss-draped limbs, was worthless. Along its margins were frequent fallen trunks, and a green scum covered much of the surface.

"I am beginning to wonder if we will ever see civilization again," Ashley said, sighing heavily. She looked about her. The water was dark and full of tadpoles. She could hear a bullfrog's deep, resonant voice at intervals. She could see mud-turtles sunning on the snags that rose above the level of the water.

But in spots, there were water-lilies—the angels of the swamp, chaste and beautiful amid their sinister and noisome surroundings.

"It is all so forlorn," she blurted out. "I—I wish I were anywhere but here."

"Do not wish for that which you do not truly want," Yellow Thunder said in a grumble. "If not for Juliana, we both would be on the riverboat. Even these marshes are more desirable than a riverboat prison."

"Yes, I know you are right," Ashley said, leaning low in order not to get snagged among a huge mass of gray moss that was draped low, from limb to limb.

Yellow Thunder knocked the moss aside, then again prodded with his cane in the water. "It should not be long," he again tried to reassure her. "There will be dry land soon. We shall dry ourselves before a fire and I will find us food. Then we shall find a white man's village."

Ashley gave Yellow Thunder a look of doubt, so cold she was numb. Her moccasins were full of muddy water that churned about at every step, and her feet felt chafed, blistered, and raw.

She glanced down at her fringed breeches and shirt. They were wet and covered with mud, and clung to her like a second skin.

She gasped, realizing that she could even see the imprints of her nipples pressing against the inside of her jacket.

Yellow Thunder glanced at her, smiling to himself when he understood her gasp of shock. He, too, had seen how her borrowed attire clung to her, and that her breasts were engraved in the buckskin as though they were now a part of it. He had fought against looking at her. Now was not the time for needs to be awakened—now when they could not be fed.

And, ah, he *did* want her, more than he had ever wanted another woman. A stolen kiss was just not enough when one hungered so for a woman.

His whole body cried out for her, not only his lips. . . .

Shaking himself out of his reverie, once again pointing his eyes straight ahead, Yellow Thunder took a wide step that took him farther away from her, his heart pounding so hard, he was afraid that if he remained at her side, she might hear it.

Ashley puzzled over why Yellow Thunder moved on ahead of her, and found it difficult to follow as quickly. The trees and woody undergrowth had seemed to disappear into thin air, and before her were more marshlands, spreading away like a green, endless sea to the horizon, an unbroken level of saw-grass and prairie canes.

It became sweaty, weary work as Ashley pushed through that monotony of mud and coarse grasses. It made her breath come hard and fast, and her muscles ache.

Groaning, wishing she could lie down and go to sleep and never wake up again, Ashley had to force one foot ahead of the other one, trying to keep Yellow Thunder in view as he trudged onward ahead of her. She was beginning to doubt that they would ever come across another human being again. Everything was deserted except for occasional cries of waterfowl.

And it seemed as though they were walking in circles. Everything looked the same—so ugly, so dead.

And then panic grabbed Ashley at the pit of her stomach. Yellow Thunder had disappeared from sight, and she could only occasionally see the long pole he carried reaching up above the marsh's growth.

When that, too, was gone from view, she was uneasy in the forsaken and unfamiliar void.

And then she sighed with relief when she came to a clearing and saw that Yellow Thunder had turned and was now coming toward her again. When he reached her, she flung herself into his arms.

"Don't do that again," she sobbed. "Please don't leave me. I felt so terribly alone when—when I didn't see you, Yellow Thunder."

Yellow Thunder placed his free hand around Ashley's waist and he drew her into a tight embrace. "Do not fret so," he said. "I went far enough ahead that I saw where the marshes end and dry land begins. It is not far, Ashley. Perhaps I should carry you? Would that make it better for you?"

Ashley crept from his arms and wiped the tears from her eyes with the back of her hand. Sniffling, she straightened her back. She had to prove to be more courageous than this. She did not want Yellow Thunder to consider her a weakling.

"No, you don't need to carry me," she said, forcing a smile. She wiped a trickle of sweat from her brow, surprised how the air had suddenly gotten so warm and steamy, while only a short time ago she had been frozen to the bone. "I can do quite well on my own. I . . . I feel foolish for having gotten frightened when I did not see you. But the alligators . . ."

"It was unwise of me not to stay close to you," he said, frowning as he gazed about them guardedly. "I should be more careful of the alligators."

He placed a gentle hand to her cheek. "It was just that I am worried about you," he said softly. "You need dry clothes. You need food, *and* rest. I cannot offer you any of these things until the marshes are left behind us."

"I understand," Ashley said, looking wide-eyed up at him, finding herself being drawn deeper into his mystery. Her pulse raced, and for a moment she forgot where they were, and the circumstances under which they were there. Yellow Thunder leaned his lips to hers and gave her a sweet kiss. Then his arm snaked around her waist and drew her even more tightly into his embrace, the kiss becoming more heated—more demanding.

They were drawn apart when they both heard what sounded like a groan coming from somewhere close by. Ashley's spine stiffened and she placed a hand at her throat, watching Yellow Thunder step away from her, his knife quickly in his hand.

Ashley jumped with alarm when she heard another groan, this time much louder and seemingly closer.

She ran to Yellow Thunder's side as he began moving stealthily toward the sound, and when they came to a clearing and discovered the source of the sound, Ashley almost fainted from the sight.

"Juliana," she gasped, her gaze raking over the girl as she lay sprawled, unconscious, beneath a tree, the lower part of her body half submerged in the swampy water, her upper half exposed. She paled and grabbed for Yellow Thunder when she saw that Juliana's right arm was swollen, a snake bite evident just above the elbow.

Yellow Thunder thrust his knife back into its sheath and ran to Juliana. He picked her up in his arms and carried her to a small patch of dry ground. There he quickly tended to the snake bite by making a small slit with his knife close to it, then sucking on the wound, afterwards spitting the venom out.

He lay her down again and began searching through the murky waters to gather herbs that grew from the depths of the water, on the trunks of trees, and on vines upward toward the sunshine that beckoned overhead.

After gathering several varieties, he went back to Juliana and spread these herbs across her wound. He held them there with a patch of moss that he had pulled from a tree, wrapping it around the wound as though it were fine lace being applied, then tied the coarse threads of the moss together at the ends.

Ashley had stood watching, fearing for Juliana, who slept much too soundly and whose lips were blue and her face swollen.

"Will she . . . be all right?" Ashley asked, as he drew Juliana up into his arms. Her head lay against Yellow Thunder's chest like a limp rag.

"Time will give you the answer that Yellow Thunder cannot," he said softly. He nodded toward Ashley. "Now it is even more important to find a white man's village. This woman needs more medical attention than what I knew to give her."

He glowered down at Ashley. "She would heal quickly if she were at *my* village so that Moon Face Bear, our village medicine man, could perform his magical rites over her," he grumbled. "Moon Face Bear's medicine is better than the white man's."

"I . . . hope she doesn't die," Ashley said, reaching over to smooth a fallen lock from Juliana's pale brow. "I wonder how long she's been lying there. And how did she get ahead of us, unless . . ."

She looked over her shoulder, frowning. "Unless we are traveling in circles, Yellow Thunder," she said, a sudden foreboding soaring through her. "Should we be close to the river again, Calvin might—"

"Do not think of things that are not positive thoughts," Yellow Thunder said, interrupting Ashley. "It is best always to have hope. That alone sometimes leads a person to the right roads of life."

He peered behind him. "And who is to say that Juliana did or did not leave the riverboat before us?" he said, glowering down at Ashley. "No matter now *when*. Now is all that is important. Let us travel onward."

He leaned his face into hers. "And remember that hope is a more pleasant companion than despair," he said softly.

Ashley nodded anxiously, took another lingering, sad look at Juliana, then lifted her chin and began walking alongside Yellow Thunder.

But too soon she found herself lagging behind again, each footstep more weary and heavier than the last. Her heart pounded as she felt herself growing weaker.

Oh, how worn and weary she was!

How could she be expected to keep up with Yellow Thunder's determined pace through the dreadful water?

Yet she traveled onward through tangles of buck brush and palmetto scrub. Often she had to step over fallen tree trunks, or make a detour around the larger ones. She could tell that this region had been heavily wooded a few years before, but in a dry spell a fire had burned among the great oaks, cedars, and magnolias; few had escaped the wrath of a lightning strike.

But many dead giants still stood and the rotting forms of numerous others strewed the undergrowth.

And then she grimaced when she again had to wade through knee-deep water, her moccasins sucking at the mud beneath them. She was so weary she could hardly drag herself along, and the swarming mosquitoes made her travels more and more difficult!

Ashley jumped with alarm when she spied a movement in the water at her right side. She glanced up at Yellow Thunder, who had not noticed or heard anything out of the ordinary.

Ashley's eyes were drawn again to the ruffling of the water at her side, and she realized that they were on the borders of a narrow channel of brown water that was an "alligator slue," what the alligators used as a highway when in search of food.

When two eyes bobbed up to the surface, and then Ashley could see the rest of the alligator that came into view beneath the water, she stopped, paralyzed with fear, and began screaming.

Yellow Thunder stopped with a start and turned to see what was wrong.

"An alligator," Ashley cried, pointing to the creature as it began swimming slowly toward her. "Oh, Lord, Yellow Thunder, it's coming for me. Please stop it. Oh, Yellow Thunder—do something!"

Ashley watched Yellow Thunder's quick reaction. He searched quickly around him for a place to lay Juliana down, and when he spied the gigantic root of a tree growing up from the water, carried Juliana there and laid her across it.

In awe of Yellow Thunder and the courage he always showed in the face of danger, Ashley watched him with a pounding heart as he approached the alligator, plunged both hands in the water, and pulled out the six-foot monster, firmly gripping it by the jaws.

But the alligator was bedaubed with clay, making it slippery, and when it gave a sudden twist and turn, Yellow Thunder lost his hold.

The beast rolled over into the slue, and with a vigorous splash of its muscular tail sent the water flying over Ashley and Yellow Thunder.

Showing no fear of the angry alligator, Yellow Thunder caught it in the same way as before, drew it out of the mud, and jumped on its back.

"Give me the rope that holds your breeches in place!" he shouted, giving Ashley a harried glance. "*A-i-i-i!* Quickly, Ashley—quickly!"

With trembling fingers, Ashley untied the rope and waded quickly over to Yellow Thunder. Her pulse raced as she handed it to him, the alligator's eyes on her, as though burning a hole through her.

Yellow Thunder tied the alligator's mouth fast shut with one end of the rope, and with the other end, fastened its legs over its back, leaving the animal at his mercy.

"Are you—going to kill it?" Ashley asked, as Yellow Thunder stepped away from the alligator.

Yellow Thunder started to answer her, but was stopped when several small alligators suddenly appeared, their soft bodies and pathetic eyes exposed as they swam toward the helpless, larger alligator.

"Oh, Yellow Thunder, those are surely this alligator's babies," Ashley said, touched deeply by the sight of the smaller alligators. She glanced then at the mother and could not help but feel sorry for it.

Her eyes widened and her heart swelled in her pride of Yellow Thunder when he went to the bound alligator, quickly cut the ropes away, and gave it a shove toward the babies. Ashley was relieved when they all swam away, soon lost from sight in the mud and mire.

Yellow Thunder slipped the knife into its sheath again, then welcomed Ashley as she came to him and gave him a warm hug. "That was so sweet," she murmured, looking adoringly up at him. Then she drew quickly away from him when she heard Juliana let out a groan of pain.

Yellow Thunder at her side, Ashley clutched at her loose breeches and hurried to Juliana, hoping that she had regained consciousness, but sighed heavily, disappointed and even more worried than ever when she saw that Juliana was still in a deep sleep, her face distorted with pain.

Yellow Thunder swept Juliana up into his arms and once again Ashley followed him through the swamp.

But soon she stopped dead in her tracks and listened intensely. She had heard something beside the normal sounds of the swampland. Her heart skipped a beat and she reached a hand to Yellow Thunder's arm when she heard the sound again.

She smiled and tears sparkled in her eyes as she listened to the sound of banjo music wafting through a break in the trees a short distance away.

# *Chapter Nine*

Ashley's footsteps and breath quickened as she clutched her loose breeches to her waist and followed Yellow Thunder toward the sound of the banjo music. Soon they reached dry land and began making their way through a corn patch. The wind rustled through the dry, faded cornstalks with a shivering and lonely sound.

But the gay music being played on the banjo made Ashley's heart sing with joy, and she hoped that soon they would be face to face with whoever was playing the instrument.

Perhaps it would be someone who could help Juliana in her time of trouble. Although Yellow Thunder had tried to work his own kind of magic on Juliana's snake bite with the herbs that he had gathered in the forest, Ashley doubted that would be enough to bring Juliana out of her unconscious state.

If the snake bite was a deadly one, Juliana might

even be dead before the next morning.

Ashley looked guardedly around her. Night was falling. The twilight was deepening into gloom, and the air was growing chilly. Overhead the swallows were taking their last flight, and birds were gathering frantically in the trees whose leaves, in advancing autumn, were just beginning to show the first signs of changing into something breathtakingly beautiful. In a matter of weeks, though, the trees would be barren of their leaves, and a long, cold winter stretched out before Ashley. This time last year she would not have had reason to wonder what winter would bring her. She had had a mother, a stepfather whom she had adored, and a beautiful house to bring her friends to.

She had even been given a party all her own just prior to the death of her parents.

She would never forget how wonderful it had felt to spin around the large parlor, where the carpets had been rolled up and placed at the side of the room, and where the furniture had been taken away, leaving only enough chairs for those who needed to rest between dances to sit upon.

The string quartet had played all sorts of music, the waltzes Ashley's favorite. . . .

But all of that had been taken from her the instant the horse and carriage had snuffed the life from her beloved mother and stepfather.

And because he had not changed his will after his marriage to Ashley's mother, Ashley's stepfather had left everything to Calvin.

Calvin had sold the house and all of its furnishings the day after his father's burial. She and Calvin had been forced to vacate the house so that the new owners could claim possession of it.

A hotel room had then become Ashley's home until she could find a cottage that she could call her own.

That had now changed, and her dreadful step-brother was responsible!

A sadness entered Ashley's eyes. The truth about her stepfather was hard to grasp—that he had been involved in slavery. Somehow it just did not ring true of the man that she had known and loved. She found it hard to believe that her stepfather could be that cold-hearted, when all that he had ever shown *her* was a devoted kindness, and love.

Ashley forced herself to cast the wonder, doubts, and hurts aside. Nothing about her stepfather mattered now. All that did matter was that she found a way to survive from day to day—and to escape the clutches of her stepbrother.

She gave Yellow Thunder a warm glance as he trudged on ahead of her, Juliana seeming to weigh no more than a feather in his arms as he carried her toward the sound of the banjo music.

Yellow Thunder gave Ashley hope . . . only he.

When they finally emerged from the cornfield, they found themselves at the edge of a small town consisting of a straggling cluster of unpainted stores, all of them wooden. Gaunt mules stood at the hitch racks, their heads bowed. There were boardwalks through the village, many with pieces shattered or missing.

What was especially distinctive about the town

was an abundance of trees. The one lonely street was lined with them, making the town look like a kind of human bird's nest.

Ashley took quick steps and began walking beside Yellow Thunder down the center of the dirt street. There were only a few men loitering about, and some children clinging to the skirts of women who had stopped to stare at the strangers coming into their town.

A lone banjo player sat in a rocker on the porch of the hotel—a clumsy one-story wooden building separated from the street only by a narrow boardwalk.

While Ashley and Yellow Thunder continued walking determinedly toward the banjo player, he did not seem to miss a note, nor did he take his eyes off the approaching strangers.

Ashley gazed back at him. He was a mulatto with handsome features. There was a touch of refinement and poetry about his slender figure as he sat on the rickety porch, playing his banjo with great facility and charm.

Soon another man came in a slow gait from the hotel and joined the banjo player. His gaze on the the three strangers, he sat down in a rocker and began rocking back and forth, all stiff and upright with his brows twisted and a cigar stump cocked up in the corner of his mouth.

Ashley noticed that both men were dressed in drab bib overalls, with a colorless shirt worn beneath them but with a bright red neckerchief tied around their throats.

Soon a stout, short elderly woman joined them

on the porch, peering with squinted eyes at Ashley and Yellow Thunder, her gaze stopping on Juliana laying limply within Yellow Thunder's powerful arms. The woman was drying her hands on a wrinkled apron. Her floor-length cotton dress was faded in color, the hem hanging loose around her feet.

Ashley noted that the elderly woman wore men's shoes—large, black, and ugly, with shoestrings laced up the front of each. Her gray hair was worn in a tight bun around her head, and her face was cratered with wrinkles.

The banjo player hushed his playing when the elderly lady placed a hand on his shoulder and nodded at him. The other man stopped his rocking and stood up beside the lady, towering over her with his extreme height, so thin he looked as though one breath of wind might blow him away.

Ashley and Yellow Thunder stopped before the porch. Ashley hung on to her breeches, seeing that they had now drawn everyone's attention. "Ma'am, gentlemen," Ashley said softly, looking from one to the other. She was glad when their gaze shifted, now looking into her eyes, focusing on the crucial problem at hand, not her dilemma with the breeches.

"We're in dire need of help," she continued. "Our friend here"—she motioned with a hand toward Juliana—"she's been snake-bitten. Perhaps you have a doctor in your town who might take a look at her? Perhaps medicate her? She's . . . she's been unconscious for quite a spell now. Please? Can you help us?"

The lady stepped forward. She placed her hands on her hips and glared first at Yellow Thunder, then at Ashley. "Where'd you come from?" she asked, her voice guarded. "I ain't seen none of you around these parts before. Where'd you come from? Young lady, how is it that you are with an Injun, dressed in Injun garb?"

Ashley glanced quickly at Yellow Thunder when the elderly lady's gaze went to him again, staring at him as though she would as soon kick him as look at him, and Ashley was reminded again of the prejudices against Indians. Even now, when it was apparent that this Indian was in dire need of assistance and had the appearance of one who was gentle instead of one who was a threat, the elderly lady was guarded in her offer to help.

Ashley felt a deep sadness for Yellow Thunder, quite aware that he saw and understood the lady's hesitation.

"Where we have been, or why we are traveling together should not matter," Ashley said, lifting her chin haughtily. "My friend Juliana may die if she does not get medical attention quickly. Please help her."

"Awright," the lady said, her heart obviously not in her decision. "Come on in my hotel. Place the lady on the sofa close beside the stove. There ain't no doctor in these parts except for what little I know of doctorin'. Let me take a look at your friend. I'll see what I can do." She extended a chubby, wrinkled hand toward Ashley. "You can call me Anna."

Ashley accepted the handshake and smiled

down at Anna. "My name is Ashley, and my friends are Yellow Thunder and Juliana," she said, smiling down at Anna. "And thank you so much for offering to help us. We appreciate your kindness more than you'll ever know."

Anna nodded and took her hand away, turning to walk back inside the hotel.

Ashley placed a hand on Yellow Thunder's elbow, urging him up the steps to the porch, and then on inside the hotel.

As Yellow Thunder gently laid Juliana down on the sofa, Ashley looked slowly around her. The room smelled of tobacco. A big stove was flanked on either side by a spittoon box—a shallow wooden affair with the bottom sprinkled with dirt and the dirt sprinkled with burnt matches, cigar stubs, old quids, and other filth. Except for a lone lantern that sat on a counter at the far end of the room, the room was dark and grimy, the sagging, uneven floor half-covered with a rag carpet.

"You're lucky to have found me," Anna said, kneeling down on the floor beside Juliana. "I knows enough about snake bites to write a book about them." She removed the herbal leaves and inspected the wound carefully. "Hmm. It's a nasty one awright. But I think she's goin' to live. It wasn't a poisonous snake that bit her. She's just had a nasty reaction to it, that's all."

She rose back to her full height, wiping her hands on her apron. "Big fellow," she said, looking up at Yellow Thunder. "Pick the ailing lady up. Follow me. I'll keep her in one of my hotel rooms for several days and tend to her. But even after she comes to, she can't be moved for a spell. She'll have to stay here with me until I says she's able to leave."

Ashley placed a gentle hand on Anna's arm. "Yellow Thunder and I can't stay that long," she said, her voice urgent. "If we leave Juliana behind, will you still see to her welfare?"

"Yes'm," Anna said, nodding. "It'd be my pleasure." She raked her eyes slowly over Ashley. "It appears to me that you shouldn't be too hasty to be on your way again. From the looks of you, I'd say a bath, dry clothes, some food, and some rest might do you some good. Spend the night, then be on your way again tomorrow. We've the room. And we've food to spare."

Ashley turned wide, pleading eyes up at Yellow Thunder. "Dare we?" she murmured, speaking too softly for Anna to hear, to know that Ashley thought the offer also included Yellow Thunder. "Or is it too dangerous to stop just yet?"

"Young lady, I don't know the trouble you've gotten yourself into, but I'd say you'll be in a lot more trouble if you don't see first to your needs," Anna said, stubbornly folding her arms across her thick bosom. "If'n you was my daughter, I'd see to it that you spend the night, then head on out tomorrow."

Yellow Thunder gazed at Ashley, then turned troubled, suspicious eyes to Anna. "You speak from the heart when you ask us to stay?" he said.

Anna paled and took a step away from Yellow Thunder. "I . . . I wasn't includin' you in my offer," she said, her voice anxious.

Ashley gasped, then went quickly to Yellow Thunder's defense. "This man you have just insulted is far better than many white men I have met in my lifetime," she blurted out, placing her one free hand on her hips and glaring down at Anna. "If you can't find it in your heart to allow him to stay in your hotel, nor shall I."

Anna's eyes widened. She eyed Yellow Thunder for a moment longer, then turned her gaze back to Ashley. "He can stay," she said in a low rumble. "But only for one night. Do you hear? And then you both get on your way."

Ashley smiled wanly at Anna's half-hearted offer, but was relieved to know that no matter how Anna felt, Ashley was going to spend at least one night somewhere besides in a swamp. She was even going to be able to eat something decent. She could smell the pleasant smells of cooking wafting from the kitchen now.

"Well?" Anna said gruffly, frowning up at Yellow Thunder. "What are you waiting for? Follow me. Bring the sick one."

Ashley watched Yellow Thunder gently pick Juliana up from the sofa. Then a thought struck her that threatened to spoil her plans to spend a night with a roof over her head. "Anna, we have no money," she blurted out, walking anxiously beside Anna as she left the outer room and began walking down a long, dark corridor. "Anna, did you hear me? We have no way to pay for a room or food."

"For one night, that's all," Anna said over her shoulder. "One night. Do you understand?"

"Without payment?" Ashley persisted, finding it hard to believe that someone who appeared as poor as this elderly lady could feel free to give out what she did possess, without demanding payment.

"That's what I said," Anna murmured. "Now go on down the corridor and choose whichever room you want. None of them's occupied." She gave Yellow Thunder an upward glance, frowning. "And find one for the Injun—separate from yours, mind you."

Ashley momentarily hung her head, blushing, then rushed away from Anna and Yellow Thunder to the room at the far end of the corridor. As she slowly opened the door, she found it as dark as a pocket. She fumbled around inside the room until she found the window, then threw open the shutters, glad when moonlight bright and serene flooded through the window and onto her anxious face.

Turning, she gazed around the room, looking at what the moon allowed. Her heart sank. The floors were no more than dirt, scarcely overlaid with a thin layering of warped boards. The bed was iron, paint peeling from it. What blankets she saw were yellowed with age, and the musty smell made her cringe and think that perhaps it would be better after all to sleep outside. She envisioned all sorts of creepy, crawling things in the room and doubted if she would get one wink of sleep the whole night through.

But the food that was cooking somewhere in the dingy house gave her cause to think twice before suggesting that she and Yellow Thunder should be on their way.

She was so hungry!

She yawned, also realizing how sleepy she was. Anything would do tonight, anything. . . .

She jumped with a start when the mulatto man with his handsome features came into the room carrying a lighted lantern in one hand and a wash basin filled with water in the other.

"I hope these will do," the man said, his voice deep and his words quite distinct. "We have no change of clothes for you, but if you will take off your garments and lay them out in the hall, they will be washed and dried for you by tomorrow morning."

Ashley was taken aback by this generous offer. She watched him set the basin of water on a table beside the bed and hang the lantern from a hook close beside the window.

"You'll find a washcloth and towel in the drawer in this bedside table," the man said over his shoulder as he walked toward the door. Then he turned and faced Ashley again. "I am called Abraham."

"It's nice to make your acquaintance, Abraham," Ashley said, going to offer him her hand. She was surprised when he kissed her palm in a gentlemanly fashion. She very slowly eased her hand to her side after he kissed it.

"Soon supper will be set in a tray just outside your door," Abraham said, then turned and left, leaving Ashley staring blankly after him.

"Is this truly happening?" she whispered, finally coming out of the trance that Abraham seemed to have put her in. "Everyone is too nice. Can they truly be trusted?"

A shudder coursed through her. Then she went to the door and opened it just as Yellow Thunder came walking down the corridor toward her.

"Take the room next to mine," she whispered, pointing toward it. "I'll see you in the morning, Yellow Thunder. Sleep tight."

He gave her a disconcerting stare, then went into the room that she had indicated. Ashley went back inside her room and anxiously removed her wet, soiled clothes. She tiptoed to the door and laid them outside on the floor, in the corridor, then closed the door again and stood over the basin of water. It was fresh, and she smiled when she spied a bar of soap floating around in the water.

"This does seem too good to be true," she murmured, then leaned down over the basin and eagerly splashed the refreshing water onto her face.

# *Chapter Ten*

When food was brought to Ashley, she cast aside all her ill feelings about having to stay in this run-down, questionable hotel and feasted on fried okra, bacon and beans, biscuits and molasses, coffee with sugar, and stewed dried apples, until she had felt as though her stomach might pop.

Now she sat stiffly on the bed, clutching a blanket around her shoulders, having given up trying to get a wink of sleep. Too many things stood in the way of her relaxing that much. Fearing who might climb through the window in the night, she had closed the shutters, which had taken the moon from her view. The lantern cast only a faint light around the room, yet it was enough to see cockroaches crawling across the ceiling, up and down the walls, and occasionally attempting to crawl onto her body, stopped by her staying alert enough to slap them off.

She was beginning to worry about having given

up her clothes so easily. Even though they were too large for her, and had suffered many rips and tears while they made their way through the swampy forest, they were all she had, and she should not have parted with them anymore than she would have parted with her life! Her further travels depended on her getting her clothes back.

Perhaps again she had trusted too much, yet these people in this small village continued to be genuinely friendly and seemed to inspire trust.

Yet still she could not cast aside the foreboding that seemed to be with her constantly now, and she had to wonder how Juliana was doing. Anna had seemed knowledgeable about snakebites, and perhaps knew enough to save Juliana's life. Yet Ashley was uncomfortable about having to leave Juliana behind tomorrow.

Ashley's thoughts went to Yellow Thunder, and how he might be faring under these less than desirable circumstances. He had not been as readily accepted in this hotel as she and Juliana had. She had to believe that he had only stood up to the humiliating reaction to him for her sake, so that she could get some badly needed rest and a proper meal in her stomach.

Ashley lay back down on the bed, trying to force her eyes shut, knowing that she terribly needed to go to sleep. There were many days ahead of her when she might not have the chance to sleep in or even in a room. If she could only forget the cockroaches. . . .

She bolted upright and slapped a cockroach away from her arm, shuddering with distaste as it scrambled away from her across the bed.

"I can't bear to stay here another minute," she moaned, climbing from the bed. She clutched the blanket around her shoulders, grimacing as she made her way across the roach-infested floor.

When she got to the door she slowly opened it and leaned her head out, looking from side to side. A lantern hanging from the ceiling midway in the corridor gave off enough light for Ashley to see that she was alone in her midnight explorings.

She glanced at Yellow Thunder's closed door. Smiling to herself, she tiptoed from her room, closed the door behind her, then crept to Yellow Thunder's door. She hesitated a moment, then lightly knocked, stopping and listening for any sounds of movement in the room.

When she didn't hear anything, she knocked again, hoping that if he was asleep, this time the knocking would awaken him. She felt wicked to the core for having come to his room in the middle of the night like this, yet she had only come to see what he was doing to fight off the fretful creatures of the night. She so desperately wanted to be able to go to sleep. She was feeling giddy from being so tired—so sleepy, as one might feel after having too much to drink.

When there was no response to her second attempt at arousing Yellow Thunder, a sudden fear grabbed at Ashley's insides.

What if he was gone?

What if he had left her behind, to fend for herself?

The thought terrified her, for she knew that somehow her stepbrother would find her, especially if she went back to New Orleans.

It tore at her heart how she had been forced to leave her beloved lace-making supplies behind—*and* her precious laces packed in a trunk. But not even for them could she risk returning to New Orleans. She saw no way at all now of ever getting her belongings. Calvin could have someone watching for her return.

She thought gratefully of Yellow Thunder—without him, she was alone in the world.

Desperation made her open the door. She sighed heavily with relief when she discovered Yellow Thunder lying on the floor on a blanket, asleep. The moonlight was spilling through the window onto him, revealing his total nudity to Ashley. She was embarrassed, yet a strange sort of heat spread within her at the sight.

When he turned to lie on his side in his sleep, the muscles stirred and rippled down the full length of his lean, bronze body. From this angle, Ashley could see his bold nose, his strong chin, and the slope of his hard jaw—everything about him beautiful, even perfect.

Her gaze wandered lower, marveling over the expanse of his sleekly muscled shoulders, his flat belly, and his slim hips. She cringed when her gaze stopped at the scars on his chest, remembering again Calvin's wickedness, and Yellow Thunder's sacrifice for her.

But, thankfully, because of the herbs that Yellow Thunder had placed on the wounds, they were nearly healed now, leaving only the scars that would surely remain there forever to mar his lovely, muscled, copper skin.

She wrenched her eyes away, then blushed when she saw that part of a man's anatomy that she had only seen once before in her life—and that had been while being forced to watch Calvin rape Juliana.

Seeing Calvin nude, and that part of him that had invaded Juliana's body, had repelled her.

But seeing Yellow Thunder in this way sent a strange sort of thrill through her.

Something within her made her want to go and run her fingers over the sleekness of his flesh, to curl up next to him and awaken him with a kiss.

Then, ashamed of her wild thoughts and wanton behavior, she turned to go. She did not get the door opened before she felt strong arms encircling her waist, causing her blanket to drop away from her.

"You came," Yellow Thunder said huskily. He had realized she was there the moment she had entered the room, yet not knowing why she was there, he had pretended to be asleep.

When she had turned to flee, he had not been able to help himself from stopping her. He had not been able to go to sleep at first because of the crawling creatures in the room. After he had opened the shutters at the window, bringing the moon's glow into the room as though it were a bright light, and the bugs had scrambled back into their hiding places, he still had not been able to go to sleep. His mind had been tortured with wanting Ashley and worrying about her welfare. It seemed that she had felt his thoughts and had come to him, as though bidden.

"Yes, I came," Ashley said, gazing into his eyes, her heart pounding. "I felt so alone. And there were so many disgusting cockroaches running around in the room. I couldn't go to sleep. I had to see how you were doing. I'm sorry if I awakened you. I'll go back to my room now and leave you in peace."

She started to lean over to rescue her blanket from the floor, but Yellow Thunder's fingers on her shoulders kept her standing there, facing him. She tried not to look down, embarrassed that they both were standing there without any clothes on.

None of this seemed real to her.

Had she truly been living a normal life only a month ago, awakening every morning knowing what life had in store for her?

Oh, how quickly it had all changed!

Now her every heartbeat seemed to beat only for this handsome, wonderful Indian!

"Do you not know that I have not had a moment's peace since I met you?" Yellow Thunder said, placing a gentle hand to her face.

Ashley gasped. "I'm sorry for that," she said, lowering her eyes. "I didn't mean to interfere in your life. It . . . just happened."

"The interference is not what I am referring to when I speak of having no peace after having met

135

you," Yellow Thunder said, placing a finger to her chin and forcing her eyes up, so that they met and held his. "It is you, the woman, who has troubled my heart—the very core of my being. How can I have any peace within my soul when I sorely ache with wanting you? I see in your eyes that you feel the same. When we kissed, did you not feel it, also? To touch you . . . to *look* at you, is to love you. Tell me you are feeling the same for me. *Techila*, I love you, Ashley. *Techila*."

Ashley was at a loss for words, so completely surprised and moved was she by his confession.

How could she deny that her body turned to liquid every time his eyes touched her?

She had never felt so alive as when she was with him.

She did not know how to react to her own feelings—her frantic need of him.

These feelings that being with him aroused were all new to her.

"Tell me what is in your mind at this moment— what is in your *heart*," Yellow Thunder said, brushing her lips with a soft kiss. "Tell me, my woman. Tell me. Never fear telling me your feelings. Did I not tell you mine, for you? Let us share our thoughts, as though we are one being— one soul. It was meant to be, or you would not have come to me tonight. It is our destiny to share our lives. Tonight we shall travel to a place of bliss, if you will only allow it."

His mouth closed hard upon hers, his lips coming to hers in a meltingly hot kiss. With his arms enveloping her, drawing her against his muscled body, she could not hold back this wild, exuberant passion that was claiming her.

She twined her arms around his neck and returned the kiss. When his hands moved between them and cupped her breasts, gently kneading them, and then one of his hands traveled lower and found her warm and secret place and began caressing her, strange new sensations were born inside her. She clung to him, his lips now at the hollow of her throat.

Throwing her head back, she sighed with pleasure when he moved his mouth lower, to a breast, and began sucking the nipple to a throbbing tightness.

And then he suddenly swept her up into his arms and carried her to his blanket on the floor. As he lowered her to the blanket, where the moonlight was bright and silver, Yellow Thunder's gaze swept over Ashley, his heart throbbing within his chest as he saw just how exquisite she was. Her breasts were gently rounded, her waist was slim, her legs slender. Her body was sinuous, her facial features were perfect. Her long and drifting hair, the color of a savage sunrise, now lay spread out beneath her as he laid her on the blanket. He knelt down beside her, his hands moving slowly over her.

She smiled sweetly up at him as his eyes locked with hers in a silent understanding.

"You are not afraid?" Yellow Thunder said, moving over her, one hand at the juncture of her thighs, slowly caressing her most sensitive pleasure point. "You came to me tonight. Do you give yourself up to the passion I offer you—willingly?"

Ashley's heart thudded wildly within her chest, yet she could not say that she was afraid, nor ashamed for what she was ready to do. Being with him in every way seemed so natural, as though she had never lived any life without him. Her body ached for something that was mysterious to her, and she had to believe that only Yellow Thunder held the key to the answers that she sought.

"I have never experienced anything like these feelings before," Ashley murmured, reaching up to place her hands to his shoulders, gently drawing him down, closer to her. "I have needs I never knew before. And I now know that is because I had never met *you*. I want *you*, Yellow Thunder. I . . . love you."

She drifted toward him as his arms swept around her, drawing her against the warmth of his body. He held her close and kissed her softly as he gently parted her thighs with a knee. She could feel the fire of his passion as it probed into the untouched valley of her womanhood.

Her body absorbed his bold thrust within her, at first shocking her with a brief instant of pain. But the pain turned slowly into an exquisite, sweet rapture, and as his body plunged into hers with rhythmic thrusts, burying himself more deeply, she clung to him, returning his kiss, hungrily.

As their bodies strained together, Ashley's breath quickened. She abandoned herself to the pleasure that was spreading into a delicious tingling heat through her, blocking out everything but these blissful moments with the man she loved.

She had never known such joy—such total happiness—as now. She had never felt as loved, as needed, as now.

And she wanted to give back, as well as take.

Yellow Thunder caught Ashley's hands and held them slightly above her, against the floor. He kissed her eyes, her nose and throat, and then again her lips, each kiss bringing him closer to that sought-for release—closer to that moment of teaching his woman the true meaning of passion.

He wanted to give her much more than that.

In time, he wanted to give her the sky, the earth, the moon.

She was already all of those things to *him*!

As his passion rose, his whole body seemed fluid with a raging heat. He placed his fingers at her buttocks and lifted her closer to him as he continued his strokes within her. He kissed her long and hard, then forced his tongue through her lips, her mouth opening to receive it.

Ashley felt as though she were floating, and then it seemed as though she were overcome by an unbearable sweet pain. As Yellow Thunder's lips moved away and he laid his face against her chest, a cry of pleasure escaped from between her parted lips as she felt Yellow Thunder's body tremoring wildly within hers, his groans filling the midnight air with a sweet agony. . . .

And then all was quiet. Yellow Thunder rolled away from her, then drew her against him again, where they now lay side by side, the moon no longer spreading its soft light over them. Ashley gazed out the window and saw a dimly luminous ring around the moon. Her mother had taught her long ago that these signs of the moon portended a furious storm.

Yet she could not fear tomorrow and what it might bring in the wonder of this moment. . . .

# *Chapter Eleven*

With her buckskin outfit now clean and smelling as fresh as the outdoors, and with a belt that Anna had given her now holding her oversized breeches in place, Ashley crept into the room where Juliana lay awake, but far from well enough to travel.

Ashley knelt down beside the bed, cringing when out of the corner of her eye she saw a cockroach scamper into hiding beneath some peeled wallpaper on the far wall. She reached a gentle hand to the threadbare blanket that lay across Juliana up to her chin, and smoothed the wrinkles from it.

"You're going to be fine," Ashley murmured, smiling as Juliana offered her a weak smile. "It's just going to take a few more days for you to get your strength back."

"I know," Juliana said, in scarcely a whisper. She reached a trembling hand to Ashley's arm. "And I will be fine. Honest. You and Yellow Thunder go on and get as far away from Calvin Wyatt as you can. I doubt if he'll ever rest until he finds you."

"Strange as it may seem, Juliana, instead of running away from him, in a sense I'll be following him," Ashley said, her voice drawn. "Yellow Thunder has got to find the chopper's settlement, and as you know, that's where Calvin's riverboat is headed."

"Don't go with Yellow Thunder then," Juliana said, her eyes anxious. "Go . . . in a different direction." She gripped her fingers more tightly on Ashley's arm. "Ashley, who is to say what Calvin will do if he finds you, *or* me? Since we were both abducted and taken on board his boat, he is insane enough to believe that he now owns us. You saw the whip marks on Yellow Thunder's chest? Calvin might do worse to us." She lowered her eyes. "If raping me wasn't enough, he . . . he will think of some other vile scheme to force upon me. I know it as well as I know I am lying here so ill *because* of him."

Juliana lifted her pleading eyes to Ashley again. "Please don't go near Calvin Wyatt," she said, a keen desperation in her voice. "Please, Ashley. If you value your freedom *and* sanity, stay . . . far . . . from Calvin Wyatt."

"I promise you that he won't lay a hand on me again," Ashley said, her voice stern. "I can guarantee you that, Juliana. But what about you? What are you going to do once you are well enough to travel again? Where will you go?"

"I'm not sure," Juliana said, sighing heavily. "But don't you worry about me, either, Ashley, as far as Calvin Wyatt is concerned. If he ever tries anything with me again I—I swear I will—kill him."

Ashley stared down at Juliana for a moment, stunned by her words—harsh words that did not match the soul of the one who spoke them.

Yet Ashley understood. Calvin had changed Juliana's life, and her outlook on life, forever.

As he had her own, Ashley despaired.

"I must go now," Ashley said, taking Juliana's hand and squeezing it affectionately. "Yellow Thunder is waiting for me. He told me to give you his regards."

"I think you are wrong to join Yellow Thunder on his journey to find his sister," Juliana said, clutching tightly to Ashley's hand. "Especially if it might bring you face to face with Calvin again."

"There are many reasons why I must go with Yellow Thunder," Ashley said, a heated blush coloring her cheeks a rosy red. "And I can honestly tell you that I will be perfectly safe while with him. He now knows who his true enemy is and won't allow Calvin to take advantage of him again—*or* of me. I am sure that when Yellow Thunder rides with his Indian companions, he is a valiant warrior who knows how to deal with his enemies. I trust him, Juliana, implicitly."

"Trust is sometimes not enough," Juliana said, easing her hand from Ashley's. "I doubt I shall ever trust again."

Ashley gave Juliana another quiet stare, fearing for her, yet she knew the time had come to say her final farewell. She hoped that God in his mercy might guide Juliana into a safe, secure, and happy life, far away from the threat of Calvin Wyatt.

"Please take care of yourself," Juliana said, reaching out for Ashley as she rose to her full height next to the bed. "I'll keep you in my prayers, Ashley. And also Yellow Thunder. If not for him and his courage in boarding the riverboat to find us incarcerated, we'd still be there. I owe him so much, Ashley. And also you. If you had not found me in the swamp, I would more than likely be dead by now."

"But you're not and you will soon be leaving this place to seek your own way in the world," Ashley said, leaning down to give Juliana a soft hug. "I'll be thinking about you. I hope our paths will meet again—at a happier time."

Juliana returned the hug, then Ashley turned and left the room, willing herself not to cry. She had to be strong, in every way, to show that she deserved to be with Yellow Thunder on his search for his sister. Last night, she had found such bliss in his arms, and had also discovered a wondrous sort of peace that came with loving Yellow Thunder and being loved in return. Since last night, having proven their love for one another, Ashley felt as though she *did* belong with Yellow Thunder.

She could not envision a life without him now.

He was the center of her universe—of her life.

As she stepped out onto the porch into a morning that was gray with low-hanging dark clouds, Ashley searched with her eyes until she found Yellow Thunder. Warmth flooded her, and she paused before going any farther when she saw him waiting beneath a large elm tree. A bundle of food that Anna had given to them both earlier in the morning was slung across his right shoulder. She noticed that someone had been kind enough to give him a cotton shirt to wear, and his breeches were fresh and clean, the buckskin fabric clinging to his muscled legs like a second skin.

Just to look at him was to experience all sorts of wondrous feelings.

Recalling what they had experienced in one another's arms did not cause her to feel shame, but instead an intense feeling of—yes, of *belonging*. No one could ever convince her that what she had shared with him was wrong, nor that it mattered if her plans to marry him one day would seem mad in the eyes of most white people.

Fate had brought them together, and neither fate nor any enemy would tear them apart.

There was more activity in the village this morning. Abraham was playing his banjo, another man was playing a fiddle, and a third man was singing along with the music. Other men were loitering around outside the ramshackle buildings, some smoking corncob pipes, others just leaning against posts, watching and listening.

Ashley noticed that there were no women among those idling the morning away. She caught sight of several in the back yards of the establishments, some hanging clothes across a line, others bent over a washtub, scrubbing clothes on a scrub board.

But Ashley's attention was drawn to something else, which had already caught Yellow Thunder's undivided attention—three young boys playing a game of craps on the packed earth of the street in front of the saloon that sat not all that far from the hotel.

As Ashley watched the game, she left the porch and began walking slowly toward Yellow Thunder, as taken by the activity of the youngsters as her beloved Osage warrior. Two of the boys played against each other, the third youngster looking on with wide and eager eyes. The players knelt on the street opposite each other, and the game continued until the unlucky boy had lost all of his money, five or ten cents at a bet.

The two remaining boys then went against each other as the game continued. It was played with two dice, which each player would in turn shake in his hand, and then give a little throw along the street.

Every throw was accompanied by a half-articulate exclamation and a snap of the fingers. The thrower lost or won according to the number of dots that turned up on the dice.

Ashley stepped up next to Yellow Thunder, her gaze again following his. "That game is called craps," she said softly. "It's a way of gambling."

"It is not so much the game that fascinates me," Yellow Thunder said, turning his eyes away from the youngsters. He gazed down at Ashley, as their eyes met and held. "It is the foolishness of the parents who allow the boys to waste time in such a way, and also money. These boys should be learning the skills of their fathers. They should be preparing themselves for adulthood in productive ways. What they do today is wasteful and bad."

"Yes, I think so, too," Ashley said, nodding. She ran her fingers through her hair and let it flutter back down onto her shoulders, then flipped it back, so that it hung long down her back. "Are you ready, Yellow Thunder, to go on our way? Did you manage to find a horse? Did you tell the owner that we could come later and pay him for it and the reason for the urgency?"

"There are no horses," Yellow Thunder said, his gaze shifting, to the broken-down, bony mules that stood at the hitching rail, their heads hung. "Only mules. They would slow us down instead of help us."

Ashley looked over at the mules and grimaced. Greenhead flies were lighting on the pitiful-looking animals like a swarm of bees, biting and sucking their blood.

She looked quickly away. "The poor things," she murmured, shivering uncontrollably. "And, no. They certainly wouldn't hurry our travels."

"Then we must continue on foot," Yellow Thunder decided, looking toward the forest and the murky swamp that lay just beyond the village. "We must fight the swamps again, to make our way back toward the river." He turned his eyes back to her. "There is no other way." He placed a gentle hand to her cheek. "You do not have to go with Yellow Thunder. Stay here with Juliana. When I have achieved my goal, I will return for you."

Ashley lifted her chin stubbornly. "No," she said. "I won't do that. Even though you've promised to return for me, circumstances might make that impossible. I'm afraid that I would never see

147

you again. I don't think I could bear that, Yellow Thunder."

"I keep my word, *always*," Yellow Thunder said, leaning his face down into hers. "I say I will return. I will return."

"It is not your word that I doubt," Ashley said, swallowing back a lump that was growing in her throat. "It is circumstances that I fear—circumstances that could keep us apart forever. My stepbrother, for one."

"Yes, it *was* foolish of me to even consider leaving you behind," Yellow Thunder said gravely. "It is because of your stepbrother that I must keep you with me at all times, to make sure that he does not imprison you again."

He placed a hand on her elbow. "*Hiyupo*, come with me," he said softly. "We have said our goodbyes to these people and Juliana. It is best that we be on our way."

He cast a quick glance at the sky. "The weather may be our worst enemy today," he said. "Let us get as far as we can before it attacks us."

Ashley suddenly remembered having seen the hazy ring around the moon the previous night. She nodded and fell into step beside Yellow Feather. When Anna came out onto the porch and began waving, Ashley gave a quick wave, and then another one to Abraham as he laid his banjo aside and gave her a silent stare.

Then she and Yellow Thunder once again entered the swamp, trying to stay at its outer fringes where they did not have to go any deeper than their ankles. As they continued on, Ashley realized the vast loneliness of the setting, with only an occasional glimpse of plantation fields or a scattering of cabins.

But more often than not, there was the vast land of nothingness again, except for the green, slimy water and the lacy moss that draped from tree to tree, an occasional snake slithering away across the top of the water, gliding smoothly and effortlessly.

After traveling for several hours, Yellow Thunder grabbed Ashley's hand and stopped her. She followed his worried gaze and saw a black cloud rising in the west, and what seemed to be smoke approaching them. She gasped and grabbed Yellow Thunder's hand, for never had she seen such a black smudge in the sky, and down low such a queer, yellow glimmer.

Then she remembered having read reports of such a sky in the New Orleans newspapers, and what it portended.

"A tornado!" she screamed, paling. "We must find cover!"

Yellow Thunder placed an arm around her waist and forced her onto the ground and dragged her with him into the water. They flung themselves low, only keeping their heads slightly above the murky water.

They clung to one another as the funnel made a track about one hundred yards wide close by them, taking everything before it.

The trees that were a little decayed were twisted off, leaving only stumps, and trees that were sound were jerked right up by the roots, no matter how big they were.

It cleared everything right down to the ground, and struck some birds trying to take flight, taking their feathers off as cleanly as if they had been plucked off by human fingers.

Just as suddenly as the tornado had come, everything then became quiet and peaceful again. Ashley moved shakily to her feet alongside Yellow Thunder. She was quite shaken by the ordeal, pale and weak in the knees.

She looked down at her buckskin attire and groaned, seeing that it was filthy again, and her skin was so cold it felt as though someone had submerged her in a bucket of ice cold water.

Yet these problems were trivial.

She was just glad to be alive!

She flung herself into Yellow Thunder's arms. "Hold me," she murmured. "We came so close to being killed. Oh, Yellow Thunder, hold me. I want to feel you next to me."

Yellow Thunder held her tightly, yet he offered no comment. His gaze moved to the heavens, thinking that perhaps he was being punished for something, or being tested! He looked into the gray sky and said a silent prayer to *Wah-Kon-Tah*, his Great Spirit, asking forgiveness for whatever transgression he was receiving punishment for, and asked his Great Spirit to spare him and his woman any more trials.

Then he placed his hands on Ashley's shoulders and held her away from him. "We won this battle with nature," he said. "The next time we may not be as lucky. Are you still certain that you want to go with me on this perilous journey of the heart?"

"Yellow Thunder, I want to be nowhere but with you," Ashley said, then sighed with pleasure as he drew her into his arms and gave her a sweet and lingering kiss.

And then they went on their way again through the swamp, stopping only once to eat from the food that Anna had prepared for them.

When twilight began to settle in over the land, they knew that they had to find shelter. The swamp was no place to be at night.

They searched and searched, then felt relieved when they saw lamplight up ahead.

They began making their way toward it.

# *Chapter Twelve*

A rude wind buffeted the trees and soughed wearily through them. The gloomy, darkening skies of dusk and the bleak and boisterous wind added to Ashley's foreboding as she kept close beside Yellow Thunder as suddenly before them lay the great Mississippi River, a score of boats resting along its banks.

"Water Gypsies," Ashley said aloud, having learned of these dwellers in the great river valley through her friends in New Orleans. She stopped with Yellow Thunder and gaped openly at the boats, wondering if among them might be someone they could trust, at least for this one night.

"What are water gypsies?" Yellow Thunder asked, arching an eyebrow.

"These are people who have left the normal way of life behind them and who have chosen to live in houseboats," Ashley explained.

"They have found the world of the white man not to their liking?" Yellow Thunder asked. "Yet, they do not hunger to possess the land of the red man?"

"It seems that something has changed their minds about their choices in life," Ashley said, raking her eyes slowly over the flotilla of houseboat refugees. The boats varied in size and construction, each having been built according to the means of its owner, his chance whims, and the materials he may have had on hand.

Some boats were hardly bigger than an ordinary skiff and were roofed with canvas stretched over loops. To get inside, the dwellers would have to crawl through a narrow opening. Other boats were large, convenient, and made homes by no means to be despised. They had several rooms and were very likely as nice inside as the parlor in any gentleman's home.

Some river people called their floating homes "shanty boats"—they were rudely built, got little care, and were expected to go to pieces in a few years.

A good many of the boats had a paddlewheel at the stern. The bit of deck, fore and aft, was not protected with railings.

Ashley's gaze shifted to a wreck half submerged nearby. Close beside it was a peddler's boat, a sign painted on its sides stating that it had medicines for sale and that it carried a general stock of merchandise.

Alongshore, neighboring the boats, were many nets, lines, and other fishing tackle. Some of the men were overhauling their tackle, others were loafing, still others were out in their boats pulling up the lines they had set.

"Let us go and see if there is someone among these boat people who might share the warmth of their dwelling and food with two strangers," Yellow Thunder said, placing a gentle hand on Ashley's elbow and walking her onward toward the boats.

In truth, he did not like asking anyone for anything, especially a white man. But for Ashley, he felt that he must. He did not feel that it was safe enough just yet to make a campfire out in the open, fearing that should Calvin or his men still be searching for them, the fire would draw them to it—as it had the last time Yellow Thunder had foolishly made a fire to warm his woman.

Taking refuge among people of Ashley's own kind seemed the only way to keep her safe from Calvin Wyatt, at least until Yellow Thunder no longer had the need to stay close to the river on which Calvin's riverboat was traveling.

If Yellow Thunder was correct in his thinking, the path of that riverboat would eventually lead him to his beloved sister.

If not, he feared that Bright Eyes would be lost to him forever.

Lanterns had been lighted and were swaying in the breeze at the prow of many of the houseboats, sending a golden, shimmering light across the gently splashing waves of the water beside them. Ashley and Yellow Thunder found many eyes following them suspiciously as people moved onto their decks, to stare at the approaching strangers.

Looking guardedly around her, seeing too much in the eyes of these people that made her uncomfortable, Ashley took Yellow Thunder's hand and steered him toward the boat closest to them. It was a little vessel hitched to the shore, a plank serving as a gangway from land to deck.

Suddenly someone stepped out onto the deck of this boat, causing Ashley and Yellow Thunder to stop with a start, a shotgun aimed at them.

Shaken and speechless, Ashley stared at the elderly woman, having never seen anyone quite like her before. She was stooped-shouldered, with a face deeply pitted with smallpox scars, and she wore a long cotton dress that was faded with age and very wrinkled. Her gray hair hung in wiry strings almost to the deck of her boat, and a corn-cob pipe hung from one corner of her mouth.

"You stop right there," she said in a grumble, her pipe bobbing between her lips as she spoke. "Don't you'uns take another step. Or you'll soon be food for the alligators yonder in the swamps."

"We mean you no harm," Ashley finally managed to say, the words stumbling awkwardly across her lips. "My friend and I have only stopped to ask for some food, and a moment by your stove. Our food supply has run out, and I'm chilled to the bone. My feet are wet and cold. Could you please lend a hand? We would be eternally grateful."

The elderly lady's shaggy eyebrows fused together as she frowned, looking from Ashley to Yellow

# Cassie Edwards

Thunder, then gazing more intensely at Ashley. "Where'd you find this Injun?" she said in her raspy voice. "I ain't never seen a white woman bein' an Injun's travelin' companion before. And where'd you come from? Who're you *runnin'* from?"

Ashley laughed softly, yet kept a nervous eye on the shotgun. "Ma'am, you're asking questions too quickly for me to remember one from the other," she said. "As for my traveling companion. I am trying to help him find his sister. Someone came to his village and abducted her."

The elderly lady slowly lowered her shotgun. "Do you think she's here? In one of the houseboats?" she asked quietly, gazing suspiciously over her shoulder at the other boats.

She then looked at Ashley again, and slowly at Yellow Thunder. "I ain't seen any Injun squaws wandering around on the decks of any of these houseboats," she said, gumming the stem of her pipe.

"No, you've misunderstood," Ashley quickly said. "We only came upon this flotilla of boats by accident. We're headed for the chopper's settlement. That's where we think we'll find Yellow Thunder's sister."

The lady kneaded her chin thoughtfully. "Chopper's settlement, huh?" she said, frowning. "Yep. Makes sense. Out there all alone, havin' only each other for companionship, those restless lumberjacks could be guilty of all sorts of meanness."

Ashley and Yellow Thunder exchanged knowing glances, then followed the woman as she motioned

156

with a hand for them to come on board her boat.

"My name's Petulia," the lady said over her shoulder. "Just call me Petulia."

"That's a pretty name," Ashley said, wanting to keep the conversation going, feeling more comfortable with the situation that way.

Yellow Thunder's silence unnerved Ashley, yet she thought that she just might understand. All of these things that he was becoming involved in which included white people surely went against his grain, in that he seemed to be the sort who preferred anything over having to mingle with white people. His childhood had introduced him to their selfish, unkind ways.

Yellow Thunder did not seem the sort, either, to let down his guard all that easily, and because he had these past few days made Ashley believe that he did so only because of her. If he had continued in his search for his sister alone, he most certainly would not have come to a houseboat, asking for food and warmth. He probably knew the art of fasting as a young man among those of his own age in his Osage tribe and could use these skills now, if not for her.

She was touched that he cared so much for her and that he had put full trust in her. That gave her a sweet feeling of belonging, as though she were truly one with him.

"Come on inside and sit yourself down beside the stove and get yourselves warm while I prepare us a bite to eat," Petulia said, taking her pipe from her mouth and placing it, bowl up, in a tin can. "It won't be long. I was midst preparin' it when I saw you comin' toward my houseboat. And there's plenty to eat." She laughed throatily. "I always make enough to feed an army. What I don't eat, I feed to the fish. That makes a fat catch for me when I decide I want fish for my evenin' meal."

With Yellow Thunder at her side, Ashley followed Petulia into the houseboat, feeling the floor sagging beneath their weight. The ceiling was low and brown with smoke, the walls papered with yellowed newspapers.

She looked slowly around her. The small room was sparsely furnished, with only two overstuffed chairs, the stuffing hanging from them in yellow globs. Also there was a table that was littered with all assortments of papers, framed pictures, and chipped cups and saucers. A cot hugged one wall, with yellowed and stained blankets draped carelessly across it.

A pot-bellied stove glowed orange in a corner with a bucket of chopped wood sitting on the floor beside it.

"Pull those chairs over close to the fire and make yourselves comfortable," Petulia said as she stood her shotgun up against the wall, then placed a wad of snuff inside her upper lip.

Yellow Thunder and Ashley moved the two chairs over beside the stove. Petulia lit a lantern and sat it down on top of the papers on the table, then waddled away and into another room, cackling.

"She is strange, to say the least," Ashley said softly, smiling weakly over at Yellow Thunder. She noticed how stiffly he sat in the chair, his arms folded tightly across his chest.

She reached a hand to his cheek and gently touched it. "Perhaps we should leave," she murmured. "I don't want you to be uncomfortable on my behalf. Please let's go. Surely Calvin isn't still searching for us. Let's go and find a place to set up camp, Yellow Thunder. It isn't fair that you should be doing something that you detest. It's enough that you have lost a sister and mother at the hands of white people. You should not have to be humiliated over and over again by them because of your concern for me. I am concerned for *you*. Let's go now, Yellow Thunder, before Petulia comes back into the room."

Yellow Thunder took her hand and kissed her palm, then held it over his heart. "We stay," he said thickly. "You eat and rest, and then we will go on our way. My woman, my heart leads me to do what is right by you. So accept these moments away from the murky waters of the swamp. Let your moccasins and feet get dry and warm. Let your stomach get comfortable with food. Let your eyes close with sleep. Then we will continue our search for the chopper's settlement."

"Whatever you say," Ashley said, so badly wanting to move into his arms and rest her cheek against his powerful chest. She hoped that the time would come when they would find a quiet, sweet peace in which to have their moments of sharing and loving with a clear mind and heart.

At this moment it seemed an impossible dream.

But even being with Yellow Thunder at all was like existing in a fantasy world. She feared that she might awaken at any moment and discover that she had been dreaming, and that Yellow Thunder was indeed a figment of her quite vivid imagination.

Yellow Thunder unclasped her hand and she brought it back to rest on her lap. She became aware of pleasant smells coming from the kitchen, and while waiting for Petulia to bring them her proffered meal, she looked slowly around the room again, this time getting a closer look since the lantern was casting more light on things.

Soon a warning flashed through Ashley. She could tell that she and Yellow Thunder were in the presence of someone who practiced voodoo. She had read many accounts in the New Orleans newspapers of witches living in the swamps who practiced voodoo, and the paraphernalia used by them. Ashley's heart pounded with fear when her gaze fell upon several voodoo rings hanging from a hook on the wall—rings made of feathers twisted into a band or rings fifteen inches across. Tied to them were many little bags made up of a piece of cloth with wax on both sides, and all kinds of feathers curled around the wax. These rings and bags were made to be hidden under the doorstep or in the bed of the person the witch wanted to harm.

Ashley wanted to flee right then and there, but she did not have a chance to explain what she had discovered to Yellow Thunder. Petulia was there, offering Ashley and Yellow Thunder a plate spread generously with food, and a pot of coffee and two cups which she set on the table beside them.

"Eat your fill and remember there's more where this came from," Petulia said, cackling as she waddled back into the kitchen.

Ashley stared down at the food, wondering if it was safe to eat it.

What if the old witch had placed a potion in it? Or some poison?

Before she could warn him, Yellow Thunder scooped a large bite of the food into his mouth. She scarcely breathed, fearing that at any moment he might collapse before her eyes, dead from the poison.

When he stayed perfectly healthy and continued eating, Ashley turned her eyes back to her own plate and slowly lifted her fork, still pausing before taking her first bite. It was a strange combination—pokeweed and sour-dock greens with fat pork and cornbread. In a corner of the dish lay a vinegar pie, which might just as well be poison, to Ashley's taste.

Sighing heavily, and so hungry she was weak, she dove into the food and ate and ate until the plate was clean—except for the vinegar pie that she just could not force herself to swallow.

Petulia waddled into the room, a shawl draped over her rounded shoulder. "I've got to leave for a spell," she said, smiling when she spied the plates that were, for the most part, empty. "I'm going to go and get a jar of buttermilk. I keep it lowered in the depths of the river for good-keeping. It's down the river a mite, but I'll be back before you can bat an eye." She cackled as she left the houseboat.

"We've got to get out of here," Ashley whispered harshly. "We can't stay here. Petulia practices voodoo. I don't trust her. She might cast a spell on us if she gets a reason to. I don't want to give her the opportunity to get a lock of our hair or cut off a portion of one of our fingernails while we're sleeping, for her to use in her voodoo."

She grabbed Yellow Thunder's hand. "Come on," she pleaded. "Let's go."

"I do not fear her magic," Yellow Thunder said, refusing to budge. "Sit. Stay. You have eaten. Now you rest."

Frustrated, Ashley sat back down.

Again her eyes roamed over the room. She paled and gasped when she caught sight of a tiny rag doll partially exposed beneath a pile of dirty clothes in a corner of the room. The doll had long, flowing golden hair—and a pin sticking in one of its arms. She stared at it a moment longer, knowing the meaning of the pin.

"That does it," she declared. "I'm not staying another minute in this place."

She bolted to her feet and went and got the doll. She took it to Yellow Thunder and showed it to him. "This doll represents someone that Petulia dislikes," she explained. "The pin in the doll's arm is supposed to be the same as sticking a pin, or knife, in a real person. This is Petulia's way of practicing voodoo, and I would hate to know her other ways."

She took the doll and placed it where she had found it, and was relieved when she found Yellow

Thunder standing behind her when she rose back to her full height.

"We will leave—not because of this woman's magic," he said. "But because of how it frightens you." He placed a comforting arm around her waist. "*Ho-yupo*. Let us leave before she returns."

Ashley flung herself into his arms and gave him a quick hug, then held his hand as they crept outside and down the plank, hurrying to the dark shadows of the forest beyond. Ashley shivered as the damp night air stung her cheeks, yet she was glad not to be able to see the lanterns of the houseboats behind them any longer.

But her eyes were wide and fearful as once again she found herself following the outer fringes of the murky swamp, again at the mercy of the night.

# *Chapter Thirteen*

They found a high spot of land after leaving the houseboats behind, and Ashley spent the night huddled beneath a tree, snuggled in Yellow Thunder's arms.

Not pausing to eat breakfast, they fled onward the next morning, now following the banks of the Mississippi, still hoping to find the chopper's settlement.

When Ashley did not think that she could travel another step before exhaustion and hunger claimed her, she and Yellow Thunder's luck seemed to suddenly change. They came across a bent little old man who was just pushing his raft away from shore to travel on the river.

Before the man had a chance to board his raft, Ashley broke away from Yellow Thunder and went to him, taking hold of his arm. "Sir, may we join you on your raft?" she asked breathlessly, her eyes pleading with him. "We've no horse, nor other means of transport. We've been traveling solely on foot. Please allow us to share your raft, at least for a short distance down the river." She lowered her eyes and dropped her hand away from him, then gazed at him again. "I am so tired of walking, sir. It would be so nice to be able to sit a spell on your raft."

The bent little man had a face that was covered with warts. He looked guardedly from Ashley to Yellow Thunder, squinting as he studied them. "Where you headed?" he asked, spitting over his left shoulder.

Yellow Thunder stepped up beside Ashley. He held his chin proudly high. "We are searching for a place that is called chopper's settlement," he said flatly. "That is our destination."

The old man clutched hard to the rope that held the raft in place. "What's your business there?" he said, his voice slight as he gazed up at Yellow Thunder, who towered over him.

"I am searching for Bright Eyes, my sister," Yellow Thunder said, gazing past the old man at the raft. He could tell that this was the man's home, for there was a small room of warped planks built on it. Two cows and a calf were his traveling companions, secured by a rope to the house. The space on the raft was sparse, yet it would carry just three people.

Yellow Thunder thought back to his village, where many canoes were always available for travel down the river. The canoes had been made with much pride; he guessed that this strange vessel had been made with equal pride by this aged man. Yellow Thunder could tell that it pleased the old man that someone was interested in traveling on his raft. It showed in his squinting gray eyes.

"Your sister, eh?" the old man said, kneading his chin thoughtfully. He spat over his shoulder again, then raked his fingers through his sparse gray hair. "The chopper's settlement, eh?"

The old man gestured toward his raft. "Yep," he said, without further thought. "Come on board my raft. I'll take you there. Be glad to."

He smiled at Ashley, and then Yellow Thunder. "My name's Frog," he said, reaching an eager hand toward Ashley, shaking it, then shaking Yellow Thunder's. "Glad to make your acquaintance."

Ashley told Frog their names as she and Yellow Thunder boarded the raft with him. She sighed as she sat down on the log floor, not even caring that she was having to share the small space with the cows and calf.

In fact, she enjoyed looking into the dark, round, trusting eyes of the calf as it ambled closer to her. As the old man used a pole to send the raft out into deeper waters, Yellow Thunder settled down beside Ashley. Enjoying herself enough to forget the hunger and weariness that was plaguing her, Ashley began stroking the calf's brown-speckled head, giggling when the calf reached its tongue out to lick her.

"Such a sweet thing," Ashley murmured, then turned her attention back to Yellow Thunder. "Did you hear what Frog said? He's taking us to the chopper's settlement. Perhaps your search will soon be over. I pray that you will find your sister, and that she will be well and unharmed."

"She will never be the same again," Yellow Thunder said sadly, watching the land darting by as the raft now floated freely down the middle of the river. "Now that a white man has touched her, she will forever feel tainted by it. She may not even be looked upon with favor by one of her own kind. If not, she may choose death over life. And that troubles me, Ashley. She deserves all that is good, for *she* was everything that was good."

Ashley placed a gentle hand on his arm. "Oh, Yellow Thunder, I am so sorry," she murmured. "You have been made to suffer so much at the hands of white people. How can you find it within your heart to love me? To touch me? When you look at me, do you not see that my skin is white?"

Yellow Thunder placed a hand to her cheek and she leaned into it. "*Ah-hah*, your skin is white," he said thickly. "But your heart is pure. It is what I feel when I am with you. Not what I see." He smiled as he leaned his face closer to hers. "Yet, that is not entirely so. I am touched by your loveliness as well as your generous, kind heart. You are perfect in every way, *mitawin*."

Ashley's heart thundered at his nearness and his sweetness when he talked to her. She leaned away from him, for if she didn't, she would surely kiss him, and she didn't want to embarrass him in front of the stranger.

167

"You called me by an Indian name," she said softly. "What did you say? What does *mitawin* mean?"

"It can mean two things in the Osage language," Yellow Thunder said, easing away from her. He drew his knees up to his chest and wrapped his arms around them. "It can mean my woman, or it can mean—wife." He smiled at her again. "Today, it meant my woman. Soon, it will mean my *wife*."

Tears swelled in Ashley's eyes. "Do you know just how much I love you?" she asked, softly enough so that Frog wouldn't hear her. "My darling, I didn't know such a love could exist. It wouldn't have for me if I had not met you." She wiped tears of happiness away from her eyes. "I will gladly be your wife whenever you say, wherever you say. I want nothing more in life than to be with you always."

She moved closer to him, content for the moment, even forgetting the hungry pangs at the pit of her stomach and the weariness of her legs and back. At this moment, she was with her beloved, and she was forcing herself not to think about what might happen once they reach the chopper's settlement.

She would not worry about Calvin possibly catching her and Yellow Thunder, selling Yellow Thunder on the auction block, and taking her as his love slave, even eventually forcing her to marry him.

No, she would not think of the worst that could happen—only the good. Yellow Thunder would find his sister. He would take her away from the life of slavery. Ashley would go with Yellow

Thunder and Bright Eyes to their Osage village. There she would learn the Osage ways as Yellow Thunder's wife.

The winds were calm this day. The raft was following the river far back into the woods, the Mississippi running swift and deep, full of logs ever gliding through the water, moving smoothly and mysteriously through the silent wilderness, with only a soft plunk, plunk, as they struck one another.

The views along the river were beautiful. The occasional bluffs on either side of them looked like mountain ranges, and then again they were traveling alongside tangles of trees, with an occasional break in them, where a lone house could be seen and a garden patch of dried out, drooping cornstalks.

To Ashley, this day the river was a stream of romance, full of change and fascination. Whether it rose or fell, it carried the raft safely in its bosom.

Ashley leaned with the raft as it began making a turn in the river, and then she paled and gasped when up ahead, around the bend, she caught sight of tall steamer smokestacks with their black smoke rising into the sky. The steamer came into full sight as the raft made its complete turn in the river.

"There it is!" she said, giving Yellow Thunder a nervous shake of the arm. "And it's Calvin's, for sure. I see the name on the side of the boat."

Yellow Thunder moved quickly to his feet and went to Frog. He placed a hand on the man's slight shoulders. "Quickly take your raft to the land," he said in a flat command. "Now, before those on the riverboat spy us in the water."

Frog nodded, his eyes wide as he peered at the riverboat in the distance. He placed his pole deep into the water and turned the raft toward land, then with the aid of the pole, guided the raft toward shore.

Ashley stood beside Yellow Thunder, waiting for the raft to get close enough to land so that they could jump off and wade the rest of the way on foot.

She peered with a pounding heart at the riverboat. As it swung about in the river and pushed its bow to the shore, black roustabouts promptly left the boat and wrapped a rope around a tree. Scampering about, the roustabouts then laid a couple of planks from the boat to the land.

Ashley scarcely breathed as she watched, along with Yellow Thunder, as several women were hustled off the boat, wearing "captive straps" cut from the hind leg of a buffalo hide. The women were forced to stand in a cluster together, awaiting their doom.

When the raft was only a few feet from land, Ashley and Yellow Thunder thanked Frog for his assistance. They fled from the raft and followed the shoreline upstream on foot, passing through dense groves of cottonwoods. They lost themselves in the thick brush along the riverbank after they got close enough to the riverboat to observe the women being herded toward a score of structures loosely grouped among the trees.

The dwellings had been put up in tent fashion, the sides made of boards, the roofs of canvas. Farther back still from the river, some cabins stood among the weeds, willows, and rank swamp growth that was infested with mosquitoes, snakes, frogs, and alligators.

Pigs and chickens wandered about as the enslaved women were lined up in front of the tent-like houses. Ashley cringed and Yellow Thunder gritted his teeth when many unkempt men came from the dwellings and began running their hands over the women, while Calvin stood on board his riverboat, watching, a smug look on his face.

Ashley realized without a doubt that these women had been brought to be sold to the choppers as though they were no more than bags of potatoes. She glared up at her stepbrother, hating him with all her soul.

"While the men are distracted by the women, we have the opportunity to search their houses for my sister," Yellow Thunder said, glancing over his shoulder at the tent-houses. "But we must hurry. Once a woman is bought by a particular man, he will be eager to take her to his dwelling. You can see in the eyes of these men how long they have been without a woman. This gives me hope that perhaps my sister is not here—that I will eventually find her somewhere else, where she will not have been forced to live such a life of degradation as these men offer."

Ashley knew by the tone of Yellow Thunder's voice that he was torn. A part of him wanted to find his sister in the chopper's settlement, to end

171

his search, and to be able to return her to a normal life with his people. Yet she knew that he dreaded the fact that he might find her here, beaten down, a woman he would no longer recognize. . . .

Ashley just wanted it to be over for Yellow Thunder, so that the haunted look would leave his eyes, so that he could begin a new chapter of his life.

Following his lead, Ashley went with Yellow Thunder into the chopper's village, stealthily going from dwelling to dwelling, surprised to find no women at all there, nor any signs that there were ever any women in the houses. This had to mean that this was the first time slavery had been a part of these lumberjacks' lives—and that Yellow Thunder's search here for his sister was in vain.

They found many of the houses in disarray. The one in which she and Yellow Thunder were standing was filthy, with fruit and vegetable peelings piled high on the kitchen floor, with soiled dishes stacked beside the wash basin. The aroma was so unpleasant, it stung Ashley's nose.

"We have wasted time by coming here," Yellow Thunder said. "My sister is not here, nor has she ever been."

He went to a window and stared from it, seeing the river on one side of the settlement, a thick forest on the other side.

"She is nowhere near here," he said, his voice full of pain. "Calvin has sold her elsewhere."

The failure in Yellow Thunder's eyes and voice made an ache in Ashley's heart. She touched his cheek gently. "I'm so sorry," she murmured. "So very, very sorry."

Yellow Thunder turned his moody eyes to her. "Do not be sorry," he said. "You are not the cause of my failures. Fate is the cause. My sister is gone from me, forever, because of the ugly, sharp fangs of fate."

"And Calvin," Ashley interjected.

Yellow Thunder frowned down at her. "*Ah-hah*, and also Calvin," he grumbled. "And one day, he will pay."

The bitterness in Yellow Thunder's voice almost made Ashley flinch. But she didn't have time to react to it. Yellow Thunder had her by the arm and was ushering her toward the door.

She drew away from him when she glanced over her shoulder and her gaze fell on a blanket draped over the back of a chair. She was recalling the cold dampness of night.

Without further thought, she grabbed the blanket, then went on outside with Yellow Thunder. They ran toward the safe cover of the forest.

Suddenly Yellow Thunder changed direction when he spied several horses in a corral.

"Come," he said, giving Ashley a nod over his shoulder. "We will no longer travel on foot."

With a thumping heart, Ashley ran with Yellow Thunder to the horses. As he chose one for himself, she caught the reins of a gentle mare and was soon leading her away into the forest, alongside Yellow Thunder and his strawberry roan.

When they found cover behind a huge boulder that had fallen from a bluff overhead, they stopped and watched as the last of the women were grabbed by the men and ushered away.

"I wish there was something I could do to keep them from this fate that has befallen them," Yellow Thunder said sadly, watching one of the women as she struggled with a man who did not wait until he got her inside the privacy of his house to have his fun with her. He dragged her with him to the ground and threw up her skirt.

"Lord," Ashley gasped, turning her eyes quickly away. "These men are animals. It's so disgusting. Yellow Thunder, I could have been among them, if not for you."

She felt gentle hands on her waist and crept into Yellow Thunder's arms as he drew her against him.

"Finding you has been a bright moment in my life," Yellow Thunder said. "You have eased the pain I carry within my heart over the loss of my sister. And even though we did not find her today, I feel somewhat victorious because I saved you from the clutches of those evil men. And, Ashley, I will not give up searching for my sister. I *will* find her."

She clung to him, at least for the moment feeling at peace with herself. "Where will you look next?" she murmured.

"That I do not know," Yellow Thunder said, easing her away from him. He gazed up at the trees, seeing the traces of color coming into them. "It is time now for the buffalo hunt. I must return to my people and participate in the hunt. My father depends on me to ride at his side, to prove to our people that I am fit to be their chief. I must kill the first buffalo, even before my father, as he killed the first buffalo for his people long ago, when my mother carried me safely within her womb."

Ashley was looking over his shoulder when she grew weak in the knees and grabbed Yellow Thunder, dragging him down onto the ground beside her. "Calvin was searching the land with his spy glass," she said, her voice filled with panic. "Lord, Yellow Thunder, he could have seen us. Perhaps he *did*. What if he saw the horses?"

Yellow Thunder took Ashley by the hand and together they led their horses into the darker shadows of the forest. When Yellow Thunder thought that they were out of range of the spyglass, he lifted Ashley onto her horse. He then mounted his own steed in a quick leap, and with Ashley at his side on her borrowed mare, rode away in a lope through the forest.

When they reached a wide stretch of meadow, they urged their horses into a hard gallop.

After riding for the rest of the day, Ashley was so bone-tired and hungry, she almost fell from her horse.

Seeing Ashley weaving, Yellow Thunder became alarmed. He drew a tight rein and grabbed Ashley's horse's reins from her hands, tied them to his, then reached for Ashley and drew her over onto his lap.

"I'm so tired," she murmured. "I'm so . . .sleepy."

"It is not safe to stop just yet," Yellow Thunder said, kissing her brow. "We must get farther away from the river. Lean against me, my love. Sleep.

Soon I will find you a place to rest. Soon I will find food. Soon."

Ashley nodded and snuggled against him. Her eyelashes fluttered as her eyes closed. She was vaguely aware of the sound of the horses' hoofbeats as hers trailed along beside Yellow Thunder's.

# *Chapter Fourteen*

As the sun sent its last streamers of light through the thick leaves of the trees overhead, Yellow Thunder drew his horse to a stop, having finally found the perfect place to make camp. While Ashley lay limply on his lap, his one arm supporting her against him and a blanket draped snugly around her, he looked around, glad to have found this enchanting place on the banks of a clear and rippling river that was alive with fish.

The river was surrounded by copses of the most luxuriant and picturesque foliage. Lofty elms spread their huge branches, as if offering protection to the cherry and plum trees that supported festoons of grapevines and their purple clusters of grapes.

Beneath these, the green carpet of grass was decked with wild flowers of all tints and various sizes, from the wild sunflowers with their thousand tall and drooping heads to the lilies that crept beneath them.

A deer rose from a quiet thicket close by and bounded out and over the underbrush which hemmed in and framed this little picture that had been most masterfully created by *Wah-kon-tah*, Yellow Thunder's Great Spirit.

Yellow Thunder's chest swelled with pride, glad to know that he had now entered a land that he was more acquainted with—the land of plenty, land that had been blessed by the Great Spirit at the beginning of time.

Gazing down at Ashley, concerned over how soundly she slept, he held her tightly and slipped easily from his saddle.

The fish flipping occasionally from the water reminded Yellow Thunder that he and Ashley had not eaten since the night before. He was anxious to catch several fish and get them cooking over a fire, hoping that food would help bring Ashley out of her lethargic state.

With eager steps, Yellow Thunder carried Ashley beneath the umbrella of a tall oak and laid her gently on a thick carpet of grass, then drew the blanket over her. He bent on one knee beside her, and his heart leapt when she stirred slightly, then turned on her side and curled up, still sleeping.

Yellow Thunder sighed heavily and gazed down at Ashley a moment longer, touched to the core of his being by her loveliness. Then he went back to the horses and secured their reins around a tree limb.

Knowing that he and Ashley had traveled far

enough from the chopper's settlement now to build a fire, he wasted no time in gathering wood and stacking it in the center of several large stones that he had placed in a circle.

Soon flames were leaping into the sky and he had a spear fashioned from a tree limb, its ends sharpened to a narrow point, for spearing fish.

He eyed Ashley again, then took his spear to the river where catfish teemed at the rocky bottom. He had never seen such large catfish before, and Yellow Thunder's eyes widened. He could almost taste them as he raised his spear and took aim.

When a fish swam up close to the embankment, Yellow Thunder tossed the spear, striking home as he speared the catfish squarely in the middle of its back.

The catfish began swimming round and round, as though crazed, flipped once or twice out of the water with the spear still sticking out of its back, and then dropped back into the water with a large splash and lay quiet as Yellow Thunder reached into the water and grabbed it.

Smiling, Yellow Thunder continued fishing until he had speared four more catfish, then carried his prizes back to the campfire.

When the moon filled the night with its silver light, the air was filled with the pleasant aroma of fish cooking on a spit over the fire.

He stopped and knelt down beside Ashley, smoothing a fallen lock of her hair back from her brow as he gazed at her. She was his main concern now and it seemed that he had been thoughtless in pushing her beyond her limits.

But they had had no choice but to keep moving.

He was only one man. Calvin had many at his disposal. To have been stopped by them again would have been the end of his *and* his woman's existence. They would have imprisoned him this time where there would have been no means of escaping. They could have used Ashley in many evil ways.

His jaw tightened angrily, knowing that one day soon Calvin and his men would become the hunted. And not by Yellow Thunder alone. When he chose to go after Calvin, many warriors would be under Yellow Thunder's command. Calvin would be forced to tell all truths, especially about where Bright Eyes had been taken.

*Ah-hah*, Calvin would pay for all of the transgressions of his life, especially against the Osage, Yellow Thunder vowed to himself.

But also for transgressions against Calvin's stepsister, Ashley!

Ashley sucked in a heavy breath and sniffed as she slowly opened her eyes. As she became fully awake, she gazed up at Yellow Thunder, whose eyes were on the fire and whose mind seemed to be millions of miles away.

She glanced past him, her stomach growling almost unmercifully as she caught sight of the fish roasting over the fire, the pleasant fragrance almost driving her wild. She had not had warm food in her stomach since she and Yellow Thunder had eaten Petulia's meal, and all the time they had been eating it fearing it might be laced with poison.

This fish cooking over the fire looked even better to Ashley than the fried chicken dinners that her mother had always prepared Sunday afternoons when Ashley was a child. She could hardly bear smelling it and not eating it.

"Yellow Thunder, I'm . . . so hungry," she blurted out through parched lips.

She wondered how long she had been asleep. Even after having slept, she felt lethargic. Perhaps all of her recent terrible experiences had finally taken their toll on her.

She had never been forced to endure much sadness in her life, except for her father's death long ago and her mother's recently. Except for that, everything had been handed to her on a silver platter.

Lately, she had been introduced into a new sort of life—perhaps what most might call the *real* world, because it was becoming more and more apparent to Ashley that not too many people had been as blessed as she.

Yellow Thunder turned with a start and his face beamed when he found Ashley awake. He leaned over her and placed his arms around her, helping her to a sitting position. "*Mitawin*, you are awake," he said, his gaze raking over her, his hands touching her as though he could not believe that she *was* awake and apparently all right. He had begun to wonder if there was more to her lethargy than just being overly tired. He had been thinking about the food that they had consumed on the houseboat, and that perhaps it had been tainted with something

181

that took awhile to work its evil magic on a person's body.

Yet he had not had any ill effects from it, and now he knew without a doubt that he was the cause of Ashley's weakened state, and that he had driven his woman too hard and had neglected her need of nourishment for too long.

He drew Ashley into his arms and held her tightly. "Do not ever give me such a scare again," he said, his voice drawn.

"I'm sorry if I frightened you," Ashley said, clinging to him. "I was just so tired—so sleepy. But I believe I'll be all right now. Except for a slight lethargy, I feel rested enough."

"Your lethargy is caused more from hunger," Yellow Thunder said, quickly drawing away from her. He went to the fire and lifted the stick on which the fish was speared.

"I have cooked us a feast," he said, laughing over his shoulder.

"I've never smelled anything as good as that," Ashley said, shivering as the night breeze nipped at her face and arms. She drew the blanket more snugly around her shoulders, then let it flutter back away from her, forgetting everything but the fish as Yellow Thunder placed a large chunk in her hands.

She did not take the time to wait for him to sit down beside her. She ate ravenously.

She watched out of the corner of her eye as Yellow Thunder ate as hungrily as she, smiling at him as he glanced her way with his midnight-dark eyes, the fire's glow dancing within them.

And when she was full enough, Ashley tossed the bones into the flames of the fire and stretched her arms over her head. "Now I feel wonderful," she said, sighing.

Then as she lowered her arms, she stared down at herself, and at how dirty and wrinkled the buckskin garment was. Yet when the breeze blew against her face and arms again, she doubted if she could stand to be away from the fire long enough to give herself a badly needed sponge bath.

However, she knew that she must. She could smell herself, an unpleasant aroma, to say the least. She glanced down at her buckskin attire. It had been put through more than any one garment could normally withstand, with rips and tears and stains of all sorts spoiling the buckskin fabric of the shirt and the breeches.

She eyed the moccasins on her feet. Although they were just as stained and worn, she also had no choice but to put them on again after her bath.

But she *could* give them a good washing in the stream and let them dry overnight by the fire.

Hopping to her feet, she began walking briskly toward the river, then felt her knees buckling and realized that although comfortably fed, she was still weak from the ordeals of the past several days. When she felt a strong arm around her waist, she turned a warm smile up at Yellow Thunder.

"You are always there for me, aren't you?" she murmured. "I love you so for it, Yellow Thunder. Never could any woman expect a man to be as thoughtful—as sweet—as you are to me."

"There never was, or will be again, another woman like *you*," Yellow Thunder said thickly, helping her to the horse. "You have proven capable of many things. You are worthy of being an Osage princess. One day soon you will live the life of a princess."

Ashley turned to face him. Smiling warmly, she gazed up at him. "I wish it were now," she murmured. "Why can't it be now, instead of a tomorrow that may never even come?"

Yellow Thunder placed his hands at her waist and drew her against his hard body. "You want it to be now?" he said huskily. "Then so be it."

He lowered his mouth to hers and gave her a gentle kiss, then whispered into her ear. "From this day forth, you are my princess—my beloved," he said. "I shall care for you as never before. I shall fill your days with happiness and hope."

Ashley twined her arms about his neck and brought his lips close to hers. "You are my knight in shining armor," she whispered, brushing his lips lightly with her tongue. "My darling, from this day forth, I shall care for you as never before. I shall fill your days with happiness and hope."

Yellow Thunder leaned slightly away from her, staring down at her with a keen puzzlement in his eyes. "A knight—in what did you say?" he asked, his eyebrows forking.

Then he threw his head back with laughter. "Never mind explaining it to me," he said, now gazing with amusement down into her eyes. "I am now recalling the children's stories that my adopted white father read to me before I was sent back to my true people. There were tales of knights, of palaces—and of princesses."

He wove his fingers through her hair and laughed softly. "The princesses in those books did not have hair the color of flame," he said, his eyes twinkling. "It was usually golden, like the wheat that grows wild in the prairie, or black, like the raven's wing. But never red."

"Does the color of my hair truly matter to you?" Ashley asked, her lips curving into a pout.

Yellow Thunder framed her face between his hands and moved his lips close to hers. "Do you truly think that it would?" he asked, then gave her a kiss that melted her insides into something that was spreading deliciously sweet within her.

She twined her arms about his neck and returned the kiss, but then suddenly wrenched herself away from him when she again realized how dirty she was and how unpleasant she smelled.

She smiled awkwardly as she began backing away from him. "You don't truly want to touch and kiss me now," she said, making a wide turn around him and heading once again toward the river. "Let me make myself sweet-smelling for you. Let me make my hair smell like flowers, instead of dust and grime. I want to feel like a princess while in your arms, not like someone you have saved from the gutters of New Orleans."

Yellow Thunder was already lifting his fringed shirt over his head, soon tossing it aside. "Nor do I wish to smell like the horse that I have been traveling on," he said huskily. "*Ah-hah*, we shall refresh ourselves with the clear waters of the river, and then, my woman, I will show you what you can expect every day from your knight in shining armor."

Ashley did not go on to the river. Instead, she turned and went back to Yellow Thunder. Running her fingers down his bare chest, she looked seductively up into his eyes. "I do not want a knight in shining armor," she murmured. "I am pleased enough with my handsome Osage warrior."

Yellow Thunder grabbed her into his arms and gave her a savage kiss, then they reluctantly parted and began making themselves sweet-smelling in their separate ways.

# *Chapter Fifteen*

Yellow Thunder had made a lean-to out of poles and their one blanket, the opening of the lean-to facing the fire. Ashley lay on the thick grass beside Yellow Thunder, and the warmth of the fire reached into the lean-to like a warm caress, mingling with the warmth of Yellow Thunder's hands as he moved them over her, touching and caressing the valleys of her desire.

Smelling sweetly like the river, the water having deliciously soothed her aching flesh, Ashley breathed in the scent of Yellow Thunder's body, smelling wonderfully of pine, for he had used pine needles to dry himself after his daring swim in the cold waters of the river. She had watched him, amazed that he was able to withstand the cold water, while she had found it almost too much just to splash the water over her.

But now, they were finally together, and Ashley was being awakened anew to feelings that had lain dormant within her until she had met her handsome Osage warrior. She was aflame with longing as he leaned over her, his hands moving over her, his fingertips circling her breasts, just missing the nipple each time so that they strained with added anticipation. When he bent his head and his tongue took the place of his fingers, her breath quickened as his lips now teasingly brushed the creamy skin of her breasts.

And then his hands cupped her breasts, urging the nipples into aching tautness. He kissed each nipple in turn, sucking on them.

And then his lips moved slowly lower on her body, down over her ribs and along her flat, smooth belly, moving his mouth over her flesh until she groaned.

Twining her fingers through his thick, black hair, she urged his lips back to her mouth and touched his tongue with hers.

He then kissed her, his mouth urgent and eager. With a groan he pulled her against him, placing his hands beneath her buttocks so that he could bring her hips to his, crushing her against his hardness.

Ashley was fast becoming delirious with sensations, welcoming him as, with one maddening thrust, he drove himself deeply inside her. Her whole body quivered and she clung and rocked with him as he sculpted himself to her moist body and pressed endlessly deeper into her soft folds.

As his body moved rhythmically against hers, her gasps of pleasure became long, soft whimpers. She gripped him tightly as his lips slithered down her neck, and when he began sucking one of her nipples again, she drew in her breath sharply and gave out a little cry of passion.

Flesh against flesh in gentle pressure they moved. Yellow Thunder was fighting to go more slowly, wanting these moments to linger on into the night, yet he was almost beyond coherent thought, quickly sinking into a chasm of desire from which there was no escape, except after allowing himself to experience the ultimate of rapture with her, that which was drawing closer and closer. . . .

With a groan he pulled her harder against him, again kissing her with a drugged passion. His hands dug into her hips, lifting her closer and filling her more deeply with his throbbing hardness. He felt himself coming even more dangerously close to the bursting point. He moved his lips from her mouth and buried his face into the sweet fragrance of her neck, groaning as he gritted his teeth, holding back . . . holding back. . . .

Ashley's heart was pounding. She was fast becoming delirious, all of her senses yearning for the promise that Yellow Thunder was offering her. The sureness of his thrusts was fast fueling her desire into a flaming inferno within her.

She framed his face between her hands and drew his lips back to hers, and as they kissed she felt the explosion of ecstasy claim her and trembled with the pleasure that rushed through her.

Yellow Thunder was aware that her passion had peaked, so he let himself go. As she strained her hips up at him, he felt the great shuddering in his loins, and the joy that ensued.

Their bodies jolted and quivered together. They clung, and their kisses became feverish.

And then his body subsided exhaustedly into hers and they lay there, clinging. Ashley urged his lips apart, and sensually touched his tongue with hers. Her body tremored with renewed ecstasy when Yellow Thunder sought her bud of pleasure at the juncture of her thighs and began caressing it. She closed her eyes and drew her mouth away from his, the rapture building again as she felt his manhood hardening again within her and soon stroking her slowly, yet surely.

Her pulse raced and she felt lightheaded with ecstasy as once again she felt the wondrous splashes of bliss overwhelming her. She clung to him as he pressed endlessly deeper within her, the sureness of his caress making her delirious with the feelings he had introduced her to. She emitted a soft cry of sweet agony as once again she found total paradise within her lover's arms. She smiled against his muscled chest when she felt his pleasure also in the way his body stiffened, then plunged over and over into her, his groans breaking through the silence of the midnight hour.

Afterwards, this time, Yellow Thunder rolled away from her and lay at her side, his arm resting over her perspiration-damp stomach, his fingers gently stroking her flesh just above that line of hair that led downward, to her throbbing center.

"It was wonderful," Ashley whispered, combing her fingers through his damp hair. "Oh, how I do love you, Yellow Thunder. How could I have ever lived without you?"

"You lived, but you did not love," Yellow Thunder said, gazing into her eyes as he rolled her onto her side, to face him. "Neither did I. As it is expected of a virile Osage warrior, I did have women before you, but only to quench the hungers of the flesh. None of them meant anything to me, but for that moment shared in the privacy of my dwelling. When morning came, the women were forgotten, because none of them stirred my heart as you do."

Ashley paled as Yellow Thunder so nonchalantly spoke to her of his experiences with other women. Of course she had to have known that he had not gone without women. He *was* a virile man, with the needs and hunger of a man.

Yet understanding did not make it any easier for her to accept his being in somebody else's arms, and she did not want it to enter their conversations, or their lives.

Somehow, she had wanted to believe that he had been as virginal as she.

Yet with further thought, she was not so sure she would have preferred that at all. She would not want to think that her man was anything but passionate. If not, he would truly be less a man in her eyes, for he was the age when he should have found victory in bed with women.

"You have grown so quiet," Yellow Thunder said, placing a finger at her chin and lifting her moody eyes to his. "Did my words of other women hurt you?"

"A little," Ashley murmured, fluttering her eyelashes nervously up at him. "Yes, Yellow Thunder, a little. I love you so. That is why."

"You do not have to hurt any longer," Yellow Thunder said, drawing her close in his embrace. "You are the only woman in my life now, and for always. Let us not think about yesterday— only our tomorrows. They belong to us, *mitawin*, only us."

"You are all I need to fill my heart with happiness," Ashley murmured. She had never felt so at peace with herself, or so loved. Her stomach growled, and she giggled as she leaned away from Yellow Thunder. "But perhaps I do need something else to eat. I am suddenly ravenously hungry again."

Yellow Thunder kissed her brow. "Making love enhances one's hunger," he said, then drew on his fringed breeches that had been washed and already dried by the fire. "I think I know exactly what you need. You stay here in the warmth of the fire. I will return shortly."

Ashley turned over onto her stomach and propped her face up with her chin, smiling at Yellow Thunder as he gave her another stare, his gaze raking over her nudity.

Then she looked into the soft, rolling flames of the campfire, her mind moving unwillingly to things that threatened to spoil this night that she would remember forever.

Her stepbrother, for one. She had been so afraid that he had seen her and Yellow Thunder's escape into the forest. They had truly taken a risk by stealing the horses.

Then her thoughts went to Juliana, wondering how she was and where she would go once she left the old hotel. She had seemed so alone in the world, and since she had not shared the secrets of her life with Ashley, she did not know if Juliana had any family.

Ashley sighed heavily, realizing that she probably would never see Juliana again. And that saddened her.

Yet she had seen in Juliana something stronger than she had ever seen in any of her girlfriends in New Orleans, or in her earlier years in New York. This gave Ashley hope that Juliana would know how to care for herself. Certainly, Juliana would keep a watch over her shoulder from now on, to ensure that no one would have a chance to abduct her again.

"Food for my woman," Yellow Thunder said, moving to his knees before the lean-to.

Ashley rose to a sitting position, her eyes widening when she saw the bunches of grapes that Yellow Thunder was offering her. They made her mouth water just looking at them.

Taking a bunch of grapes, she started to place one in her mouth, but stopped when Yellow Thunder came to sit down beside her and very gingerly placed one at her lips himself.

Smiling seductively at him, her eyes soon locking with his, Ashley took the grape and it liquefied deliciously in her mouth as she began chewing it.

At the same time, she placed a grape at Yellow Thunder's lips and watched him clamp his perfectly white teeth onto it, soon chewing and smiling at her, also.

This was repeated many times, and after the empty stems were thrown into the fire, Yellow Thunder removed his breeches and drew Ashley into his arms again.

Moving to a sitting position, he lifted Ashley onto his lap, her arms twined around his neck, her legs straddling him.

Her heart pounding, Ashley leaned her breasts against his chest, then sucked in a wild breath of air and closed her eyes in ecstasy as Yellow Thunder pressed his thickened manhood up inside her and began thrusting himself upward in rhythmic strokes as she clung to him.

As he drove in swift and sure, Ashley threw her head back in abandon, her hair drifting down her back until its tips brushed Yellow Thunder's thighs. She groaned as his hands moved over the glossy-textured skin of her breasts and gently kneaded them.

He then lifted her up away from him and laid her down on her back on the grass. His lips brushed the creamy skin of her breasts, and her ragged breathing became slower as he made his way down her body, soon touching her throbbing center with the tip of his tongue.

The pleasure was so intense that Ashley did not dare to breathe. As his tongue caressed her, she shivered, and tremors cascaded down her back. She rolled her head back and forth, the fevered ecstasy within her building.

She was glad when he moved over her and parted her thighs and soon magnificently filled her with his hardness, moving with the slow thrusting of his pelvis, the sureness of his caress lighting the fires of desire within her.

He framed her face between his hands and kissed her softly, and then feverishly as his body began to quiver and quake into hers.

She clung to him, the blissful rapture soon fully claiming her, making her cry out with a sweet agony.

Afterwards, Ashley lay breathlessly happy within Yellow Thunder's arms, feeling safe and fulfilled—but not able to brush away thoughts of what might happen tomorrow to take away from this happiness again.

There seemed to always be something there to spoil their happiness.

# *Chapter Sixteen*

*Several Days Later—*

Ashley had fallen instantly in love with this wilderness that Yellow Thunder called The Ozarks. As she rode onward, Yellow Thunder's village finally in sight a short distance away, she marveled again over her surroundings. This was a land of virgin, fragrant forests interspersed with rolling prairies, gushing springs, and crystal-clear streamlets. It was a land of ferns and flowers; of hills, dells and verdant valleys.

And now, as she readied herself in her mind to meet Yellow Thunder's chieftain father, she squared her shoulders and sat more upright on her horse. Her heart pounded and her throat was dry at the thought of facing a powerful Indian chief—even of entering an Indian village.

She kept her eyes straight ahead now as they came upon the outskirts of the village, but not before she had seen that it was a village of sturdy tepees nestled among pines, aspens, and silver birch.

Closer to the river, only a few feet from the village, the leaves of huge cottonwood trees swayed in the mid-afternoon breeze. The smoke of the many campfires drifted lazily from the foliage.

As they rode into the village, they were met by an entourage of people shouting and running toward Yellow Thunder, their eyes showing their happiness to see him. Dogs and children followed behind the adults.

Yellow Thunder smiled down at the youngsters who now ran in a lope beside his horse as he continued toward his chieftain father's dwelling—a tepee that was much larger than those of his tribesmen, with a door in the east, since all good things came from the east.

Yellow Thunder glanced at Ashley, seeing her uneasiness. He then looked at his people again, noticing that they were now quiet, their questioning gazes on Ashley.

But he ignored all of this, for he knew that in time they would all, including Ashley, become acquainted, and friendships would be formed among them all.

Who could not love Ashley? he thought, as he recalled their times alone together these past days. She was everything he wanted in a woman, and more.

And he was sure he knew how she would feel about his people! Who could not love them, he thought, again feeling pleasantly warmed with the memory of how quickly he had been accepted back into his tribe after living the life of a white boy for four winters of his life. Then, and now, he had been gathered inside the hearts of his father's people, as though one with them.

And so shall my woman, he thought firmly.

At his father's dwelling, Yellow Thunder dismounted and went to help Ashley down from her horse. He was aware of the half-circle of people around him and Ashley, everyone still only silently watching, no one taking upon themselves to ask why this white woman was there. He knew that everyone had anxiously waited to see if he would bring back Bright Eyes and that most had to be disappointed that instead it had been a woman who had the skin coloring of what some Osage called their enemy.

Not taking the time to explain why he had not found Bright Eyes, knowing that in time they would all be told, and anxious to see his father, though the news he brought about Bright Eyes was anything but good, Yellow Thunder placed a hand on Ashley's elbow and ushered her toward the entrance flap of this large and stately tepee.

Ashley swallowed hard, so afraid that Yellow Thunder's father would disapprove of her and order his son to banish the white woman from the village.

The thought of that possibility terrified her, not only because of the embarrassment that would cause her, but also because her dream of being with Yellow Thunder for the rest of her life would never come true.

Hopefully, Yellow Thunder and his father had a better understanding than some fathers and sons she had known. Calvin and Ashley's stepfather had argued often. She had even felt that Calvin had no respect whatsoever for his father.

And now she understood why, even though Calvin himself was not a man who earned respect.

Now she cared nothing about either of them!

This was her new life, her new beginning. Now if only the chief accepted her and what his son had planned for her. . . .

She quickly noted that the tepee, a fine lodge of eighteen skins, was brightly painted with all sorts of emblems—the bright, yellow sun, the jagged forks of lightning, and many more things that she did not have the time to interpret.

She bent low and entered the tepee as Yellow Thunder held the buffalo hide entrance flap aside for her, then stepped in with her, allowing the flap to drop back in place behind them. She quickly noted that within the tepee, a well-built fire was burning cheerfully, and she was quite taken with the luxuriant comfort of the lodge—the soft buffalo robe couch upon which she had been silently motioned to sit, the sloping willow back rests at each end of the couch.

In their proper places were oddly shaped, fringed and painted parfleches and cooking utensils, the parfleches well-filled with dried berries, choice dried meats, and tongue and pemmican. The earthen floor was covered with woven mats and animal skins.

Over the bright fire the evening meal was steaming in a large, black pot, emitting fragrances that reminded Ashley that she and Yellow Thunder had not eaten since the early morning meal.

But she soon forgot her hunger when, out of the shadows, came a tall, lean man clothed in a handsome dress of deer skins, neatly garnished with broad bands of porcupine quill-work down the sleeves of his shirt and his leggings, and—fringed with scalp-locks, which sent Ashley's heart to racing with fear.

She looked away from what to her was a dreadful sight, although it must be something of value and meaning to the Osage, and looked at the chief's hair. It was graying, but was very thick and flowed over his shoulders. In his hand he held a beautiful pipe.

Although he was obviously nearing the age of sixty, Ashley thought that he was handsome and very dignified—just what she would have expected in Yellow Thunder's father.

She sat stiffly on the couch, her hands folded tightly in her lap, as Yellow Thunder went to his father and gave him a warm hug, then came with his father back to the fire.

Yellow Thunder waited for his father to sit down on a platform piled high with comfortable robes opposite the fire from the couch, then sat down himself beside Ashley. His legs crossed, his back straight, he leaned his weight on his hands, which he rested on his knees.

Ashley became unnerved under the close scrutiny of the chief as he lay his pipe aside, his midnight-dark eyes never leaving her.

"This woman," Chief Eagle Who Flies said, nodding toward Ashley. "You bring her to our village instead of Bright Eyes? Why is that, my son? What is she to you, or to your father?" His gaze moved slowly to Yellow Thunder. "You did not find your sister. Your search was in vain?"

Yellow Thunder held his gaze steady with his father's. "*Ah-hah*, my search was in vain," he said, his voice drawn. "I followed my heart and still I did not find her."

Yellow Thunder's gut twisted when he saw the instant hurt in his father's eyes, feeling helpless because of it. He was a son who had let his father down, yet he had done everything within his power to find this chief's beloved daughter, cutting his search shorter than he would have wished only because he had to return to his village to lead the buffalo run that was imperative for the survival of his people when the moon was cold on the earth at night and the sun had lost its ability to warm during the daylight hours.

Yellow Thunder turned his eyes to Ashley. He smiled at her, trying to reassure her, for he could tell that although he had tried to prepare her for these awkward moments with his father, nothing had seemed to build that sort of courage within her heart.

And he understood. Many people had been intimidated by the powerful chief, Chief Eagle Who Flies.

It was Yellow Thunder's place now to ease the tensions in this lodge of the chief and to create a bond between his woman and his father that no one could ever break!

"*Ahte*, fate drew me and this woman together," Yellow Thunder said, addressing his father as he took Ashley's hand for reassurance. "Our hearts are now as one." His eyes locked with his father's. "It is my wish to soon make her my wife. She has a good, warm heart for our people. She will be as one with them, also. Will you give your blessing, *ahte*? Although her skin is white, I have found that her heart is pure. She is someone easily loved, *ahte*. Soon you will see this and take her into your arms as though she were your flesh and blood."

Chief Eagle Who Flies moved his gaze to Ashley. He looked her slowly up and down, in his eyes a guarded expression.

Then he lifted a hand toward her. "*Hiyu-wo*," he said.

Ashley glanced quickly at Yellow Thunder. "I do not understand what he is saying to me," she whispered. "Please tell me quickly, Yellow Thunder, what he said. I don't want to disappoint him. I don't want him to think I am ignorant."

Yellow Thunder leaned closer to her. "He says to come forward," he whispered, his eyes never leaving his father.

"Oh, I see," Ashley said, her knees weakening at the thought of approaching the powerful chief. But she knew that this was required before she was accepted—*if* she was!

Dying a slow death inside, Ashley moved to her feet and went to the chief and stood before him, their eyes holding. She was suddenly aware of the clothes that she wore. Although Indian buckskins, they were in a frightful state, which had to detract from her usual pleasant appearance.

Oh, what a horrid way to meet one's future father-in-law! She would have preferred to be dressed in silk and lace.

"You come to my village with hopes of marrying *micinksi*—my son?" he said, realizing that if he chose to use an Indian word, he must quickly translate it for the white woman.

And he did not mind. He understood the cultures were different. And he was looking past her soiled buckskin, admiring this woman, seeing her through the eyes of his son, as though he, this old chief, were young again and looked for women who was pleasing to the eye *and* to the heart.

"I want nothing more than to be with your son, and to make him happy," Ashley murmured, nervously clasping her hands together behind her.

"And how did you meet?" Chief Eagle Who Flies asked.

Ashley glanced quickly at Yellow Thunder, quietly seeking his help with her pleading eyes.

Yellow Thunder rose to his feet and went to Ashley, taking her hand and urging her down on the blankets beside his father's resting platform. He took it upon himself to explain exactly the first moment he had seen Ashley, and the circumstances of their first actual meeting.

"And so you were a part of the same family that abducted my wife and son many moons ago?" Chief Eagle Who Flies said, angrily folding his arms across his chest. In his eyes was condemnation as he stared at Ashley. "Did you know about this?"

"I only knew Peter Wyatt a few years," Ashley quickly answered. "My mother married him after the death of my true father, and after the death of Peter Wyatt's wife—the woman who took Yellow Thunder from the arms of your wife those many years ago. I knew not of the circumstances, except that I did hear someone say something about an Indian having once been a part of the family, and his name."

She turned smiling eyes to Yellow Thunder. "His name was Yellow Thunder," she murmured. "When I met Yellow Thunder and realized exactly who he was, my heart went out to him, and then I . . . fell in love with him."

Chief Eagle Who Flies relaxed his arms away from his chest. He lifted his pipe and lit it again with a small twig that he held into the flames of the fire. "I understand now," he said, taking a puff and letting the smoke roll from between his lips. "And I will not interfere in this that you wish to do, *micinksi*. Your choices have always been wise. I am sure it is no different in your choice of woman. *Hoye*, I am in agreement with this that you wish to do."

Yellow Thunder grinned from ear to ear, then the smile was lessened when his father began speaking again.

"You will lead the buffalo hunt without me this season," Chief Eagle Who Flies said, resting the bowl of his pipe on his knee. "The burdens I carry within my heart are too heavy. This season, the entire village will not participate. It is not the time to forget those who are stealing our people at every opportunity. We will lessen their advantage. Some warriors, all children, and many women will stay behind in the safety of our village. It will be left to a select few to bring home enough meat to last the duration of the long winter." He shook his head slowly back and forth. "*Nah*, I cannot venture far from this village. I must always stay where Bright Eyes can find me, in case she is able to escape those who abducted her."

Yellow Thunder's heart went out to his father, and he realized this sacrifice his father was making by not riding with the others to hunt the powerful buffalo. His father had always looked forward to this season, when he could ride his horse with the other warriors, to prove to them that even though he was aging, his abilities were not.

*Ah-hah*, Yellow Thunder thought regretfully to himself, his father was making a great sacrifice, and Yellow Thunder was going to be given much of the glory that his father could have had.

"Please go now," Chief Eagle Who Flies murmured, waving with his pipe toward the entrance flap. "We will talk again tomorrow before you leave for the hunt."

Yellow Thunder gazed at his father for a moment longer, then took Ashley's hand and drew her to her feet and ushered her from the tepee.

Ashley felt the sadness that Yellow Thunder was feeling, by just looking into his eyes. She leaned closer to him, her insides warming deliciously when he slipped an arm around her waist. She went with Yellow Thunder to a close-by tepee, one that was only slightly smaller than the chief's, yet was as brightly decorated.

Once inside, Yellow Thunder got a fire going in the fire pit, placing some dried sweet grass on the live coals, then bent over its fragrant smoke, rubbing his hands over it.

Ashley bent to her knees beside him and draped her arm around his neck. "Try not to dwell on sadness," she encouraged him. "You did all that you could. I feel certain that you will find your sister one day. But for now, please do not let it ruin your life. You have the buffalo run to look forward to. You have . . . me."

Yellow Thunder turned warm eyes to her. "*Ah-hah*, I have you," he said, placing his hands to her waist and lowering her to the warm pelts beside the fire. His mouth covered her lips with a sweet and lingering kiss.

Ashley sighed and twined her arms around his neck, wanting to give Yellow Thunder the sort of loving that would make him forget everything.

Everything but her.

# Chapter
# Seventeen

Ashley was stunned when Yellow Thunder drew away from her, their kiss and their passion cut short.

"What's wrong?" she asked, her voice quavering. "Is it something I did—or perhaps did not do? Being here with your people is so new to me. I—I can't be expected to know how to act, or to react, to everything."

Yellow Thunder held her face between his hands and looked softly into her eyes. "It is nothing you did, or did not do," he said regretfully. "It is just that this must wait. I have things to tend to before we are free to make love in my dwelling."

He pulled her face close and kissed her, then stepped fully away from her. "You will find water in the paunch of the buffalo," he said, gesturing toward a buffalo paunch that hung from a pole just inside the entranceway. "It is adjusted so that the water bag is easily tipped and the water can run out freely. The water is kept fresh with sprigs of mint." He then gestured toward a wooden basin that sat close to the paunch. "You may refresh yourself with the water. I shall return shortly."

Ashley nodded in acquiescence. She watched Yellow Thunder gather a breech clout and fresh, clean moccasins, and now realized why he was delaying their lovemaking. He was a man of intense cleanliness. He was going to go and take a bath in the river. He expected the same of her in his absence, except that she would be bathing in the protective cover of his dwelling.

After he left, she glanced around her, wondering what she would change into after her sponge bath, then spied a lovely fringed shirt that would fall below her knees.

Smiling, she grabbed the soft, buckskin top, and laid it close to the wash basin. For a towel, she chose a blanket that was rolled neatly up with others against the wall of the tepee.

Then she proceeded with her bath, not having any trouble at all getting the water poured from the strange looking paunch. Again she smiled when a sprig of mint rolled with the water into the basin, its fragrance sweet and clean as it wafted up.

She enjoyed the bath, even washing her hair. Though there was no soap, the mint seemed to have done the trick, for she smelled even better than when she had used scented soaps.

After she drew the soft buckskin shirt over her head, and it hung neatly to below her knees, she began searching around the tepee for a hairbrush, smiling when she found something similar, surely meant for the hair, with the long bristles of a porcupine fashioned onto a stick.

While drawing this crude brush through her waist-length hair, her heartbeat quickened. She had heard a noise outside the entrance flap, and she hoped that Yellow Thunder had returned. Already it seemed hours since his departure.

Just how long could a bath in the river take? Surely he was as anxious to return to her as she was to be with him.

This time they would be able to make love without worrying about her stepbrother suddenly arriving to imprison them again—or worst yet, to kill Yellow Thunder, and take Ashley away.

When the entrance flap was pulled aside, Ashley moved quickly toward it, then stopped, disappointed to find that it was not Yellow Thunder entering the tepee. Wide-eyed, she watched a lovely Osage maiden carry a large tray of food into the dwelling and place it on the floor beside the fire. Then, without even a word or glance toward Ashley, the girl left again.

This gave Ashley cause to be uncomfortable. If this one maiden looked past her, as though she were not there, how would the rest of Yellow Thunder's people treat her? She so badly wanted to belong, yet she recalled the prejudices against the Indians in the white community.

How could she expect it to be different for a white woman in an Indian community?

She could be regarded not only as an intruder, but as the *enemy*.

Not wanting to dwell on such thoughts, she made herself recall, over and over again, how quickly Yellow Thunder's father had accepted her. Ashley settled down on a thick bear pelt beside the fire and laid the hairbrush aside. She eyed the food hungrily, seeing an assortment of meats, and even some berries and slices of apple. It was hard not to eat, for the sight of the food was tempting and the aroma of the baked meat made her stomach growl.

But she refrained from eating, knowing that it was surely brought to this dwelling for Yellow Thunder.

She would wait for him.

She waited and waited, eyeing the entrance flap, and then the food. She reached a hand out to the food, then drew it back quickly. The temptation was becoming greater by the minute, especially since it was taking Yellow Thunder so long to return!

Her eyes shifted slowly to the food again, and she was past caring for whom the food was intended. She could not stand the ache in her stomach any longer.

And Yellow Thunder was wrong to stay away from her so long! It did not take this long to take a bath.

As she stuffed her mouth with the delectable morsels of meat, jealousy stung her heart and she wondered if Yellow Thunder had gone to a woman, taking the time to explain Ashley's presence in his dwelling. She grew angrier and ate more quickly at the thought of Yellow Thunder being with another woman, even if it was to explain her presence in his tepee. She had to wonder if he also was telling the woman that this white woman with the hair the color of a savage sunrise was going to share his blankets forever.

Was he explaining that this woman whose eyes were the color of the grasses of spring was going to be his *mitawin*?

Feeling blue and dejected, and no longer wanting any food, Ashley pushed the tray away from her and drew her knees to her chest, locking her arms around them.

She was no longer looking at the entrance flap. She was even beginning to feel that Yellow Thunder was going to spend the first night back at his village in a tepee other than his own.

Tears scalded Ashley's eyes at the thought of him speaking softly in another woman's ear while he was familiarizing himself with the woman's curvaceous copper body. Perhaps he had decided that that was what he wanted, instead of this woman whose heart was bleeding at such a thought.

Suddenly, Ashley's gaze shifted upward and her heart skipped a beat when Yellow Thunder entered the dwelling in a brief breech clout, a young brave accompanying him, the lad's arms filled with an assortment of objects.

Her pulse racing, Ashley slowly rose to her feet as the boy came to her and began laying these things at her feet as Yellow Thunder watched, his eyes filled with a soft glow, his lips curved in a sweet smile.

"These things I bring to you tonight are things that are most dear to the Indian women and most gratefully accepted as gifts from the man who wishes to marry her," Yellow Thunder said, bending before Ashley as he began spreading the gifts out for her to see while the boy kept laying them on the floor of the tepee.

Now realizing what had taken Yellow Thunder so long, and grateful that it had nothing to do with another woman, Ashley was breathless as she gazed down at the gifts. She placed her hands at her throat, tears near as she looked from item to item.

There was a snow-white doeskin dress, beautifully decorated with pink and blue beads and porcupine quills, and knee-high moccasins similarly decorated.

There was a rolled-up bundle of satin-soft buckskin, surely enough for two dresses, and a pair of moccasins.

He had also brought her strings of beads, brass rings, silk handkerchiefs, needles made from bone, thread, and earrings.

The young lad left quickly once everything was removed from his arms.

Yellow Thunder rose to his full height and stepped around the gifts. He took Ashley's hands in his, his eyes dark and imploring as he gazed down at her. "You are pleased?" he asked softly.

Ashley smiled through sparkling tears up at him. "Yes, so very much," she murmured. "How do I say thank-you in the Osage language?"

"*Pilamaye*," Yellow Thunder said.

Ashley eased one of her hands from his and placed it gently to his cheek. "*Pilamaye,*" she murmured. "Thank you, my darling, for everything."

"You do accept the gifts?" Yellow Thunder said, a strange sort of light appearing at the depths of his eyes.

"*Ah-hah,* I gladly accept the gifts," Ashley said, smiling through more tears up at him. "Everything is so lovely. I will wear everything that you have given me with a happy heart. I shall use the thread and needle with eager fingers. I want so badly to please you. I want to be everything to you."

Yellow Thunder moved his hands to her face and gently framed it between his fingers. "The acceptance of such gifts constitutes a marriage," he said softly.

Ashley's eyes widened in surprise, and her heart soared. "We . . . are now officially man and wife?" she said incredulously, while more than willing to accept this way of bonding with her beloved.

She felt comfortable that in the eyes of her God she was married.

And also in the eyes of Yellow Thunder's.

"*Ah-hah,* we are," Yellow Thunder said, once again taking her hands and leading her to the other side of the fire, where the pelts were piled higher to make a comfortable bed on which to place his bride.

He led her downward, onto her back, and lay down beside her, turning her so that their eyes could meet. "A ceremony witnessed by my father and our people will come later, after the buffalo hunt . . . and another search for my sister," he murmured. "Does that please you also, my woman?"

Ashley felt as though she were floating, her happiness was so intense. "Everything you do pleases me," she murmured, reaching a hand to his hairless, broad chest, smoothing her palm over the rippling muscles. "I love you so, Yellow Thunder. So much, sometimes, it frightens me. So many things could happen. This world we live in seems so crazed. One cannot count much on the future. I . . . I wonder if that will ever change? If ever there will come a time when there is total peace among people? If so, oh, how I wish we could be transported now to be a part of such of a society."

"Greed will last until the end of time," Yellow Thunder pronounced softly. "And as long as there is greed, there will be wars and prejudices. Let us take from one another that which makes us happy now, though it will be hard not to worry about what might be for the future generations of our people. Even our children, after we are walking hand-in-hand in the land of the hereafter, will be wishing for such things as we are now speaking of for them. Let us pray that their wisdom will be strong and enduring enough to get them through the difficulties that lie ahead."

"You speak of children with such pain in your voice," Ashley murmured, searching his eyes with her own. "Children should be a reason to smile, not frown. Our children, Yellow Thunder, will be given everything within our power to give. The love given them will guide them throughout their lives. They will survive better because of it."

"*Ah, hah*, love *does* help break down barriers," Yellow Thunder said, a smile quavering on his lips. "Did it not for us?"

"Nothing could have stopped this that has happened between us," Ashley said, drifting into his arms. She snuggled close, taking much comfort from him as he enveloped her within his strong arms. "Our love was meant to be from the beginning of time. It was written in the stars, their brilliant fires in the sky leading us to one another, sparking fires within us that nothing can ever snuff out."

"That is so," Yellow Thunder breathed out against her cheek as he bent his mouth, seeking the sweetness of her lips. "We have talked enough. My lips are thirsty for the taste of you. My fingers ache with the need to feel you."

His mouth closed hard upon hers, dazzling her senses as his lips seared into hers with an intensity that left her breathless and shaking. She became a tempest of emotion, trembling with a building passion as she let him part her thighs, then begin caressing the damp valley of her desire.

He rained kisses on her face and closed eyelids, and a delicious languor stole over her as his fingers pleasured her, her moans of pleasure firing his passions.

In her hazy, desire-gripped state, she did not know when, or how, their clothes were removed, only welcoming the wondrous press of his hard body against hers as he moved atop her and drew her into a torrid embrace.

As he kissed her with fire, his hands molding and kneading her breasts, she parted her thighs for him and felt a tremor from deep within when she felt the thickness of his shaft enter the soft, yielding folds of her femininity.

Her breasts pulsed warmly beneath his fingers, the world melting away.

She locked her legs around his waist, opening herself more widely to him and her hips responded in a rhythmic movement, matching his.

Tremoring with pleasure, she gripped him tightly, then held her head back and sighed when his lips lowered to suckle one of her nipples.

Ashley caressed the skin of Yellow Thunder's back lightly with her fingertips, then placed her hands at his hips, pressing her nails only lightly into the flesh of his buttocks.

Again Yellow Thunder took her mouth savagely in his, enjoying the sweet, warm press of her body against his. He could feel the curling of heat growing in his groin and could not hold back any longer.

His climax was intense, the whole universe seeming to explode around him as he cried out his released passion.

Ashley's climax was wonderful and long, and then a great calm filled her as she lay limply within Yellow Thunder's arms, his breath teasing her ear as he pressed his cheek to hers.

And then Yellow Thunder rolled away from her and lay on his back, his eyes closed, his chest still heaving with his uneven breathing.

Ashley turned on her side to face him and moved her hands lightly over his abdomen, laughing softly as her mere touch seemed to make his skin ripple with pleasure. "I do love you so," she whispered, her lips following the path of her fingers as she leaned over Yellow Thunder. "You are so strong, so virile, so . . . noble."

She sat up then, and smiled down at him as he opened his eyes and gazed up at her with eyes still hazed over with passion. "And you are *mine*," she said, giving him one firm, quick nod of the head.

"Yours to do with as you please," he said, chuckling low. He leaned up on an elbow and with his free hand cupped her breast within his palm. "Also, this allows me to do with you as I please?"

"Always," Ashley said, sucking in a wild breath when he drew her down low enough so that he could flick his tongue around her hardened nipple.

But he soon eased away from her and sat staring into the flames of the fire. "Tonight we find pleasure with our bodies," he said thickly. "Tomorrow we find pleasure in the hunt. We must find the buffalo. Without the buffalo my people could not survive. It is our food, our clothing and shelter. The bones and horns are our tools, the hair our ropes."

He gazed over at Ashley and reached a hand to her face, gently touching her cheek. "The buffalo is the Osage's life—the Osage's *power*," he said, his jaw tight.

Suddenly he rose to his feet and slipped his breech clout on, then handed Ashley her doeskin dress. He beckoned to her to rise, and together they stepped outside.

The moon was new. The stars were bright, like millions of tiny fires in the sky.

"Tomorrow will be good," Yellow Thunder said throatily. "*Ah-hah*, it will be good."

*New Orleans—*

Juliana moved through the corridor of the mansion with a lifted chin, glad to be well again and proud to have found employment in an affluent home just outside of New Orleans, where she could hide from Calvin yet still have the estate grounds where she could breathe fresh air and contemplate her future.

As far as she was concerned, Calvin had ruined her chances of finding a man who would truly love her after he discovered that she was no longer a virgin.

Now, she did not care.

She only wished to have a place to eat, sleep, and think her days away, until that day when she might trust herself to be seen in crowds and along the streets of New Orleans.

Until then, she wanted the solace that this wonderful old mansion and its owners lent her. Her duties were minimal, mainly seeing after the maids to make sure they were carrying out their duties.

As now, she had been told to go and check on one of the oldest maids, who spent most of her day in the kitchen where she could be useful even though she was blind.

The elderly blind lady had come down ill earlier in the day, and the doctor had already been there and gone, saying that it was just old age causing the blind woman's fainting spells. There was not much one could do, except let nature take its course.

Stepping lightly up to the elderly lady's door, Juliana did not stop to knock. The door was ajar, and a faint lamplight was spilling out from the crack of the door.

Pushing the door open more widely, Juliana stepped gingerly into the room, recalling when she was so ill and would have died, if not for Yellow Thunder and Ashley. So often, she wondered if they were well and if they had found Yellow Thunder's sister.

It was such a tragic thing, this thing called slavery.

Seeing the elderly lady lying so still on the bed, the covers pulled up just beneath her chin, made Juliana almost turn around and leave, but a low, raspy voice stopped her.

"Is someone there?" the voice asked in heavily accented English.

Juliana turned with a start and walked slowly toward the bed, the lamplight on the table beside the bed soon revealing to her the color of this woman's skin.

Copper. The same color as Yellow Thunder's.

The lady was an Indian!

Juliana knelt beside the bed and reached under the covers until she found one of the lady's frail hands. "My name is Juliana," she murmured. "I'm new here. We didn't get a chance to meet before you took ill. Are you feeling better now?"

"I have not been the same since I was taken from my people so long ago," Star Woman said, her voice quavering as she looked sightlessly toward Juliana's voice. "Now that the end is near, I need to be back with my people. The burial rites of the white people are not the same as the Osage. I . . . I need to be taken back to my people. Can you do this for me? Star Woman is no longer any use to your people. She will only be in the way. Please? Can you take me back to my village so that I may touch my husband's face again?"

Star Woman closed her eyes and looked away from Juliana. "My son," she said, sobbing. "He is gone from my touch forever. He was wrenched from my breast when he was an infant. His lips no longer suckled from my breast, nor did his heart share my love. Star Woman became a slave. I do not know what happened to my Yellow Thunder. He may have died while being forced to live the white man's life. My son. My son."

Juliana's heart began to pound, and an anxiousness was building up inside her the more this elderly Indian woman spoke. Juliana realized that she had not found the sister that Yellow Thunder was searching for, but she had, instead, found—his mother!

She could hardly speak, she was so stunned by this discovery, yet she had to assure Yellow

Thunder's mother that he was safe with his people again. This alone might make the elderly Osage woman's last days more acceptable.

Juliana had to find a way to return Star Woman to her people, her son, and her husband. She had been searching within her mind for a way to pay Yellow Thunder back for his part in rescuing her.

What better way than this?

Juliana clutched Star Woman's hand more tightly. "Your name is Star Woman, the mother of Yellow Thunder?" she asked, her voice drawn.

Star Woman turned her face back toward Juliana. She opened her eyes, yet saw only light and shadow. "*Ah-hah*, that is so," she murmured.

"Star Woman, your son Yellow Thunder is well and is living once again with his people," Juliana blurted out, watching the elderly woman's face go from despair to happiness in one blink of an eye.

"Yellow Thunder is with his people again?" Star Woman gasped. Then she grew wary. "How do you know this thing? You tell me the truth?"

"The full truth," Juliana said, and then they talked for hours and hours, with Juliana, in the end, promising Star Woman that she would go to Yellow Thunder and Chief Eagle Who Flies, to tell them that she was alive and where she was living, since she did not seem strong enough herself to make the journey. Juliana had graciously taken Star Woman's earnings to procure a scout who would take her to Yellow Thunder's village, since Juliana did not have enough money herself to pay for such arrangements.

As Juliana rose from the floor, Star Woman reached for her hand. "Tell Chief Eagle Who Flies that his wife still dreams of him," she said, a sob lodging in her throat. "Tell my son that my arms hunger for his embrace."

"I will," Juliana said, swallowing hard. She bent low and gave Star Woman a hug, then left the room with all sorts of plans crowding her brain. Leaving would mean that she would lose her job— her security.

But she would not consider her losses when others had so much to gain!

Smiling, she went to her room and gathered up her meager belongings, then crept outside and stole a horse. She knew an Indian scout who lived up the road just a short distance.

Billy Two Arrows.

His reputation was known far and wide—and he was Osage!

Still somewhat weak from her ordeal in the swamp, Juliana's legs trembled as she pulled herself up into the saddle. Then, with the wind behind her and the moon laying a silver path before her, she rode hard from the large mansion that she now understood dealt in slavery.

# *Chapter Eighteen*

*Several Days Later*

The search for the buffalo had already taken a full day and night. It was now early in the morning, and a thick haze of glittering frost flakes filled the air through which the sun shone dimly. Where they had made camp, the lake's placid waters reflected autumn's variegated colors. Overhead wheeled great flights of passenger pigeons, as well as ducks and geese going south.

They broke camp, and Ashley continued the journey beside Yellow Thunder on a beautiful black colt, the color of a storm cloud in summer. Yellow Thunder had asked Ashley to accompany him on the buffalo hunt, haunted by the memory of his sister's abduction into a life of slavery. It would not happen to his woman. He had sworn to her that he would die defending her against any who would do her harm.

Now she stayed at his side, leading the long procession of horses and people following behind them.

Yellow Thunder wore a wolf fur jacket over his buckskin attire, matching the hooded jacket that he had given Ashley to wear to ward off the chill of the quickly advancing winter breezes. Ashley not only was entranced by Yellow Thunder's noble handsomeness, but was now also in awe of all the Osage people. Nothing in this world could possibly surpass them in beauty and grace. They were the most cleanly in their persons and elegant in their dress and manners. Ashley did not believe that anyone would be able to appreciate their richness and elegance without seeing them in their own country.

Even their horses were treated with reverence. Yellow Thunder's steed was a prancing white stallion. He had lavished much care upon this horse, grooming and decorating it with a fine blanket, bridles trimmed with quill work, eagle feathers, and a sweet grass wreath.

The trappings of Ashley's own black colt, which Yellow Thunder had prepared for the long travel ahead, were especially gorgeous. A blanket of soft-tanned skin was fringed and hung to her horse's knees. Belly-bands were wide braided belts; porcupine quill work in lovely colors bordered both sides. The colt's tail was braided and tied with a red buckskin ribbon, and eagle plumes fluttered with every movement. There was also a wreath of sweet grass around her mount's neck, perfuming the air as it moved in a brisk trot across the weaving, knee-high grass of the meadow.

Ashley looked straight ahead again, proud to be a part of this cavalcade of travelers. After the lodge of each of those who had joined the hunt had been taken down in the Osage village, the lodge poles had been divided into two bunches, the little ends of each bunch fastened upon the withers of a horse, leaving the butt ends to drag behind on the ground on either side.

Just behind the horse, a brace was tied across to keep the poles in their places, and then upon the poles behind the horse was placed the rolled-up tent and numerous other articles of the household. On top of all of this rode two, three, or even four women and children.

The hundred or more horses bearing their loads were drawn out for miles, creeping over the grass-covered meadow and through the forest, and three times that number of men rode along in front or on the flanks.

Matching Yellow Thunder's silence, as they awaited the return of the scouts who had been sent ahead to report back their first sight of the buffalo, Ashley thought back to two nights before, when Yellow Thunder had requested her presence at his side at the Mystery Lodge of the Osages. It was there that the problems of the tribes were discussed, and this particular meeting had been called to discuss plans for the buffalo hunt.

Ashley had been impressed by the Mystery Lodge. It was built a short distance from the main dwellings of the tribe and was covered with beautiful skins. On the front had been painted a replica of the Good Spirit, while on the back had been painted the Evil Spirit. In the center of the enclosure was a fireplace and a line running east and west, representing the path of Grandfather Sun.

That night, among the subjects discussed, were the good or bad fortunes of the tribe. Everyone knew not to disturb the meditations of the tribal council. Anyone entertaining such thoughts was told the lodge was guarded by four spirits—that of the black bear, the elk, the lynx, and the panther, who could read the mind of persons contemplating such mischief.

Ashley had sat breathlessly still as she watched a ceremony which had been explained to her by Yellow Thunder before he entered the Mystery Lodge with her. He had told her that, before embarking upon a hunting expedition, the Osage prayed to invoke the favor of *Wah-kon-tah* in their endeavors. If they observed a bad omen, such as a bad dream, the whole thing would have been called off.

The favorable sanction of the Great Spirit were necessary for the expedition's success.

Two approaching horsemen drew Ashley quickly from her thoughts. When Yellow Thunder raised a fist in the air, an instruction for everyone to stop, Ashley waited breathlessly along with him until the two warriors drew rein before him. She strained her ears to understand what they were saying, but they were speaking quickly to Yellow Thunder in the language of the Osage.

But by the way Yellow Thunder's eyes lit up, she knew that the news was good.

Buffalo had been sighted! The hunters had found the buffalo!

There would be meat for the pots in the village of the Osage, even through the long days and nights of snow and ice-covered ground to come.

Everything then seemed to happen so quickly that it was a blur in Ashley's mind. They had to travel only a short distance before making camp at the juncture of two rivers. Before Yellow Thunder departed with the other warriors and became lost to her view as he rode over the crest of a hill a short distance away, he explained to her that this was a crossing place for the great buffalo runs each fall when, as regularly as the coming of the north wind, thousands of the huge, hairy beasts migrated into the area to escape the cold winters of the northern plains. The herds of the lumbering bison began to move instinctively toward the warmer climate of the Texas Territory, stopping from time to time to forage on the lush grasslands of the Ozark Plateau.

Soon the women were hard at work unloading the bundles from the horses, erecting the tepees, in rows of seven lodges to the row, with their entrances facing east, because to the Osage all good things came from the east.

Then, just as quickly and methodically, a hunting bonfire was built, and the women erected long poles held up by notched branches, making scaffolds on which the sliced buffalo meat and the hides would be hung to dry.

Suddenly Ashley stiffened, and she looked toward the ridge over which Yellow Thunder and the other warriors had disappeared. She could hear the bellowing of the buffalo.

A shiver went through Ashley and she hugged herself when she envisioned the Osage warriors startling the buffalo. She hungered to get even one glimpse of Yellow Thunder. She had understood why she could not accompany him as he went to battle the buffalo. She would have slowed him down, and she could have been the cause of both of their lives being endangered.

But at this moment, nothing would stop her from leaving the campsite to see what was happening over the crest of the hill.

Then she realized that she was not alone. Suddenly, on all sides of her were many children and women, walking deliberately toward the ridge, carrying large cutting tools and dragging traverses behind them. They went past her and disappeared over the crest of the hill before she could get to it. When she reached the hill herself, she stopped and stood frozen on the spot when she found herself witnessing a sight that made her feel ill.

Her knees almost buckled beneath her as she watched the slaughter of the buffalo, the women and children following along the route of the massacre, skinning and butchering the fallen animals, then walking her way again, hauling the hides and meat on traverses back to the camp.

She tried to focus on something besides the death spread across the land and was grateful to find Yellow Thunder among the hunters. Seeing him so magnificently proud on his white stallion took away the horrors she had seen. She reminded herself again of the importance of the buffalo to the Osage. Without it, they would not survive!

Her heart pounded with admiration for Yellow Thunder as she watched him atop his white stallion. With his ash bow in his hand and his quiver of arrows slung on his back, he was racing along another ridge opposite the one where Ashley stood.

With his long bow, which he seldom bent in vain, he sped his whizzing arrows to the target.

She was in awe of the apparent ease and grace with which Yellow Thunder had drawn the bow, killed the buffalo, paused briefly, then with an ear-splitting whoop galloped on after the herd to make another kill.

She could tell by watching Yellow Thunder and the others that the horses had been trained to approach the animals on the right side, enabling the riders to shoot their arrows to the left. The horses ran and approached without the use of halters, which were hanging loose upon their necks.

This brought the riders within three or four paces of the buffalo, making it easy to shoot the arrow with great ease and certainty to the heart.

Ashley sucked in a wild breath of air as her attention was drawn once again to the huge, shaggy beasts as they charged madly by below her. They passed with a thunderous pounding of hoof and rattle of horns, causing the ground to tremble as if from an earthquake. Just behind the herd rode the hunters, their long hair streaming in the wind, guiding their trained mounts here and there in the thick of it all, singling out this fat cow or that choice young bull, shooting their arrows or slaying the beasts with lances twelve or fourteen feet in length.

Again Ashley looked at the land dotted with dead beasts, while other great animals stood head down, swaying, staggering, as the life blood flowed from their mouths and nostrils.

As the women continued with their task of butchering and removing pelts, no one cheered the hunters, nor spoke, nor laughed. It was too solemn a moment.

As the sky began to lose its luster and the sun swept down toward the horizon, the warriors came together and began riding away from the buffalo. Ashley shaded her eyes with her hands and looked past the Osage warriors to see what remained of the buffalo.

She sucked in a breath of air, gasping, staring. In the distance, as far as she could see, the earth was black, as though covered with a great, moving black cloud—the surviving buffalo. She could hear the faint roar of their pounding hooves and realized that although many had been slain today, those that lived outnumbered the dead by thousands.

Yellow Thunder reined in beside Ashley. With his bow slung over his shoulder, he reached a muscled arm down and grabbed Ashley around the waist, bringing her onto his horse with him. Without a word, he took her on into camp where there were already long scaffolds of drying meat set up and many hides and pelts pegged out on the ground to dry.

"It was a profitable day," Yellow Thunder finally said, helping Ashley down onto the ground. He slid easily out of the saddle and walked toward his tent, which had been erected by one of the Osage maidens assigned to the task.

Ashley went with him, finding a fire and food cooking in a pot over it. She felt guilty for not having been the one to prepare all of this for her beloved.

But in time, she would know how everything was done and Yellow Thunder would have cause to be proud of her, as she was of him at this moment.

After removing his bow and quiver of arrows, Yellow Thunder turned to Ashley and held her face between his hands. "*Mitawin*, you are pale," he said softly, looking into her eyes. "Is this caused by the spilling of blood?"

Ashley lowered her eyes, not wanting to confess such a weakness to him, yet she had no choice. He would understand that everything would come in time—her acceptance of all of his customs and rituals.

She lifted her eyes slowly, locking with his. "*Ah-hah*, somewhat," she softly confessed. "Does that make you less proud of me?"

"*Nah*," Yellow Thunder said, smiling at her usage of the Osage word. "My pride in you runs deep and forever. Do not fret so over things. In time, you will know all things Osage. I will be your teacher."

She crept into his arms and sighed, welcoming the feel of his hard body against hers. She was relieved that he smelled only of the out-of-doors, not of death, since he had not touched the animals that he had slain. Only his arrows, and the knives of the women, had made contact with the buffalo.

"Tonight there will be celebration," Yellow Thunder said, holding her at arm's length. "There will be food, and then tales of the adventures of our warriors, long into the night. And then, my woman, there will be time for us, alone . . ."

Ashley smiled timidly at him, yet she was filled with a reckless passion that was heating her insides to an inferno at the mere thought of being with him again intimately.

# Chapter
# Nineteen

The moon was new and just cresting the horizon when Ashley joined Yellow Thunder beside the great outdoor bonfire. The Osage people sat in vast numbers close to the fire, listening to the tales of the elders and to the prayers sent forth to the Great Spirit by Moon Face Bear, the medicine man who had accompanied the hunting party.

The people had also gathered to sing songs, especially the song of the wolf, the most successful of hunters.

Ashley felt fresh and clean from her quick plunge into the river with the other women of the village, yet still chilled clear through to the bone. She had been determined to join them in the daring escapade so as not to look weak. The other women still had not included her in their conversations or activities, and she was eager for them to accept her.

Ashley drew her blanket more closely around her shoulders, snuggling into its warmth. Yellow Thunder sat down beside her on a blanket that he had spread for their use, and she inhaled the fragrance of pine needles emanating from him. She smiled at the thought of him bathing also in the dusk of the evening and in the bone-chilling temperatures of the river.

She could envision even now how his muscles rippled as he swam effortlessly through the water, and how his midnight-dark eyes would gleam in the light of the newly rising moon.

Ripples of pleasure swam through her at the thought of being with him in the water, swimming alongside him, knowing that she would never feel the coldness of the icy river, only the warmth that radiated from him.

Her thoughts shifted, back to the time when they *had* joined one another in a swim—when they had leapt overboard from the river boat.

She thought of Juliana, wondering again how she was and where she might be—and with whom.

She prayed that Calvin had not found her. Recalling how Calvin had ravaged Juliana's body made Ashley feel ill. She reached for Yellow Thunder's hand, remembering the good that had resulted from her abduction. She had met Yellow Thunder. Without him, she would have thought the world a wicked place, and surely she would have lost all hope of finding a life of joy and peace.

She had found this all with Yellow Thunder. She prayed that Juliana would also find such a life, with such a man.

"It is a good night for stories," Yellow Thunder whispered, leaning closer to Ashley so that only she would hear him. "The air is cool. The stars are bright. The fire is warm."

"What will the stories be about?" Ashley whispered back, shoulder to shoulder with Yellow Thunder.

The water rippled over rocks in the most shallow part of the river close to the campsite. Fish flipped toward the light of the moon, then fell back down into the water with a great splash. A loon laughed its hysterical call in the distance, echoing back to itself across the river.

"The elders who have joined the hunt for the buffalo will tell stories of past hunts, and about men and women of virtue who were known for their endurance and spirit," Yellow Thunder said, as one of the elders rose to stand with bent shoulders beside the fire, his voice a monotone as he began telling his personal tale.

"The stories tonight will be of adventure, discovery, and victory," Yellow Thunder added, smiling at Ashley. "But no one will voice too loudly their happiness over the success of the hunt. Though it was a great event today, with many pelts and much meat taken, it is not good to raise our voices too loud about our victory. The animals who died are pitied within our hearts and minds. If not for the need to survive, none would ever be felled by the Osage. The buffalo are a proud and noble beast. The Osage never forget that."

Ashley was touched deeply by Yellow Thunder's feelings for the buffalo, making the scene of the massacre less horrific. It had all been done out of necessity, not greed.

Yellow Thunder leaned even closer, until his breath was warm on Ashley's ear. "It will be hard not to cry out to the heavens when I sink my arrows into the flesh of the white buffalo when I find him," he whispered. "It is something so long lived for, and desired. It will take much restraint not to flaunt the hide of the white buffalo to all those who have hunted him as long as I. But, as now, I must be silent, to show respect to the elders and their stories, and then the medicine man who will soon lift his voice to the dark heavens, for *Wah-kon-tah* to hear, that we may receive blessings for tomorrow's hunt."

Ashley silently nodded, then sat proudly with him the rest of the evening through the stories, the prayers, and then the songs. She feasted with the rest of the Osage as large platters of food were passed around for everyone to eat from with their hands.

Her stomach contentedly full and her heart warmed by her growing knowledge of the Osage ways, Ashley went back to their tent with Yellow Thunder, at peace with herself and the world. She was filled with a bliss that she had never known before. Everything seemed so right now.

Yet she was frightened by it all. It did not seem that things could stay this perfect for long.

She would take from this moment what she could, she decided, thrilling inside when Yellow Thunder took her hand and led her to the fire. He paused beside a thick pile of plush pelts that he had placed beside the fire pit.

Ashley's heart raced when Yellow Thunder smiled down at her and gently eased the blanket from around her, letting it fall to the floor around her ankles. She trembled when his fingers went to the hem of her buckskin dress and slowly lifted it up over her body. The warmth of the fire caressed her bare flesh.

Yellow Thunder began moving his hands over her body, curving them over her breasts. His lips then took over, moving over her silken flesh with butterfly kisses.

Ashley almost melted on the spot when his lips surrounded one of her nipples, sucking it to a stiff peak, his tongue circling it teasingly.

She threw her head back in rapture as he knelt before her and his tongue and mouth proceeded lower. She giggled when his mouth crossed over the sensitive part of her stomach.

Then she moaned and wove her fingers through his hair nervously when his lips found her throbbing center and kissed her there, then flicked his tongue over the mound of pleasure, making her almost delirious with sensation.

As the pleasure mounted and his tongue coaxed her to an even more intense rapture, so did her heartbeat race. She became afraid of the rapid beat, and placed her hands on his shoulders, urging him away.

As he moved back to his full height, he did not come to her with further caresses and kisses. Instead, he began undressing slowly before her, smiling at Ashley as he saw the flush on her cheeks, knowing that she was becoming as aroused as he and was anticipating the peak of passion they could bring one another to.

After his clothes were discarded, Yellow Thunder took a step closer to Ashley. He took her hand and led it to his manhood, sighing throatily when her fingers encircled his throbbing shaft.

He held his legs apart and closed his eyes as Ashley began moving her fingers over him, and then his knees almost buckled beneath him with pleasure when he felt her mouth close over him, her tongue tickling the sensitive underside of his shaft.

Wild with pleasure, Yellow Thunder put his hands on her shoulders and held her in place as he began moving gently within her mouth, the intensity of the feelings momentarily making him forget where he was, or how the pleasure was being given—only that he was almost mindless now with the rapture that was flooding him.

Yellow Thunder enjoyed this for just a moment longer, and when he felt the familiar heat in his loins, rising, spreading, moving, he jerked himself quickly away from her and just as quickly eased her down onto the pelts, moving atop her.

The fire was warm and gave off a faint, dancing glow. The pelts were soft and pliant beneath Ashley's back, Yellow Thunder's hands like magic on her body, caressing her, causing her to weaken with a building desire.

His mouth sought hers, eager, hot, and searching, then bore down hard upon hers with raw passion. With a moan of pleasure she returned his kiss, her arms slowly twining around his neck.

Yellow Thunder surrounded her with his strong arms and crushed her to him so hard that she whimpered, and her body yearned for the promised ecstasy that he was offering her. Her blood surged and she drew in her breath sharply, then cried out when she felt him enter her with one quick, deep thrust. When he began moving rhythmically within her, her hips responded, rising and falling as his body coaxed her hips into rhythmic movement.

Yellow Thunder's fingers became entwined in her hair, reveling in the touch of her soft, creamy flesh against his, her body pliant in his arms. He darted his tongue moistly into her mouth, his hands moving down her body, cupping her buttocks with his hands. Her flesh was smooth and hard as she strained into him, making it easier to fill her more deeply, more magnificently.

When his mouth left her lips and he held his cheek against hers, breathing hard, she was aware of how his body was reacting, realizing that he was near to his peak of passion.

She felt her own spiraling need growing, and the wondrous rush of pleasure that suddenly gripped her, sending her thoughts somewhere outside of herself, her mind gripped with ecstasy.

Then their bodies subsided against each other, and they lay cheek to cheek, breathing hard.

"How wonderful you make me feel," Ashley finally said, stroking his back with her fingertips.

He rolled away from her and turned on his side, as she turned on hers, to face one another. "You

239

make my days and my nights complete," he said, gently touching her face. "Today I conquered the buffalo. Tonight *you* conquered *me*."

Ashley crept into his arms and hugged him fiercely. "I was yours, my darling, that first time our eyes met and held in the chapel," she whispered, breathing in the wonderful manly scent of him. "Did you know then that it would not be the last time? That there had to be much more than that?"

"*Ah-hah*, I felt it deeply within my soul, yet I could not allow myself to linger on those feelings, for I thought it impossible ever to be near you, yet alone touch and kiss you," Yellow Thunder said, smiling into her eyes as she leaned slightly away from him to look up at him. "Remember? I thought you had married Calvin. When you lit the candles, how did I know it was for another purpose?"

"The candles were for my mother and stepfather," Ashley said somberly. "It is to keep their memory alive."

"Inside my heart I am forcing memories aside of my white adoptive father, who became your stepfather," Yellow Thunder said, moving to a sitting position. He looked into the fire, recalling too much that he did not want to think about—the total rejection of his adoptive white mother and father when they had explained to him that they no longer wanted him. He had felt as though he would never be wanted again, by anyone. It was the memory of his acceptance back into his true people's hearts that made him soar with an instant happiness.

He gazed at Ashley and reached a hand to hers, bringing her up to sit beside him. Now he had her—his woman, his wife. All that had happened to him as a child was nothing now to him.

"If I could only find my sister now, everything would be right in my world," he said sadly, holding Ashley snugly against his side. "And also, I must not forget the white buffalo that I have hunted for so many moons. I feel that it is now possible for me to find him. If I was given you for a wife, then why should I not be favored with the white buffalo to bring home to my people, to bring them good fortune because of my gift to them?"

He smoothed a fallen lock of her hair back from Ashley's eyes. "*Ah-hah*, tonight I feel as though I can do anything my heart desires," he said, smiling down at her. "Because of you, *mitawin*. Because of you."

He held her face between his hands and lowered his mouth to her lips and kissed her reverently.

# Chapter
# Twenty

*Two Days Later—*

The hunters always started before sunrise. Ashley stretched and yawned as she stood beside the large open-air fire, where a whole forequarter of a buffalo was already suspended from a tripod above the blaze. A woman had been assigned to give it an occasional turn during the hours required to thoroughly roast it.

Ashley had just returned from an early expedition with the women of the tribe, glad to have finally been befriended by one of the women of her age.

*Pahaha*, whose name meant "curly hair," had taken pity on Ashley as she traveled with the women on a salt-hunting expedition. Some of the Osage women had been assigned this day to find salt in the saline springs of the Ozark Plateau, for the Osages often combined their hunting expeditions with salt-making.

They had not wandered far this early morning when they found the crystals of salt mixed with sand. Pahaha had explained to Ashley, in her mixture of Osage and English, that in the drier seasons of the year, the Osage were sometimes able to secure salt in pure form. But this year, when rain had fallen in abundance, they had been forced to find the salt among the grains of sand along the river bottoms.

Never thinking that even this small item that she had taken for granted, brought up in a household of white people, was so hard to come by for the Indians, Ashley had watched in fascination the process of dissolving the salt out of the sand in water and then boiling the salty water to evaporate the water, leaving only the pure salt.

More and more she grew to admire the Osage, who lived the simplest form of life, yet who were strong in their pride in their way of life.

This humbled Ashley, and she wished that all of the white community could experience how the Indians had to live, how hard they had to work just to put food on their table. Surely, if everyone saw the hardships of the Indians up close, as she was, surely the Indians would no longer be condemned as "dumb redskins," as so many labeled them. It took much intelligence and endurance for the Indians even to survive.

Pahaha came to Ashley with two sticks that had meat speared on their tips. "*Hiyu-wo*," Pahaha said, offering one of the sticks of food to Ashley and keeping one for herself. "Come and sit with me and eat before we do more chores of the morning."

Her stomach aching from emptiness, Ashley accepted the gift of friendship. "*Pilamaye*," she said softly, proud that she remembered the word that meant thank-you.

Snuggled into her wolf-fur coat, Ashley sat on a blanket beside the great roaring fire with Pahaha and many other women, who were already gnashing at their own sticks of meat with their teeth, obviously as hungry as Ashley.

Ashley took her first bite, savoring the taste of the meat, although it was a bit greasy to her liking. Thus far, the day seemed perfect. The sun was warm on her face, and the sky was intensely blue overhead, as she chewed vigorously. But then she noticed a void among those eating. The elders were sitting on the outside of the women, enjoying their morning meal, but there were no young boys in sight.

It was strangely quiet without them, as though the young braves had been plucked from the face of the earth.

"Pahaha, where are those young braves who were not a part of the buffalo hunt this morning?" Ashley asked, gazing at the beautiful Osage maiden, whose raven-black hair was worn long and loose to her shoulders, yet differed from the other women's in the way it curled and waved beautifully instead of hanging straight.

Of course—that was the reason for her name, Curly Hair, Ashley realized.

Ashley understood why the men each evening offered Pahaha so many gifts, to try and entice her into courtship. She was ravishingly lovely, with her smooth and perfect copper features and wide, vivacious eyes. She was petite, and her hips swayed only slightly as she walked, yet she was quite seductive in manner.

Ashley had been relieved when Yellow Thunder had paid Pahaha no heed, for she had half-expected that Yellow Thunder's eyes would stray now and then to the lovely Osage maiden. It seemed impossible that any virile man could *not* give her a second glance.

Yet Yellow Thunder had taken Ashley for a wife, not Pahaha, and her heart sang that she could be chosen over such a lovely maiden.

"The young braves?" Pahaha said, arching an eyebrow. "They go on their own expeditions today without the interference of mothers, fathers, uncles, and cousins. It is a time of friendship between the young braves of our village. They learn much today which will help them be more skilled in the buffalo hunt in the future."

Ashley bit the last of the meat from the stick and laid the empty stick on the ground. She enjoyed the food, then relaxed more, taking advantage of this moment of rest, for soon she was going to be taught many more things by the women who did not follow the men on the hunt today. There were many more chores besides gathering the buffalo from the blood-strewn land. Ashley was glad to be a part of the hunt in this way.

Two days in a row watching the buffalo falling in great heaps on the ground was more than enough for her.

"The boys are hunting their own prey today," Pahaha said, tossing her food stick into the fire, then wiping grease from her lips with the back of her hand. "Rabbit-hunting is great fun for the boys. The smaller boys get the tails of the rabbit. They will bring the tails to the camp, and the fluffy tips will be dyed in pretty colors, to be worn for hair ornaments. The skins will be saved to make into winter hunting caps. Or perhaps they will kill a porcupine. When a porcupine is skinned, the quills, hair, and tails are saved. The quills will be dyed by the women for our decorative work, the hair for head roaches, and the tails for hair combs."

"*Ah-hah*, I have used such a comb," Ashley said, her eyes widening. "Tell me more, Pahaha."

Pahaha folded her arms across her chest, protected from the morning chill by a full-length fur robe. "The fur of the skunk is cut into strips and used for neck ornaments," she said, giggling when she heard Ashley emit a gasp at the mention of the word "skunk."

"The scent bag of this animal is carefully preserved, and the liquid kept for disinfectant purposes. A drop mixed with paint and smeared on the body keeps away ailments."

"Also everyone for miles," Ashley said, also giggling. She was glad to have this light-hearted moment with Pahaha. Except for her sensual moments with Yellow Thunder, and listening to the tales being told around the evening fires, everything about this hunt was serious—frighteningly serious, sometimes, to her. She had feared she was a nuisance to these active, hard-working people—until Pahaha had taken pity on her and made her feel as though she belonged.

"*Ah-hah*," Pahaha said, her eyes dancing. "The smell sometimes sends me away from those who wear the disinfectant. Unless it is a handsome warrior who stands near me. Then I allow it."

"You are beautiful, yet not married," Ashley murmured. "Have you not yet found that perfect warrior for yourself?"

"*Ah-hah*, there is one," Pahaha said, getting a dreamy, faraway look in her eyes. "His name is Red Loon. He is Yellow Thunder's best friend, a devoted Osage warrior."

"But Yellow Thunder has not mentioned Red Loon to me," Ashley said, eyeing Pahaha questioningly. "I have yet to meet him."

"He is one who has been assigned to stay separated from the tribe for now, to secretly search among the other tribes of this area for our stolen horses, and . . . and Yellow Thunder's sister," Pahaha said somberly. "Although Yellow Thunder was told that a white man stole his sister from her dwelling during the midnight hour, we have not forgotten the possibility that perhaps our Indian enemies were responsible. This is what Red Loon has been sent to find out. This year he must miss the thrill of the buffalo hunt with his blood brother Yellow Thunder." Pahaha lowered her eyes.

"And Pahaha must miss the thrill of Red Loon's presence."

Then Pahaha lifted her eyes, smiling bashfully at Ashley. "I speak too openly of a brave who has yet to share his heart solely with me," she said, yet Ashley was not listening.

The talk of Yellow Thunder's sister and her abduction had again catapulted Ashley back to the terrors on the riverboat, where Juliana had been so savagely raped.

She was remembering the women incarcerated in the hold of the ship, and how they were man-handled and bid upon at the chopper's settlement.

She could not believe that anyone but her step-brother was responsible for the slave trade in these parts.

"There are so many ways the young braves grow wise in trailing, stalking, covering, disguise, and all the arts of a good hunter," Pahaha was saying, pulling Ashley back to the present. It was Pahaha's way of shifting the conversation away from a subject that might make them both uncomfortable.

Ashley listened intently, glad to have her mind filled with something besides that which tore at her heart.

"Some of the lads, before their teens, join the men in their hunt for big game," Pahaha was saying. "At an early age, physical strength is developed from long-distance walking, running, and climbing. Even long hours of crawling or walking in a stooped position have to be endured."

There was a noticeable activity suddenly around them, drawing Ashley's attention away from

Pahaha. The other women had begun another part of their long day's duties.

Several buffalo carcasses had been brought into the camp and the women were preparing them, making use of nearly every part of the buffalo.

Ashley, following Pahaha's instructions, helped prepare the buffalo, willing herself not to faint from the strong odor of the blood, or the sight of it. With deft fingers, she helped cut the skin along the underside of one of the bulls, cutting from its chin to the end of its tail. The skin was pulled to each side as it was removed, providing a clean place to pile the meat to be smoked and dried.

The intestines were then removed, the contents squeezed out, and the casings turned inside out and cleaned. The paunch was emptied of its contents, cleaned and made ready to receive the melted tallow, after which it was placed in a mold of clay until the tallow cooled and hardened to hold its shape. Then the paunch would be dried, forming a useful vessel.

"The horns of the buffalo will be fashioned into spoons, tools, and utensils," Pahaha explained as she worked beside Ashley. "The brains will be saved for tanning the skins, and the sinews taken from along the backbone will be made into bow-strings and sewing thread."

Pahaha paused for a moment when she saw how pale Ashley had become, then led her away from the others. "You will be all right?" she asked, frowning into Ashley's ashen face.

"Is it the blood? It is something you do not like?"

"I'm fine," Ashley said, wiping a bead of perspiration from her brow with the back of her hand, shuddering when she saw the blood on her hand as she brought it slowly down again. "But I must admit, it will take some time for me to be at ease with such chores as this."

"You have never prepared buffalo before in your white community?" Pahaha asked innocently.

"Not so much as a chicken," Ashley said, laughing softly. "But I am learning. And I shall overcome my discomfort while doing so. I must prove to Yellow Thunder that I am strong—not a weakling who nearly faints at the sight of blood."

Pahaha giggled, then nodded as she encouraged Ashley to walk with her beside the river. "In due time, everything of the Osage way of life will be natural for you," she said. "You will understand that every part of the buffalo is important for our survival, and what part is the most prized of all."

"What is that?" Ashley asked, so badly wanting to learn, to show that she was serious in her interest to learn.

"The tongue, liver, and fetus of the buffalo, when present, are delicacies almost equal to the marrow in the bones which are roasted and cracked," Pahaha said, weaving her long, lean fingers through her hair that was fluttering in the gentle breeze of morning.

Ashley gulped hard at the mention of the fetus of a buffalo being looked on as a delicacy, and changed the subject. "The hides," she said quickly. "How are they prepared?"

Pahaha stopped and knelt down to pluck a wild flower, then resumed walking again alongside the river as she sniffed its spicy fragrance. "The hides of the animals are stretched well above the reach of straying wild animals and village dogs to dry," she explained. "We women, with our fleshers and scrapers, will remove all excess animal tissue from them, leaving only the pure skin, which will be used for floor coverings, robes, blankets, and lodge coverings, or tanned for moccasins and dog harnesses."

A sudden commotion to Ashley's right side, just beyond where the dwellings sat in their rows of seven, made her stiffen, a scream frozen in the depths of her throat. A buffalo, as white as the snows of winter, had appeared on the crest of the nearby hill, for a moment standing still, snorting puffs of white breath into the cool, clear morning.

"Yellow Thunder's white buffalo," Ashley whispered. "Lord, it's the white buffalo."

And then something seemed to spook it. It came tearing down the hill in the direction of the Indian camp. Women and children began scattering and screaming in its wake.

When the buffalo reached the camp, in its terror it ran wildly around, stopping behind one lodge one moment, then turning with a start and running in a different direction the next moment. The women continued to scream, the children bawled, and the elders shouted words of command to them. Some were already firing arrows at the frightened white beast.

Ashley grabbed Pahaha's hand and half-dragged her from the river behind the protection of a nearby tree. Their eyes widened as they watched everyone else ran for safety. Those nearest the river jumped into it; others hunkered behind trees, trembling.

The buffalo loped on, unharmed, threading its way between the lodges, kicking out wickedly at them as he passed. Ashley thought that for all his great size and odd shape, he was quite agile and quick on his feet.

She held her breath and placed her hands at her throat as the arrows whizzed in the air, but still none harmed the buffalo as he continued to wind in and out of the lodges.

Then, almost as quickly as it had arrived, it disappeared over the ridge, leaving a strange silence behind it in the camp.

Slowly, cautiously, everyone came out from hiding.

No one was hurt. Not a lodge was overturned. But it was obvious that most of the women's daily work had been destroyed. Long scaffolds of drying meat and many hides and pelts pegged out on the ground to dry had been trampled.

Yet this was nothing as to what could have happened. The frenzied buffalo could have left much death behind.

"You are all right?" Pahaha asked, as she turned to Ashley, gently touching her cheek.

"Are you?" Ashley said, still in awe of what she had just witnessed. It was as though the buffalo had appeared from out of nowhere, like an apparition, just to put alarm in the hearts of the Osage for the havoc they were wreaking on the buffalo's own kind.

Then she turned once again and stared at the hill, over which the white buffalo had fled. The buffalo kill was much farther away today than in days past. It was many miles from the campsite. Ashley realized that Yellow Thunder would not have had a chance to see this beast that seemed to haunt his midnight dreams.

But at least he would know it existed!

In time, he would be able to search for it, knowing the search would not be in vain.

# Chapter
# Twenty-One

*Several Days Later—*

The buffalo hunt behind her, Ashley knelt over a spread buffalo skin along with many other women, scraping the fleshy side with a sharpened bone— the shoulder-blade of a buffalo, sharpened at the edge like an adze.

The winds had turned colder, and the mid-afternoon sun was welcome on Ashley's face as she laid her scraper down on the ground and rose to her full height, taking the time to snuggle her full-length fur coat beneath her chin.

For a moment she forgot the busy women all around her, among them sweet Pahaha, and gazed solemnly at Yellow Thunder's father's large tepee. Yellow Thunder had been there all day at his father's side, softly chanting, after having found his father ailing seriously upon their return from the buffalo hunt.

The moment Ashley had looked down upon Chief Eagle Who Flies, she had recognized symptoms of the same illness that one of her favorite aunts had died from in New York. Shortly after her aunt had had a seizure which had left her paralyzed on one side, another seizure several days later had claimed her life. Yellow Thunder's father was similarly paralyzed. When he tried to talk, his words were garbled, as though his tongue twisted as he tried to form each word.

Even though Ashley had not known Chief Eagle Who Flies very long, it still pained her immensely to see him so ill. And her heart went out to Yellow Thunder, who felt utterly helpless as he sat vigil at his father's side.

Ashley had gone ahead and worked with the women because she had felt as though she were an intruder on these private moments between father and son.

Moon Face Bear's services had been requested, and the medicine man had come and gone from Chief Eagle Who Flies's dwelling. Everyone was anxious to see if his powers were great enough to make Chief Eagle Who Flies well again. Ashley knew they were not.

Wanting to busy her hands and her mind, Ashley lifted her assigned skin and carried it to one of several small holes that had been dug in the ground. A fire had been built with rotten wood to produce a great quantity of smoke without much blaze. Here the various skins would be smoked.

Ashley laid the skin across several small poles that had been stuck in the ground over the hole and drawn and fastened together at the top. She wrapped her skin around the poles in the form of a tent, then sewed the skin together at the edges to secure the smoke within it.

Aching from her full day of labor with the other women, Ashley placed her hands at the small of her back and groaned as she stepped away from her skin, which the smoke was already touching in a soft caress.

Again she looked toward Yellow Thunder's father's dwelling, then sighed heavily as she began walking toward it. She wanted to at least let Yellow Thunder see her, to remember that she was there if he needed her. It did not seem right for him to bear his sadness alone.

Yet perhaps that was another way the Indian culture differed from the white people's, she thought. Perhaps they did not want to share their sorrow.

And surely this loss was greater for Yellow Thunder than most. He had been taken from his parents at a young age, been denied their love and devotion. He had been allowed to return to his father, to renew these feelings between father and son. And now he perhaps could not bear the thought of having to say goodbye again, this time forever.

"It would be much easier if his mother were here," Ashley whispered to herself as she stopped just outside the entrance to the tepee. "Yellow Thunder would at least have her."

Ashley smoothed the entrance flap aside and stepped quietly into the tepee. She peered into the gloom of the interior of the dwelling, where the fire had been allowed to burn down to glowing embers. The air was heavy with the scent of the sweet grass that was being used to purify the air. Yellow Thunder was kneeling beside a platform, on which lay his father, whose eyes were closed in heavy sleep. Yellow Thunder's head was bowed, but his chanting had ceased.

Tears came to Ashley's eyes as she gazed at the back of the man she loved, seeing his normally broad and proudly straight shoulders now bent. He was dressed in only a brief breech clout, and his raven-black hair hung long and loose down the perfect line of his back, his copper flesh a golden sheen in this softer light.

Swallowing hard, afraid that she should not be there, Ashley began tiptoeing across the mats on the floor, then fell slowly to her knees beside Yellow Thunder when she reached him.

He did not look her way, but seemed to sense that it was she, for one hand reached out and sought hers, grasping it tightly.

"He is no better," he said thickly, his eyes slowly lifting to gaze upon the ashen face of his father. "Listen to his breathing. It is now hard for him to take each breath.

"He is going to die," he said, a deep sadness having robbed the usual sparkle from his midnight-dark eyes. "In my heart and soul, I must prepare myself for his death. My *mitawin*, come into my arms. Help lessen my burden."

Ashley felt guilty for having misinterpreted his intentions earlier, when he had not asked her to stay with him. Surely he had wanted her all along, yet was so shocked by his father's sudden illness that he had not thought to voice his need.

"I am here, always, for you," Ashley whispered, turning to him, twining her arms around his neck as he drew her into his embrace. "Tell me what I can do to help. I will do anything you ask. Anything."

"You are doing all that I wish, for now," Yellow Thunder whispered, stroking her soft hair. "My wife, my wife . . ."

A commotion outside the tepee drew Ashley and Yellow Thunder apart. There was a strained silence among his people, and all that could be heard was the sound of approaching hoofbeats. Yellow Thunder and Ashley rose to their feet and together walked to the entrance flap. Yellow Thunder brushed it aside, allowing Ashley to leave ahead of him.

When Ashley recognized the woman on one of the approaching horses, her heart leapt into her throat. "Juliana?" she said, her eyes wide. A sudden feeling of relief rushed through her, filling her with joy that Juliana was alive and well.

Then Ashley had to wonder what Juliana was doing there—what purpose had caused her to make the long journey to Yellow Thunder's village?

Her gaze shifted to Juliana's riding companion. His facial features and shoulder-length black hair looked Indian, yet his attire was that of a white man. His breeches were dark and made of broadcloth, his shirt and jacket of a red plaid flannel. But he also wore a beaded Indian headband to hold his hair back from his face.

Ashley's eyes were drawn downward, where two huge pistols were holstered at each of his hips and close by, sheathed to his right thigh, was a huge knife.

She gazed up at his face again, seeing a sternness in his features, yet the gentleness in his dark eyes was surely why Juliana had trusted him.

Yellow Thunder moved to Ashley's side, his eyebrows arching in surprise when he recognized Juliana and Billy Two Arrows, a half-breed scout who was in part Osage and who had on occasion helped Yellow Thunder round up horse thieves.

Yellow Thunder had not asked Billy Two Arrows to join him on his hunt for his sister. That hunt had been too personal—something that Yellow Thunder had wanted to do for himself.

Juliana and Billy Two Arrows reined in their horses close to where Ashley and Yellow Thunder were standing. Juliana, dressed in man's breeches and shirt, with a wide-brimmed hat holding her hair within its crown, slid out of the saddle and ran to Ashley.

"Lord, it's so good to see you," Juliana said, hugging Ashley tightly.

"Juliana, I am so relieved to see *you*," Ashley said, returning the hug. "You don't know how often I have wondered about you—where you might be, and with whom. And to suddenly find you here in Yellow Thunder's village is little short of a miracle."

Juliana stepped away from Ashley and looked her up and down, a slow smile touching her lips as her eyes then locked and held with Ashley's.

"I knew that you'd be all right," she murmured, giving Yellow Thunder a quick glance. "I knew that he would ensure it."

Yellow Thunder took a step toward Billy Two Arrows as the scout dismounted and smiled widely at him. "My friend, what brings you so far from New Orleans?" Yellow Thunder said, giving Billy Two Arrows a quick hug, then stepping back, a hand clasped onto the scout's shoulder. "It is many sunrises since we last joined on a hunt."

"That is so," Billy Two Arrows said.

"And this time?" Yellow Thunder asked, "you bring a woman on a hunt? You bring my friend Juliana with you?"

Juliana heard what Yellow Thunder was saying, then stepped away from Ashley and went to Yellow Thunder, peering up into his dark eyes, anxious to reveal the reason for this mission.

Yellow Thunder dropped his hand from the scout's shoulder and turned to face Juliana. He gave her a quick hug, then stepped away from her, his eyes still locked with hers. "You are well," he said softly. "That is good. And you have come to my village for that reason? To show Ashley and Yellow Thunder that you are well?"

Juliana brushed her hat back from her brow with a forefinger. "No, not for that," she said, smiling up at him. "I have come to tell you some news that will make you so very happy."

"News?" Yellow Thunder said, an eyebrow again arching.

"Yes," Juliana said, then blurted out her tale of discovery, watching Yellow Thunder's eyes light up with the news and his face twitch into a broad smile.

"My mother?" he finally said. "You have . . . found my mother?"

"I'm so glad to be the one to bring you the news," Juliana said, placing a gentle hand to Yellow Thunder's cheek.

"You found her, yet she did not return home with you?" Yellow Thunder said, his heart pounding with an eagerness to see his long-lost mother.

Juliana's smile faded and she dropped her hand to her side. "She is alive, but not strong," she murmured. "And . . . and she is blind, Yellow Thunder. I did not want to risk bringing her on the long journey. She feared trying it. And . . ."

Yellow Thunder placed a hand to Juliana's shoulder when she hesitated with her words. "And . . . ?" he said thickly. "What are you not telling me?"

"She is still a slave, Yellow Thunder," Juliana rushed out. "She is not free to travel anywhere. She belongs to a white man. She was bid on and paid for all those long years ago, only moments after you were snatched from her arms."

Yellow Thunder's jaw tightened and he eased his hand from Juliana's shoulder, circling the fingers of both hands into fists at his sides. "She is still enslaved, and she is blind," he repeated through clenched teeth.

Ashley went to Yellow Thunder and slipped an arm around his waist for reassurance. "At least you know that she is alive," she said softly.

"That is not enough," Yellow Thunder growled. "That . . . is . . . not enough. The white man will soon see that she is of no further use to him and he will rid himself of her—possibly by killing her."

Ashley paled, realizing that Yellow Thunder was right. "What are you going to do?" she asked, peering up at him, seeing the angry fire in the depths of his eyes.

"I must go for her," Yellow Thunder said, "Not only for her will I do this, or for myself, but for my father. He may never see his daughter again, but perhaps he can die with a smile on his lips and in his eyes if he can just once more see his wife."

He spun around and faced Ashley. "*Ah-hah*, I must go for my mother," he said. "I must free her. And you will accompany me. I will not chance parting with you for the length of time required to do this."

"I will gladly go," Ashley said, straightening her shoulders as she gazed with determination up at him. "I will help with your mother's escape."

Yellow Thunder and Ashley's eyes held in a silent understanding for a moment, and then Yellow Thunder turned to Billy Two Arrows. "You will accompany me and my woman on this journey of the heart?" he asked solemnly.

"You knew that I would, if asked," Billy Two Arrows said, a stern hand on a holstered pistol.

"We must leave the horses behind and go by canoe," Yellow Thunder said. "It is the fastest way to New Orleans, and it is the quietest."

"That is true," Billy Two Arrows said, nodding.

Juliana stepped up beside Billy Two Arrows and placed a gentle hand on his arm, then looked up at Yellow Thunder. "I want to go also," she said softly. "I know the habits of those who own the plantation where your mother is enslaved. I can assist you in that way, by telling you when is the safest time to try the abduction."

"*Ah-ha*, that is wise and I appreciate your kindness," Yellow Thunder said, nodding.

"It is the least I can do to repay you for helping me escape not only the evil clutches of Calvin, but also dying from the snakebite," Juliana said, then turned her eyes to Ashley. "And I hope by doing this that I am somehow repaying you. I owe both you and Yellow Thunder my life."

"You know that you didn't have to do anything as payment for what we did for you," Ashley said, stepping up to Juliana and drawing her into her gentle embrace. "That you are alive and well is payment enough."

They embraced for a moment longer, then Ashley eased herself from Juliana's arms. "And do you think that I could ever forget that it was you who chanced getting the key from the guard in the riverboat, which not only freed Yellow Thunder but also myself?" she murmured. "We owe you, Juliana. We shall forever be grateful."

Juliana's eyes misted with tears, grateful to have found a friend like Ashley. But she had not come to the Osage village only to renew acquaintances. She had brought such wonderful news for Yellow Thunder! There was even more that Yellow Thunder must be told.

Juliana turned her eyes up at him. "Yellow Thunder, I have brought a message from your mother for you," she said softly. "She says that you are still in her heart as though you had never been taken from her."

Yellow Thunder's throat tightened and he fought the threat of tears that were pressing against his eyes, touched deeply by Juliana's words, and so relieved that he would soon see his mother again.

His only fear was that his father would not last until his wife was returned to him.

"I also have a message from your mother for your father," Juliana said.

# Chapter
# Twenty-Two

Kneeling beside Chief Eagle Who Flies's sleeping platform, with Ashley on her right side and Yellow Thunder at her left, Juliana gazed down at the ashen face of what had once been a most powerful Osage chieftain. She was recalling everything that Star Woman had said about her husband, as she remembered him in his youthful days.

Star Woman's descriptions of her husband had in fact actually described Yellow Thunder, for the son was an exact replica of his father.

Juliana also recalled how lovingly Star Woman had spoken of Chief Eagle Who Flies, and how she had said that she had never stopped thinking about him, dreaming every night of the embraces and kisses they had once shared.

Dreaming about the man she loved had kept him alive inside her heart and had kept her going through the years when she had been faced with much hardship and sickness, and when loneliness finally proved to be her worst enemy.

"Father?" Yellow Thunder said, breaking through Juliana's thoughts. "Someone is here with a message from mother—from your *wife*, Star Woman. Father, please hear me. Your beloved wife is still alive. This woman who stands at my side has seen and talked with mother. She has brought you a message from her. If you hear me, please show me some sort of a sign."

Ashley held her breath, her eyes eagerly wide as she gazed wistfully down at Chief Eagle Who Flies, fearing that he was in a coma, perhaps never to recover. She had seen her aunt lapse into such a state, where she knew nothing and no one. Her aunt had seemed to be in a drugged sleep the last days and nights of her life.

If this was what Yellow Thunder's father was experiencing, the news of his wife had come too late.

And it was almost certain now that Chief Eagle Who Flies would never see his daughter again.

Yellow Thunder's heart pounded like a distant drum as he watched carefully for his father to make some gesture with his eyes, his mouth, or his hands to indicate that, even though he was in a strange sort of sleep, he could hear.

But too soon, disappointment assailed Yellow Thunder, for his father did not respond in any way to the news. He still lay stone quiet, his hands limply resting on the blankets that were drawn up almost to his chin, his eyes quietly closed.

A determination seized Yellow Thunder. "I cannot give up," he said, his voice drawn. "I must give my father a reason to live for at least a few more days, so that my mother and father's hands can clasp, sealing again the bond that was ripped apart all those years ago."

Ashley covered her mouth with a hand, stifling a gasp behind it as she watched Yellow Thunder, in his desperation to be heard, place one hand beneath his father's head, and the other behind his back, to brace him as he forced his father into a sitting position.

A sick feeling swam through Yellow Thunder to feel his father's body so limp within his hold and to see his left arm and hand hanging weakly, like a leaf dangling from a limb, waiting for a breeze to detach it and send it spiraling to the ground below to rot and wither away into nothingness.

This made Yellow Thunder even more determined that his father would be awakened to hear the news, to have something to grasp onto, to keep hope alive within his heart.

Finding his father's weight heavier in his unconscious state, Yellow Thunder finally managed to get the chief to a standing position. Grasping onto his father for dear life, Yellow Thunder began dragging his father back and forth across the mats.

Billy Two Arrows, who had until now only stood in the shadows of the tepee, came and stood on the chief's other side, helping Yellow Thunder in his attempt to awaken his father.

Ashley and Juliana's hands searched for and found each other's. They clung together as they watched what seemed to be an impossible task.

Ashley's heart cried out to Yellow Thunder to let it be, to accept what the good Lord had handed him.

Her disheartened gaze went to Chief Eagle Who Flies. His devastating illness having robbed him of his dignity, yet she could see that he still held some nobility. His beautifully-beaded buckskin clothes clung to shoulders and chest that had not yet wasted away with illness. On his healthy side, he still looked as strong and as vital as before.

But the way his head was hanging and his feet were dragging proved that too much had been taken from him ever to be the same again.

Suddenly there was a sound that seemed to escape from some deep well. Ashley's eyes brightened and her pulse raced when she saw Chief Eagle Who Flies's lips move and realized that the sound had come from him.

Yellow Thunder's heart thrilled with the sound, and when his father emitted another low rumble of protest over what was happening to him, Yellow Thunder grabbed him away from Billy Two Arrows and clutched his father to him, holding him on his feet by sheer will.

"Father, you do hear me, don't you?" Yellow Thunder asked, his lips only a fraction away from his father's ear. "Make another sound that I can glory over! Let me know that you are able to comprehend what you hear."

Ashley gasped with happiness when Chief Eagle Who Flies's eyes slowly fluttered open. "Yellow Thunder, your father's eyes . . ." she said, pointing to his father.

Yellow Thunder held his father partially away from him, and almost shouted with joy when he found himself being frowned at by a father who had only moments ago seemed ready to enter his grave.

"I hear . . . and . . . I feel," Chief Eagle Who Flies managed to say, when his tongue would allow it. He tried to jerk himself free from his son, but fell limply again within his strong grip.

"What . . . is . . . this?" Chief Eagle Who Flies then said, only barely audible through his harsh breathing. "Why . . . is . . . everyone staring at . . . me? Who is . . . the white woman standing . . . beside . . . Ashley?"

Feeling an inner strength that he had never known existed, and elated by his father's partial recovery, if even for only a limited time, Yellow Thunder picked his father up and carried him to his platform, easing him down onto it.

"The white woman's name is Juliana," Yellow Thunder said, gently drawing a blanket over his father. "She has brought you some news. It will please you, Father. So . . . please you."

Yellow Thunder gestured toward Juliana, then stepped aside as she came and knelt on the floor beside Chief Eagle Who Flies's platform.

Ashley moved to Yellow Thunder's side and leaned against him, welcoming the strength and comfort of his arm as he snaked it around her waist and they watched the tender scene being acted out before her.

"I have brought you a message from your wife, Star Woman," Juliana said softly, seeing the shock of the news registering in the chief's old eyes.

Chief Eagle Who Flies lifted his trembling right hand and tried to lean upon it, but it fluttered back onto the pelts when his strength again failed him. "My wife?" he said, his words slurred, his tongue twisting with the effort. "You have . . . seen my wife?"

Juliana strained to understand him, feeling so sorry for him. His condition was nothing like she had expected, but she had not known of his failing health until now.

Then she proceeded with the news that she had carried to him. "Yes, I have seen and talked with Star Woman," she said softly. "She sends her love. She told me to tell you that she still dreams about you."

Tears streamed from the chief's old eyes, and he emitted a strange sort of choking sound from the depths of his throat. "She is alive," he struggled to say. "She dreams of me?"

Yellow Thunder stepped away from Ashley and knelt quickly beside his father, opposite Juliana. Ashley soon followed, kneeling down beside him.

"Father, I am going to find Mother," Yellow Thunder said, clasping his father's stronger hand. With his free hand, he wiped the tears from his father's copper face. "I will bring her to you. You will be together again. You will love again."

Chief Eagle Who Flies showed a brief contentment and peace on his face and in his eyes, but then his expression changed into a strange sort of fear and anxiousness. He looked wildly up at Yellow Thunder. "When she last saw me, I was a young, healthy man," he said, his words still garbled, yet audible enough for Yellow Thunder to understand. "She must not see me this way. Let her remember me as I once was. Yellow Thunder, this I ask of you. Do not . . . allow her to see me like this."

Ashley swallowed back a rising lump in her throat, and tears threatened to spill from her eyes. She felt the old man's pain that she heard in his voice and saw in the desperation of his eyes.

And she understood.

Then she smiled sweetly at Yellow Thunder when he found just the right words to say to make things at least partially acceptable to his father.

"Father, I *will* bring mother to you," he said. "But do not fret so. She cannot see. The years have also taken their toll on her. She is . . .blind. She will not be able to see the change in you."

Chief Eagle Who Flies was stunned speechless by the news of Star Woman's blindness, and deeply saddened over it, but then it seemed a blessing that now, when husband and wife would be reunited, she would not be able to see the change in her chief.

"My wife is blind, and her husband is a cripple," Chief Eagle Who Flies finally uttered. Then he sighed heavily. "Go for her. Bring her to me. Let me touch her face. Let me kiss her lips . . . one . . . last time."

"I will leave now for New Orleans, by canoe," Yellow Thunder said, leaning over his father and giving him a gentle embrace. "I will bring mother to you soon. Soon, Father, your lips will touch, your hearts will become as one again."

Chief Eagle Who Flies patted Yellow Thunder on the back with his stronger hand. "*Ah-hah*, soon," he said, then welcomed the blanket beneath his chin as Yellow Thunder arranged it snugly beneath it. He also welcomed Ashley's heartfelt hug and her kiss on his cheek.

Then he closed his eyes and allowed sleep to claim him again, a smile locked on his lips as he began dreaming of that beautiful maiden of so long ago and how she had stolen his heart the first time their eyes met. He could see her dancing around the fire with the other maidens, her eyes locked with his. He could feel her hands on his face as she had come to him, her lips sweet as she had kissed him.

He trembled inside, as though a young man again, as he dreamed of their first time together. His heart pounded in his sleep as he felt again that rush of desire as their bodies tangled and soared above the clouds, joining the eagles in flight as they found that ultimate pleasure.

Yellow Thunder stood a moment longer beside his father's sleeping platform, watching his father's facial expressions in his sleep, wondering what he was dreaming about.

But when Ashley's hand circled Yellow Thunder's, reminding him of his own midnight dreams that had stirred him to passion, he smiled and knew his father was recalling those sweet times with his wife, when they were young.

Then, with Ashley's hand in his, Yellow Thunder led her from the tepee, Juliana and Billy Two Arrows following them.

"One canoe is all that we will need," Yellow Thunder said, leading them quickly to his own dwelling. "Gather up many pelts," he said to Ashley. "We will place them in the bottom of the canoe for mother to sleep upon for her return travel to our village."

He looked over his shoulder at Billy Two Arrows. "Go and explain to my warriors what we are doing and ask for their assistance in preparing the canoe for travel," he said.

Billy Two Arrows nodded and hurried away.

Juliana rushed around the tepee with Yellow Thunder and Ashley, helping gather up what was needed for the trip. Then there was someone else in the tepee.

Ashley turned and smiled as she found Pahaha standing there, her face sweet and soft in the glow of the dim fire in the fire pit.

"I have heard about Star Woman, and that she has been found," she said, looking anxiously from Ashley to Yellow Thunder.

Yellow Thunder turned and faced her as he was busy affixing a sheathed knife at his waist. "Mother is alive, but not well," he explained.

"I wish to help in some way," Pahaha said softly. "I shall sit with your father while you are gone. I shall see to all of his needs. Will that please you, Yellow Thunder?"

Yellow Thunder's lips tugged into a soft smile. "*Ah-hah*, that would please me," he said. "With you at my father's side, my worries will be lessened."

Pahaha's eyes were dancing. "I shall go to him now," she said. "May the Great Spirit bring you and your mother home safely."

Pahaha turned to leave, then turned around again and hurried to Ashley. "Be safe, my friend," she whispered, hugging Ashley, then left quickly.

When the sky was smeared red by a dazzling sunset, Yellow Thunder and Billy Two Arrows were drawing paddles through the water, sending the large canoe constructed of buffalo skins and green cottonwood trees down the long avenue of the river. Ashley and Juliana were huddled warmly beneath the same bear pelt in this same canoe, sharing each other's warmth, fears, and hopes.

# Chapter
# Twenty-Three

The journey down the river had been silent. Yellow Thunder's anxiousness to see his mother and to release her from her captivity kept conversation at a minimum. He had determinedly, almost without ever pausing to rest, drawn the paddle rhythmically through the water, his eyes always set straight ahead, awaiting that moment when Juliana would tell him that the plantation showing through the trees was the one where he would be reunited with his mother.

There had been no trace of doubt in Yellow Thunder's mind or heart that he would not succeed in releasing his mother. Now that he knew where she was, after all the years of being separated from her, nothing would stand in the way of his being with his mother again.

Ashley sat quietly beside Juliana, having just awakened from another brief nap. These naps were needed, since they had traveled the full night through on the river. The air was very still and mild, and the soft blue sky was unsullied by a single cloud. As they moved through the water, close to the bank, she could hear the lowing of cattle and the crowing of cocks from the distant farms and plantations.

Seeing a grand old house with huge pillars through the break in the trees on her right side, Ashley stiffened and glanced over at Juliana, to see if she would nod yes, indicating that was the plantation they were seeking.

"No, that's not the one," Juliana said, understanding Ashley's silent question in her eyes. "But I know that plantation. It's just up the road from the one that we are going to."

Ashley's pulse raced as she watched Juliana reach a hand to Yellow Thunder's shoulder, tapping it. She smiled as she watched Yellow Thunder's eyes light up as Juliana told him that their journey was soon over, and that it would be best to beach the canoe just around the bend up ahead.

Only briefly did Ashley think about how hungry she was, since they had not taken the time to stop and prepare the morning meal. The dried jerky that Billy Two Arrows had brought with him in his buckskin travel bag had only whet her appetite more.

Although the houses they had passed had been set far back from the river, the wondrous smells of frying bacon, eggs, and boiling coffee had managed to reach the river, almost sending Ashley's stomach into spasms.

She held her breath and grabbed the side of the canoe when Yellow Thunder and Billy Two Arrows changed the course of the vessel, heading it toward shore. The air seemed charged with anticipation and excitement as they quickly beached and secured the canoe, and everyone climbed from it onto rocks and sand.

"This way," Juliana whispered, reaching her hands to her hat and drawing it low over her brow. She did not want to reveal herself to these people, knowing now what they were capable of. She wanted nothing to do with them.

Ashley rushed to Yellow Thunder's side, her eyes widening when he removed his huge knife from its sheath.

She looked over her shoulder as Juliana fell into step with Billy Two Arrows, then smiled to herself when she saw the scout reach for one of Juliana's hands and hold it as they moved stealthily from the shore into the shadows of the trees that reached away from the river. It was obvious by the way he held her hand and gave her occasional warm glances, that Juliana and Billy Two Arrows had become more than just traveling companions. Juliana had finally found her own knight in shining armor—her own Indian warrior, with whom she could share the rest of her life.

This made a splash of joy touch Ashley's heart, for she would never forget how Calvin had abused Juliana. Now Juliana could perhaps forget the ugliness of that moment and find peace and happiness in the arms of her warrior!

Ashley's knee-high moccasins cushioned her feet against the vine-strewn ground, where occasional thorns reached up from the vines and the long, stringy feelers that were woven like many twisted and gnarled fingers across the ground beneath her.

She moved relentlessly onward, forgetting the uncomfortable ground cover, too glad now to be in an even more wooded area that would help keep them from being seen as they approached the plantation that they even now could see through a break in the trees. Huge, white columns graced the lovely house that sat closer to the river than the others Ashley had observed while traveling down the wide Mississippi.

After leaving the Osage village, they had traveled down more than one river to finally reach the Mississippi. Ashley had become guarded as Yellow Thunder and Billy Two Arrows had guided the canoe into the waters of the big river, knowing that it was possible to come head to head with her stepbrother as he continued dealing with slavery along the shores of the great, muddy river.

When they finally came to a clearing, where they could get a full view of the plantation, Yellow Thunder knelt low behind the thickness of a cluster of bushes, separating them to take a closer look.

Ashley crouched close beside him. Aware of Juliana and Billy Two Arrows moving to hunker low beside her on her other side, she peered ahead, scarcely breathing as her gaze took in what the others were so closely scrutinizing. The great mansion was at the front of the plantation grounds, the slaves' quarters behind it. Behind the quarters were fields, and behind those was an uncleared cypress swamp, where in the winter some time ago slaves had most likely been put to work chopping trees and operating the plantation's sawmill.

But to Ashley's surprise, the slaves' quarters were apparently abandoned, the small shanties having fallen into disrepair, some leaning precariously sideways as though they might collapse beneath even a slight gust of wind.

The yard around the abandoned slaves' quarters was a gritty slope of stone and gravel, with a speckling of grass growing on it, and it was strewn with sticks, old shoes, and similar litter.

"They don't seem to deal in slavery any longer," Ashley said softly as she moved closer to Yellow Thunder. "As you can see, the slaves' quarters are abandoned. That means . . ."

"Yes, that means that those who remain as slaves live in the house," Juliana said, interrupting as she went to stand on Yellow Thunder's side, Billy Two Arrows leaning close to hear. "This is why I did not know that my employers dealt in slavery. Their slaves—what is left of them—are much older now and are treated more as servants. Your mother has a room, alone, at the far back of the house, close to the kitchen. Her duties are mostly making the pies each day. One does not need one's eyesight to make pie dough, or to roll it out. It is done by touch."

"My mother," Yellow Thunder said, his heart soaring just to say the word "mother" and know that he would soon be with her. "Does she ever leave the house? Will I have the opportunity to get her without having to enter the house? I had thought all along that I would be stealing her from slaves' quarters. That would have been much more easily done than having to enter the white man's dwelling."

"It was my mistake for not having explained earlier," Juliana said somberly. "But even I did not know about the empty slaves' quarters until now. After I discovered your mother at the house, my thoughts were too filled with coming to you with this information to take the time to assess the full situation."

She paused, thinking hard, then smiled up at Yellow Thunder. "Your mother *does* leave the house on occasion," she said, beaming. "Although I was not employed long enough there to have noticed the habits of most employees, I do remember having seen your mother leave the house on occasion to take a stroll in the front yard, touching and smelling the flowers that line the drive that leads up to the house. That was my only acquaintance with her until the one night I talked at length with her and saw her close enough to see that she was Indian."

"Then she will leave the house today?" Yellow Thunder said, his heart racing at the thought of going to her, leading her away from the house, then into the arms of her long-lost son!

"I'm not sure," Juliana said solemnly. "The reason I became acquainted with her in the first place was to look in on her after she had fainted earlier in the day. She was weak then. I am not sure how she fares now."

"If it is necessary, I will enter the white man's dwelling," Yellow Thunder said, clutching his fingers more tightly to the handle of his knife. He glanced down at Juliana. "Now tell me the habits of the others. Will we have an opportunity to enter the house without being seen? Will we have to wait until the sky darkens?"

"As I said, I was not employed there long," Juliana fretted. "But I believe that it is the habit of the family to go into New Orleans each day about mid-morning—the man, woman, and two children together. I imagine they spend a good portion of the day shopping. They are rich, and surely find all sorts of ways to squander their wealth on each other."

Yellow Thunder's gaze moved to the stable. "Can you tell if they are gone now?" he asked.

Just as the question rolled across his lips, a horse and carriage left the stable, the driver taking it to the front of the house. Soon after, the family departed the house and boarded the carriage. As the carriage lumbered down the long drive, Star Woman providentially appeared, feeling her way with a long, narrow stick as she cautiously made her way down the steps from the porch.

"I remember now," Juliana said eagerly. "Star Woman liked to commune amongst the flowers right after the family left in their carriage."

Juliana squinted as she watched the elderly Indian woman finally reach the ground, then begin walking shakily toward the flowers that the frost of the approaching winter had not yet killed. "She is still not too well," she murmured. "See how she shakes as she walks?"

Yellow Thunder's eyes were misting with tears, his heart aching at the sight of his mother. When they had last been together, she had been young and vital. He had been only a babe, suckling at her breast.

Yellow Thunder lifted his eyes to the sky, silently asking *Wah-kon-tah*, why this had been allowed to happen.

"We must not wait any longer," he said.

Yet he knew he had to be cautious. Too much lay at stake for any careless recklessness at this time. He gazed intently into Juliana's blue eyes. "Tell me the activities of the others who live in the white man's dwelling," he said.

"For the most part, the others are elderly, like your mother," Juliana said. "I was the youngest among them. I don't think they will oppose a strong young man like you. In fact, they would more than likely be glad to see that she was being given a way to escape. If they could escape, themselves, I am certain they would."

"Are there no overseers?" Yellow Thunder further questioned.

"None, as far as I know," Juliana said softly. "And I imagine it is because these people have been at the plantation for so long, they are trusted to remain there until they die."

"Even so, *I* shall go for your mother," Billy Two Arrows quickly interjected. "It would be less conspicuous if I was seen entering the grounds, for I am dressed as the white men dress. Perhaps I will be mistaken for a temporary gardener or a stable hand."

"Go with speed, then," Yellow Thunder said, clasping a hand to Billy Two Arrow's shoulder. "Bring my mother to me, my friend. I will be indebted to you forever."

Billy Two Arrows smiled at Yellow Thunder and nodded. Then, as Yellow Thunder dropped his hand from his shoulder, Billy Two Arrows moved stealthily from the cover of bushes and ran across a wide open space, until again he was able to use the large trunks of oak trees as a shield as he approached Star Woman from behind.

Everyone watched with bated breath from behind the bushes as Billy Two Arrows stepped around the oaks to face Star Woman. . . .

# *Chapter Twenty-Four*

Star Woman stiffened, realizing that someone had just stepped up next to her. Always before, she had been left alone on her outings to walk among the blessings of *Wah-kon-tah*. The touch and smell of the flowers always catapulted her back in time to those happy days spent with Eagle Who Flies in the forest.

Star Woman leaned heavily against her cane, and with her free hand reached out to feel for the intruder. "Who is there?" she asked, her voice unsteady, gasping when her hand finally made contact with someone's face. She flinched and drew her hand quickly away. "*Hoh. Iho.* Speak your name or else leave me in peace."

"I am a friend," Billy Two Arrows quickly stated. "Star Woman, I have brought you news that will gladden your heart."

"News?" Star Woman said, squinting her old eyes, growing angry again over not being able to see. "What is this you have to say? And who are you? How do you know my name?"

"I am Billy Two Arrows," he said, growing uneasy over having to take so long with her, afraid of being seen. "I am a friend with your Osage people. I have come to tell you news of your son, Yellow Thunder."

Star Woman's mouth opened in a startled gasp. "Yellow Thunder?" she said, her voice quavering. "What of . . . my son? How could you know about him?"

"He is near," Billy Two Arrows quickly explained, reaching for Star Woman's arm to guide her way to Yellow Thunder. "I will take you to him."

Star Woman's heart skipped several beats and the shock stole her breath.

She grew limp and drifted to the ground in a dead faint.

Yellow Thunder had been watching attentively, growing more uneasy by the minute. When he saw his mother crumple to the ground, nothing could keep him away from her, not even the fear of being seen and taken captive.

"No, Yellow Thunder!" Ashley cried as he bolted away from her and raced across the straight stretch of meadow that reached to the mansion.

Ashley knew that no matter what she said or did, he was going to go to his mother. She chewed on her lower lip as she watched him finally reach her, then kneel down and lift her into his arms. A moment later he was racing across the meadow again, with his mother lying limply within his powerful embrace.

Billy Two Arrows ran on ahead of Yellow Thunder and arrived just moments ahead of him. "Hurry back to the canoe," he said, taking a look over his shoulder and heaving a sigh of relief as Yellow Thunder reached the safety of the bushes.

At the canoe, everyone waited for Yellow Thunder to place his mother gently upon the spread pelts, then in a blink of an eye, the canoe and its eager passengers were escaping up the long avenue of the river, toward home.

Ashley knelt beside Star Woman, while Juliana held the old woman's head on her lap. Placing a damp cloth on Star Woman's brow, Ashley dabbed it lightly, watching and hoping for a sign of her awakening. Ashley hoped Star Woman's unconscious state was only from having fainted—not from any other illness which might keep her from awakening to discover that she still had a son and that a husband awaited her arrival at the Osage village.

"How is she?" Yellow Thunder asked, peering down at his mother over his shoulder, yet keeping up a steady rhythmic motion with his arms, not for even one moment ceasing to move the paddle steadily through the water.

"She still hasn't awakened," Ashley said, looking solemnly up at Yellow Thunder. "If she doesn't soon, I . . . I don't think she will."

"We will find a place to make camp soon," Billy Two Arrows said. "After we are far enough up the river. And then, Yellow Thunder, you can work with your mother yourself."

Yellow Thunder nodded, then turned his eyes straight ahead again, the happiness he had thought to feel upon finding his mother robbed at finding her in such a sorry state.

Ashley continued bathing Star Woman's brow, and then again became aware of her growing hunger. She was glad when the canoe was finally headed toward shore, and soon camp was made.

Billy Two Arrows soon had meat cooking over the fire after a successful search for a rabbit. Yellow Thunder was kneeling over his mother, continuing to speak in the low tone he had used ever since she was carried to land and placed on several pelts beside the warmth of the fire.

Ashley gazed at Yellow Thunder with building pity. He seemed to think that perhaps Star Woman would hear him somewhere in the darkness where her mind had fled upon the shock of realizing that her beloved son was near. Ashley knew that Yellow Thunder was thinking that he might awaken her by the sheer force of his will.

But she was beginning to doubt that anything would reach through that dark void.

Suddenly Yellow Thunder's voice was stilled, and in its place Ashley heard a slight gasp. She moved to her knees so that she could see Star Woman's face more clearly, and Ashley's heart skipped a beat when she saw her eyelashes begin fluttering, and then her eyes slowly opening.

Yellow Thunder drew Star Woman up fully into his arms, and laid his cheek against hers, so that when she became fully awakened, the first thing that she would be aware of was the nearness of her son.

"Mother?" Yellow Thunder said, his voice breaking as he found her sightless dark eyes gazing up into his. "Mother, it is I, Yellow Thunder. I have come to take you home, to your husband. Please say that you understand."

Ashley was filled with much emotion as she watched mother and son reunited.

Star Woman breathed raspily, her heart racing out of control. She felt that it could not be possible that this man who was holding her ever so tenderly within his arms was her son, her beloved Yellow Thunder. It was strange how life seemed to have raced by in a flash, turning him overnight into a warrior of thirty winters, instead of a child of only a few sunrises.

Her hands trembled as she lifted them and began familiarizing herself with Yellow Thunder's facial features. Tears streamed down her cheeks when she felt how identical his cheekbones and lips were to his father's.

Ah, she marveled to herself, what smooth skin, and what a beautifully shaped nose, also like his father's.

*Ah-hah*, she thought. This *was* her son, for what other man could be so much the same as Chief Eagle Who Flies?

"*Micinksi*, my son," Star Woman said, placing a hand at the nape of Yellow Thunder's neck and drawing his lips close to hers. She kissed him, then hugged him with all of her might. "My son, it is true. You are here. You are alive. You are taking me home. It has been so long. So very, very long."

"I will tell you much about many things later," Yellow Thunder said, cradling her within his arms and smiling sweetly at Ashley over his mother's shoulder. "Soon you will be home. There you will be safe. There you will be reunited with your husband."

Yellow Thunder's smile faded, knowing that she had to be told the truth about Chief Eagle Who Flies's health soon. But he thought that it was best to delay the telling. The shock of having Yellow Thunder back had sent her into a tailspin of emotions.

Knowing that her husband lay near death might do the same, and this time she might never awaken from the shock.

"Your father? My husband? He is still as handsome?" Star Woman said, easing from Yellow Thunder's embrace.

"*Ah-hah*," Yellow Thunder murmured.

"A man as virile as my Eagle Who Flies must have taken many wives through the years after losing his first," Star Woman said, her voice not taking on any tone of sadness or jealousy at such a thought.

"Not many," Yellow Thunder corrected. "Only one."

"Oh?" Star Woman said, arching a heavy, gray eyebrow. "And she still warms his bed? Will she share his blankets with me, his first wife?"

"She is no longer sharing father's blankets," Yellow Thunder said softly. "She now walks the roads of the hereafter."

There was a great pause, and then Star Woman smiled sightlessly up at Yellow Thunder, a contentment evident as she relaxed against him. "The food," she murmured. "It is almost ready? Your mother's heart is pleasantly full, but her stomach is empty."

Billy Two Arrows heard her comment and nodded at Yellow Thunder. "Tell her that soon she will be eating."

"He calls himself Billy Two Arrows," Star Woman said, looking sightlessly around her. "I know of his presence. But I sense there are others nearby. Who are they, my son?"

Juliana knelt beside Star Woman, taking the old lady's hand and placing it to her face. "Do you remember me?" she said softly. "Juliana? I am the one who took your son the news of your whereabouts. I came with him to guide him to the plantation where he could find you. It makes me so happy, Star Woman, that you have been reunited."

Star Woman's old eyes misted over with tears. She reached a hand to Juliana's shoulder and drew her close enough to hug her. "*Pilamaye*, thank you, my child," she said, choking back a sob. "Because of you, my prayers have been answered. And because of you, I will also be reunited with my beloved husband. *Pilamaye*. *Pilamaye*."

"It was my pleasure to do this for all of you," Juliana said, then went and sat back down beside Ashley.

Yellow Thunder nodded at Ashley, a silent bidding for her to come to him and his mother. When she got there and knelt down before them, Yellow Thunder took his mother's hands and placed them on Ashley's face. "Touch this woman and know her well, Mother," he said thickly. "You will be learning of the woman who is now my wife."

Star Woman's lips parted in a gasp, then tugged into a gentle smile as she moved her fingers slowly over Ashley's face. "My fingers see that she is beautiful," she murmured. Then her hands went to Ashley's long and silken hair, whose texture differed much from that of the Indian maidens.

Star Woman's smile faded as she continued weaving her fingers through Ashley's hair. "This woman is white," she said dully. "My son, you are sharing your blankets with a woman with white skin?"

"*Ah-hah*, that is so," Yellow Thunder said matter-of-factly. "She is the woman who stole my heart, so I offered her my blankets in exchange. And Mother—she is wonderful."

Ashley sat all tensed up, afraid of not being accepted by Yellow Thunder's mother, then sighed with relief when Star Woman placed a hand at the nape of her neck and drew her close for a hug.

"My son, if your heart says this white woman deserves your love, then so be it," she said. "I will treat her well, my son, as mothers should do wives of their favorite sons."

Yellow Thunder laughed softly. "But, Mother, I am your only son," he said, his eyes gleaming.

"*Ah-hah*, I know," Star Woman said, her smile a genuine thing as she looked sightlessly at Ashley. "I know, and that makes it even more special to have a daughter-in-law at my age of sixty winters."

Billy Two Arrows brought several sticks bearing offerings of speared meat at their tips and handed them around. Soon the whole rabbit had been devoured and the bones discarded into the crackling blaze of the fire.

"I must excuse myself for a moment," Ashley said, blushing as she peered over at Billy Two Arrows, and then Yellow Thunder.

Yellow Thunder frowned as she escaped into the forest, not wanting to take his eyes off her, yet he forced himself to relax, convincing himself that nothing would happen to her during the short time she needed to spend in the privacy of the bushes.

He inhaled a nervous breath and then made his mother more comfortable against him. They could not linger much longer. They had not gotten that far from the plantation. Once his mother's disappearance was discovered, who was to say what those who owned her would do?

He hoped that they would see it as convenient for them. If she were gone, it would not be up to them to rid themselves of her. After all, she was almost past the age of being of service to them. He cuddled her close, missing those years that they could have had together, sharing so much. . . .

Ashley felt much better after having found relief behind the bushes. She paused for a moment, staring at the Mississippi only a few short steps from where she stood. The lure of the river seemed to beckon her to it. She badly wanted to jump right into it for a bath, but she knew better. She knew the dangers.

Yet she would at least lean over the water and splash her face and cleanse her hands of the grease left there from eating the rabbit. What could that hurt? she thought as she knelt on the sandy bank.

Before she had her hands in the water, something caused her back to stiffen and her heart to pound erratically. She could hear a sound that was quite familiar to her. It was the sound of paddlewheels splashing in the water! A paddle-wheeler was approaching!

Ashley stumbled to her feet, her pulse racing as she began scrambling clumsily from the riverbank, then stopped, stunned, when the riverboat cruised on past her and she was able to make out the name painted boldly on the side.

"Calvin!" she whispered, suddenly frozen to the spot at the sight of the great white boat so close to her—and so close to where the campfire was burning brightly. "Oh, Lord, what if . . . he saw?"

She turned around and began running blindly through the forest, her eyes wide and searching, glad when she saw the camp just ahead, through a break in the trees.

# Chapter
# Twenty-Five

Shadows had begun to fall and move like wavering ghosts in the forest on each side of this smaller, narrower river as the canoe slid endlessly onward. They had left the Mississippi River behind at daybreak, finding safety from Calvin's riverboat in the smaller, shallower river where larger vessels could not pass.

Ashley sat on the floor of the canoe with Star Woman, cradling her head on her lap as the elderly woman slept. She felt relieved that Calvin had not seen the camp the day before. Once again, she had found a reprieve from Calvin's evil.

Ashley gazed down at Star Woman, wondering how she would react when she was among her own people again. Although it seemed that Star Woman had clung to the beliefs of her people and to their language, Ashley could not help thinking that she would have almost as many adjustments to make in the Osage village, as she herself had had.

Thirty years made quite a difference in one's habits and thoughts.

Yet, still, Star Woman had lived among the Osage the first thirty years of her life.

Ashley glanced up at Yellow Thunder, his back to her, as his powerful arms methodically drew the paddle through the water in cadence with Billy Two Arrow's paddle on the opposite side of the canoe. She knew that her beloved was torn by conflicting feelings—feelings of joy for having found his mother, and sorrow at her loss of sight.

No doubt he was also worried that he might not bring his mother to her husband in time. If the old chief died before Yellow Thunder's return, Ashley was afraid that Yellow Thunder would blame himself for having failed his father.

Juliana touched Ashley's arm, drawing her attention away from her worries and concerns to Juliana's welcoming smile.

"Are you all right?" Juliana murmured. "You have been so quiet for so long." She glanced down at Star Woman, then back up at Ashley. "Is it because you are afraid you might disturb Star Woman? Or is it something else?"

Ashley nodded. "It is many things, not just one that is troubling me," she said somberly. She leaned closer to Juliana. "Mainly I am hoping that we are not too late—that Chief Eagle Who Flies is still alive. So much lies in balance. Yellow Thunder is carrying a burden much too heavy for just one person. I know him well. If he should fail in even one of his endeavors, he would find this hard to accept. Oh, I pray that Chief Eagle Who

Flies is still alive. If not, I—don't know what to expect."

Juliana took Ashley's hands in hers. "Yellow Thunder is a strong man, filled with much courage," she reassured her. Juliana glanced up at Billy Two Arrows with tenderness in her eyes. "He is like Billy. They seem to have been made from the same mold." She smiled at Ashley again. "Do not despair, Ashley. Yellow Thunder will bear up to anything that happens. He has had a lifetime of learning how."

"Yes, I know you are right," Ashley said, sighing heavily. "Yet still I worry so about him."

"That is because you love him so much," Juliana murmured, squeezing Ashley's hands affectionately. Once again she peered up at Billy Two Arrows, her eyes sparkling into his as he turned a quick glance her way.

Ashley had seen the quick exchange and smiled as she drew her hands away from Juliana to pull the fur robe more smugly up to Star Woman's chin.

"You've fallen in love with an Osage warrior, haven't you?" Ashley whispered, leaning her face closer to Juliana's. "I see it in your eyes, and I hear it in your voice when you speak Billy's name."

"Yes, I love him," Juliana whispered back, her face coloring with a blush. "After we leave Yellow Thunder's village, I plan to stay with him—be his woman."

Ashley leaned over Star Woman to give Juliana a warm hug. "I'm so glad," she said. "So very glad. Not only because I am happy that you have fallen in love with a man who seems to be as warm in his feelings as Yellow Thunder, but also because you will have someone to look after you. Calvin wouldn't dare approach you now. Billy wouldn't allow him to."

"*Hoh*, we are almost there," Yellow Thunder said, drawing Ashley and Juliana apart. He gestured toward the reflection of fire in the darkening sky. "The fires of my people burn well tonight. They reach to us, to guide our way home."

Ashley's pulse began to race as she looked heavenward and also saw the reflections, and then looked around Yellow Thunder, her heartbeat quickening when she caught sight of the great outdoor fire in Yellow Thunder's village through a break in the trees.

She leaned closer to Yellow Thunder. "Shall I awaken your mother?" she asked softly.

Yellow Thunder cast her a quick glance, his brow furrowed with a frown. "*Nah*, do not," he said, his glance shifting to his mother. "Let her sleep until I have time to go into my village to learn of the welfare of my father. Then I will return and take her to him. Either way, whether father has already started his long journey on the road to the hereafter, or whether *Wah-kon-tah* has touched his heart with a few more beats so that he can look a last time upon the face of his wife, mother will be taken to my father. But I must know, myself, the attitude which I should adopt with her. One of sadness and grief, or one of anticipation and happiness."

Ashley nodded and moved her legs slightly, so that Star Woman would not be disturbed when the canoe was beached. She waited breathlessly as the canoe headed toward shore. She scarcely breathed as the thump of the canoe jolted her, watching Star Woman for any signs of awakening.

When she saw that Star Woman still slept soundly, Ashley sighed with relief and sat quietly by as everyone but herself and Star Woman left the canoe.

The sun was hidden now behind the distant hills, the valleys below purple with dusk as Ashley sat there, anxiously waiting for Yellow Thunder's return. She watched him until she could not see him any longer, then began singing softly to pass the time more pleasurably, hoping the news would be good upon Yellow Thunder's return.

Yellow Thunder broke into a run, leaving Billy Two Arrows and Juliana behind, when he heard the soft drone of a drum in the distance and voices singing sorrowfully in unison with the beating of the drum.

Yellow Thunder's heart raced and his breath came in short rasps, knowing that the sounds he was hearing were evidence of what he was about to come face to face with.

His father was lying on his death bed! And his father's people were sharing their songs with him!

The drum represented his father's continuing heartbeat, meaning that when the drum ceased its beats, so had his father's heart!

"*A-i-i-i,*" Yellow Thunder shouted, expelling the torments from the depths of his soul with this cry that echoed back at him, over and over again through the forest that surrounded him.

"*Ahte*, Father!" he then cried. "Wait for your son! Wait for your wife! Do not leave us yet!"

When Yellow Thunder reached the outskirts of his village, he stopped and stared at the crowd that hovered around the lodge of Moon Face Bear, their tribe's medicine man. His knees grew weak and his jaw went tight, certain that his father lay in Moon Face Bear's large lodge, dying!

With another tormented cry, he broke into a mad run and burst through those who made way for him as he moved determinedly toward the medicine lodge. When he finally reached it, he stopped short, his eyes wide, seeing how the lodge skin had been raised all around, so that the Osage people could see what was going on inside the lodge.

Yellow Thunder stood as though frozen to the ground, also now among the observers, watching the medicine man. Moon Face Bear's hands had been purified by the smoke of burning sweet grass and he was removing the wrappings of a sacred pipe stem, singing, he and those elders seated in the lodge singing the appropriate song for each wrap.

At long last, the long stem with its tufts of brilliant feathers lay exposed. After reverently filling it, Moon Face Bear held it upward in the direction of the heavens, then down toward the earth, and then pointed it to the north, south, east, and west as he prayed for health to return to Chief Eagle Who Flies.

Out of respect to Moon Face Bear, Yellow Thunder did not interfere in his healing ritual. He stepped aside as the medicine man rose, holding the stem of the sacred pipe extended in front of him, dancing slowly and deliberately out of the lodge, the elders falling in place one by one behind him.

So then did the women and children follow along once Moon Face Bear left the medicine lodge, soon forming a long, snakelike procession, dancing along and weaving in and out and around the lodges of the camp, singing the various songs of the medicine pipe.

After each song was finished, the singers rested a little before another was started, and in the interval, people talked and laughed, believing in the efficacy of their prayers and devotion and the powers of the medicine pipe.

Then everything was quiet again as the songs and dancing ended and the people stopped to watch Yellow Thunder enter the medicine lodge alone.

Billy Two Arrows and Juliana were among the observers as Yellow Thunder knelt down beside the sleeping platform on which his father lay, bedecked in his finest regalia from his head to his toe, his headdress of many feathers on a platform beside him, where everyone could see its grandness.

By the way Yellow Thunder's father was lying, there was no indication of his father's paralyzed left side. His hands were folded together, resting atop him. His moccasined feet were placed closely together.

Yellow Thunder gazed at his father's closed eyes, yet was glad to see some movement beneath the lids and sorely relieved when his eyes fluttered open.

"You have returned?" Chief Eagle Who Flies said in a low mumble, as he gazed up at Yellow Thunder, his voice noticeably weaker than when Yellow Thunder had last spoken to him.

Yellow Thunder noticed, too, that his father's breathing was more shallow. "Where . . . is . . . Star Woman? I willed . . . my . . . heart to continue beating until . . . I could touch the softness of her face . . . and . . . lips again."

"She is not far," Yellow Thunder quickly assured him. "I first wanted to see if you felt well enough to receive her at your side. You do. I shall go for her."

"Quickly, my son," Chief Eagle Who Flies said, wheezing as he lifted a bony, trembling hand toward Yellow Thunder. "I . . . have not long in . . . this world."

Yellow Thunder nodded, then turned and fled from the medicine lodge. He pushed his way through the crowd, realizing that people were reaching out for him, wanting comfort by merely touching him, yet forcing himself to ignore them. He had heard the weakness and desperation in his father's voice. He had seen the pallor of his sunken cheeks and eyes.

Yellow Thunder already felt the absence of his father. Ah, what an ache it had already formed around his heart!

And how sad it would be if only moments after two who had been so in love for so long ago were reunited, they were separated again.

The only comfort for Yellow Thunder at this moment was the knowledge that his father and mother would not be saying final goodbyes just because his father was no longer of this earth. They would one day walk the roads of the here-after hand in hand.

*Ah-hah*, that made these upcoming moments bearable, to know that there was never an end for those who truly loved!

His mother would know this, also, and be able to accept her husband's last moments, knowing that one day they would meet again.

When Yellow Thunder reached the canoe, he found his mother just awakening in Ashley's arms. Ashley peered questioningly up at him.

"*Ah-hah*, my father is still alive," he said thickly, his eyes momentarily locking with Ashley's, seeking comfort in their depths.

Then he gazed with warmth down at his mother. "Mother, father is asking for you," he said, lifting her gently into his arms.

Ashley stepped out of the canoe and followed alongside Yellow Thunder toward the village as he softly and gently explained Chief Eagle Who Flies's condition to his mother.

When tears began streaming down Star Woman's face, Yellow Thunder humbly bent and

kissed them away, making Ashley stifle a
sob in her throat. She was more conscious
than ever of the compassion of this man
whom she had chosen to be her mate for
eternity.

Soon they were in the medicine lodge. Yellow
Thunder carried his mother to Chief Eagle Who
Flies's sleeping platform, then helped her to her
feet.

Chief Eagle Who Flies gazed up at his wife, and
Ashley was stunned that he did not flinch at seeing
her so changed. He was proving that he was a man
of wisdom and courage, for although tears glim-
mered in the corners of his eyes, he remained noble
and proud as he reached out to Star Woman and
took her hand in his.

"My wife," Chief Eagle Who Flies said, bringing
her hand to his lips and softly kissing it. "My . . .
precious . . . wife. You have come to say hello and
goodbye to your husband?"

Star Woman held back the rest of her tears, not
wanting these last moments with her husband to
be spent in crying, but in rejoicing over their
reunion.

"No more goodbyes," she said, moving to her
knees beside the sleeping platform. "That is too
final, my husband. We have been brought together again for a purpose. We both know which road
to choose for our travels in the hereafter. Your
road is mine. Mine is yours. Forever, my husband.
Forever."

Star Woman reached her free hand to Chief
Eagle Who Flies's face and smoothed her fingers

slowly over his features, smiling as she encountered the many changes. Ah, but even wrinkles did not take away his handsomeness!

"My wife, move into my embrace," Chief Eagle Who Flies said in a raspy whisper, his words only barely audible. "Let our arms fill one another's. Let our lips feel again the marvels of a kiss. This I will take with me on my journey until you come to me again, in death."

Ashley wiped tears from her eyes with her fingers and sighed when Yellow Thunder helped his mother up, so that she could lean over and move into her husband's embrace.

Yellow Thunder remained there, his hands softly holding his mother in place, while watching with a wondrous song in his heart as his mother and father embraced, and then kissed.

Then Yellow Thunder eased his mother away when his father began coughing. He held his mother next to him and waited for his father's coughing spell to cease.

His heartbeat quickened as his father reached over among his belongings beside his sleeping platform and took from them the great medicine bag of his forefathers.

Chief Eagle Who Flies held the bundle up, toward Yellow Thunder. "My son, before it . . . is . . . too late, I must hand this over to you for safekeeping," he said, coughing between each of his words. "To this medicine bag pay the greatest homage. Look to it for safety and protection throughout the rest of your life. Never . . . go . . . into battle without it. From this day forth, never be without your medicine. It is a part of your past—a part of *me*. I will be with you always, my son. Always."

Yellow Thunder accepted the medicine bag, a bundle made of the skin of the otter and ornamented with ermine, containing a collection of charms. This bundle contained such magical objects as a bag of cedar leaves, a braid of sweet grass, a buffalo tail, an amulet, and the skin of a hawk.

"Thank you, Father," Yellow Thunder said, holding the bag to his heart. "I will guard it with my life. It will be a part of all my tomorrows."

Chief Eagle Who Flies reached his good hand toward Yellow Thunder. "*Hiyu-wo*, come to me," he said, his breathing more shallow, his voice raspy. "Give your father one . . . last . . . embrace."

Stepping away from his mother and forcing tears away, Yellow Thunder bent low over his father. Clutching the bundle with one hand, he put the other beneath his father's frail neck and hugged him, feeling no less manly when he then placed his lips to his father's in a kiss that frightened him so much his heart leapt to his throat— for his father's lips were cold!

Trying not to show that he was shaken by this discovery, Yellow Thunder rose back to his full height and carefully guided his mother to Chief Eagle Who Flies once again, seeing how she sorely trembled as she gave her husband a last hug and kiss.

Yellow Thunder's eyes wavered as she turned weeping, sightless eyes up at him, knowing that she, also, had been aware of the coldness of her husband's lips.

"Star Woman, *techila*, I love you," Chief Eagle Who Flies said in barely a whisper. He reached a hand to Star Woman again and smiled as she entwined her fingers through his.

"*Mitawicu*," Chief Eagle Who Flies mumbled, as his eyes slowly drifted close. "I take . . . this woman . . . for my wife. . . ."

Yellow Thunder shuddered as he heard his father inhale a great breath, then breathe not again.

# Chapter
# Twenty-Six

*Two Weeks Later—*

Winter came in a sudden blast from the north. The wind blew blustery and cold around the corners of the tepee. The morning light was just beginning to creep down the smoke hole, meeting the slow spirals of smoke that rose from the fire in the fire pit that Ashley had built while Yellow Thunder still slept soundly on a thick pallet of furs spread close to the warmth of the fire pit.

Drawing her fur robe more snugly around her shoulders, Ashley sat down facing the fire, watching its flames curling around the logs that she had carefully arranged in the fire pit. There was something relaxing about the crackling and popping of a fresh new fire, in which the wood gave off a pleasing aroma. There was something soothing about watching the fire stroking the logs.

An involuntary shudder soared through Ashley at the thought of the sad days just left behind. The preparations for the burial, and then the ceremony itself, had taken several days. Since then, the mourning period had been observed, in which Yellow Thunder had hardly spoken a word to Ashley, not drawing her into the most secret places of his heart where he silently mourned his chieftain father.

If it had not been for Pahaha, and her sweet and generous nature, Ashley would have felt misplaced among the Osage people.

And yet she had not complained. She knew the worries and concerns that had been transferred to Yellow Thunder upon the death of his father.

Ashley sighed heavily, knowing that these burdens and concerns would not be that hard on her husband if he had been able to bring his sister back to the village under his protective custody. Also, there was much talk and concern now among his people that something may have happened to Red Loon, one of Yellow Thunder's most valiant warriors and dear friend. Neither Red Loon nor the warriors accompanying him on the mission to search for those responsible for the stolen Osage horses had returned.

They had been gone far too long now. Scouts had been sent out to find them, but even the scouts had been gone much too long.

But one thing in Yellow Thunder's favor was the fact that his mother was in her rightful place among her people. When she had absolutely refused to join him and Ashley in his dwelling, saying that young people should not be bothered by an old blind woman, Yellow Thunder had assigned some women and children to erect his mother a tepee close to his, so that he would be there for her at a moment's notice, when he was not traveling across the countryside on missions for his people.

And he would be leaving soon, as soon as he put his mourning behind him. He still could not rest until he found his sister. Nor would his conscience allow him to forget those women that had been left behind at the chopper's settlement.

Ashley smiled softly at the thought of something pleasant that had just entered her mind, pushing everything else aside.

Juliana had left with Billy Two Arrows. He had promised her that he would build her a new cabin when they returned to New Orleans. He had also promised to give her everything she desired to furnish it.

Ashley's smile slowly faded when she could not help worrying still about Calvin, should he hear of Juliana's good fortune.

He alone could ruin it.

So caught up in her thoughts was she that Ashley did not hear Yellow Thunder stirring awake behind her. She closed her eyes and trembled with ecstasy when she felt his hands smoothing the fur robe away from her shoulders. Then he gently turned her to face him, his gaze raking slowly over her, soaking up the sight of her silken nakedness.

Having not expected this, thinking that he was still in mourning even today, Ashley sucked in a wild breath of rapture when she discovered him still nude, as he always slept each night.

Then she shot him a downcast look through her lashes, trying to fight back the building passion when his hands molded her breasts. "I've missed you," she murmured, the warmth blossoming within her as his thumbs tenderly circled the soft pink crests of her nipples.

"I have not been away except in spirit," Yellow Thunder said hoarsely. "Was my silence so hard to bear, *mitawin?*"

"At times the silence caused me much pain," Ashley murmured. "Yet I was reminded of the pain you were having to bear and that made me feel guilty for my own." She lifted her eyes to his, apology in their depths. "Then your pain became mine."

"The pain for us both is now behind us," Yellow Thunder said, the fingers at the nape of her neck urging her lips to his. "There will be no more mourning. My father is well on his way to the hereafter. He smiles down on me from up there where everything is wonderfully peaceful and gives me his blessing to resume my life today, as it was before he died."

"Never will your life be the same," Ashley said, his mouth so close, his breath so warm on her lips. "You are now a powerful chief. Your life will never be totally yours, or mine, again. You belong to your people."

"*Ah-hah*, that is so," Yellow Thunder whispered back. "Yet even though I am the chief of our people, my time with you will be separate—will be private and passionate. A chief needs a woman's love, as do those who are only warriors. Perhaps even more, for he needs to find release from the pressures that come with the duties of being chief. *Mitawin*, I will need you so often, you will perhaps even tire of me."

He leaned away from her, his eyes twinkling. "Will you pretend a headache or a chill to keep me at arm's length on nights you are weary of my persistent need of you?" he teased. "Or will you welcome me, always, with opened arms?"

"Always I will welcome you to my blankets," Ashley said, giggling at his description of women pretending headaches and chills to avoid their duties to their husbands.

She did not see their lovemaking as a duty. To her it would always be wonderful.

Yellow Thunder's lips brushed her throat, and then the peaks of her breasts. Ashley's pulse raced. She closed her eyes and threw her head back in ecstasy, her hands clinging to his sinewed shoulders as he eased her down onto her back on the pallet of furs.

As she lay there, his hands worshipped her flesh as they moved over her. An incredible sweetness swept through her and she trembled when he began caressing the warm, moist valley at the juncture of her thighs with his fingers.

His mouth smothered her moans of pleasure as he kissed her, and when he moved atop her, she

311

did not dare breathe, for she knew what to expect next—that which would take her to the ultimate of joyous bliss.

She twined her arms around his neck and clung to him, his lips now pressed against her slender neck, his warm breath stirring her hair.

Her heart pounded when she felt his hot, pulsing desire probing where his fingers had already aroused her. She opened herself to him and gasped with rapture as he pushed into her, soon magnificently filling her. As he plunged more deeply with his steady, rhythmic strokes, she locked her legs about his waist, the wonder of their joined bodies causing her to feel as if she were floating.

His hands swept down her body again in a soft caress, igniting fires in their wake. Her fingers rediscovered the contours of his face, the slope of his hard jaw, the high cheekbones, and the bold nose.

She buried her face next to his neck as his steel arms enfolded her. She trembled with readiness, so familiar with his lovemaking now that she understood why he had slowed the thrusting of his pelvis.

He always did this just prior to . . .

She had no more time to think. His movements had speeded up, moving deeper, moving faster. She clung and rocked with him, the rapture within her spiraling, spreading, swelling. . . .

Their bodies jolted together and their lips met in an explosive kiss as once again they found the way to heaven and back within one another's arms.

With a fierceness Yellow Thunder held her, then rolled away from her and lay on his back, panting, his eyes closed.

Ashley moved to her side and molded her body against his, laying an arm over his chest, where she could still feel his heart pounding almost out of control.

"It was wonderful," she whispered. "I love you so, Yellow Thunder."

He said nothing, only reached for her hand and twined his fingers through hers.

"Yellow Thunder, how do you say the word 'husband' in Osage?" she asked, leaning up on an elbow.

He smiled at her. "*Mihigna*," he said, speaking the phrase slowly and eloquently.

"*Mihigna*," Ashley said, sighing as she lay her cheek against his chest. "I love the sound of that word. I love being your wife."

Ashley was aware of Yellow Thunder's sudden silence. She gazed up into his eyes. "What are you thinking about?" she asked softly.

Yellow Thunder turned his eyes down to hers, somewhat wavering. "You may not like my sharing these moments with someone else, even in thoughts," he said carefully.

"Yellow Thunder, I am not a selfish or jealous person," Ashley said, smiling sweetly up at him.

"*Nah*, you are not," he said, smoothing his fingers through her thick, long hair. "It was foolish for me to think for even one moment that you would mind that I was thinking about my mother, who only recently lost her husband. It is sad, this

313

loss. She had only just found him again after thirty winters of separation."

He turned and placed his hands at Ashley's waist and drew her atop him, so that she was straddling him. He gazed into her eyes, his hands resting on her thighs. "I am yours for many, many savage sunrises," he said determinedly. "Nothing will tear us apart. Nothing."

A loud, piercing scream caused Ashley to jump with alarm, then move quickly away from Yellow Thunder. She dressed as quickly as he, and together they rushed from their tepee, thick fur robes draped around their shoulders.

One step outside the tepee, they saw who had screamed, and the cause for it. The scouts that had been sent out to find Red Loon and his companion warriors were returning with many bodies draped over their horses behind the riders.

Ashley's gaze moved in a jerky fashion toward Pahaha, who was tearing at her hair and her flesh with a knife, having seen her beloved Red Loon lying across a horse, his scalp removed.

Seeing Pahaha injuring herself in such a way stunned Ashley. For a moment she stood, staring, frozen to the spot. Then she broke into a mad run and went to Pahaha, struggling to take the knife away from her.

Pahaha fell to the ground, sobbing, and pounding her fists against the ground. Blood seeped from the wounds on her arms, and long pieces of hair that had been cut raggedly hung loosely over her shoulders.

Ashley went to her knees beside Pahaha and placed a gentle arm around her waist, urging her back to her feet. "*Hiyupo*, come with me," she murmured, guiding Pahaha through the gathering crowd of wailing Osages. "Come to Yellow Thunder's dwelling. Let me comfort you there." Ashley cast Yellow Thunder a troubled glance as he was removing Red Loon from the horse.

"Who is responsible?" Yellow Thunder asked, his throat tight, his heart pounding as he tried not to see the dried blood where his friend's scalp had once been. Hate was burning his insides, the need for revenge heating up to an inferno!

One of his warriors stepped forward. "Before Red Loon died, he spoke the name Black Buffalo," he said solemnly. "Our arch enemy of the Kickapoo tribe is responsible for this." He raised a fist over his heart. "He must die!"

"Black Buffalo?" Yellow Thunder grumbled, the name like poison on his lips. "He is kindling the dangerous fires of warfare, and, *Ah-hah*, he will die."

"We ride now to find him?" the warrior asked anxiously.

"*Nah*," Yellow Thunder said, carrying Red Loon toward his friend's private tepee. "Respect will be paid Red Loon and the others and then we will go and seek our vengeance!"

"It will be as you say, my chief," the warrior said, turning away from Yellow Thunder to assist the others in removing all the slain warriors from the horses.

315

Holding his tears at bay, yet unable to still his thunderous heartbeat, Yellow Thunder carried Red Loon into his tepee and laid him down beside the fire pit that held only cold ashes. As though Red Loon were alive and well, Yellow Thunder began talking to him as he prepared the fire.

And once the tepee was warm and cheerful, Yellow Thunder knelt down beside Red Loon and began a low chanting, suddenly immersed in another mourning period.

Ashley led Pahaha into Yellow Thunder's dwelling and guided her down beside the fire, onto the pallet of furs. She gazed into Pahaha's eyes, fear clutching the pit of her stomach when she could not get any response from Pahaha, who seemed now to be in a self-induced trance.

Not certain what she should do, Ashley jerked off her fur robe, and then hurried to the paunch of water that was hanging just inside her door. With trembling hands, she poured some water into a wooden basin, grabbed a cloth, and went back to Pahaha.

Ashley dampened the cloth in the water and wrung it out, her eyes now glued to the gashes on Pahaha's arms, wondering how on earth Pahaha could have done such a thing to herself. As she dabbed at the bloody wounds, she flinched when Pahaha began rocking herself back and forth, her eyes closed now. From deep within her came sounds so haunting they gave Ashley cause to tremble. The sounds were a mixture of moans and wails, coming out in the form of chanting. And the more Pahaha chanted, the louder she became.

Soon a heavy hand on Ashley's shoulder made her jump with a start. She turned her eyes quickly up, then sobbed and dropped the wet cloth into the basin of water. She rose and flung herself into Yellow Thunder's arms. "I'm so glad you're here," she sobbed. "I don't know what to do. And . . . and I feared that you were going to close me out again with mourning over your dead warriors, especially Red Loon. I don't think I can bear it, Yellow Thunder, if you ignore me again. Please don't." She clung harder to him. "Oh, please don't, darling. I need you. You need me."

Yellow Thunder held her tightly against him, his cheek against hers. "*Ah-hah*, that is so," he said thickly. "We shall share this mourning as though we are one body, one soul."

When he lifted her chin with a forefinger so that their eyes could meet and hold, Ashley smiled up at him, glad then when his lips came to hers gently, sweetly, reverently.

They wrenched themselves apart when they heard a voice behind them.

"I hear much that reaches my heart with sadness," Star Woman said, standing just inside the entrance flap, leaning heavily on her cane. She moved slowly toward Ashley and Yellow Thunder, then past them, stopping to stand over Pahaha, whose wailing still poured from the depths of her soul.

Star Woman laid a gentle hand on Pahaha's shoulder. "*Hiyu-wo*," she murmured. "Come with me to my dwelling. Let me help you with your burden of sadness. Let me sing to you. Let me hold you in my arms."

Pahaha turned her weeping eyes up at Star Woman, touched deeply by the blind woman's words. Slowly she rose to her feet and was soon engulfed in comforting arms. Then, leaning against Star Woman, she left the tepee with her.

Yellow Thunder gazed down at Ashley and smiled. "My mother holds magic in her words and touch," he said. "It seems that only she could have drawn Pahaha into her heart at this time. It is good for them both, so alone are they now."

Ashley leaned into Yellow Thunder's embrace, silently praying that she would never be alone, never be forced to live without *her* beloved warrior.

# Chapter Twenty-Seven

*The Next Day—*

A long series of monotonous howls, shrieks, groans, and nasal yells, emphasized by a succession of thumps upon drums, made Ashley want to scream. Yet she stood still, willing herself not to do anything that might upset Yellow Thunder.

Witnessing his mourning at first hand, she almost wished that she had not made a fuss over having been left out the last time. For what she had stood there watching had made her stomach queasy. Yellow Thunder had taken it upon himself to prepare his warrior friend for the resurrection of his spirit. She had stood at Yellow Thunder's side as he had cleansed Red Loon's body of all the blood and dressed him in full battle array, his crown of feathers fortunately hiding the mutilation of his head beneath it.

Now Yellow Thunder was preparing Red Loon's face, the war paint he was applying, shining brightly beneath the glow of the fire in the fire pit.

When that was done, Yellow Thunder left Ashley's side long enough to gather up all of Red Loon's honorary symbols—his buckskin clothing with its pictorial representations of his victories in war on the front and back; his bow and quiver; his lance and shield.

Yellow Thunder laid these aside, then placed Red Loon's medicine bag around the dead warrior's neck, where it lay suspended from a strip of leather, resting on his powerful chest.

Yellow Thunder turned to Ashley and offered her a faint smile of reassurance as he took her by an elbow and guided her from the tepee to stand among the congregation of people who were waiting for one of their greatest and most honored warriors to be brought from his tepee to be taken to his final resting place.

With Star Woman at her side, Pahaha stood among those waiting, her eyes bloodshot from crying, her hair cut even shorter now, to show proof of her mourning.

Ashley wanted to go to Pahaha and offer her moral support, yet she felt as though she might be intruding on Pahaha's grieving, since it was so obviously intense and heart-wrenching.

The wails and shrieks and drumbeats continued while Yellow Thunder went solemnly to Red Loon's tepee and ran his knife down two full lengths of the buckskin covering, then slowly began rolling this portion of the tepee upward, stopping when a large hole was exposed, revealing the waiting warrior inside on the high, pelt-covered platform.

After tying back the rolled-up portion of the tent so that it would remain in place throughout the rest of the ceremony, Yellow Thunder turned to two young braves who had stepped up behind him, their fringed buckskin colorfully beaded and spotlessly white.

Yellow Thunder nodded to each of the young braves, motioning them into the tepee. They went in through the entrance way, not the space that Yellow Thunder had cut open with his knife.

Ashley watched, wide-eyed, as the braves soon came out again, each of them carrying his share of Red Loon's weapons and honorary symbols.

Everyone grew silent as several warriors entered the tepee through the entrance way and approached the hole that Yellow Thunder had cut. Other warriors then stepped forward, Yellow Thunder among them. Red Loon was handed carefully through the hole to Yellow Thunder and the waiting warriors and was gently held there until the warriors who had been inside the tepee came out again, through the entrance way. Red Loon had not been carried through the entrance way so that no one would ever have to cross the path of his journey to the hereafter.

The dead warrior was then carried with much respect and love toward his final resting place, while everyone followed behind. Ashley fell into stride with the others, just behind Yellow Thunder. She paused, wide-eyed with wonder, when a sharp pain shot through one of her bottom teeth, at the far back of her right jaw. She grabbed at her jaw when she was shaken by another pain, which left a dull ache in her tooth and the gum surrounding it.

Ashley placed her tongue over the aching tooth. She remembered now that it had hurt her while she was eating, after she bit down on a sliver of bone in the buffalo stew.

During the meal, the pain had finally subsided and she had forgotten all about it until now. Now the pulsing pain made her frown, fearing that the only way this could be remedied would be the extraction of the ailing tooth.

Inhaling a nervous breath, Ashley resumed walking with the Osage people, the pulsing tooth annoying, yet perhaps a godsend, for it was helping to take her mind off the sadness of the moment.

Yet she wished that time would pass more quickly. Perhaps Yellow Thunder, in his wisdom, knew a way to medicate her tooth. He knew so many ways to use herbs. Still holding her throbbing jaw, Ashley gazed upward at the position of the sun in the sky.

Soon it would be noon—the time of decision for Red Loon and the other warriors who had died in the massacre led by Black Buffalo.

Yellow Thunder had explained this part of the funeral ceremony to her earlier this morning. He had said that the dead warriors would be taken to some place of higher elevation and propped upright in a sitting position where they would be exposed to the views of Grandfather Sun as the sun rose high in the eastern sky. If Grandfather Sun recognized these warriors and approved of their spirits' ascent, the spirits would leave the bodies at exactly noon, or when the sun was directly overhead.

Yellow Thunder had further explained that if Grandfather Sun failed to recognize the warriors, or disapproved of them, their spirits would be condemned to earth where they would take up their abode in the bodies of screech owls. As the condemned spirits suffered, their weeping and wailing would be heard at night when their hosts flitted about the woodlands.

The drum began its droning beats again in the distance, seemingly keeping time with the footsteps of the warriors as they walked through the village toward the river.

Solemnly, the procession continued up a slight rise in the land, then stopped when they came to a scaffold that Yellow Thunder and some of his friends had prepared at dusk the prior evening for this solemn ceremony.

An involuntary shudder raced across Ashley's flesh as her gaze traveled slowly down the long line of scaffolding that already bore the bodies of fallen warriors, Red Loon the last of those to be propped upright in a sitting position on the high scaffold, where he would be exposed to the view of Grandfather Sun.

Ashley's pain had worsened. Her whole jaw seemed to be on fire, making her only half aware of the rest of the ceremony, during which songs

were sung and words were spoken aloud over the
dead.

Still only half aware of what was happening, her
whole mind controlled by the pain now, Ashley felt
a strong hand on her elbow as Yellow Thunder led
her away from the scaffolding and down the hill.
She moaned softly and closed her eyes as the jaw
began an even fiercer throb.

Though Yellow Thunder was walking beside
Ashley, his mind was elsewhere. His eyes were
flashing fire in their depths. He had decided that
*this* time no mourning period would be practiced.
He could not wait to attack Black Buffalo later,
for that would only give the Kickapoo renegade
the opportunity to work his evil on other innocent Osage tribes—or perhaps even on his own
Kickapoo people. When there were horses to be
stolen, Black Buffalo missed no opportunity, not
even if it was his neighbor Kickapoo's.

*Ah-hah*, Yellow Thunder thought bitterly to
himself. He must work fast to seek his vengeance on the renegade. He had already instructed
his warriors to prepare themselves for war as
soon as they returned to the village. If the Osage
warriors attacked Black Buffalo now, while Red
Loon and the other fallen warriors were fresh on
their journey to the hereafter, Red Loon and his
companions would be there in strong spirit to join
the battle, perhaps even guide a few arrows into
the hearts of their enemies!

The thought made Yellow Thunder smile, and
then his smile was replaced by a frown when he
heard Ashley emit a soft groan. He quickly glanced

down at her and saw how she cupped her jaw in her hand, her eyes hazed over with pain. Her face was unnaturally flushed, which meant that she probably had a fever.

He stopped and placed his hands at her shoulders, turning her to face him. "*Hoh!* You are in pain," he said. He lifted a hand and touched her hand, which still held her jaw. "It is a tooth?".

Ashley smiled weakly up at him and nodded her head. "*Ah-hah*, it is a tooth," she murmured. "It hurts so badly, Yellow Thunder. Do you have a way to make it feel better?"

Yellow Thunder nodded. "*Ho-iy-aya-yo*," he said, suddenly whisking her up from the ground and into his arms. He carried her more quickly toward the village, past those who were moving slowly for the most part, their heads hung.

Ashley twined her arm around Yellow Thunder's neck and laid her pulsing jaw against his powerful chest, the fur of his robe soft against her cheek. Already she felt better, but she knew that was only because she was being held within his powerful arms. Just being with him soothed her. She felt that while under this special magic, anything was possible. Even getting rid of this dreadful toothache!

She looked suddenly up at Yellow Thunder. "I don't want to lose my tooth," she blurted. "Tell me I won't have to, Yellow Thunder."

"Only time will give you the answer," he said, frowning down at her. "But I shall do all that I know to do. Then, if what I have done is not enough, I shall call Moon Face Bear to our lodge. He will sing and chant over you. If that does not help, then I know the skill of removing teeth quickly and painlessly."

"No," Ashley moaned, placing her jaw against the soft pelt again. "I don't want to lose the tooth. I would be too ugly then to share your blankets." ·

Yellow Thunder stopped abruptly and gazed down at her with his midnight-dark eyes. "Never could you be ugly," he said fiercely. "You are beautiful inside and out. And *techila*, I love you. For always, *mitawin*, even if every tooth in your head is removed."

Yellow Thunder took her into their dwelling and set her down on a thick pallet of furs next to the fire pit. Gently he took her fur robe from around her shoulders, then eased her down onto her back, covering her with a blanket. "You lie still," he said softly. "I shall return shortly. Soon you will feel much better."

The throbbing was worse. Ashley closed her eyes, curling up on her side as tears streamed down her cheeks. She soon welcomed the black void of sleep.

Carrying a small buckskin bag, Yellow Thunder came back into the dwelling. He sat down on the pelts beside Ashley and slightly shook her to awaken her.

Ashley awakened with a start, then remembered the pain. She groaned as she looked pitifully up at Yellow Thunder.

"Open your mouth," Yellow Thunder softly commanded as he pinched into his fingers a bit of powdery substance from inside the buckskin pouch. "What I have here will make you better quickly."

Ashley stared at the powdery substance for a moment, and hesitated. But the pain was too severe now to question him about what he was going to use to medicate her tooth. She opened her mouth and turned it toward Yellow Thunder, pointing out the pulsing tooth to him.

Then she closed her eyes as Yellow Thunder began applying the powder all around the affected tooth. She sighed heavily as his fingers caressed her gum over and over again with the powder.

When the pain began fading away, and she felt that she could breathe easily again, Ashley opened her eyes and stared with relief up at Yellow Thunder.

Yellow Thunder smiled down at her. "You are better?" he asked.

Relieved, she nodded.

"Pahaha shared her store of wild licorice root with us today, so that I would not have to take the time to search for this root myself while you are in such pain," Yellow Thunder said, applying just a little more powder to her gum. "Always the root of the wild licorice is the remedy used by the Osage for teeth ailments. It is good that it also works for women with white skin and hair the color of a savage sunrise."

Ashley lay back down on her back and closed her eyes as Yellow Thunder moved his hand away and pulled tight the strings on the small buckskin pouch. "*Ah-hah*, I am also glad," she said, sighing heavily. "You never think to appreciate a mouth that isn't in pain, until you have experienced a throbbing toothache such as I have just had."

Yellow Thunder placed his palm to her brow and frowned. "Still you feel feverish," he said in a low growl. "You stay in bed. You get rest."

Ashley nodded and closed her eyes, glad that the sad funeral ceremony was behind her, as well as the ache in her tooth. Right now all she wanted to do was sleep and forget everything ugly in the world.

But she did not even get close to sleeping when she heard the pounding of a horse's hoofbeats coming into the village, and soon someone shouting Yellow Thunder's name just outside his tepee.

Yellow Thunder went to the entrance flap and jerked it aside. He recognized one of the scouts he had sent to find Black Buffalo's whereabouts. "You found where he makes camp?" he asked his scout.

"We did not find Black Buffalo," the scout said, winded from his hard ride on the horse. "But we did find other men—*white* men, headed this way. It is the man known as Calvin, the man you tracked in New Orleans, thinking that he would take you to your sister. He is with many other white men, and well armed."

Ashley had heard what the scout was saying and scrambled quickly to her feet. She hurried to Yellow Thunder's side and listened with an anxious heartbeat as the scout told them something else.

"The woman called Juliana is among those traveling this way. But not of her choice. She is tied and gagged and is being forced to walk ahead of the horses. She looks near to exhaustion."

A strange spinning in her head quickly dizzied Ashley, and she felt her face drain of color.

Yellow Thunder gazed down at her. Their eyes met, exchanging surprise—and fear.

Then Yellow Thunder left Ashley and began shouting orders to his warriors as they moved into a tight circle around him, their eyes anxious.

After everyone had listened to their chief's commands, and began readying themselves for travel, their assortment of weapons shining beneath the waning afternoon sun, Yellow Thunder went to Ashley and ushered her back inside the tepee.

"I will return soon," he said, taking Ashley over to the pallet of furs and easing her down onto them. "You stay. You wait."

"I can't," Ashley argued, trying to rise to her feet, yet unable to because of the force of Yellow Thunder's hands holding her in place. "I must go and help Juliana!"

"You are not feeling well," Yellow Thunder said in a growl. "You stay. I will bring Juliana to you soon."

Each time Ashley opened her mouth to argue, he placed his hand over it to stifle the argument. Then he moved away from her and gave her a stern look. "You stay," he said firmly.

Ashley said no more. She watched with an aching heart as he gathered up his weapons, put on his long and flowing fur robe, then left the tepee without another glance her way.

Ashley sat still on the warm pelts and listened until she could no longer hear the thunder of the horse's hooves in the distance, then scrambled to her feet and went to the door and peered toward the forest. She trembled and hugged herself with her arms, the wind's edge as sharp today as Yellow Thunder's orders.

Yet still she did not know just how long she could stay behind, feeling useless, and helpless.

# *Chapter Twenty-Eight*

Unable to stay behind any longer, worrying about Yellow Thunder and what Calvin might do to him should he capture him, Ashley rushed around the tepee. She changed into a looser buckskin dress that would make it easier to ride a horse, then yanked on her knee-high moccasins.

After slipping on her hooded wolf-fur coat, she snuggled the hood around her face and tied it securely beneath her chin with a thin strip of buckskin. She then stared at Yellow Thunder's weapons, fear rushing through her at the thought of being forced to use one.

With a stubbornly set jaw, she chose a rifle, then fled from the tepee and to the horses. She was soon urging her steed into a hard gallop toward the forest, where she had last seen Yellow Thunder and his warriors heading.

The wind was sharp and cold against her face. Her hands were like ice as she clutched the horse's reins, wishing now that she had a pair of the butter-soft gloves that she had left behind in New Orleans when she fled Calvin's wrath.

Everything in her life had changed that day. And even though she had known fear and hardship while with Yellow Thunder, she would still choose a life with him.

As she rode onward, squinting to keep out the winter wind, her heart pounded and she kept gazing ahead, wondering if she were too late. What if she couldn't find Yellow Thunder before he was attacked by Calvin and his men?

Ashley was suddenly aware of other dangers in addition to Calvin. The shadows were deepening in the forest. The late afternoon was waning into night. If she didn't find Yellow Thunder soon, she could get lost in the forest. Although many of the forest animals were already hibernating for their long winter's sleep, there were those that might still be foraging around for food. She and her horse might be scented by a panther, or perhaps a hungry bobcat, or a pack of wolves.

The thought terrified her, but Ashley continued riding onward, weaving her horse in and around the trees. She breathed much more easily when she saw a wide meadow through a break in the trees ahead.

But as she reached the meadow, the sight that met her eyes made her feel faint. She drew her horse to a shuddering halt and slid out of the saddle, trembling as she watched the battle that had just begun a short distance away. Yellow Thunder and his warriors were fighting many white men, one of them undoubtedly Calvin.

As the savage sunset splashed its orange rays across the land, it revealed much blood, and the bodies of both Osage warriors and white men fell from their steeds to lie lifeless on the ground.

With a rapid heartbeat, Ashley stared grimly as the horses plunged together, the hooves of the mighty steeds muffled by the springy sod beneath them. The guttural cries of the wounded seemed to split the air in half.

It all passed in a blur to her as she watched the glittering lances of the Osage and the brightly polished weapons of the white men flash in the fading light of evening. She cringed as arrows whizzed through the air and shots rang out. She watched as men drove rifle butts into their enemies, or knives through their hearts.

She watched as some of the charging Osage warriors rode skillfully, low along the sides of their horses, protecting themselves against the rapid gunfire.

She grew ill when a white man was scalped only a few feet from where she stood. Yet even as she cried out against such barbarity, she knew this battle would have never happened if Calvin had not become so greedy.

Ashley trembled uncontrollably as her eyes sorted through the warring men, glad to see that Yellow Thunder was still among the living.

She then searched with her eyes for Calvin, and her heart seemed to drop to her feet when she found him. She gasped. An arrow had just pierced her stepbrother's chest. He was grabbing at the arrow, trying to dislodge it, his eyes wild.

Ashley stifled a scream behind her hands as she watched Calvin fall from his horse, then lie there, so still, so very still.

Ashley knew that she should be relieved to see Calvin dead. Yet even so, tears welled up in her eyes. She stared at Calvin's lifeless body for a moment longer, and then something else came to her in a flash.

"Juliana!" she whispered harshly to herself, placing a hand to her throat as her eyes searched wildly about her. "How could I have forgotten about Juliana? She was with Calvin and these men. Where is she? Oh, Lord, let her still be alive!"

And what of Billy Two Arrows? she wondered desperately to herself. No one had mentioned anything of *his* welfare.

But Ashley had to assume that he was dead. Billy would have fought Calvin to his last breath to save the woman he loved. The thought of such a courageous, valiant man as Billy Two Arrows being dead made tears splash from Ashley's eyes. She would never forget his laughter, nor the friendship that she had seen shared between Yellow Thunder and Billy Two Arrows.

And the way Juliana had looked at Billy with the same love and respect that Ashley always felt when she gazed upon her handsome, noble Osage chieftain.

Her gaze was drawn back to Calvin. Horrified, not believing what she was witnessing, she saw Yellow Thunder kneeling over his dead body.

Her heart thundering wildly within her chest, she watched him remove Calvin's scalp. It was such a brutal, savage act—something that she would never have expected of her husband.

Yet there was no denying what she had seen. Yellow Thunder was holding his prize up into the air for everyone to see, a look of victory in his midnight-dark eyes as the surviving warriors circled around him.

No matter how much Ashley wanted to look away from the sight, she willed herself not to and forced herself to understand this part of Yellow Thunder that had led him to take the scalp of her stepbrother.

Calvin was his enemy.

"No," she silently corrected herself.

Calvin was not just Yellow Thunder's enemy, he was also an enemy of the white community—of *all* people, white *or* red-skinned!

The news of his death would be welcomed by both the Indians and the white people, far and wide, for Calvin was the lowest form of animal that could walk the face of the earth. He stood for everything bad.

Still shaken by the sight, Ashley sighed heavily and tried to compose herself enough to go to Yellow Thunder to reveal her presence to him now that the fighting had ceased. Yellow Thunder's victory over Calvin had stricken fear into the hearts of those white men remaining alive. They had retreated and were even now fleeing for their lives across the darkening meadow.

Ashley's eyes widened when she discovered someone standing on the far side of the killing field. The more she stared, the more her pulse raced, for she saw that this person was not a man—it was a woman, her hands bound with buckskin thongs, her mouth gagged with a neckerchief tied over it. A rope dangled from her bound wrists, lying on the ground like a snake beside her.

"Juliana!" Ashley gasped.

Then she screamed the name out loud when she saw the slight figure suddenly crumple to the ground.

Yellow Thunder had stepped up to his horse and secured Calvin's scalp to his saddlehorn when Ashley's scream caught him by surprise. He turned with a start as she raced by him. His mouth went agape when he followed her steady stare and saw Juliana lying on the ground, perhaps dead.

He had thought Ashley was back at his dwelling, safe from the bloodshed which he now knew that she must have witnessed. He sighed heavily as he glanced at the scalp, hoping that she could understand his need to take it. Then he broke into a run after her.

When Ashley reached Juliana, she fell to her knees beside her and placed her fingers at her neck to check her pulse beat. When she felt one, she went limp with relief. Juliana was still alive, yet perhaps in worse shape than when Ashley and Yellow Thunder had found her in the swamp, near to death because of the snake bite. Juliana looked worn and haggard, her eyes dark and sunken, her lips cracked and parched.

"Why did he have to do this to you?" Ashley cried, trying to will her fingers not to tremble long enough for her to untie the ropes that had cut so deeply into Juliana's wrists that blood was dried on them.

Yellow Thunder appeared suddenly on Juliana's other side. He jerked the gag from Juliana's mouth, shouting at one of his warriors to bring water. He looked at Ashley, their eyes meeting and momentarily holding. Then both resumed trying to bring Juliana out of her unconscious state.

"Lift her head just slightly from the ground," Yellow Thunder instructed Ashley. When she did as he asked, he allowed only a trickle of water at a time to enter Juliana's mouth from a buffalo paunch that a warrior had brought him.

Ashley scarcely breathed as she watched and waited for Juliana to show some signs of recovering. She cradled her friend's head gently on her lap, her heart heavy.

Juliana emitted a soft cough. Her hand went to her mouth, and she coughed into it as her eyes slowly fluttered open. When she discovered Yellow Thunder and Ashley there, she burst into tears.

Ashley rocked Juliana slowly back and forth. "You're going to be fine," she murmured. "There, there. You are safe now. Please don't cry. Juliana, please don't cry."

"It is best that she does," Yellow Thunder said. "It will release her torment, and then she will be able to tell us why she was with Calvin. She will be able to tell us the fate of Billy Two Arrows."

The mention of Billy made Juliana's eyes grow wild, yet her crying softened into tormented sobs. She closed her eyes and reached for Yellow Thunder's hand, clutching it desperately. "Calvin and his men came and burned our cabin," she cried. "Billy and I were both dragged from the cabin. I was tied and gagged."

Juliana paused, almost choking on the words that she did not want to say. "They . . . shot Billy," she said, her words sounding strangled. "They left him there to die."

Juliana then looked wildly at Ashley. "Why?" she cried. "Why would they kill him? It wasn't necessary. I—I had already agreed to guide Calvin to Yellow Thunder's village if they would spare Billy's life. They said they would, and then—then they shot him!"

Juliana slowly shook her head back and forth, her eyes closed. "I was forced to leave him anyhow, and bring Calvin to Yellow Thunder," she said, her voice low and drawn. "I was told that if I tried to fool them by taking them in the wrong direction, they would each one take turns . . .with me, then they would kill me slowly. I . . . I had no choice."

Her eyes opened again. She stared up at Yellow Thunder, reaching a trembling hand to his face. "I'm sorry," she murmured. "So very, very sorry."

Yellow Thunder sighed heavily, then drew her into his gentle embrace. "I am sorry about Billy Two Arrows," he said. "As for your apologies, there is no need. You did what you were forced to do. But now it is all over. Calvin is dead. He will never force anything upon you again."

Then Yellow Thunder eased her away from him, his eyes still holding with hers. "You say Calvin did not know the location of my village?" he said, raising an eyebrow. "You are certain of this?"

Ashley's heart pounded as she remembered what had taken Yellow Thunder to New Orleans, and why he had been trailing Calvin. If Calvin had not known where Yellow Thunder's village was, then surely he was not responsible for the abduction of Yellow Thunder's sister after all.

She knew by the look in Yellow Thunder's eyes, and by the tone of his voice, that he had also come to this realization, and was finding it hard to accept. For if Calvin had not been responsible for his sister's abduction, who had been?

"He did not know where your village was," Juliana said, wiping tears from her cheeks with the back of her hand. "He went to great lengths to get the answer from me. Had he known, there would have been no need to come to the cabin, to force me and Billy into telling him."

His jaw tight, his eyes haunted, Yellow Thunder rose to his feet and inhaled a deep breath. He had wasted much time in going to New Orleans to follow the wrong man.

Yet, had he not gone there, he would have never met Ashley! For that he was grateful, but otherwise, he was angry over having been misled by a close associate—Billy Two Arrows!

*He* had been the one to tell Yellow Thunder about Calvin Wyatt's association with slavery.

Had he been purposely misled? Or had Billy Two Arrows himself been misguided by someone, on purpose, to lead Yellow Thunder away from the full truth about his beloved half-sister?

He gazed at Calvin's horse, which was standing close by, grazing on a thick stand of grass. His eyes narrowed as he stared at the bulging saddlebags. Perhaps he could find some answers there, among Calvin's personal belongings.

In wide strides, he went to the horse and opened one of the saddlebags and rummaged through it. Finding nothing of importance there, he went to the other side of the horse and ran his fingers through the belongings in the other saddlebag. His eyes brightened when he felt a small book, hoping it was perhaps a journal kept by Calvin. His white adopted father had kept daily journals. Many evenings, Yellow Thunder had watched him make entries in them. His adoptive father had even taken the time to teach Yellow Thunder how to read and write.

Taking the small, hand-sized journal from the saddlebag, Yellow Thunder flipped it open. He squinted into the darkening sky, then gazed back down at the pages that lay open before him. There was just enough light to read by.

Helping Juliana to her feet, Ashley moved slowly toward Yellow Thunder, then stopped next to him and gazed down at the same pages that he was reading.

She grew pale and breathless as she read Calvin's entries. She was stunned that he had found some sort of dark pleasure in boasting about things that a normal person would not talk about, much less put in writing. She paled when she read his account of having paid a man to run down her mother and Calvin's very own father with a carriage and team of horses.

She read further as he explained why the murders had been necessary. It was because Calvin's father had discovered his son's misuse of the riverboat he'd given him.

When Peter Wyatt had discovered that his son was using the riverboat for illegal slave trading, he had threatened to disinherit Calvin.

Calvin recounted the whole tale in his journal and how he had killed his father before the will had been changed in his disfavor.

Ashley shook her head back and forth as she looked away from the journal, fighting back the nausea that the full truth had caused. Calvin was a greedy man with a twisted mind, one who had no morals. Nor had he felt any love or devotion toward his parents.

He had killed his father and his stepmother for their money and the full possession of his father's riverboat.

The more Ashley thought about what Calvin had done, the more she became blinded with rage and frustration. But then her mood softened. This journal proved her earlier feelings about her stepfather—that he was a good, God-fearing man and that he had had nothing to do with slavery after all, except for that one time, when he had acquired his Indian son through these means.

Tears of relief came to Ashley's eyes. She was glad that Peter Wyatt's name was cleared, and that she was free again to think lovingly of him.

Yellow Thunder was recalling the gentle voice of his adoptive white father and the love and warmth Peter Wyatt had shared with his adopted Osage son. Yellow Thunder had even seen tears in Peter's eyes the day that Yellow Thunder had been handed over to his true people. Yellow Thunder had known then that Peter had loved him as a father does a son.

And now, how good it was to know that Peter Wyatt was innocent of the crime of slave trading after all. Yellow Thunder was free to think of him with respect again.

And he had been right to accuse Calvin of having abducted his sister, although now it seemed that Calvin had not actually dealt in Indian slavery.

Ashley read a few more passages in the journal, her hatred for Calvin building within her heart when she discovered other things that the fiend bragged about. He had dirtied his hands with all sorts of evil doings. But the worst of all for Ashley was the murder of her stepfather and beloved mother!

"Calvin deserved to die!" Ashley suddenly cried, yanking the journal away from Yellow Thunder. She began tearing the pages from the journal, tossing them into the wind. "But my mother didn't! She was sweet! She was everything good in the world! She shouldn't be dead! She shouldn't!"

Stunned by Ashley's outburst, Yellow Thunder grabbed the journal away from her and dropped it on the ground.

He drew Ashley into his arms. "You must forget," he said, holding her tight. "Your life as you knew it is over. I am your life now, *mitawin*. My people are your life. Place your grief behind you and rejoice in what you now have."

"How can you stay so calm after what you have just discovered?" Ashley sobbed, leaning back, so that she could look into his eyes. "How . . . can you . . . ?"

"I was taught self-restraint as a child after I was returned to my people," he explained. "I practice it well. I am now chief. I must show control and strong will at all times."

Ashley gazed past him at the scalp swaying on his saddle, then up into Yellow Thunder's eyes again. "I'm glad that you took Calvin's scalp," she hissed.

Yellow Thunder drew her into his embrace again. "Such bitterness I hear," he murmured. "Let it go, *mitiwan*. Let it go."

Ashley cried for a moment longer, then the sound of coughing behind her drew her back to that part of herself that was not selfish, remembering Juliana and what she had just been through.

Ashley moved from Yellow Thunder's arms and drew Juliana into the comfort of her own. "In time, we shall all forget Calvin and what he has done to us," she whispered, stroking Juliana's waist-length black hair. "In time."

343

The sun had dropped over the horizon, and the swift, black night was cloaking everything. Yellow Thunder was proud that he had been some comfort to his woman, yet there was no comfort for himself, for as he looked into the darkness, he despaired over ever learning who *had* abducted Bright Eyes.

Where was she now? How could he ever expect to find her?

He held his head in his hands, trying to fight off any thoughts of his half-sister being dead.

Even Billy Two Arrows's life had not been spared the wrath of such a man as Calvin Wyatt.

*Nah*, he could not cast aside his despair and anger all *that* quickly!

# *Chapter Twenty-Nine*

*That Next Evening—*

Many drums pulsed in the velvet darkness of the night. The light of the great outdoor fire reached high into the dark heavens. There had been much scalp-dancing during the day, and it continued long into the night.

Ashley had sat with those who were not participating in the dance, watching, in awe of this dance that she would have thought would be a spectacular show of fierce exultation and triumph over the death of the Osages' enemy. Instead, those participating in the scalp dance had blackened their faces, hands, and moccasins with charcoal, and wore their plainest buckskin for the ritual.

It had been a solemn spectacle, participated in by those who had lost a relative in the battle against Calvin Wyatt, or those who had slain the enemy.

Elderly men had held the scalps of the enemy tied to willow wands in front of each of the men, and the other warriors who were not participants in the scalp dance stood in a line on each side. Plaintive songs were sung in a minor key.

Ashley shifted her weight, trying to get more comfortable on the pallet of furs some distance from the warmth of the fire. Her heart pounded as she waited for Yellow Thunder to take his turn in the scalp dance. Even though he was the chief, he had chosen to be last.

The scalp he had taken as a prize of victory today was the most celebrated—her stepbrother's.

Ashley swallowed hard, not wanting to look at Calvin's scalp again, yet she knew that to prove herself worthy of being an Osage chieftain's wife, she must sit quietly by, observing even this most gruesome of celebrations while hoping that this would be the only time that she would be forced to do so.

She prayed often that there would soon be a joyous peace between the Osage and the white communities.

But she doubted that would ever happen. When one greedy white man was cut down, another was there to take his place. Ashley knew that her future would be scarred by many terrible experiences because she was white and married to an Indian.

But she was ready for the challenge. For Yellow Thunder, she would even give her life, if it ever came down to that choice.

She jumped with alarm when a young brave stepped forward and threw a huge armful of rye grass upon the fire, causing it to blaze with a sudden roar and burst of great flames.

Then a warm hand slipping over hers made her turn and smile weakly at Juliana who sat at her right side, touched by Juliana's gesture of friendship even though Ashley knew that Juliana was hurting inside over the loss of her beloved Billy.

But Ashley knew the importance of Juliana being a witness tonight to the scalp dance. Her hatred for Calvin ran perhaps even more deeply than anyone else's. Calvin had not only robbed Juliana of her virginity, but also of the man to whom she had given her heart.

Ashley twined her fingers through Juliana's and leaned closer to her. "Are you all right?" she whispered. "It's been a long and tiring day. No one would think badly of you if you went on to the tepee and rested there. Please feel free to do that, Juliana. You must still be exhausted from your ordeal."

"I'm fine," Juliana whispered back. She glanced at Calvin's scalp swaying on the willow pole and slowly smiled. "I'm fine now that I know that evil man is dead. He can never ruin my life again. I'm finally free of him."

Ashley turned her eyes quickly away from Juliana when she heard a commotion at her left side. When Pahaha rose to her feet and began running away from the site of the celebration, sobbing, Ashley bolted to her feet and went after her.

Just as Pahaha reached the outer fringes of the forest, where the dark purple shadows hovered, ghostly and eerie, Ashley caught up with Pahaha and took hold of her wrist to stop her. Pahaha's eyes were tormented as she turned and stared at Ashley.

Breathless, Ashley stared back, then finally regained her wind. "Why did you run from the others?" she asked, releasing Pahaha's wrist, gently touching her cheek instead. "Pahaha, tell me what's the matter. Why is it that you could no longer sit with the others? Why are you crying?"

Pahaha wiped tears from her cheeks, but a sob lodged in her throat. "Soon there will be another scalp dance," she said softly. "When Black Buffalo is found and captured, my people will celebrate his death—because of Red Loon's death. I . . . I am not sure I can bear being brought so close to the reality again of Red Loon being dead. I . . . I only want to place it behind me. I have already mourned until the tears I have left within me hurt when they spill from my eyes. I want . . . no more pain, Ashley. I only want to remember happy times with Red Loon. That is the only way I can bear waking up each day and going to sleep each night. The scalp dance for Black Buffalo will make me live my beloved's death all over again within my heart, Ashley. Tell me that you understand."

Ashley shifted her gaze to Pahaha's short, ugly hair which she had cut to prove her grief to her people. And although Pahaha wore a heavy fur coat to keep her warm on this cold night, Ashley still remembered the slash marks that were just now healing after Pahaha had inflicted them on her flesh upon hearing about Red Loon's death.

Ashley was finding it very hard to understand many of the practices of the Osage, wondering if she would have the courage to inflict such pain upon her own person if anything happened to Yellow Thunder.

She had her own way to mourn her dead. The Osage had another.

She understood that this also was something that she would learn to accept. In time, she would know all of their practices and would have to accept them or lose everything that she loved in life—Yellow Thunder, now the embodiment of all that life was to her.

"Perhaps Yellow Thunder can find another way to celebrate his victory over Black Buffalo," Ashley tried to reassure Pahaha, drawing her into her embrace. "We shall hope so, anyway, shan't we?"

"I know of no other way," Pahaha said, sighing heavily.

A sound near where they were standing, a snapping of twigs in the dark depths of the forest, made Ashley's heart skip a beat. Her pulse raced, knowing that no one but she and Pahaha were away from the great outdoor fire and scalp dance.

If someone were in the forest, it was not someone of the Osage village.

Pahaha slipped from Ashley's arms and, from instinct, reached beneath her buckskin dress and grabbed a knife from a sheath that was attached to her right thigh.

With a stealthiness that Ashley had never seen in Pahaha before, the Osage girl began creeping into the forest, the knife raised in the air, ready for its death plunge.

Ashley looked cautiously from side to side, her heart pounding so hard that it seemed to echo in her ears. Then she followed quietly behind Pahaha, hoping that Pahaha had enough skill with the knife. Ashley would have felt much better had it been a gun, for one had to get much too close with a knife to protect oneself, which meant that the enemy would have a much better chance at stopping Pahaha, than she the enemy.

They did not have to go much farther. Someone suddenly stumbled out of the forest and fell to the ground, moaning. A horse soon also came into sight, its saddle empty.

Ashley stood as though glued on the spot as she stared down at the man, Pahaha standing beside her, seeming to be scarcely breathing as she lowered her knife to her side.

When the man raised his head and turned his face upward so that the light of the moon spiraling down through the leafless limbs of the trees overhead illuminated his features, both Ashley and Pahaha gasped in unison.

"Billy Two Arrows!" Ashley cried, falling to her knees on one side of Billy, Pahaha on the other.

They placed their hands at his shoulders and slowly turned him over onto his back, then Ashley lifted his head onto her lap.

"Billy, we—we thought you were dead," Ashley said, smoothing his hair back from his eyes, for his headband had slipped from his head and now hung loosely around his neck. Her gaze moved slowly over him, not able to see any signs of blood, then realized that was because he was wearing a jacket which covered his chest wound.

"The bullet did not enter my chest deeply," Billy said between quavering breaths. "I was carrying a small journal in the pocket of my shirt. This book . . . saved my life."

His eyes implored Ashley, and then Pahaha. "Juliana," he said in a harsh, frightened whisper. "Have you . . . seen Juliana?"

Suddenly a sweet and lilting voice spoke Billy's name close by, accompanied by joyous sobs.

Ashley turned and was surprised to find Juliana there. She fell to her knees beside Billy. Ashley moved aside and let Juliana take her place, now cradling Billy's head on her lap. Her tears splashed on his face as she clung almost desperately to him.

"My love," Juliana said, stroking Billy's face with her fingers. "You are alive. God, you are alive! When I became worried about Ashley having left the protection of the warriors at the village and came looking for her, I never expected to find you. How did you escape with your life? Everyone thought you were dead, or that Calvin would not have left without making sure that you were."

"He was carrying a small journal in his pocket," Ashley said, returning Billy's smile. "That alone saved him. It took the worst impact of the bullet."

"Billy, Calvin is dead," Juliana quickly told him. "Do you hear the sound of drums in the distance? They are being played for the scalp dance. Yellow Thunder may even now be dancing around Calvin's scalp."

"I . . . must . . . see," Billy said thickly. "Help me . . . to see."

Ashley positioned herself on one side of Billy, Juliana on the other, while Pahaha took the horse's reins. Ashley and Juliana groaned as they lifted Billy from the ground, one of his arms slung over each of their shoulders. Helping him along, they headed back toward the village, Pahaha leading Billy's horse behind them.

Just as they came into view of those who sat around the great outdoor fire, Ashley sucked in a wild breath as she watched Yellow Thunder perform his own scalp dance in unison with the beat of the distant drums. He was all muscle and movement, his face still handsome and noble, even though it had been blackened for the ceremony.

But something else about Yellow Thunder made her tremble uneasily. It was the haunting sadness in his eyes as he seemed to look past her, seemingly not aware of her being there.

And then it all changed when Yellow Thunder's gaze fell upon Billy Two Arrows. He stopped in mid-step, his lips parting in a silent gasp, the haunting sadness in his eyes replaced with wonder and joy.

All eyes moved in the direction of Yellow Thunder's gaze, and as Yellow Thunder broke into a mad dash toward Billy, there was a buzz among the people, then cheers of happiness as the scalp dance came quickly to a halt.

When Yellow Thunder reached Billy Two Arrows, he paused, then hugged him fiercely.

"*Hoh!*" he said throatily. "You were left for dead, but you are alive?"

Billy returned Yellow Thunder's embrace. "*Hecitu-yelo*, it is true that I am still alive," he said, then sensed a change in Yellow Thunder, as Yellow Thunder stiffened and stepped back away from him. "Yellow Thunder, what is it? You are not so happy to see your friend Billy Two Arrows as you were moments ago. What has changed your mind about your friend so quickly?"

"It is very good to know that you are still with the living," Yellow Thunder said, frowning into Billy's dark eyes. "But there is a question in my heart that bothers me."

"And what is that?" Billy asked.

"You are the one who led me to New Orleans to watch Calvin," Yellow Thunder mumbled. "You misled me. Calvin had nothing to do with the Indian slave trade. Why would you tell me that? You knew that this would take much of my valuable time away from my people. It is never good to be away from my people for that length of time, unless it is for a definite purpose."

"Your trust in your friend is this shallow, that you accuse me of misleading you?" Billy said, stepping away from Ashley and Juliana to stand on his own, closer to Yellow Thunder. "What reason would I have, Yellow Thunder, to do this? You are my friend. Calvin Wyatt was a stranger to me, who is now my enemy."

"What are you saying then?" Yellow Thunder asked, his eyes wavering.

"I am telling you that I received word that

Calvin Wyatt dealt in slavery," Billy said firmly. "That is all I heard. I myself concluded that he could be dealing in Indian slavery as well as white. Would you have not thought the same? A man of Calvin's ilk would not see any difference in the color of the skin, as long as he received money for the slave."

Yellow Thunder's thoughts were catapulted back to the time when he had grown to love his adopted father. Later, had not Yellow Thunder quickly accused him of being associated with Indian slavery without seeking proof first? Yellow Thunder could now see how easily mistakes could be made, especially when a person badly wanted someone at whom he could point an accusing finger!

Yellow Thunder turned away from Billy, hanging his head. Then he turned slowly around and faced him again. "For a moment, I failed you as a friend," he said, lifting a heavy hand to Billy's shoulder. "But that is behind us now. We will not look back, only forward."

Billy smiled at Yellow Thunder. "That is good," he said, then clutched at his chest when a sharp pain grabbed him there. He bent into the pain, breathing hard. "My legs are weak. My chest pains me. Take me where I can rest."

Yellow Thunder stepped to Billy's side and placed one of his strong arms around his friend's waist. "Lean your strength against me," he said. "*Hiyu wo*, come. There is something that you must see. It may even take away the misery of your pain."

Billy gazed questioningly over at Yellow Thunder, then smiled warmly at Juliana as she moved to his other side, slipping her arm lovingly around his waist.

Ashley stepped up beside Yellow Thunder and felt a great calm come over her, thinking that just perhaps things were going to finally be all right after all. There was only one more obstacle to completing this pattern of wonderful things falling into place.

Finding Yellow Thunder's sister.

The reunion between him and his mother was a thing that Ashley would never forget. Now she hoped to be a witness to another miracle—finding Bright Eyes alive and well and soon back among her people.

As they all moved toward the great outdoor fire and the elderly men who still stood holding the willow wand with the scalps swaying from them, Ashley could hear the quiet as everyone waited for Billy to see the scalps.

When he did, he cast Yellow Thunder a questioning glance.

"Calvin's?" Billy said thickly.

"*Ah-hah*, one among the scalps is Calvin's," Yellow Thunder said, his eyes dancing and a smile quivering on his lips.

Billy smiled as he singled it out from the others and watched it flutter in the breeze.

"Tonight Calvin Wyatt's scalp hangs for all to see," Yellow Thunder said, his eyes narrowing as his thoughts shifted to his other enemy. "Tomorrow—Black Buffalo's!"

Ashley paled, having forgotten Yellow Thunder's plans to go after Black Buffalo. She sighed heavily, knowing that only moments ago she was counting her blessings and thinking that things were finally falling into place to form a future of genuine happiness.

How could she have forgotten the threat of Black Buffalo that lay heavy over their heads?

And there was not one thing that she could say to Yellow Thunder to change his mind.

He was hungry for vengeance—and he would not rest until he had it!

# Chapter Thirty

The morning light spiraled down through the smoke hole over the fire, casting a faint glow onto Ashley's face, awakening her.

Shivering, she turned and saw that Yellow Thunder was still asleep, so she crawled from beneath their shared blankets and hides and slipped a log into the glowing coals of the fire.

After she saw that the fire was going to take hold, Ashley went back to the pallet of furs and slipped cozily between the pelts and blankets again, then giggled when she felt a warm hand sliding over her shoulder and then down, to cup a breast within its palm.

"I awakened you," Ashley said, turning to face Yellow Thunder. His hand now moved in a light caress across her abdomen, stopping where her blood seemed to be throbbing at the juncture of her thighs.

Closing her eyes, Ashley sucked in a wild breath

of delight, the pleasure spilling forth within her as Yellow Thunder thrust his fingers inside her and moved them rhythmically, as though it were his magnificent shaft filling her.

"*Ah-hah*, you awakened me," Yellow Thunder said, brushing a kiss across her parted lips. "But even in my dreams I was touching and kissing you. I am never without you, *mitawin*. Never."

Ashley twined her arms around his neck and urged his lips to hers. She kissed him passionately, her pulse racing as he positioned himself above her, soon replacing his fingers with his thrusting manhood.

Opening herself more widely to him, Ashley lifted her legs and locked them at her ankles around him. As his hips moved, sending his hardness more deeply within her, her hips moved with him. She clung and rocked with him, her tongue darting between his lips, finding his tongue responsive and sweet as their tongues touched, tip to tip.

Ashley was trying not to think about what was going to happen today, knowing that this time she could not join Yellow Thunder.

He had laid down the law. He had said that she could not go with him to strike against Black Buffalo.

Billy Two Arrows would be among those warriors who were going to stay behind to guard the village. Billy had even been instructed not to allow Ashley to leave the village, no matter what her excuse might be.

Fear was already gripping Ashley, knowing

that Black Buffalo had a reputation for being a fierce leader of his band of renegades—of those Kickapoo who had detached themselves from their tribe to be free to wreak their own sort of havoc on the Ozark settlers or their neighboring enemy tribes.

Horse stealing had become Black Buffalo's specialty, the path of his raids being swept clean of good horses. Red Loon and the other Osage warriors had paid for trying to intervene in Black Buffalo's activities.

Now, Yellow Thunder was going to be riding into the face of danger, and Ashley feared that he might not be the victor this time over his enemy. Black Buffalo was practiced in killing and plundering, and Yellow Thunder was a man of peace, whose life was guided by love and trust, not by hate and greed.

Ashley hoped to keep Yellow Thunder with her for as long as she could this morning, to postpone his departure. If she could get by with it, she would even tie him up and keep him there with her, forcing someone else to lead the Osage into battle against Black Buffalo.

But no matter what ways she would conjure up inside her troubled mind, she knew that she must give in to this thing called fate and see how it would affect her and Yellow Thunder's destiny.

"You make love, yet your mind is elsewhere," Yellow Thunder said, pausing in his thrusts to gaze into Ashley's eyes. He reached a hand to her brow and smoothed her hair back, leaning to kiss her brow.

"Why do you worry so over things that you cannot control?" he whispered against her flesh. "*Mitawin*, you must have more faith in your husband. I vow to you that I will be victorious over Black Buffalo. *Wah-kon-tah* will be with me in spirit, as you will be with me in my heart. How can I lose with such powers accompanying me into battle? Tell me that you will not despair so over this that your husband must do."

He framed her face between his hands and forced her gaze to lock with his. "Tell me, *mitawin*," he said throatily. "Tell me now."

Ashley swallowed hard, so wanting to show him that she did have faith in his abilities to lead, but afraid that her voice would betray her. "I love you," she murmured, instead. "And I believe in you."

Tears burned at the corners of her eyes, then she flung herself into his arms. "I just wish you didn't have to go," she cried.

"This will not be the only time that I will have to leave you behind, to fight battles to protect our people," Yellow Thunder said, easing her away from him so that he could look into her eyes again. "The life of the Osage is not easy. There are many predators, both white-skinned and red. It is my duty as chief to keep those predators from overpowering my people. So, my sweet one, you must accept this part of my life, as you have my other beliefs. When you saw me place a scalp on the saddle of my horse, and realized whose it was, you accepted that. So shall you accept when I must don my war paint."

"Yes, I know that I must," Ashley said weakly.

She cleared her throat nervously. "But never shall I not fret over it. That is my nature, Yellow Thunder—to worry about those I love and that which I have no control over. You will have to learn to accept that part of me, as I am forced to accept these things about you that trouble me deeply in my soul."

"And so it shall be between us," Yellow Thunder said, nodding. He smiled slowly. "I worry also about things. You, especially. So if you did not show concern about me, I would be disappointed."

Ashley relaxed and sighed, then laughed softly as she twined her arms about his neck and brought his lips to hers. She kissed him softly and sweetly, then moaned with pleasure against his lips as once again he filled her magnificently with his thick shaft. She closed her eyes and felt the fever rising within her, her blood heating up with each of his thrusts, her heart singing.

Then his mouth slithered down from her mouth and clasped the nipple of one breast, his tongue swirling around it, causing it to throb and rise into a tight peak against his lips.

Yellow Thunder could feel the heat rising in his loins, and the spiraling, spinning sensation within his brain. He placed his hands beneath her buttocks and lifted her into him as he bucked more wildly within her.

Perspiration laced his brow, and his breathing came in short rasps. He laid his cheek against the soft pillow of her breasts and allowed himself to accept the bliss that Ashley's body offered.

As he clung to her, he plunged maddeningly within her, mindless with the pleasure.

Ashley clung to him, weakened by rapture, the fires of his passion transferring to her as his hot, pulsing desire plunged over and over within her. Suddenly she felt a tremor from deep within and gave herself up to the delicious languor that claimed her.

Afterwards, Ashley lay within Yellow Thunder's embrace, clinging, knowing that when she let him go, he would soon leave to join the other warriors to prepare themselves for the warring that lay ahead of them this day.

"Tell me about him," she suddenly asked.

Yellow Thunder rolled away from her to lie at her side. "Tell you about who?" he asked, gently stroking her cheek with his fingertips.

"Black Buffalo," Ashley said, her eyes anxious. "Tell me about him. What he looks like. Why he has turned into a renegade instead of an honorable warrior like you?"

Yellow Thunder moved to a sitting position. Ashley rose with him, placing a blanket around both of their shoulders so that they shared its warmth.

"I have known him for many moons," Yellow Thunder said, his voice drawn. "But never were we friends. He was always driven by evil ways. His appearance speaks for itself, as to the ways of his past."

He gazed at Ashley, unsmiling. "He is not a pleasant man to be with, or to look at," he said grimly. "Some moons ago, he became afflicted with a crooked mouth, one that droops at the corner. This is because he spoke unkindly and maliciously of another who had passed on to the land of ghosts. The spirit of the injured one returned in a state of resentment and startled Black Buffalo with a quick whistle. In his fright, Black Buffalo turned quickly in the direction of the sound, and the side of his face was drawn down at the corner."

"My goodness," was all that Ashley could say, mesmerized by the tale. She had learned that the Indians had a way of coloring their versions of tales of their enemies while speaking about them around midnight fires, when stories were being told by the elders. This sounded like one of those tales cleverly plotted and put together.

"No innocent person can hear these whistles of the ghosts," Yellow Thunder said, shifting his gaze to stare into the flames of the fire. "But the guilty one hearing it is always marked for life. The guilt of this person is thus proven."

He turned to Ashley and twined his fingers through her hair, enjoying its softness. "It is bad form for anyone to speak harshly of another unless of their arch enemy," he said softly. "The habit of speaking slowly and carefully with guarded words is the polite custom of the Osage."

"And so Black Buffalo is ugly?" Ashley asked.

"He is not only ugly, but also has ugly ways," Yellow Thunder said angrily. "Killing Red Loon was one of his worst mistakes. He will pay!"

An uncontrollable shiver raced across Ashley's flesh at the grim, angry sound of Yellow Thunder's voice. She flinched when he moved quickly to his feet and began walking toward the entrance way, with only a blanket thrown around his shoulders and without moccasins.

"Where are you going?" Ashley asked, rushing to her feet, a blanket secured around her own shoulders. "You haven't eaten. You haven't taken the time to dress."

Yellow Thunder turned her way, frowning. "No food is required before today's battle, and I will return later for my clothes," he said softly. "Some warriors even refrain from making love before warring. They say it steals their strength. With Yellow Thunder, he feels more powerful after leaving the blankets with his woman."

Ashley went to him and stood on tiptoe to kiss him softly, then stepped away again, her eyes filled with wonder. "You have yet to tell me where you are going now, without your clothes," she murmured. "Is it a secret meeting?"

"*Nah*, no secret meeting," Yellow Thunder said, his eyes gleaming into hers. He smiled slowly. "Do you not know that never will I keep secrets from you? You are a part of me now, of my thoughts, moods, and desires. I go to the sacred sweat lodge to meet with my warriors and the old medicine man, Moon Face Bear. Moon Face Bear will pray with those of us who will soon be leaving for warring, and will pray for us during our absence. Moon Face Bear has medicine of great power and has found favor with the Sun during the many winters and summers of his life. In him and *Wah-kon-tah*, we warriors will entrust our lives."

Ashley flung herself into his arms and kissed

him again, then stood away and watched Yellow Thunder leave the tepee. A sob broke free from the depths of her throat, and she sat down on the rich pallet of furs, her hands running over that space that was still warm from the body of her beloved.

She looked upward, through the smoke hole, seeking a glimpse of the sky, and after she found it, she stared at the bright, clear blue of it and found some solace in her prayers to her own God.

Yellow Thunder joined the others on their way to the sacred sweat lodge, smiling a silent welcome to each. Then at the entrance of the lodge, each of them dropped their robes or blankets, their only coverings, and stark naked crept through the low doorway and sat themselves around the interior, in silence, while red-hot stones were brought in and dropped in a hole in the center.

Moon Face Bear began to sprinkle the rocks with a buffalo tail that had been dipped in water, and as the stifling hot steam enveloped the warriors, the medicine man began singing a song of supplication to the Sun, in which all soon joined. Moon Face Bear then filled the medicine pipe, lighted it with a coal which was passed in to him, and as the pipe was passed around, each warrior, after blowing a whiff of smoke toward the heavens and the earth, made a short prayer to the Sun, to Old Man, and to Mother Earth.

This lasted for many hours. Then the warriors left the sacred sweat lodge, feeling blessed and ready for warring.

# *Chapter Thirty-One*

Leaving the songs of the women behind in the Osage village, Yellow Thunder led his warriors onward, riding over the meadows and through the dark forests that paralleled the Arkansas River. The warriors wore their plain, everyday leggings, shirt and moccasins, and heavy fur jackets, the fur worn to the inside for warmth.

Tied to each saddle were their beautiful war clothes, and in a small parfleche were their eagle-plume headdresses. If there was time before going into battle, these war clothes would be donned.

If not, they would be carried into the fray. They were considered to be great medicine, especially the shirts. Upon them had been painted their owners' dreams, some bird or animal that had appeared to the owner during the long fast that the warrior had made before he changed from a careless youth to a responsible warrior.

They rode from morning until late afternoon, then led their horses up a high butte and stopped. Below, they got their first look at Black Buffalo's camp. Through the naked branches of the cottonwoods down below could be seen the dark, smoke-blackened tepees, their peaks releasing the drifting, lazy smoke up into the breeze.

Not far from the lodges, several war horses grazed within a crudely erected corral. In the center of the camp were pieces of rotten logs and brush, so closely laid that not a glimmer of fire could shine through them. This was a fire normally used for cooking or to warm themselves while on the trail in order not to betray their presence to a passing enemy.

Yellow Thunder's gaze shifted. Some distance from the camp, in the forest, women were bundled against the cold, stooping and bending, tying and hauling the wood they had gathered that would feed their fires of warmth and light.

Yellow Thunder's jaw tightened as his gaze shifted again, this time watching children scampering around and through the wood-gathering party, chasing one another in mock battles with limbs for lances and rifles.

Yellow Thunder looked cautiously around the camp for signs of the renegades, finding only a few loitering and chatting beneath a willow tree.

Otherwise, it seemed that the other renegades must be asleep in their dwellings, resting now in order to ride all night on raids.

Yellow Thunder glanced over his shoulder at his men, nodding a go-ahead. Since the women and children were far enough from the village at this moment, he would not command his warriors to take the time to don themselves in war paint or clothes. It was best to strike the camp now, while the women and children were not in the midst of the death and devastation. Yellow Thunder never wanted to harm women and children.

Today all he truly wanted was to see Black Buffalo and his warriors pay for the wrong done to Yellow Thunder's valiant warriors—especially his best friend and blood brother, Red Loon!

Yellow Thunder's right hand reached up and he circled his fingers around his father's medicine bag, which was now his, ready to carry it into battle with him, trusting it to protect him as long as it hung securely around his neck from a leather thong.

Then he grabbed his bow from his shoulder. He held on to it tightly as he thrust his moccasined heels into the flanks of his mighty stallion. *"Takpe!"* Yellow Thunder shouted. "Attack!"

With shrill yelps, he began sliding his horse down the bluff in a cloud of dust, his warriors following his lead. They raced on into the camp, swirling around the men and snatching away the weapons from those who were running from their dwellings.

*"Huka-hey!"* The war cry of the Osage filled the air, over and over again.

Yellow Thunder smiled broadly when he realized that he and his warriors had appeared so suddenly that the Kickapoo horses were stampeding, breaking down the fence and tumbling over it in a frenzy.

Some of the Kickapoo renegades ran and got their horses and mounted them in a leap.

The renegades then became a frieze of wild riders, the horsemen sitting forward on their horses's withers, their naked legs hanging stirrupless, their stocky bodies balanced as if they were part of the steeds they rode, bows and quivers and long lances visible.

Yellow Thunder slid headfirst to the ground from his horse, pulling his arrows from their quivers. He rolled behind a nearby tree and let loose sprays of arrows in the midst of the frantic renegades and their horses.

There was much shrieking and yelping, and it soon became evident that the Kickapoo were outnumbered. One after another, they tumbled from their horses to the ground.

Others turned and fled in all directions. The sudden and unexpected onslaught of Yellow Thunder and his warriors had demoralized the renegades at the very start.

The air was filled with many sounds, with the pawing of hooves, the snorting of the ponies, the outcries of pain from those wounded, and the screaming and crying of the women and children who stood huddled now at the edge of the camp, witnessing the sight of their loved ones being defeated at the hands of the Osage warriors, led by Yellow Thunder.

Out of the corner of his eye, Yellow Thunder caught the sight of an approaching horseman. His heart thudded wildly within his chest when he turned and got a full view of the enemy's face, seeing that Black Buffalo was himself trying to escape.

Dropping his bow, Yellow Thunder stepped out into the open and reached for Black Buffalo. Just as the horse sped past him, he hauled Black Buffalo to the ground with him. With fire in his eyes and a racing pulse, Yellow Thunder wrestled with Black Buffalo. Over and over again they rolled across the ground.

Then Black Buffalo soon had the advantage. He struck Yellow Thunder over the head with a rock, momentarily stunning him, and took off running toward the butte at the far edge of the village, dodging arrows and knocking down Osage warriors as he sped past them.

When Black Buffalo reached the butte, he scrambled up, but was soon dragged back down when Yellow Thunder locked his hands around Black Buffalo's ankles.

Yellow Thunder then jumped Black Buffalo and hit him hard in the chin, jolting Black Buffalo back to the ground. When his head hit the hard earth, he was rendered unconscious. He was not even aware of Yellow Thunder leaning over and yanking his medicine bag from around his neck.

Yellow Thunder stood there for a moment, smiling widely as he gazed down at Black Buffalo's medicine bag. The renegade was now a degraded man.

One without medicine was not a man at all. Yellow Thunder had rid Black Buffalo of his respect!

Yellow Thunder's smile faded as he again stared down at Black Buffalo, seeing that he was coming to. His hand went to the knife sheathed at his waist as his gaze rested on Black Buffalo's long, sleek hair.

Yellow Thunder slowly removed the knife with his free hand and knelt down beside the renegade.

But when Black Buffalo opened his eyes and yelped with fright at what he expected his enemy to do next, Yellow Thunder saw that the scalping was not necessary at all. He had won more victory over Black Buffalo than even a scalp represented.

When Black Buffalo's eyes caught sight of his medicine bag shimmering in the breeze as it hung from Yellow Thunder's hand, he himself knew that he would not be scalped. Losing possession of his medicine bag was worse to him even than losing his scalp.

Black Buffalo's respect was gone. His leadership was robbed of him as long as he no longer had his medicine bag.

Black Buffalo lowered his eyes, feeling the humiliation of the moment. In the eyes of his people, as soon as Yellow Thunder showed them Black Buffalo's medicine bag, he was no longer worthy of even looking upon their faces.

Yellow Thunder stepped away from Black Buffalo and allowed him to rise from the ground. Yellow Thunder even allowed Black Buffalo to walk away from him—away from his camp, away from his people, destined to be alone now for eternity.

Proud, his chin lifted, and carrying Black Buffalo's medicine bag, Yellow Thunder turned and moved back into the camp. The fighting was over. His warriors were standing triumphantly around the camp, Yellow Thunder had not lost a single man. Twenty enemy had fallen, and the survivors had fled.

Yellow Thunder stopped in the center of the village and gazed slowly around at the women and children cowering together, clinging, their eyes wide with fear. He saw no reason to cause them further pain and knew that for the most part, their men would eventually return—but not to resume the life of raiding. Their leader was gone. Their power was gone. Now they would become husbands and fathers again, caring only for their families, their wildness tamed by Yellow Thunder and his warriors!

"*Iho!*" Yellow Thunder said loudly. All eyes were upon him now. He lifted Black Buffalo's medicine bag into the air for all to see. "Black Buffalo's medicine has been taken from him. He is no longer a man! Now my warriors and I will leave you in peace."

There was a strained silence, and then a familiar voice spoke up from somewhere behind Yellow Thunder, making his heart skip several erratic beats.

"Bright Eyes?" Yellow Thunder said in a whisper, stunned at hearing her voice speaking his name and almost afraid to turn around to see if it really was her, or a figment of his imagination.

"Yellow Thunder, it is I, Bright Eyes," she said, running from Black Buffalo's tepee toward her brother. "Oh, Yellow Thunder, you came! I knew that you would."

Feeling as though his entire body was one pounding heartbeat, Yellow Thunder turned on a moccasined heel. His eyes lit up and tears soared to his eyes when he saw his sister running toward him. The fringes of her white doeskin dress skipped in the wind, and her long, braided hair blew back from her shoulders. The beads of her headband caught the reflection of the sun. Jangling upon her arms were silver bracelets.

And then Yellow Thunder's happiness waned when his gaze noticed something else about his sister.

He teetered from a siege of lightheadedness when he stared blankly at her stomach, which was quite heavy with child.

Then she was within his arms, clinging. "Big brother, take me home," she said, sobbing against his powerful chest. "It has been so horrible. I have been kept as a slave. I now carry within my body Black Buffalo's child."

Her words were like knives repeatedly stabbing Yellow Thunder's heart. He closed his eyes and tightened his jaw, forcing himself to accept this truth about his sister, that she would soon give birth to a renegade's child. He could hardly stand the thought. He kept trying to force himself to remember that she was safe and that was all that truly mattered.

He eased her away from him and held her at arm's length. He did not ask how she happened to be there. He knew. Black Buffalo had abducted her. And he knew why. His sister was a beautiful woman.

With a tight jaw, Yellow Thunder wondered how long Black Buffalo had watched his sister from afar before deciding to abduct her. Just thinking of his enemy lusting after his sister, and then forcing himself upon her, made him rethink his decision not to kill him.

Yet, he quickly decided, Black Buffalo was the same as dead. He had lost everything today. Everything.

It also then came to him why Red Loon had died. Red Loon had surely discovered that Black Buffalo was keeping Bright Eyes as his captive.

Yellow Thunder gazed down at his sister. "Let us go home," he said thickly, willing his eyes not to look upon that mound of disgust that was now a part of Bright Eyes and her future. He could not envision himself ever accepting such a child as a nephew—or as an Osage.

But for his sister, he knew that he must learn to tolerate and accept what fate had handed them both.

And there was much to be happy about. His sister was alive! His beloved Ashley awaited his return! Their dreaded enemy was their enemy no more!

There was much hope now for his people's future.

*Ah-hah*, he and his people were blessed, and he would find some way to even feel blessed over soon becoming an uncle.

Yellow Thunder led his sister to his horse and helped her up onto his saddle.

He then swung himself into the saddle behind her, holding her against him with his muscled arm. "*Ho-iyaya-yo*," he shouted, raising a fist in the air. His warriors answered his command by mounting their steeds and turning homeward, plodding along steadily away from the renegade camp. They rode without stopping, long into the night, then when they were a few miles back from their village, they began their war songs.

When they rode into the village, where the outdoor fires were blazing high into the midnight sky and where everyone still awaited their return, there was an instant uproar of excitement. Women and children rushed to meet the victorious warriors, followed more slowly and sedately by the men.

As the warriors drew rein and slipped out of their saddles, the women embraced and hung on to them, and presently were heard the chanting praises of a husband or son or brother.

Ashley was inside her tepee adding more meat to the stew that she was preparing for Yellow Thunder's return when she heard the uproar outside and the thundering of the hooves of the horses as they rode into the village. Her heart pounding, she rushed from the tepee. Tears of happiness pooled in her eyes when she found Yellow Thunder among those who were returning, and then her gaze locked on someone else—a girl that Yellow Thunder was treating both gently and lovingly as he helped her from his horse.

Ashley's gaze shifted, gasping, when she saw that the beautiful woman was very pregnant.

Ashley began walking briskly toward Yellow Thunder, half stumbling when she broke into a mad run. Although she wondered who the woman with Yellow Thunder was, and why he was treating her so lovingly, Ashley was not jealous. She knew the extent of Yellow Thunder's love for her. He had proven it to her enough times. That he was alive and well was all that truly mattered!

Tears streaming down her cheeks, Ashley flung herself into Yellow Thunder's arms as he turned and held them out to her when he saw her running his way. He held her tightly, his nose buried into the depths of her hair.

"I'm so glad that you're back," Ashley said, clinging to him. "So glad, my love."

Ashley could feel questioning eyes on her and found the pregnant woman closely scrutinizing her, a keen puzzlement in her eyes. She eased out of Yellow Thunder's arms and squared her shoulders, clearing her throat nervously.

Yellow Thunder followed Ashley's gaze, and he smiled when he realized why she had become so suddenly quiet. He reached a hand out and took one of his sister's hands within his and drew her close to his side. "*Mitawin*, this is Bright Eyes, my sister," he said, smiling from one to the other. "Bright Eyes, this is my wife."

Ashley and Bright Eyes gasped in unison.

Then Ashley gazed quickly up at Yellow Thunder. "This is Bright Eyes?" she asked, incredulously. "How can it be? Where did you find her, Yellow Thunder?"

"I've much to tell you and my people," Yellow Thunder said, now aware that everyone had drawn close to him, their eyes wide as they gazed upon Bright Eyes. He could tell that they were happy to see her, yet were puzzled by how she was there and how she happened to be pregnant.

"My people," Yellow Thunder shouted, drawing Bright Eyes into his close embrace at his side. "I have found Bright Eyes! She was being held captive at Black Buffalo's camp! Many things were forced upon her."

He glanced down at her stomach, frowning, then looked again at the many faces of his people.

"She is with child," he said, his voice drawn. "Black Buffalo's child. But let us look to the child as only belonging to Bright Eyes. We will love and cherish it because it came from her womb. Never think about how the child was conceived. We want the child to feel loved, not ashamed because of who its father was."

A voice broke through the strained silence, even silencing Yellow Thunder's. "Black Buffalo?" One of the warriors who had stayed behind to protect the village spoke up loudly. "Do you bring us his scalp? Will we have a scalp dance?"

Billy Two Arrows and Juliana came to stand just before Yellow Thunder. Pahaha moved in to stand beside Ashley. Her eyes implored Yellow Thunder, hating to see the scalp of her enemy and not wanting to have it hanging around forever to remind her of how her beloved Red Loon had died. She waited breathlessly for Yellow Thunder to respond to the warrior's question.

"There is no scalp," Yellow Thunder said, causing low gasps to waft through the crowd.

Yellow Thunder went to his horse and removed Black Buffalo's medicine bag from around his saddle horn, where he had attached it just after acquiring it.

Smiling victoriously, his shoulders squared, and his chin lifted, he held the medicine bag up into the air and allowed everyone to get a close look at it. "There is no scalp!" he shouted. "But there *is* Black Buffalo's medicine bag. Which would you rather I had brought to you? His medicine, or his scalp?"

There was a great silence, and then the air seemed split apart with the cheers and chants, proof that Yellow Thunder had been wise in his choice of what should be brought home to his people.

A young brave brought Yellow Thunder a long pole. He proudly attached the medicine bag to it, watching then as the boy took the pole and thrust its sharpened end into the earth in the center of the village. It was now not only Yellow Thunder's prize, but his people's.

Ashley placed her arm through Yellow Thunder's and smiled up at him, never as proud of him as now. Her husband had made a wise decision that not only affected himself but everyone in the tribe.

She turned her gaze then to Pahaha.

They exchanged warm and knowing smiles.

# *Chapter Thirty-Two*

*A Few Days Later—*

Two horses were readied for travel. Juliana embraced Ashley. Yellow Thunder gave Billy Two Arrows a hug of friendship. He then stepped back to stand beside Ashley as Billy helped Juliana onto her blanket saddle, then went to his horse and swung himself onto his own blanket.

Ashley looked heavenward and shivered, hugging her fur coat more closely around her when she studied the low-hanging gray clouds and felt the bite of the wind as it increased in its fury.

Snow.

There had been much talk of the first snows of winter being near. Today the air smelled crisp and pure, like new snow.

Ashley went to Juliana and reached a gloved hand toward her, glad when Juliana accepted this final gesture of goodbye by circling her gloved fingers around her friend's.

"You ride with care," Ashley murmured. "And if it starts snowing, please seek a quick shelter."

"Billy will know what to do if the weather becomes threatening," Juliana quickly reassured her.

"I'm glad that Billy talked Yellow Thunder out of going to the chopper's settlement," Ashley murmured, releasing her hand and dropping it inside the pocket of her fur coat. "That would not only have delayed your arrival at New Orleans, but put Yellow Thunder in danger again—and I have had enough of that to last a lifetime."

"Billy was right to encourage Yellow Thunder not to intervene in what is happening at the chopper's settlement," Juliana said softly. "This is something that the authorities in New Orleans should handle. And they will. Once Billy and I tell them everything we know, those unfortunate women will soon be set free."

Ashley cast Yellow Thunder a loving glance, then smiled up at Juliana. "If not for Yellow Thunder, you and I would be among those women owned by those lumberjacks," she said, shuddering at the thought.

"Yes, I know," Juliana said, giving Yellow Thunder an appreciative glance. Then her eyes turned to Billy Two Arrows, a rush of love soaring through her. She was eager now to begin their lives all over again without the threat of Calvin Wyatt haunting her every waking moment.

Yellow Thunder stepped up to Ashley's side and gave Juliana a pleasant smile. "You will make my blood brother happy," he said, reaching to touch her arm. "He deserves a woman like you."

Juliana leaned down and kissed Yellow Thunder's cheek, and then rode away with Billy Two Arrows, her back straight and proud.

Ashley turned to Yellow Thunder and moved into his embrace, the fur of their coats blending as though they were one. "I love you," she murmured, welcoming his lips as they warmed hers with a lingering kiss.

Then they were wrenched apart by a shrill scream coming from the tepee that had been built especially for Bright Eyes, close to Yellow Thunder's and Ashley's, so they could keep close watch on her now that she was nearing her birthing date.

Yellow Thunder and Ashley stood as though frozen to the spot for a moment, staring at each other. Then, when another scream tore through the air, they both broke into a run toward Bright Eyes's tepee.

When they got there and ran inside, Ashley paled and almost fainted when she caught sight of Bright Eyes lying on a pallet of furs close to a blazing fire in the fire pit, her dress lifted, her legs parted, the head of her child just barely exposed at the opening of the birth canal.

"My Lord!" Ashley gasped, teetering from the sight.

Yellow Thunder grabbed for Ashley, steadying her. He placed his hands onto her shoulders and leaned down into her face. "My sister needs us," he said. "There is no time to go for a midwife. The baby is already coming."

Ashley nodded her head anxiously, her eyes wide. As Yellow Thunder jerked away from her and fell to his knees between Bright Eyes's parted legs, Ashley trembled, but went to Bright Eyes's side and knelt down beside her. Ashley held Bright Eyes's hand as she gave another air-splitting scream.

Ashley was numb as she watched Yellow Thunder place his hands on each side of the baby's head. "Bear down now," he ordered his sister. "Now, Bright Eyes. Now!"

Wild-eyed, Ashley watched Bright Eyes groan and grunt. Her face was flushed, and her hair was wet with perspiration. Ashley cringed when Bright Eyes squeezed her hand so hard that it hurt, yet continued holding it, hoping that she was being of some use somehow. She had read accounts of women helping bring children into the world, asking for many sterile cloths and basins of hot water.

Today, in this Indian dwelling, there was neither, nor were any asked for. There was not time for anything but to see that the child was born without mishap, and then everything else would fall into place.

"I . . . can't." Bright Eyes cried, screaming again as she tossed her head back and forth. "I have . . . no . . . more strength."

"*Tanka*—younger sister—you must find the strength and courage to continue for just a while longer," Yellow Thunder softly encouraged. "The tip of the child's head is already visible. If you could just give another push. That would be all that was necessary to bring the child into our world."

"But do you not see, my brother?" Bright Eyes cried, as she gazed beseechingly into Yellow Thunder's eyes. "I do not want this child. Let . . . it . . . die! Let *me* die. I hated Black Buffalo. So shall . . . I hate his child! Please just leave and let me and the child die."

Ashley paled at Bright Eyes's words. She was trying to put herself in Bright Eyes's place, wondering if she would feel the same if it were she having a child of rape.

Yet, even such a child was in part the woman's, and surely could be loved. Especially after the mother carried it within her womb for nine months. Surely a bond was formed during those long months of togetherness.

No. Ashley did not think that she could hate a child that was a part of her, no matter who the father was. The child should be given a chance. The unborn child was not at fault.

"Leave me!" Bright Eyes cried.

When another pain bore down upon her, she bit her lower lip so hard from the pain that blood began streaming down her chin.

But then Bright Eyes grunted and groaned and grew red in the face, unable to control her body, it seemed, as her stomach contracted wildly and the child slipped easily from the birthing canal into Yellow Thunder's waiting hands.

Mesmerized, Ashley stared at the tiny body lying within her husband's hands, herself feeling a bond with it. And when the child made its first sound, its cries filling the tepee, a warmth Ashley had never felt before flooded her.

She unclasped Bright Eyes's hand and went to Yellow Thunder and peered down at the tiny creature as he cut the umbilical cord, its copper body shining. The child was a boy.

She looked anxiously up at Bright Eyes. "You have a son," she said, sighing. "And he is so beautiful, Bright Eyes." She inhaled a shaky breath and frowned when she discovered that Bright Eyes was closing her eyes, purposely not looking at her child.

Ashley gazed up at Yellow Thunder. They exchanged silent, woeful glances, then busied themselves cleaning the child, soon having it wrapped within a soft blanket.

Ashley washed and primped over Bright Eyes, chattering like a magpie, to try and draw Bright Eyes out of her depression.

But Bright Eyes just continued to lie there, her eyes closed, her lips clenched.

After Ashley had placed a clean buckskin robe on Bright Eyes and had her lying comfortably between clean, warm pelts beside the fire, Yellow Thunder brought the child to Bright Eyes and took it upon himself to lay it at her side.

Bright Eyes's eyes flew open wildly and she screamed up at Yellow Thunder. "Take the child away!" she cried. "Give it to someone else. I never want to see it. Never!"

Yellow Thunder gathered the child up into his arms again, frowning down at his sister, yet not scolding her. He knew that he would find a way to break down this wall that his sister had built between herself and her child.

Meanwhile, he took the child to Ashley. "Hold him," he said softly. "I will go for a woman who has recently given birth. She will feed not only her child, but Bright Eyes's, until Bright Eyes sees that it is her duty to do so."

As Ashley took the small bundle into her arms, she settled down onto a pallet of furs opposite the fire from Bright Eyes. She gazed down at the tiny, perfect face, its small lips puckered as though already feeding from a breast, then looked adoringly up at Yellow Thunder.

"Some day I want to be holding *our* child," she murmured. "Oh, how wonderful it would be, Yellow Thunder, were this child *ours*."

"We *will* have our own child one day," Yellow Thunder said, softly touching Ashley on the shoulder. He glanced over at Bright Eyes. "And so shall she soon take her child into the safety of her arms, gladly calling him her own."

Yellow Thunder turned to walk away, then swung around and glanced down at his sister again. "When your breasts begin to ache, then you will gladly place your child's lips to the swollen nipple," he said, then left.

Ashley held the child gently in her arms and slowly rocked him back and forth, never taking her eyes off Bright Eyes. She was hoping that she would catch Bright Eyes taking a stolen glance at her son, yet the whole time Ashley awaited Yellow Thunder's return with milk for the child, Bright

Eyes did not move. She just lay on her back with her eyes closed, as though dead and unfeeling.

When Yellow Thunder came back into the tepee, a lovely woman beside him, carrying her own bundle of joy, Ashley smiled up at the generous lady. She watched almost breathlessly as the woman sat down close to Bright Eyes's pallet of furs, motioning then for Ashley to bring her the child.

When Ashley took the baby to her, the woman revealed both of her breasts and soon had a child suckling at each of them. Both children made contented mewing sounds as their tiny fingers dug into the flesh of the breasts feeding them.

Ashley and Yellow Thunder sat down opposite the fire from the feeding children, waiting and hoping for a reaction from Bright Eyes.

But while the child was taking nourishment from another woman's breast, Bright Eyes still did not move a muscle, nor did it appear as though she were breathing as she lay there so tense, so guarded.

After a short while, Bright Eyes's child was placed on the pallet of furs beside its mother, and the woman left with her child to go back to her own dwelling until the next feeding hour.

Ashley questioned Yellow Thunder with her eyes. "Now what should we do?" she asked softly.

"We leave Bright Eyes and child alone," Yellow Thunder said matter-of-factly. "It is now night. It is time to retire to our own dwelling. Bright Eyes and the child must have privacy."

Ashley paled at the thought of leaving Bright Eyes with the child that she obviously hated. "But Yellow Thunder," she said, turning to face him, so that her whispers would reach only his ears, not Bright Eyes's. "It isn't safe to leave the child with Bright Eyes. What if she . . . kills him?"

"My sister has never killed even a fly," Yellow Thunder said, smiling smugly over at Ashley. "She is the sort that would even allow a snake to bite her, rather than kill it to keep it away from her. Never would she kill her own child."

Ashley's eyes wavered as she glanced over her shoulder at Bright Eyes. She found it hard, still, to trust the child with her, yet she had no choice.

Yellow Thunder drew Ashley into his embrace. "My woman, do not fret so," he encouraged. "My way is right. When the child cries, and there is no one here but Bright Eyes to give it what it cries for, she will take the child into her arms and lovingly place its lips to her breast. It is a mother's instinct to do this. And so then shall the instinct of loving one's own child take precedence over hating him, only because she hated his father."

"I hope you're right," Ashley said, moving to her feet beside him. She gave Bright Eyes and the child another quick glance, then stepped out into the cold, dark dreariness of night. She glanced up at the sky, glad at least that the snows had not come and that thus far, Juliana and Billy's journey back to New Orleans had surely not been hampered.

Now she could focus her fears on only one thing—the child, the small, sweet child. . . .

• • •

Just beyond the dark fringes of the forest, where the shadows were purple and fleeting, a figure lurked, crouching behind a thick stand of bushes. As his fingers parted the branches again, he watched breathlessly as Yellow Thunder and Ashley left the wigwam from which had been heard the cries of a newborn child.

"Because of Yellow Thunder's interference, I have lost everything that was important to me," Black Buffalo whispered to himself, glowering now at Bright Eyes's tepee. "But now I have come, and I have waited. I have heard my child's first cries! I must have my child! My child alone will breathe new life and new hope into me."

He clenched his hands into tight fists. "And I will have what belongs to me tonight!"

Weaponless, Black Buffalo knew the chance that he would be taking in entering Yellow Thunder's village. But he had come this far to claim his child, and nothing would stand in his way now.

Not even Bright Eyes. To get what belonged to him, he would kill Bright Eyes if necessary.

All that was important to Black Buffalo now was to have this child to carry on his lineage, and that of his ancestors. And he would not allow a child whose blood was in part Kickapoo to be raised by the enemy, the Osage.

Knowing that he must wait for just the right moment to enter the village, Black Buffalo drew his elkskin coat more snugly around his shoulders and moved stealthily into the darker depths of the forest, where he had left his cache of food. With a spear fashioned from a limb, he had caught himself a rabbit and had left it cooking over a smokeless fire.

Also he had gathered an assortment of nuts beneath the trees, as well as grapes that had been well preserved in the middle of the thick clusters, where frost had not yet harmed them.

Settling down beneath a willow tree, he took the rabbit from the spit over the fire and tore at the meat with his teeth. Afterwards, he quenched his thirst with the juice of the grapes.

Pleasantly full, his hands warmed over the fire before stamping it out, Black Buffalo left his temporary camp. His gaze was intense as he once again made his way through the dark forest, toward the flickering of the outdoor fires ahead at the Osage village. It was past the midnight hour now, and he expected most everyone to be asleep.

He especially expected Bright Eyes to be asleep, exhausted after having given birth.

His footsteps as soundless as a panther's, Black Buffalo stepped into the clearing that led to the village. With guarded eyes, he crept onward, and when he saw a warrior standing guard at the far side of the village, he smiled to himself and headed for Bright Eyes's tepee. He looked quickly over at Yellow Thunder's tepee, seeing only the faint light from the campfire flickering along the buckskin walls. He leaned an ear as he came closer, hearing no sounds, and smiled, glad that Yellow Thunder and his white woman were asleep. This gave him freedom to do as he pleased.

He crept up behind Bright Eyes's tepee and hugged it with his back, his heart pounding as he listened for any sounds inside it. He had not seen anyone else enter the tepee and gathered that it was still only Bright Eyes and the child who were there, and hopefully asleep.

Inhaling a deep breath, then exhaling it shakily, Black Buffalo moved stealthily to the entrance flap and brushed it aside. As he entered the dwelling, he saw that his earlier assumptions were correct. Only the mother and child were there. It looked as though both were asleep, but he was puzzled by where they were. A newborn child was usually with its mother. *His* child was lying separate from its mother. It looked as though Bright Eyes had not laid claim to her own child! And if not, why wasn't someone else there looking after it?

Stupefied by the discovery, now more anxious than ever to remove his child from its mother, Black Buffalo crept on into the tepee and when he came to the child, knelt beside it.

His heart pounding, he cautiously unfolded the blanket to see if he was the father of a son or a daughter.

To have a son had always been his dream. When he had been told of Bright Eyes's pregnancy, he had beamed with the thought of fathering a son.

And as he laid the last corner of the blanket aside, his eyes lit up with pride, for his child *was* a boy.

As Black Buffalo slowly rewrapped the sleeping child, he gazed at Bright Eyes, recalling the moments they had shared, after she had learned not to struggle within his embrace. He had thought that perhaps she had even grown to love him, for her struggles had waned into something soft and submissive within his arms.

But he had to believe that had not been at all how she had felt. She had pretended, perhaps hoping that might spare her life.

Now, she refused to hold her son, which must mean she hated it as much as she had hated its father, and that tore at Black Buffalo's heart, for he had learned to love this woman with every aching beat of his heart. Leaving her now was the hardest thing that he had ever done, even harder than having lost his medicine bag.

But he knew that his days of being with her were over. She would now only be in his way, would delay his escape with his son.

With a trembling hand, he ran his fingers over his distorted face, knowing that he was ugly and undesirable. Perhaps if he had been handsome, she could have loved him.

Smiling, he glanced down at the bundle beside him and knew that this son of his was perfect in all ways. He would have many women desiring him when he matured into a great Kickapoo warrior.

Somehow, Black Buffalo thought to himself, his son would be given all the opportunities of a young Kickapoo brave.

Somehow a way would be found to make this possible.

Slipping his hands beneath the small bundle, Black Buffalo gently picked up his son and rose slowly to his full height. He gave Bright Eyes another lingering stare, seeing her loveliness as her thick lashes lay across her copper cheek, then turned and moved decidedly toward the entrance flap.

But when he got there, he heard a movement behind him which made his insides freeze.

It was the sound of someone drawing back the string of a bow.

"Place the child down on the floor beside you," Bright Eyes said with grim softness, her heart pounding at the thought of actually losing her child forever.

She sat slowly up, her fingers trembling as she held the bow in place, an arrow ready to sing from it.

She had heard Black Buffalo enter. She had pretended to be asleep while he had taken the time with his son, to marvel over him.

This had given her time to realize just what the child meant to her. Now, the thought of losing him made a strange sort of queasiness in the pit of her stomach—especially to lose him to Black Buffalo, even if he *was* the child's father!

"I will not," Black Buffalo said defiantly. "This child is mine. He is a *son*. A son needs his father."

"That child will never know his father," Bright Eyes said, inching off the pallet of furs, rising shakily to her feet. "Now lay him down. He is mine. He is *Osage*. He will be raised Osage!"

Black Buffalo turned suddenly and faced Bright Eyes with a glower. "He . . . is . . . Kickapoo," he hissed. "He will be raised Kickapoo. Lay the bow and arrow aside, Bright Eyes. You know that you do not have the courage to shoot. You might kill the child."

Then his eyes gleamed as he smiled slowly at her. "But of course that would not matter, would it?" he tormented her. "You had placed the child away from the warmth of your blankets. You disowned it. Did you even wish it were dead? This is your opportunity. Shoot the child and the arrow would go through its slight form and pierce my heart, as well."

Suddenly everything seemed to happen in a flash, as at that moment Yellow Thunder came inside the tepee and grabbed the child from Black Buffalo's arms. He stepped aside just in time for Bright Eyes to take aim and shoot an arrow through Black Buffalo's chest. Her eyes were wild as she watched Black Buffalo clutch at the arrow, then fall dead to the floor.

"Lord, oh Lord!" Ashley gasped as she raced into the tepee, soon seeing what had happened. She stared up at Yellow Thunder, who was still holding the child, then slowly over at Bright Eyes, who still held the bow poised, as though it was frozen in her hands.

"Help her," Yellow Thunder said to Ashley, nodding toward Bright Eyes. "She fought for her son. She killed Black Buffalo."

"So the voices we heard were Bright Eyes's and Black Buffalo's," Ashley said, hurrying to Bright Eyes. "God, what if we hadn't come?"

Bright Eyes finally dropped the bow and began sobbing uncontrollably, reaching her hands out to

Yellow Thunder, for her son. "Bring my son to me," she cried. "I want him. He is mine. Please bring him to me."

Ashley stepped aside as Yellow Thunder took the child to Bright Eyes. Gently, he placed the bundle into his sister's arms. Then he watched as Bright Eyes very slowly drew back the corners of the blanket so that she could see her child.

Yellow Thunder reached an arm around Ashley's waist as his sister gasped with the pleasure of what she was seeing, then looked up at Yellow Thunder and Ashley.

"He is beautiful," Bright Eyes murmured. "My son, Yellow Eagle, is beautiful."

Yellow Thunder was touched by the chosen name for her son. In part she named him after her father, and partly her brother.

"*Ah-hah*, he is beautiful," Ashley said, sighing.

"I almost lost him," Bright Eyes said, tears splashing from her eyes.

"But now he is yours forever," Yellow Thunder said, reaching a gentle hand to her cheek.

"*Ah-hah*, forever," Bright Eyes said, then grew solemnly grim as she gazed over at Black Buffalo, then back up at Yellow Thunder. "He took much from me, but he also gave," she murmured. "Tonight he gave me back my son, for had he not come and threatened to take Yellow Eagle away, I might never have come to my senses. When I thought I was going to lose my child, then I knew that I never could give him up."

Yellow Thunder leaned a soft kiss to his sister's cheek, and then went to rid the tepee of the enemy.

Ashley knelt down beside Bright Eyes as Bright Eyes made herself comfortable again on the pallet of furs. Ashley's insides melted warmly as she watched Bright Eyes place her son's tiny lips to her breast, making the union of mother and son finally complete and everlasting.

# Chapter
# Thirty-Three

*The Next Morning—*

"Everything is finally working out for us, *and* your people," Ashley said, as she cuddled close to Yellow Thunder beneath a warm covering of blankets. "I'm feeling so lazy this morning. Why don't we just spend the full day lying here together, letting nothing or no one pull us into the rush of the day? It is so peaceful here, Yellow Thunder. I am so perfectly content."

When the soft cries of a baby came to Yellow Thunder's ears, he smiled and drew Ashley even closer with one hand, and with his other began the soft caresses meant to arouse her.

"Yellow Eagle is hungry. It is good to know that his mother will be feeding him," Yellow Thunder said, stroking Ashley's tender flesh and seeing the pleasure building as her body grew limp and her eyes closed. "My sister has now found her own happiness, in her child. My mother has found her place again in her village, with her people. And I have you with me, always to warm my bed and my heart."

He moved over her, the silken flesh of her body against his causing a tremor to soar through him. He held himself only a fraction away from her, allowing him space to continue igniting her senses as her every secret place became his.

Yellow Thunder's dark, stormy eyes swept over Ashley as she writhed in response to his fingers, then he touched her lips wonderingly with his and kissed her with a feverish desire that made her moan and reach to touch that part of him that lay hard and throbbing against her thigh.

When she circled her fingers around his manhood and began moving them on him, the heat of his passion rose within him and he groaned with pleasure against her lips.

The more she pleasured him in this way, the harder it was not to totally possess her, yet he did not want to rush this thing that was wonderful between them.

There were no demanding duties calling him from his tepee this morning. In fact, he had this day to do as he pleased.

It was time to give himself more to his woman than he had yet been allowed to because of his duties to his people and his beloved captive sister.

Today was Ashley's, he had decided before she had even awakened. He had lain there for some time, watching her and touching her before she had opened her eyes to smile her special smile at him this new morning of their togetherness.

Ashley drew her fingers away from him and then framed his face between her hands, giving him an all-consuming kiss.

Then she leaned away from him and crawled beneath the blankets, her tongue and lips making a heated path down his flesh, smiling to herself when his stomach quivered as she licked her way down to that part of him that only moments ago had been so wildly responsive to the touch of her fingers.

Knowing what Ashley was about to do, Yellow Thunder closed his eyes, his heart pounding with anticipation. When he felt the warmth of her mouth close over him, he sighed heavily, then stiffened and scarcely breathed as the pleasure mounted and spread like hot, flowing lava throughout him, spreading, spreading. . . .

"No . . . more . . ." Yellow Thunder said in a voice unrecognizable to himself. He reached beneath the blankets and placed a gentle hand on Ashley's shoulder. "It is best that you go no farther with that . . . sort of pleasuring. I am near the point of exploding."

Ashley tossed the blankets aside and crawled atop him, straddling him as she positioned herself over his throbbing hardness. She sucked in a wild breath and threw her head back in ecstasy as he lifted himself fully into her and began moving rhythmically within her as she rode him, his hands on her breasts, making a sensual thrill grab her at the pit of her stomach.

She groaned as he moved faster, filling her more deeply, his hips thrusting upward, over and over again, until she was almost overcome with a feverish heat that was touching her all over like fingers of fire.

Then she was quickly beneath him, his mouth and tongue awakening her to an even more intense pleasure. She closed her eyes and let rapture claim her as his kisses moved across her stomach, and then his mouth was hot and sweet on that secret place that was solely his.

Her fingers bit into his shoulders as he began pleasuring her in this special way, sending wild ripples of ecstasy through her. Trembling, she let him part her thighs more widely and she became breathless as he kissed her throbbing mound with a gentle and lingering kiss.

His fingers reached up and kneaded her breasts, and then again began making a slow, sensuous descent along her stomach, and then beneath her to lift her closer, ever closer as the pleasure mounted and spread like roaring flames throughout her.

Then he moved over her and she opened herself to him with a frantic need as he entered her with one maddening thrust. When he began moving rhythmically within her, she responded in her own rhythmic movement, her whole body quivering from the pleasure.

Yellow Thunder's fingers went to the nape of her neck and urged her lips to his. Her stomach churned wildly as they kissed, the press of his lips so soft, yet so demanding. Her lips parted and his tongue probed. He explored the inner edge of her lips.

And then he once again took her mouth in his, this time almost savagely, as their pleasure peaked.

Yellow Thunder's body shuddered into Ashley's as the ecstasy spread into a delicious, tingling heat, and then the delicious languor stole over him as his pleasure seemed to pass on into Ashley.

He held her close as he felt her passion peaking.

Anchoring her against him, he kissed her midst her silent explosion of ecstasy.

Afterwards, Yellow Thunder rolled away from her, yet still held her hand. "And so we found paradise together again?" he said, chuckling low. He leaned over and flicked his tongue around the nipple of one of her breasts, smiling at her as he watched her eyes close in a renewed ecstasy. "This is the way you wish to spend the rest of the day, *mitawin?* Warming the blankets with your husband?"

Ashley opened her eyes and gazed at him, reaching a hand to touch the perfect line of his jaw. "There are so many things I would like to do with you," she murmured. "It seems as though there is never enough time. I am married to a powerful chief. I must share you, always, with so many others."

"This is why it is best that you have someone else to fill your time when I am busy at my duties," Yellow Thunder said, turning on his side and drawing her body fully against his as she turned to her side also, facing him. "A child. A child would fill your lonely hours. Do you think that perhaps we made a child this morning? Or do you think we should try again now, a second time?"

Ashley's stomach growled, and she gazed over at the pot that hung low over the fire. Before going to bed the previous evening, she had prepared a stew that would cook long and slow into the night. It now smelled heavenly, filling the spaces of the tepee with its wondrous aroma of cooked buffalo, carrots, wild onions, and potatoes.

She then smiled weakly over at Yellow Thunder. "Do you think that perhaps we could eat first, then return to the blankets together later?" she said, deep within her wanting to tell him a suspicion that she felt about herself and this raging constant hunger for food that she had recently been experiencing.

The fact that she had not yet had her monthly flow this month made her wonder if she might be pregnant. She would give it a little more time, for she did not want to excite Yellow Thunder with such news, and then be forced to disappoint him should she not be pregnant at all.

But for now, she was limp with hunger.

"My woman is hungry, she eats," Yellow Thunder said, rising from the pallet of furs. He pulled on his buckskin clothes and moccasins as Ashley hurried into her own.

Ashley drew a blanket around her shoulders as Yellow Thunder placed fresh wood on the fire. When a blaze was reaching high beneath the pot of stew, warming it anew, she got two wooden bowls and spoons from their storage place at the one side of the tepee and was soon dipping the wondrous smelling stew into plates for each of them.

Ravenously, she ate, then cocked an eyebrow when she heard some children just outside the tepee laughing and squealing about something.

"I wonder what is making the children so joyous this morning?" Yellow Thunder said.

Together they went to the entrance flap and drew it aside, discovering a slowly falling snow that was already blanketing the earth in its cloak of white.

Ashley looked past the children and into the pine forest just beyond the village, sighing at the lovely sight of the limbs draped in white.

Then she watched the children at play again, enjoying their excitement at the new snow, the first of the winter. Some were even lying down and rolling in it as others thrust out their tongues, eating it as it fell in utter softness onto them.

"Let's be children again," Ashley said suddenly, smiling up at Yellow Thunder. "Darling, let's go for a ride in the snow. That would be so much fun." She locked her arm through his and stood on tiptoe. "And, darling, we are due some light-hearted moments. Since we met, it has been one challenge after another. Today let us place all challenges and memories of the long, sad days past and enjoy the snow."

"This is what you want?" Yellow Thunder said, gently placing a hand to her cheek. "To ride free through the snow?"

"*Ah-hah*," Ashley murmured. Then another thought struck her. "Unless you think it would

403

be too dangerous. Do you think the snow will become too deep for safe riding?"

"This is our first snow," Yellow Thunder said, looking up into the sky. "It will not be a heavy one. It is a time of newness when the snows fall. It is a time to enjoy. And so we *shall.*"

Ashley stood smiling and proud as Yellow Thunder beckoned for a young brave to come to him, then asked him to prepare two horses for riding and bring them to his tepee.

Then, giggling, Ashley turned with him and ran back inside the tepee and gathered up her hooded fur coat and her gloves. She watched him dress warmly as she rushed into her own outdoor garments.

She did not think much about it when he placed a sheathed knife at his waist. But she could not help stiffening when he positioned a quiver of arrows on his back, then picked up his great, fine ash bow.

"Why are you taking those?" she asked, smoothing her hair beneath her hood that was tied snugly beneath her chin. "Are you expecting to run into some sort of trouble while we are out riding?"

"It is always best to be prepared for danger, even if you are not expecting it," Yellow Thunder said matter-of-factly. With his free hand, he slipped his hood up over his head and nodded for her to follow him. "Come. The snow awaits us."

Sighing, and realizing how foolish she had been to react so quickly and carelessly to the bow and arrow, Ashley went outside with him, where two saddled horses awaited them. She smiled a silent thank-you to Yellow Thunder as he helped her onto her horse, then she watched his powerful strides as he went to his own horse and was soon sitting tall and square-shouldered in his own saddle.

Several children followed Ashley and Yellow Thunder, running and laughing, as they left the village.

Then they were left behind and it was only Ashley and Yellow Thunder alone entering a wonderland of white.

Although Ashley's face was cold, and the horses were snorting steam into the frigid air, she could not help but enjoy it, the sight something that she would remember, always. Never had she seen anything as beautiful while living in New York, and especially while living in New Orleans.

Today she was experiencing nature at its best— at its loveliest and most tranquil.

"Everything is so still," she said, brushing flakes of snow from her nose. "Besides our horses, all that seems to be moving is the snow falling softly from the heavens."

"And that is how it should be," Yellow Thunder said, smiling at her. "What you are hearing is the voice of nature. It is time for peace and quiet to reign within the forest. The Osage have put away enough supplies to last the full winter, and most animals are in their deep winter's sleep. Right now, *mitawin*, it is only you and I. Breathe in the wonders of the air, and take in the beauty of the land with your eyes. Time will pass quickly and again our people will be active in the forests, as will the animals who will be foraging also for food."

Ashley gave him another warm smile. Then, as her horse rode in a slow lope beside Yellow Thunder's, she allowed herself to absorb the beauty which surrounded her. The new snow was falling now in big, soft petals, as though from a wild plum tree. It was clinging to the bushes along the way, making them look like huddled ghosts.

As they came to a stream and crossed it, they discovered that its mouth was puckered with ice. Ashley again became lost in the wonders of nature, still in awe of the overwhelming silence, the softness of the snow on the ground and of the still falling flakes overhead.

She clutched her reins and gazed into the distance, where the frost-rimmed trees were like fairy-tale cobwebs against the gray sky.

And then all of this was disturbed by a sound that sounded like distant thunder, which became a loud rumble.

Yellow Thunder and Ashley exchanged quick glances, then peered straight ahead when they heard the sound again.

Yellow Thunder's heartbeat quickened. "That is the sound of buffalo," he said, his eyes widening. "This must be a herd that lost its way earlier and is now late to pass on to the lands of green grasses."

"There must be many," Ashley said, her heart pounding, feeling a stirring of danger in the air.

"Let us go and see," Yellow Thunder said, sinking his moccasined heels into the flanks of his horse, Ashley following closely behind him.

They rode until they arrived at a willow-bordered stream that ran out from a butte. Then Ashley's gaze followed Yellow Thunder's as he looked upward and locked on the wondrous sight of what stood atop the butte.

*"Hoh!"* Yellow Thunder cried, his whole body turning into a wild heartbeat at the sight. "It is the white buffalo!"

Ashley gazed up at the magnificent albino beast with its massive body tapering into hindquarters that were almost delicate. "Lord, it is," she sighed, unable to pry her eyes off the animal.

Yellow Thunder gazed heavenward, where a break in the sky revealed the sun winking from it. "My sun power is strong," he said, his chest thrust out proudly. "Now I must do work *for* the Sun."

When the white buffalo stirred, then disappeared toward the other side of the butte, Yellow Thunder grabbed his bow from his shoulder and rode quickly away from Ashley. "Come, *mitawin*. Be witness to my moment of glory!"

The wind blew harshly against Ashley's face, but she soon felt an intermittent tremor of warm air on her face as the sun washed the sky clean of the clouds, the snow melting just as quickly on the trees and land.

Suddenly everything had changed, even the reason for being away from the village, out in the wilderness where the mood of nature and of husbands changed with the blink of an eye.

Ashley rode onward, her husband's excitement reaching clean inside her soul.

# Chapter
# Thirty-Four

Ashley snapped her reins and urged her steed into a soft trot behind Yellow Thunder's stallion around the west side of the butte on which they had seen the magnificent white buffalo. The thundering that they had heard earlier had to be the herd of buffalo that the white buffalo traveled with. By the sound that their hooves had made, there were many of the beasts.

There was absolute quiet now. The buffalo were surely grazing on the grass that had become exposed to them after the snow melted away.

Yellow Thunder turned his gaze to Ashley, placing a hand of caution out for her to warn her that they must not frighten the buffalo into stampeding. ◆

She tightened her reins, making sure that her horse went no faster than the gentle lope in which she was already leading it.

When Yellow Thunder turned his eyes straight ahead again, Ashley swallowed hard, knowing that they would soon be able to see their target.

Her thoughts were suddenly stilled, and along with Yellow Thunder, she yanked her reins tight, drawing her horse into a shuddering halt. Her eyes widened and she gasped softly, for as far as the eye could see there were buffalo, and still more buffalo! It was a grand sight of perhaps one or two hundred magnificent beasts humped up in the biting cold on the south slope of the butte.

"Your warriors should be here," Ashley finally said, peering anxiously over at Yellow Thunder. "There are more buffalo today than they found on your last buffalo hunt."

"*Hecitu yelo,* it is true that we are seeing more buffalo today than when my warriors sought the beasts for the buffalo hunt," Yellow Thunder said, nodding. "And although we are looking upon a magnificent sight today, my warriors would not give chase even if they were here. We do not kill needlessly. What we took during the buffalo hunt was adequate."

Yellow Thunder's jaw tightened, and his eyes narrowed as the white buffalo moved into view.

And then Yellow Thunder's back straightened, and he gasped softly when he saw another white buffalo—one that had not been of this earth for many sunrises.

An albino calf!

Never in his wildest dreams had he expected to see two white buffaloes at one time, and the excitement welled within him—but not because he planned to kill them both. It was just the sight that thrilled him through and through.

"Do you see—" Ashley said, Yellow Thunder interrupting before she could finish her question.

"*Ah-hah*, I see the calf," Yellow Thunder said, and then another thought came to him that made his heart skip a beat as the two white buffaloes moved together, the larger animal licking the calf's face. If the white buffalo was the calf's mother, Yellow Thunder would not be able to kill it. He would not leave the calf motherless, without nourishment.

And he would not dare kill it. It was the special property of the Sun, born with the blessing of the Sun. It was meant to live until adulthood so that another warrior one day might have the opportunity to kill it for its special hide, so that this warrior could receive the special favor of the Sun, not only for himself but for his whole tribe.

Ashley could almost feel Yellow Thunder's despair, realizing herself the dilemma the discovery of the white calf was causing her husband. She knew him well enough to know that he would not kill for the sake of killing, and he was too kind to take the mother from the calf, or even kill the calf just to get to its mother.

She watched Yellow Thunder, and when he swung his horse around, apparently to leave, Ashley began to follow his lead, but turned and took one last look. Then she drew her horse to a halt and stared with an anxious heartbeat at the calf as it ambled up to another buffalo besides the white beast and began suckling from it.

"Yellow Thunder!" Ashley cried, reaching a hand out for him. The white buffalo moved away from the nursing calf and moved among the other grazing animals, stopping to graze also from a thick stand of grass. "Look. The white buffalo is not the calf's mother. The calf is suckling from another buffalo."

Yellow Thunder swung his horse around, and his eyes brightened when he discovered that what Ashley had said was true.

Then his spine stiffened when something else drew his attention when there appeared to be a commotion and sudden restlessness among the buffalo.

He soon saw the cause. Some wolves had appeared at the far edge of the herd, trotting around howling and yelping. Suddenly the buffalo shifted, as though one huge body, and began racing across the land snorting and bellowing, alarmed by the presence of the wolves.

Stunned by the sight, Ashley gaped openly at the stampeding buffalo. Then she screamed when Yellow Thunder rode away from her, pushing his horse into a hard gallop toward the thundering herd.

As crazed as the buffalo were, Yellow Thunder could be killed!

Afraid to follow, not being that skilled with a horse, Ashley watched with a pounding heart and weak knees as Yellow Thunder rode after the fleeing buffalo, but she soon saw what he was actually after. The white buffalo seemed to have been lost from his mind, for his gaze locked on the calf that had been abandoned by its mother and was now standing vulnerably alone, bellowing loudly as several wolves surrounded it, their sharp fangs bared as they snarled and eyed the calf hungrily.

Apparently, Yellow Thunder had seen the danger before Ashley, for he was now riding toward the cowering wolves, an arrow fitted into the string of his bow.

His knees bracing him, locking him securely to his horse, Yellow Thunder rode up close to the wolves, aimed, and sank arrow after arrow into the wolves, until each wobbled and fell over onto its side, dead.

Then Yellow Thunder yanked on his reins and drew his horse to a stop, his eyes locked with the deep brown eyes of the white buffalo calf.

The calf was no longer bellowing. He seemed to understand that Yellow Thunder had just saved him from a horrible death. And as the calf ambled up to his horse, Yellow Thunder leaned over and patted its soft head.

"Sacred animal, I will meet with you another time," he said, then gazed into the distance, able to see the adult white buffalo leading the herd.

Despair filled Yellow Thunder to think that he had lost his white buffalo to save another. But he felt twice blessed because of it, as the Sun poured its warmth from the sky, caressing his face. He had saved the albino calf, the special property of the Sun. And he could not find it within himself to go after the powerful white buffalo that had stopped and now stood still, gazing back at him, it seemed, while the mother returned to get that which she had carelessly left behind.

Yellow Thunder knew that it would be an easy chase now, since the buffalo was winded from his flight, but he felt that this had all happened for a purpose, and he would not make chase today for that coveted prize he had waited for all of his life.

There would be another time.

*Ah-hah*, he would feel as blessed today, even if he had not slain the coveted white buffalo. He had saved another, for another time.

Perhaps even for his own son, should he and Ashley be blessed with one.

Afraid that the mother might change its mind and not come for its calf if he stayed close to it, Yellow Thunder swung his horse around and rode hard away from it. When he reached Ashley he drew rein beside her and turned his horse so that he could watch the reunion of mother and calf. His eyes widened when the large white buffalo even decided to come ahead and be a part of the family reunion. It tugged at his heart to see the three buffaloes grow close to one another, licking and rubbing up against each other.

Tears splashed from Ashley's eyes, so moved was she by the touching scene, and so proud of her husband that he would allow the buffalo bull to live, knowing how much he had wanted to return to his village with the coveted pelt of the white buffalo.

Flicking tears from her eyes, Ashley gazed at Yellow Thunder. "My darling, you are so good and understanding of so many things," she said, reaching over to gently touch his cheek. "You have such deep feelings. You are such a compassionate man. Oh, how I love and admire you."

Yellow Thunder stared at the white beast a moment longer, watching it retreat again toward the other vast number of buffaloes, the mother and calf following dutifully behind him.

Then he gazed at Ashley. "Let us return to our dwelling," he said thickly. "There will come a time when my arrows will be used for other than killing wolves while in the presence of a white buffalo. I *will* have that coveted white pelt. In time, *ah-hah*, I will have it."

"*Ah-hah*, my love, you will," Ashley said, smiling sweetly at him. "I know that you will. It was just not meant to be today. What you did instead touched my heart deeply. And should your people have been here to witness it also, they would look upon you with great favor. I am certain of it, my darling."

Yellow Thunder just smiled, then released her hand and moved his horse back in the direction of their village. They rode away into the wondrous sunshine, Ashley proudly at his side.

When they arrived at the village and a lad took their horses to the corral, Yellow Thunder ushered Ashley inside the tepee and turned her to face him as they stood beside the flickering flames of the fire in the fire pit.

"I learned something important today," he said.

"And what is that?" Ashley asked, gazing into his midnight-dark eyes.

"The importance of children," Yellow Thunder

said, slowly disrobing her, her fur coat settling in a heap around her ankles. "If we did not make a baby this morning, then let us try again now."

"But . . ." Ashley said, attempting to tell him that she thought that she might already be with child, but he placed a gentle hand over her mouth, sealing her words inside her.

"Let us not talk now," Yellow Thunder said softly, as he smoothed her dress over her shoulders, moving it slowly over her breasts and then her hips.

When she was standing silkenly nude before him, he rained kisses on her lids and on her hair while moving his palms soothingly and seductively over her.

With a sob, she flung herself into his arms and their lips met in a feverish kiss. She clung to him as he slowly laid her down onto their pallet of furs. He then pulled momentarily away and slowly stripped himself as he gazed down at her with burning eyes.

His clothes now also tossed aside, Ashley placed her arms at his neck and pulled him over her. He surrounded her again with his strong arms, crushing her to him so hard she gasped. His mouth forced her lips open as his kiss grew more demanding, more passionate.

Straining her hips up at him, she emitted a cry of sweet agony as he drove in swiftly and surely, pressing endlessly deeper within her. There was not a part of Ashley's body that did not tingle with aliveness. She was aflame with longing—with a fever that he was fast feeding with his rhythmic strokes within her.

Yellow Thunder's passion and desire matched hers as his mouth again sought hers with wild desperation. His body hardened and tightened, and then he felt a great shuddering in his loins as their bodies jolted and quivered together, their passion having crested and exploded. . . .

Breathless and fulfilled, Ashley held Yellow Thunder's hand as he rolled away from her and stretched out on his back, panting. She moved to kneel beside him and smoothed her hands over his muscular body. "My darling, what I was trying to say earlier, before we made love, was that we may have already made a baby within my womb," she murmured, smiling sweetly down at him. She giggled. "But even so, this lovemaking was not a waste, do you think?"

He placed his hands at her waist and lifted her atop him, and then over to his right side where he molded her against him, their cheeks touching, their hot breath mingling.

"A child," Yellow Thunder said softly. "It will make our special world complete."

"You will make such a wonderful father," Ashley whispered, tingling all over when he ran a hand down her side, then between them, to gently cup one of her breasts. "You are such a gentle, caring man. Today, when you allowed the white buffalo to go free, I never loved you so much."

"Today," he said, as though deep in thought. "The choices I made while near the white buffalo were not easy. As I have explained before, the albino buffalo is considered a sacred thing, the special property of the sun. When one is killed, and after the hide is beautifully tanned, at the next medicine lodge it is given to the Sun with great ceremony. It is hung above all the other offerings in the center post of the lodge and there left to gradually shrivel. War parties of other tribes never dare to touch it, for fear of calling down upon themselves the wrath of the Sun."

He gazed then into her eyes, unsmiling. "A white robe from the buffalo is never offered for sale," he said softly. "None who secure it might keep it any longer than until the time of the next medicine lodge, the great annual religious ceremony. Medicine men, however, are permitted to take the strips of trimming and use them for wrapping their sacred pipes, or for a bandage around the head—only to be worn, of course, on great occasions."

"You speak of it with such great reverence," Ashley said, taking his free hand and kissing its palm. "One day, my love, you will again find a white buffalo. It will be a reward for your kindness to the buffalo today."

Yellow Thunder turned his eyes to the fire, envisioning how it might have been today. Standing over the fallen albino buffalo, he would have raised his hands to the heavens, fervently praying, promising the Sun the robe and the tongue of the animal.

He would then kneel over the animal and would take off the hide with a knife and cut out the tongue, careful to make no gashes in the pelt, for he was doing the work for the Sun.

None of the meat would be taken, for it was considered sacrilege to eat it. The tongue would be dried and given to the Sun, together with the robe.

Sighing, knowing that his choices today were good, Yellow Thunder turned back to Ashley and again drew her into his gentle embrace. "Today was good," he whispered. "Very good."

*"Ah-hah,"* she whispered back. "Very."

Their lips met in a sweet and lingering kiss.

# *Chapter Thirty-Five*

*Several Days Later—*

Great fires were burning in a wide circle in the center of the village. Within the circle the Osage people gathered, seated on pallets of fur on the ground. Though it was the early part of December, the many fires and the sun warmed the people as though it were summer. On their faces they wore pleasant smiles, and some kept time with the throbbing of the many drums in the distance by the quiet slapping of their hands and the nods of their heads.

This was the fourth day of Ashley and Yellow Thunder's wedding ceremony. She sat beside Yellow Thunder on a high platform in the midst of this throng of people, dressed in a beautiful white doeskin dress with fancy beadwork and fringes more lovely than any other that she had yet worn. Small, fluffy feathers had been shaped into flowers and placed in her hair above each of her ears, and her hair hung long and wavy down her back to her waist.

She cast Yellow Thunder a warm smile, seeing him as more handsome than she had ever thought possible in his white doeskin, the beadwork matching that which decorated her dress. The only headdress he wore was a headband with the same design of beadwork.

Ashley gazed ahead again, finally settling down inside after having been thrust suddenly into the wedding ritual, the like of which white man's civilization seldom knew. The wedding ceremony was on its last day, the vows spoken between Ashley and Yellow Thunder, the exchanging of gifts, and the vast feasts shared with the neighboring tribes of Osage already behind them.

Today there were games and dances to observe, and then . . .

Ashley gulped hard when she thought about what else was going to happen today. She was to be tattooed with the sign of a spider on the back side of her hand. Yellow Thunder had told her that this was necessary, for this was a mark of distinction among the first-class families of the tribe. Yellow Thunder's mother bore the sign of the spider, as did Pahaha.

Already Ashley had been presented with the *mon-sha-kon*, or burden strap. It had been made a certain way from certain things all of which had some significance to the Osages. Yellow Thunder had explained this also to her, saying that every highly respected woman in the tribe had a ceremonial burden strap given to her by her husband, although they were never actually used for carrying wood or other objects. The ceremonial burden strap symbolized the virtues and industry of womanhood and hung on the appropriate side of the lodge entrance as a permanent reminder of her honor, and her place among the order of things.

This she had accepted without hesitation.

But to be tattooed? In the white man's culture, tattoos were only worn by those whose reputation was in question. Women especially did not get tattooed!

Ashley straightened her back and lifted her chin proudly as many young unmarried men and women came and stood before her and Yellow Thunder. She stared more at the men than at the women as they stood in silent stateliness and decked out in their gorgeous finery, their faces strikingly painted, their long hair neatly braided. Many of the young men carried suspended by a thong from the left wrist a small mirror which kept turning and flashing in the bright sunlight, catching the eyes of the young women, apparently for some purpose.

The women were dressed in floor-length fringed robes, decorated with painted porcupine quills, and wore many strands of beads around their necks. Their hair was braided and hung long down their backs.

When the elders began beating the drums and singing the dance song, which was a lively one and of rather an abandoned nature, the dancers faced each other, rising on their toes, then sinking so as to bend the knees. Thus they advanced toward one another and met, then retreated, again advancing and retreating a number of times, all singing and smiling and looking coquettishly into each other's eyes.

The lines of men and women advanced again, and suddenly a girl raised her robe and cast it over her own head and the head of the youth of her choice.

Ashley's eyes widened and she glanced quickly at Yellow Thunder. He leaned close and whispered to her that the woman was kissing the man beneath the dress.

Ashley was surprised by the boldness of the young women, then her head jerked back around to watch the performance as the spectators shouted with laughter and the drums began to beat even more loudly than ever, the song increasing in intensity.

The women moved away from the men, smoothing their robes back in place, the lines retreating, the favored young men looking embarrassed, all of them taking their seats.

Yellow Thunder leaned close to Ashley again. "For this kiss, payment must be made tomorrow," he whispered. "If the young man thinks a great deal of the girl, he may present her with one or two horses. He must give her something, if only a copper bracelet or a string of beads."

Ashley smiled and nodded, then watched as several other young men, these dressed only in brief breechcloths, stepped before the audience of many to play the game called *canhuyapi*, meaning "wooden leg." It was a follow-the-leader game, the strongest boy being the leader.

The boys strapped themselves to long poles, similar to what Ashley knew as stilts in the white community, then began walking about, weaving in and out and around the gawking crowd. When the leader began hurrying his pace, almost running with the poles, those who could not last fell clumsily to the ground, followed by a roar of laughter from the spectators. This continued until only one boy was left, and he then became the victor and was cheered loudly for his endurance and strength.

Ashley was thinking back to earlier in the day, when the young braves of the village had been put through other tests of strength, when the contestants plunged into the icy water of the river to see how much cold they could endure.

Ashley had noticed that not all boys had equal enthusiasm for all games, but one thing they all tried to do was to mount while their horses were running at full speed. Running a few steps by the side of the horse, then grasping the mane and springing into the air, the riders had been lifted by the motion of the animals.

Another quite necessary thing for the boys to learn, it seemed to Ashley, was to mount at the back of a rider who was riding at full speed. In a battle, if a warrior was unhorsed, another could save him by riding swiftly by. The one on foot grasped the tail of the horse and leaped to the back of the rider and to safety.

This had appeared to Ashley to be hard to do, but easily practiced with gentle ponies. She understood by watching that such training developed skillful Osage horsemen.

Another game that Ashley had observed was a riding and shooting game called *hanpa kute*. A pole had been planted in the earth and a moccasin placed on top of it for a target. Riding by as fast as possible, the young braves shot an arrow at the moccasin. In order to be fair, the rider had to go by the target at full speed. If he slowed his pony down as he neared the pole, he was ruled out of the game.

Yellow Thunder had explained to Ashley that behind all of this physical activity was the further objective of tenacity and poise. In play, the young braves imagined themselves in the midst of the enemy in all sorts of conditions—on foot, surrounded, wounded, and without weapons, and with bullets and arrows flying toward them. The tighter the place in which a warrior found himself, the more resourceful he needed to be.

Nerve, pluck, and quick action were necessary accomplishments, for these could save a warrior's life.

Suddenly everything became quiet. Even the drums ceased their throbbing. Ashley was drawn back to the present when she felt many eyes on her. She swallowed hard when she discovered that she was now the full focus of attention as a warrior unknown to her stepped up to the platform and reached his hands out for her. He smiled broadly, his smooth, white teeth contrasting beautifully against the deeply coppered flesh of his face.

Ashley smiled awkwardly back at the warrior, realizing now that he must be the village artist. Yellow Thunder had told her that it took many horses, robes, and blankets to afford an artist for this special job. Yellow Thunder had boasted that he had paid double the normal price for her tattoo, for she was special in many ways, and not just because she was the wife of the chief.

Rising slowly to her feet, fear gnawing at the pit of her stomach because she did not know what pain might accompany the tattooing, Ashley took the artist's hands and allowed him to lead her down from the platform.

She could feel Yellow Thunder's eyes on her back as she then knelt down beside the fire, where two young braves had placed several pouches on a white doeskin pelt spread out on the ground.

"Hold your right hand out to me," the artist said in mixed English and Osage, yet clear enough for Ashley to understand. "Hold it steady while I apply charcoal from the sacred redbud to it."

When the artist saw that Ashley's hand slightly trembled, he took it in one hand and held it steady, as with his other hand he began smoothing the charcoal across the back of her hand.

He gazed into Ashley's wavering eyes. "This will pain you very little," he said as he picked up his wing-bone tattoo needle. "Just breathe easily and sit still while I place the beautiful design of the spider on your hand. This tattoo will last a lifetime. It is the symbol of the Grand Hankah and all the

425

mysterious powers related thereto."

Unable to feel relaxed about this strange ritual, and the fact that she would have to live forever with the tattoo, Ashley's voice felt frozen at the depths of her throat. She just slowly nodded, her eyes anxiously wide as the artist placed the needle against her skin and began pricking out the geometrical figure of the spider.

She sucked in a nervous breath, glad that the pain *was* slight, and glanced over her shoulder at Yellow Thunder, seeing the pride in his eyes as he smiled reassuringly at her.

She returned the smile, then looked slowly around her at the people who were looking on, warmth and love in their eyes. She realized then just how intense the hush was among these people and understood that what they were witnessing was something they revered. She was now becoming special in *their* eyes, someone they would now feel easy about drawing into their affairs, as one of them.

Even Ashley was having stronger feelings for these people. And that was good.

She was carrying a child that would be in their image, for she would not think of her child in any other way than being an exact replica of its father. Be it a son or daughter, she would think of it as having lovely copper skin, eyes as dark as midnight, and raven-black hair.

This would forever prove her worth to these people!

"It is almost finished," the artist said, smiling into Ashley's eyes. He laid his tattoo needle aside, then very gently rubbed the redbud charcoal into the tiny openings in Ashley's skin.

He brought her hand close to his face and blew the excess charcoal away, then held her hand up before her eyes and waited for her approval.

Ashley's eyes widened and a slow smile crept onto her face as she stared at the lovely tattoo on her hand. She reached her other hand to it and ran her fingers slowly over the geometrical figure of the spider, seeing that it most definitely would not rub off.

She then gazed up at the artist. "Why, it is most lovely," she murmured. "I do like it so."

The artist's eyes twinkled with happiness and he took Ashley by the other hand and drew her up to her feet. Smiling broadly, he then held her tattooed hand up for everyone to see.

There was much shouting and praises lifted into the air, everyone very pleased not only with the end result of the artist's work, but also with Ashley's attitude about the tattoo.

A warm arm was suddenly there around her waist, and the artist eased his hand away from Ashley as she turned and moved into Yellow Thunder's gentle embrace. "I truly do like it," she murmured, as she clung to him amidst the clamor of people now closing in on her and Yellow Thunder.

She soon had to relinquish her hold on Yellow Thunder and found herself being hugged by everyone, one at a time, and she found that she was smiling so hard and long that her jaws were beginning to ache.

When the sun began dipping low in the sky, and the fires had burned down to softly glowing embers, the winds blew harder into the village, the excitement waned, and everyone began to disband, some to neighboring villages, others to the tepees of this village.

Yellow Thunder lifted Ashley up into his arms and carried her to their tepee. They disrobed one another and fell to the floor in a lover's tangle, their lips and hands awakening each other to passions kept stilled during the long four days of the wedding ritual.

"How did I last so long?" Ashley whispered, her fingers searching and finding his throbbing hardness. She began to move her hands on him as Yellow Thunder stretched out on his back and enjoyed it. "Although we took time to sleep the three nights of the ceremony, it was with others. Now we have full privacy, my husband. Let me show you just how much I have missed you, and oh, how much I love you."

Yellow Thunder's pulse raced and his breath quickened when he felt the softness of her mouth closing down over him, where he so unmercifully throbbed with a building pleasure. He closed his eyes and groaned, his head rolling as her mouth and tongue worked their magic on him. And when he felt as though he might explode from the pleasure, he framed her face between his hands and drew her away.

"Lie on your back," he said, looking at her with passion-hazed eyes.

As though in a spell, mesmerized by the nearness of him, Ashley nodded and lay down on the soft pelts. Her heart pounded as he moved beside her and began moving his hands over her, caressing her from her breasts to that damp valley where her life now seemed to be centered. His fingers stroked her, and then he positioned himself so that he could part her flesh with his fingers, giving his lips and tongue more access to that part of her that held the secrets of her own pleasure.

He reached his hands up and kneaded her breasts as his tongue paid homage to her tight bud of desire, flicking over and around it, until Ashley groaned and began to writhe with pleasure.

When he thrust his tongue within her, it seemed as though the sun might be within her, spreading its delicious warmth throughout her, growing hotter, spreading, building, and peaking. . . .

She tossed her head wildly back and forth when she could not help going over that edge into ecstasy. She bit her lower lip to stifle a scream of delight that was surfacing from deep within her.

And then the most magnificent of feelings overwhelmed her when she felt him enter her in one strong thrust, filling her, answering that cry of her body that only moments ago he had aroused within her.

Their lips met in a frenzied kiss. Ashley placed her legs around Yellow Thunder, drawing him even more deeply within her, arching herself higher and harder against him. She rocked and swayed with him, and then, too soon, their passions fused, as though one body, one soul, one heart.

Shortly afterwards, while Ashley was still clinging to him as he lay so wonderfully atop her, she whispered something into Yellow Thunder's ear that made him beam, his eyes revealing his happiness.

"A baby?" he then said, rolling away from her, and lifting her atop him, so that she straddled him. "You are certain?"

"*Ah-hah*, my darling, I am with child," Ashley said, smiling down at him, her hair draping over her shoulders, just barely revealing the nipples of her breasts through the silken tendrils.

Yellow Thunder drew her down so that their lips could meet in a lingering, sweet kiss.

# Chapter
# Thirty-Six

*Several Months Later—*

Awkward from her pregnancy, Ashley walked slowly beside the river a short distance from the village, inhaling the sweet fragrance of spring. The air was warm and the breeze light, making it possible for Ashley to shed her heavy fur garments. She did not even have to wear a shawl today. She placed her hands to her abdomen, the buckskin fabric of her dress soft against her flesh, the ball of her stomach that pressed tightly against the inside of her dress quite large now.

"The months have passed quickly," she whispered to herself, smiling contentedly when the child within the protective cocoon of her womb gave her hand a quick kick.

She could not help but marvel over how she could feel the child move around inside her, and at how even at this moment she could feel what might be an elbow or knee rolling past her hand.

Then her child lay quiet again.

"Perhaps sleeping," she whispered, then strolled onward.

As she gazed at the river, she could see tiny fish darting about like streaks of sunshine just beneath the surface of the crystal-clear water. She watched a water spider skip its way across the surface, and then listened to the soft sounds of a mourning dove from somewhere close by.

When a dove fluttered down from overhead and landed close to her and began prancing softly about, gathering dried pieces of grass into its mouth, Ashley smiled. The sweet bird was building a nest, perhaps even already heavy with eggs. This was what spring was all about—new beginings, love, and sweetness.

"And also the spring buffalo run," Ashley said, stopping to stare through a break in the trees just a short distance away. Through this she could see where a meadow began that reached beyond the forest to purple-hued bluffs, then more meadows and pine forests.

Yellow Thunder was out there somewhere, having left several days ago for the buffalo hunt. Ashley had been one of the few women left behind for various reasons.

She had become quite subdued in her activities of late. She wanted nothing to happen to this child that was conceived out of such love. This child would be cherished not only by its parents, but also by the whole Osage tribe.

It was a future leader of these wonderful people.

Ashley resumed her walking again, seeing this as valuable to the well-being not only of herself, but also her child. Every day she got her special exercise by taking short strolls in the forest where she was learning how to commune with nature, just as her beloved husband did.

Each bird, animal, tree, and flower meant something special to her, even the rocks and the earth.

The sun slipped through the branches overhead, illuminating an ocean of daffodils only footsteps away. Ashley sighed and went to them.

Bending slowly, holding the small of her back with the effort, she knelt down before the cluster of precious yellow flowers and began plucking them for a bouquet for her tepee. She would keep them there until Yellow Thunder's return, drawing some comfort from them.

Tears misted her eyes, for these flowers reminded her of her mother, suddenly making Ashley sorely miss her. In New York, always around Easter, her mother's garden of spring flowers had drawn people from all over the city just to look at it. The peonies, snapdragons, iris, lilies, and so many more flowers had flooded her mother's yard with great splashes of color.

But the daffodils had taken precedence over the rest, for they seemed the most gentle, the most sweet of them all. They had been the centerpiece of her mother's dining table from the moment one burst into full color until the last dropped from its stem.

Her hands filled with as many as she could

carry, Ashley rose slowly to her feet again and turned back in the direction of the Osage village. When she got to the outer fringes of the forest, she turned a smiling face to Bright Eyes as she came walking toward her, Yellow Eagle snuggled in her arms.

As Bright Eyes came to Ashley and stopped, admiring the flowers with her wide, dark eyes, Ashley in turn continued admiring Yellow Eagle. He was Indian in all of his features, and Ashley hungered even more for a son that would be an exact replica of Yellow Thunder. That way, she would never be without Yellow Thunder, even when he was far away on a buffalo hunt.

"*Hoh*, the flowers are so pretty," Bright Eyes said, then turned her eyes up at Ashley. "Their color is more brilliant this year. Perhaps it is because the winter was so mild and spring was allowed to reveal itself earlier than normal."

"*Ah-hah*, they are pretty," Ashley said. Smiling, she pulled one of the flowers from the bunch and broke off part of its long, lanky stem, then took it upon herself to place the flower in Bright Eyes's hair, just above her right ear. "And so are *you*."

They laughed softly together, then Bright Eyes turned back in the direction of the village with Ashley.

"You are not going to resume your walk?" Ashley asked, glancing over at Bright Eyes.

"*Nah*, my walks grow shorter each day," she said, puffing with the effort to carry Yellow Eagle.

"Why, he seems too heavy for you to walk anywhere with him," Ashley said, glancing down at the child. "How he has grown!"

She reached her free hand over and smoothed her fingers over the tight, fat skin of one of Yellow Eagle's legs. "I hope my child is half as healthy," she said, giggling. She glanced down at her breasts, so much larger and rounded. She laughed softly and blushed as she gazed at Bright Eyes. "I surely have enough milk to ensure my child's health," she murmured.

"As you know, I was as large, and the milk supply was never lacking for my son's tiny lips," Bright Eyes said, shamefully recalling the time, right after his birth, when she had refused to feed him and that she had actually allowed another woman to place her breast at the mouth of her son.

Loving her son now so much, Bright Eyes found it hard to believe that she had been so cold toward the tiny infant that had just left the womb in which it had been sheltered for nine months.

Since then, she had taken her son to her own bosom and had scarcely allowed anyone ever again to even hold him. She feared losing him. To lose her son would be the same as dying herself.

Bright Eyes's jaw tightened with the thought of Black Buffalo. She never connected her son with Black Buffalo. To Bright Eyes, he had never existed.

The child was hers, only hers.

"You're such a wonderful mother," Ashley said, now walking with Bright Eyes into the activity of the village. "I hope to be half as dedicated to my child as you are, Bright Eyes."

Their conversation was cut short when Pahaha came walking toward them, helping Star Woman along, the elder woman's sightless eyes squinting into two narrow slits. Star Woman was chattering like a magpie to Pahaha, always full of questions about what everyone was doing and about the weather, whether it was a beautiful day or one of gray gloom.

Ashley's heart always ached when she saw the helplessness of her husband's mother, and saw that it had worked out quite well for Pahaha and Star Woman. Sweet Pahaha had offered to share her own tepee after Star Woman had absolutely refused to move in with her son, to interfere with his life with his new wife and future son.

Although most elders did live with their families, Star Woman did not want to be in the way. She understood that it was not the same between herself and her son—not since they had been separated all these years. She did not want to force herself upon her son the duty of looking after her, as most elders forced upon their children.

This way, living with Pahaha, she retained a measure of the independence she had found while living as a slave woman to the white people. Although a slave, she had been given her own private quarters, away from the others, because she had done special things for the family. No one had known how to bake as well as she, or, until she had gone blind, how to sew lacy fabrics as well.

Now her fingers were gnarled and twisted with a crippling disease. She felt useless, except that

while with Pahaha, she at least had companionship and was made to feel worthwhile because
she offered back the same sort of companionship. Pahaha had vowed never to love again, and
it seemed that she was quite sincere in this promise. She offered no man any smiles. She was as
happy as was expected of one who had lost her
very heart.

Ashley could see Pahaha stiffen when she gazed
with a tight jaw at the child within Bright Eyes's
arms. Ashley wanted to reach out and touch
Pahaha's heart, telling her that she must forget
this hate that she carried around with her for the
father of this child.

Black Buffalo was dead.

And it was not this child's fault who his father
was!

Ashley couldn't understand why Pahaha
couldn't see this. Carrying around such a hate
was somehow the same as keeping Black Buffalo
alive, and that was bad for Bright Eyes as well as
Pahaha.

"Who is standing near?" Star Woman asked,
reaching out a hand and discovering the daffodils. Her gnarled fingers moved slowly over them,
studying their shape.

Then her face brightened into a smile. "Daffodils," she murmured. "My favorite flower of the
spring. Ah, if only I could see them. Seeing them
through my fingers is not enough. To see their soft
petals, and the wondrous yellow color. That would
be wonderful. Wonderful."

Ashley glanced down at the daffodils, remembering what she was going to do with them—enjoy them while her beloved was away.

Then she looked slowly at Star Woman, pitying the old lady's inability to enjoy everything at full capacity.

Without further thought, Ashley placed the bouquet in Star Woman's hands, helping to circle the crooked fingers around them. "Mama, they are yours," she said softly, the word coming easily for her, since Yellow Thunder's mother had come to mean so much to her. "Please take them. Enjoy them."

Tears came to Star Woman's eyes as she drew the flowers toward her, so that she could rub them against her wrinkled face. "Thank you, daughter," she murmured, swallowing back a sob of gratitude. "You are so kind."

Pahaha smiled at Ashley, silently thanking her with a nod, and then her eyes moved to Ashley's swollen abdomen. "And how is our child this morning?" she asked, never letting a day pass without asking Ashley this a dozen times.

Pahaha was anxious for the child's arrival. Her duties to this child would give her something else to fill her lonely hours since she had promised Ashley that she would be her mid-wife. She would also always be there to see after the child when Ashley wanted time alone with Yellow Thunder.

The child, in a sense, could become partially Pahaha's own—the child that she would never have with her beloved Red Loon.

"I have been kicked quite often this morning."

Ashley said, gently pressing her fingers around the ball of her stomach. "I am sure I am carrying a son—a son who will excel at any challenges he may face. Already he challenges me each and every day."

Yellow Eagle began to whimper and squirm within Bright Eyes's arms. Ashley gazed at the child, then slowly at Pahaha, whose attitude had changed from loving to sour, in the way she glared down at the baby with a pinched look on her usually lovely face.

She then glanced at Bright Eyes, knowing her hesitation at allowing anyone to get near her child, much less hold him, and thought that just perhaps now was the time to change both of these women's attitudes about children.

Taking it upon herself to make these changes, Ashley very decidedly lifted Yellow Eagle from Bright Eyes's arms and just as decidedly and determinedly shoved the child into Pahaha's unwilling embrace, giving her no choice but to hold him as Ashley just as quickly drew her arms away again.

There was at first shallow breathing between these two women and looks of wonder at Ashley as they questioned with their startled eyes what she was doing. And then there was a moment when Pahaha's reluctance began melting away into acceptance as the child reached up and touched her face, sending a thrill clean into her heart from the tenderness with which the child touched her.

Bright Eyes took a step forward to retrieve her

439

child, then when she saw the change coming over Pahaha, and knew the good of this change, she hesitated and very quietly stepped back to stand quietly beside Ashley again.

When the baby smiled up at Pahaha and then emitted a soft laugh, tears formed in Pahaha's eyes and she clutched the child closer to her bosom. She began slowly rocking him back and forth in her arms, talking softly to him.

Ashley turned to Bright Eyes. "Is it not good to see your child giving pleasure to someone else?" she murmured, then drew Bright Eyes into her embrace and softly hugged her.

"*Ah-hah*, I now understand how selfish I have been," Bright Eyes said, her tears wetting Ashley's cheek.

Then everyone's attention was drawn elsewhere when a lone rider appeared at the edge of the village.

Ashley stepped away from Bright Eyes, her heartbeat quickening when she realized that it was Yellow Thunder.

She looked past him and saw no other warrior, causing her pulse to race and her throat to become dry. Yellow Thunder would not be returning unless he had been injured somehow, or had been stricken ill.

But when Yellow Thunder came closer and Ashley saw a travois being dragged behind the horse and saw what was upon the travois, a thrill soared through her. She clasped her hands together before her and sighed as tears of joy splashed from her eyes.

"The white buffalo," she whispered. "My husband found the white buffalo again, and this time he did not hesitate to sink a spear into its flesh. The white pelt that is on the travois is proof."

She lifted grateful eyes to the sky. "Oh, Lord, *and* Great Spirit, thank you, thank you, thank you."

# *Chapter Thirty-Seven*

*A Few Months Later—*

At the far edge of the Osage village, smoke spiraled slowly into the morning light from a stone chimney that covered most of one side of a two-room log cabin. The autumn leaves of the forest framed the cabin with brilliant orange, red, purple, and yellow. Occasionally, one of these leaves would break free and spiral slowly to the ground. Squirrels sniffed through the pile of leaves, searching for fallen acorns.

One by one the Osage people gathered about this new addition to their village, their chief having only one month ago presented the cabin to his wife so that she could enjoy some semblance of the life that she had left behind to make her more comfortable and to give them more space for the child that was soon to join their lives.

The declaration had just moments ago been

made to the Osage people that a child had been born to Chief Yellow Thunder and Ashley, and everyone gathered around the cabin to get their first look at the future leader of their people.

Ashley lay in the bed that Yellow Thunder had made for her, its mattress a thick cushion of wondrously soft pelts and blankets. Her face flushed from having just given birth, her smile gentle and filled with awe of the child that lay at her breast, she watched his lips suckle her nipple, his tiny fingers kneading her breast contentedly, as though he was well acquainted with the practice of nursing from his mother.

Her body still seemed to throb from the effort to give birth to her first child as Ashley gazed up into the midnight-dark eyes of Yellow Thunder. She smiled softly at him and reached a hand out for him.

"My darling, the name you gave our son is so appropriate," she said, recalling the many times her unborn child had kicked her inside her womb. "Kicking Wolf. *Ah-hah,* I like the name."

Yellow Thunder sat down on the bed beside Ashley and took her hand in his, hardly able to wrench his eyes away from his son, who was an almost exact replica of himself in all of his features.

Except one.

When Kicking Wolf opened his eyes, Yellow Thunder saw Ashley, for the green of her eyes had been transferred to her son.

"He is beautiful, isn't he, Yellow Thunder?" Ashley said, gazing proudly at her son again.

"Absolutely beautiful."

"Handsome," Yellow Thunder corrected. "Boys are handsome. Next we shall have a child that we can call beautiful. We shall have a daughter."

"If that would make you happy," Ashley said, then looked slowly around the room, still amazed that her husband could be so generous.

She loved her new home, this house able to open its heart to the world with the windows that she had requested be a part of its construction.

She had managed to buy some lace from a traveling salesman, and lace now sheltered every window with its delicate flower designs, inviting quiet contemplation.

Seeing the lace had catapulted her back to a time when lace-making was of prime importance in her life. She still loved lace, but now her husband and child filled her every thought and desire.

She gazed at the windows. They were coaxing the first traces of morning light to come inside, enough to see the pieces of furniture that Ashley had managed to acquire from travelers who came by from time to time with their covered wagons. She had traded her fancy beadwork to the women, who were entranced by it, picking up a chair and a table here and there, and even several pieces of china and silverware.

She felt as though she were in heaven, having a husband, a true home, and now a child.

She did not see how she could ever ask for more than this, for she had already found paradise on this earth.

The crowd outside the cabin was beginning to

chant and sing. Yellow Thunder leaned down and kissed Ashley softly on the lips, then smiled at her. "It is now time," he said. "My people wait."

Ashley knew what was expected of her. She must at least for a few moments be parted from her son, so that Yellow Thunder could share their child with all of his people.

Pahaha entered the bedroom, smiling from ear to ear. "When I made the announcement of the birth of your child, everyone was so very, very pleased," she said, going to kneel down on the opposite side of the bed from Yellow Thunder. "Is Kicking Wolf ready? Are you going to take him now, Yellow Thunder?"

Yellow Thunder nodded at Pahaha as Ashley made sure the blankets were in place around her child, then allowed Yellow Thunder to pick him up in his arms.

Ashley's smile wavered, and tears burned at the corners of her eyes as he left the bedroom. She felt suddenly left out and could hardly bear it.

She turned eager eyes to Pahaha. "My robe," she said anxiously. "Get my robe. I want to go with them."

Pahaha placed a hand on Ashley's arm. "No, it is best that you stay in bed," she advised. "You have just given birth. Rest. Yellow Thunder will return the child soon to your arms."

Ashley rose slowly to a sitting position, brushing her blankets aside. "Pahaha, I want my robe," she said determinedly.

Nude, she swung her feet over the side of the bed. She was able to see into the outer room now and saw that Yellow Thunder was almost at the door. "And hurry," she fussed. "I want to stand at Yellow Thunder's side as he presents our child to his people."

Ashley did not call to Yellow Thunder to stop, for she wanted to surprise him by suddenly being there with him, a devoted mother and wife.

Pahaha sighed heavily, then rushed around the bed and grabbed Ashley's robe from a chair and eased it around her shoulders as Ashley managed to get to her feet.

Ashley slipped her arms into the sleeves of the robe, and tied it in place at her waist. Then Pahaha clung to her as she walked slowly from the bedroom and out into the living quarters just as Yellow Thunder was ready to open the front door.

"Yellow Thunder, wait for me," Ashley said, smiling at him as he turned with a start and saw her there.

Her knees were weak and she felt lightheaded, yet she pushed her way across the room until she was finally at his side.

Yellow Thunder gazed down at Ashley with utter amazement, then laughed throatily, knowing that he should have expected his wife not to stay in bed for long. She was a determined, most stubborn woman—a quality that he much admired about her.

Pahaha stepped aside as Ashley clung to Yellow Thunder's arm. "I'm ready," she murmured, holding her chin proudly high. "Let's show off our son, Yellow Thunder."

His shoulders proudly squared, Yellow Thunder

opened the door. Ashley steadied herself at his side and stepped out with him, to be met by thunderous applause, chants, and singing.

After Yellow Thunder unwrapped Kicking Wolf, he held the child in the palms of both of his hands and raised him high for everyone to see, causing a great hush to fall over the crowd, and then great sighs of adoration.

"Your future leader!" Yellow Thunder shouted. "His name is Kicking Wolf!"

Yellow Thunder then gave Ashley a lingering smile. "Thank you," he whispered, for only her to hear.

"You're welcome," she whispered back, beaming.

Then she added also in a whisper, "I love you dearly."

When Yellow Thunder lowered their son and offered him back to Ashley, then bent low and gave Ashley a kiss for all of his people to witness, she felt a joyous bliss all through her.

They went back inside the privacy of their house and placed Kicking Wolf in his small crib that stood at the side of the bed.

Then Ashley and Yellow Thunder went to the bedroom window, which she could boast of being paned with glass, and stood in a sweet embrace, witnessing another glorious savage sunrise together.

Not far from the cabin, there was a garden of huge, golden sunflowers, their heads bent as though in a silent prayer of *pilamaya*—thank you.

Dear Readers:

I hope that you have enjoyed reading *Savage Sunrise*. My next Leisure book in the continuing *Savage* series will be *Savage Illusion*, to be released in six months. *Savage Illusion* promises to be filled with much adventure and passion!

I would love to hear from you all. Please send a legal-size self-addressed stamped envelope to:

CASSIE EDWARDS
R# 3 Box 60
Mattoon, Il. 61938

Warmly,

*Cassie Edwards*